Killing Time

Novels by Thomas Berger

Killing Time

A Novel by

Thomas Berger

Little, Brown and Company

Boston   Toronto   London

LIBRARY OF CONGRESS CATALOGING-IN-PUBLICATION DATA

Berger, Thomas, 1924–
    Killing time: a novel/by Thomas Berger.
        p.   cm.
    ISBN 0-316-09147-2
    I. Title.
    [PS3552.E719K5   1990]
    813'.54—dc20   89-27369
                                    CIP

10 9 8 7 6 5 4 3 2 1

*Published simultaneously in Canada
by Little, Brown & Company (Canada) Limited*

PRINTED IN THE UNITED STATES OF AMERICA

To Bernard Wolfe

NOTE

READERS are earnestly advised not to identify the characters in the narrative which follows—criminals, policemen, madmen, citizens, or any combination thereof—with real human beings. A work of fiction is a construction of language and otherwise a lie.

Some years ago a notice was posted at the entrance to Sala B of the Uffizi Gallery in Florence: "Please don't touch the pictures! It is dangerous for the works of art, it is punished by law, and finally it is useless."

—THE AUTHOR

Killing Time

Chapter 1

AT ABOUT eight-thirty on Christmas Eve the Arthur Baysons were letting themselves into the apartment of Mrs. Andrew Starr and her daughter Wilhelmina, usually called Billie. Betty Bayson, Billie's sister, retained her own key even though she had been married for some time and lived in the suburbs.

Betty called out her habitual threshold greeting as she managed to slide the key from the lock and elbow the door open without unsettling her armload of Christmas gifts. Arthur of course gave her no aid whatsoever, lumbering along behind. He was sometimes innocently inconsiderate.

"Hi!" shouted Betty, already seeing the body of a man lying supine on the floor of the living room, the blood on the carpet, the red-and-cream-striped screwdriver handle in his left temple. Arthur in his awkward way tripped slightly on the corpse's left shoe.

Betty continued for some time to repeat her greeting, which eventually took on the sound of an animal cry, though her expression did not change. She was pale and fine-featured as a child though well into her twenty-third year.

Arthur was more upset by Betty's noises than by the dead man at his feet. He placed his wide white hand on her shoulder, but she tore away and ran through the kitchen-dining room, where the table was set for the Starrs' traditional Christmas Eve supper, through ten feet of dark hallway to the larger of the two bedrooms, and there, switching on the light, she saw the nude body of her sister Billie. Billie lay across the bed in the attitude of a spring twisted in the opposite direction from its natural spiral, a monstrosity of arrested motion and deviated line. From beneath the bed protruded her mother's feet and ankles: Betty knew them from the shoes. She also recognized from them that her mother was dead.

Arthur wandered in, carrying the parcels that Betty had dropped in the hallway. He was resisting the horror with a grimace that in another context might have been a thin smile. Under such control he made no further adjustment at the sight of the new bodies. Still carrying the gifts, which were wrapped in bright green paper and tied with silver ribbon, he returned to the living room, put the packages carefully onto the sofa, and telephoned the law.

Hardly had he put down the instrument when the front doorbell rang. Arthur's brain was now coursing with life: he doubted the police, for all their two-way radios, could move so swiftly, and stepped to the bay window of this ground-floor apartment, from which one could sight a caller on the stoop.

He more than half expected to see the returned murderer as he peered cautiously through the gauze curtains, but instead, in the light of the streetlamp at the curb, recognized his father-in-law, Andrew Starr. Arthur hastened to press the button that opened the outside lock, and stood at the apartment door to receive the older man.

Starr had obviously shaved and otherwise made a supreme effort to be at his best: clean shirt, the collar standing away from his scrawny neck; ancient gray topcoat with antediluvian dirt deep in its fibers but devoid of surface lint; shoes encased in rubbers though the evening was utterly dry. He was a periodic alcoholic and by his drinking had estranged himself from his wife and family. For years Starr had lived alone in a furnished room and saw his family only on the major holidays. He worked as a stock clerk for an auto-parts supplier.

It always depressed Arthur to see Starr; and Starr, for his part, was usually leery of Arthur. Today, however, Arthur looked steadily at his father-in-law as if he were an object of special value, and Starr found himself wondering whether by the end of the evening, after the gifts had been exchanged—in his topcoat pocket, wrapped in tissue, was a combination penknife and nail file for Arthur—whether he might successfully beg a five-spot off him.

"Merry Christmas," said Starr in his voice that had been both weakened and made rough by years of ardent fluids.

"They are all dead," said Arthur. He gently seized Starr's thin arm through the worn sleeve of the topcoat.

Starr showed no understanding of the situation even after he had been led to the bedroom and peered at his elder daughter and wife. Reality spoke little to him unless his veins hummed with drink, and he had not had a mouthful since noon. He was even secretly bitter that he had abstained for the sake of his family and now his sacrifice had been proved nugatory. He returned to the living room and sat on the sofa, still wearing his hat and coat.

Betty stood by the front window, staring quietly across at the lighted windows in the buildings opposite. Arthur, who went to the toilet three times during the ensuing quarter of an hour, wondered at the Starrs' apparent calm, admired them for it. Once as a boy, when his dog had been killed by a truck, he and his mother had wailed interminably; and his father, returning from work, had joined them.

The first police car arrived discreetly, sirens silent and red lights extinguished. However, with the appearance of a second patrol car, wailing and flashing, an anonymous private automobile full of detectives in mufti, and an ambulance, people began to collect in the street and study the uniformed man who had been posted on the stoop.

Inside, Starr was asked his name three times by as many individuals. The first two were patrolmen, and though they made some effort to appear neutral, he was conscious of their great hostility towards him. Policemen always had his number though in all his years of degeneration he had never run afoul of the law. The third questioner was a man of about Starr's own age and even grayer of hair. His eyes were blue-gray and he wore a gray suit with a maroon sweater beneath it. His manner was equable, even tingling on the sympathetic. He sat down alongside Starr on the couch and groaned, as men their age often do when taking the weight off.

Starr liked him but regarded him warily; he was obviously a detective, from his clothes. He was older than the others and therefore probably the boss. Starr thus thought it politic to address him as "inspector."

"Do you know me?" the detective asked, and at Starr's disclaimer, he said: "Then why did you call me 'inspector'?"

Starr was suddenly too terrified to explain his innocent process of reasoning. He had not had a drink in more than nine hours. Chin trembling, he said: "I didn't do it. Look for that boarder."

"Well," said the detective, who was a lieutenant of Homicide named James T. Shuster though he saw no need to admit that to Starr, whom he had immediately assessed as guilty, whether or not of the crime at hand. "Well now, Andy, if you are referring to the man on the floor, as you very well know he is also dead. Was there another boarder? No? Ah then." He patted Starr's shaking shoulder. "Then you mean that after dealing with the persons in the bedroom, he came out here and inserted a deadly weapon into his own head?"

Starr began to cry, but noiselessly, and no one else in the crowded room took notice of him. Betty and Arthur had already talked with the lieutenant, and when after listening briefly he had turned away from them, they continued to relate their stories to a tweed-jacketed young man who Betty could see found her attractive.

Shuster decided to press his advantage with Starr. "This boarder Appleton," he said. "Not a bad-looking devil, was he? Probably had a cup of coffee now and again with your wife, passed the time of day with your daughter." He dug his thumb into the sensitive hollow just below Starr's shoulder cap, not so much to hurt him then and there as to suggest what could be done in the future.

But Starr's psychic wretchedness had rendered him for the moment physically anesthetic. Nor was he moved in the least by Shuster's implications as to his wife and daughter. He naturally assumed his wife had been sleeping with the boarder, and perhaps Wilhelmina had also done so, and they all quarreled and murdered one another. He knew only that he had not been involved, that he had come to this unpleasant place to exchange gifts, to eat Christmas Eve supper, and to borrow money from whichever member of the family, including the boarder, he could tap, and with it to spend Christmas Day in the company of a bottle. He continued to weep for himself; though, dehydrated, he produced few actual tears.

The police photographer had taken pictures of the body of Appleton the boarder, and the medical examiner having finished his preliminary business, the corpse was placed in a sort of sleeping bag and taken outside to the ambulance. Its appearance at the door put an end to the crowd's joking conjectures that a brothel-raid was in progress. A short, anxious man climbed the stoop and applied to the patrolman for entrance to the house, claiming that the fourth-floor apartment was his legal residence. He was taken into the hallway for questioning and eventually allowed to proceed upstairs.

Betty Starr was embarrassed by Arthur's possessive hand upon her forearm and subtly disengaged it. A detective who introduced himself as "Tierney" had drawn up chairs for the Baysons and himself.

"Mrs. Bayson," he said, "any time this becomes too distressing for you, just let me know." He had dark curly hair and his eyes were red-brown, almost amber.

"I have reserves of strength, Mr. Tierney," she responded, and Arthur looked at her in surprise at this turn of speech, though he had always admired her fluency; he believed himself inarticulate.

"Good," Tierney replied, consulting his notebook. "Could

6

you be more specific about Wilhelmina's modeling, or Billie as you call her."

"For a long time she refused to do underwear." Betty shook her head vigorously, dramatizing refusal. "Stockings and shoes, but not underwear. She had nice legs and especially shapely feet, not long ones like mine." Betty looked down at the extremities in reference and waited for Tierney to make a flattering disagreement, but he remained silent and she continued, a short-lived edge to her voice.

"But after a while I guess she decided there wasn't anything morally wrong with it, at the beach nowadays the bathing suits are as brief as anything a girl wears beneath her clothes." Betty stared at Tierney, ready to avert her eyes from his, but still he studied the notebook. "Anyway, underwear fees are highest of all."

Arthur stirred uneasily. Billie had modeled exclusively for the cheaper magazines which appealed to the prurient of eye. Once, in a barbershop, he had watched a pimpled man stare at a picture which he recognized, two seats away, as a bare-breasted likeness of his sister-in-law. But he endeavored now to put the subject aside, so as not think badly of the dead.

Tierney of course knew from experience that murdered models were rarely of the type who figure in the pages of high-fashion magazines. He had already made quite an accurate estimate of Billie from an examination of her wardrobe.

He said: "I imagine your sister had lots of gentlemen friends. Can you name some?" Tierney had been a patrolman and a precinct detective and now was with Homicide. He was brave: he had once disarmed a fanatic who brandished a live grenade. He had gone to college for one and a half years. But he did not understand women as well as he would have liked. He felt that he could communicate more feasibly with his fellow man. He did not understand that Betty had made instinctive efforts to flirt with him and was now about to give him up as hopeless.

On the one hand Betty would have liked to reveal Billie's looseness, but on the other she was loyal, and perhaps also spitefully reluctant to emphasize her sister's popularity with men. Finally she named but two of the horde: Bobby Cox, a salesman, and Vic Carbo, a prosperous used-car dealer.

"But that was last year," Betty added, "and the year before. I haven't kept up with Billie's affairs lately."

Tierney changed the subject. "This boarder Appleton, his room was the one at the end of the hall on the left? And that was Billie's where she and your mother were found, and your mother's clothes were kept in there also, right? But where did your mother sleep? Billie had a single bed."

"Out here," Betty said in a strong voice, pointing to the sofa where her father sat with the older detective. "That opens into a double bed."

It was the sight of her father, weeping, that made Betty suddenly break down. Since the age of twelve, she had nothing but contempt for her male parent. But seeing him show this unprecedented evidence of humanity reminded her that she was now, except for him, bereft of immediate blood-relatives. Betty put her head into her lap.

Tierney patiently waited for the waterworks to finish, then brought up the subject of former boarders. Betty eventually named those she could remember.

On the sofa, Shuster said to Starr: "I guess you ought to go downtown, Andy, I really think you ought to. This place makes you nervous. Too many memories, eh? Hell of a thing to happen on Christmas Eve. These your packages?" Referring to the gifts, which were still in the corner of the sofa where Arthur had dropped them.

Overpitifully, Starr said no and emptied his pockets of the little tissue-wrapped packets he had brought along for each member of the family: the penknife for Arthur and cheap compacts for the three women. For the sake of his wife, who was not really obliged to entertain him on Christmas Eve—they had been separated for years and he did not contribute to her support— he had also remembered Appleton in a small way, with a pack of cigarettes.

Shuster unwrapped each of the gifts and stared at it suspiciously, learning nothing, but pounding home by still another means the suggestion that Starr was guilty. Shuster did not actually yet believe that Betty's father had committed the murders; it was simply his strategy always to put maximum pressure at the weakest point in any circuit, working as if he were a flow of water or electric power. He was immune to the fact that he and Starr were of the same generation and thus had at least an affinity of time. He would not have been a police officer had he any strong interest in human connections as opposed to disjunctions.

He said now: "Well, you hardly went broke on your Christmas buying, did you, Andy?"

He leaned close to Starr, smelling the man's feckless, musty odor, and said: "I'm going to send you downtown, my boy, and we're going to kick the shit out of you all night and tomorrow."

Shuster had made his first mistake. Terrified by implications, Starr was capable of a stubborn resistance to direct statement.

His spine appeared from nowhere, and he said defiantly: "All right. I don't have anything to hide."

Shuster had gone in too deep to back out. He directed an

officer to take Starr to police headquarters; but with discretion, unmanacled, uncharged, for questioning only. Into the man's ear, he added: "If he wants a lawyer, delay. Delay till I get there, and don't give the name to the reporters."

The officer asked significantly whether there were special instructions.

Shuster had learned his lesson. "Yes," he said. "Leave him alone. Don't even take his arm."

Starr walked proudly to his daughter and kissed her forehead. He had not offered to do that in years, and Betty would have fended him off if he had. Now, however, she said, "Dad." Then he shook hands with Arthur and left the apartment, walking firmly. Because of that posture and the seemingly respectful distance at which the officer followed him, some of the people in the street took Starr for a detective. But this was not true of the newspapermen who had arrived long since and were waiting outside for Shuster to give them entry. They rushed at Starr like concupiscent dogs trying to mount a bitch, and before his escort could interfere, had got all his particulars.

Chapter 2

ON CHRISTMAS DAY, Joseph Detweiler rose early as usual, washed and shaved at the corner washstand with which his room was provided, used the toilet down the hall, and made a cup of instant coffee by means of a hotplate. It was technically illegal to operate such a device in one's room, but Detweiler had explained his needs to the superintendent and got special permission to use the apparatus. People were naturally sympathetic to Detweiler and usually favored him. Bus drivers would even accept dollar bills from his hand; newspaper vendors, sitting sourly in their stalls, gave him directions without complaint. Detweiler was not aware, however, that he received special treatment. He assumed that everybody was habitually pretty nice to everybody else.

Following the coffee, with which he took nothing to eat, Detweiler performed a series of exercises that acknowledged the unity of mind and body, involving both muscle control and mental discipline. Though under the average height and slender, after years of this regimen he was remarkably strong.

Hours later he put on his outdoor clothes, walked to the nearest subway station through the winter sunshine, boarded the first train that pulled in, and as it lurched into motion he began his work, which was out of the ordinary.

Shuster had spent the night at the office, sleeping on a lumpy studio couch in his underwear. He was up at seven and breakfasted in a never-closed beanery near police headquarters. Later in the morning he telephoned home and told his wife not to expect him at the family Christmas dinner that was scheduled for midday. After expressing a ritualistic disappointment, he asked her to distribute to their kids and grandchildren certain packages that she would find on the floor of his wardrobe and to look for her own gift on a shelf in the garage. He liked to have fun with his old woman, to whom he had been married for twenty-seven years: the big box in the garage contained a note, embedded in several cubic feet of wood shavings, which directed her to look for a particular mason jar in the basement. The jar contained another note and so on. At the end of the trail was a small parcel lying beneath the Christmas tree, which would yield up a string of pearls that had cost him no small sum.

But he was relieved to miss his dinner. His son had married a small dark girl whom Shuster did not like. She seemed to be a type of Communist and usually managed when in his presence to bring up the subject of the alleged brutality of the police. Shuster's daughter, on the other hand, was married to a cop who served on the Vice Squad and went about midtown inciting whores to pick him up, take him to their rooms, and strip for him, at which point he would show his badge and make the arrest.

Arnold pretended in front of his wife to dislike the work and had once asked his father-in-law to put in a good word for him with Homicide. But when Shuster had so done, Arnold muffed the subsequent interview with the captain; on purpose, Shuster was convinced. And henceforth he believed that Arnold either climbed into bed with the hookers before the arrest, as they usually claimed before the judge, or, what was perhaps worse, got some weird satisfaction from eyeing them. Whatever, a veteran Vice-Squad man was an oddball, though Shuster had no sympathy for prostitutes. He regarded any sort of lawbreaker with contempt.

Shuster had told Tierney he could stay at home until midafternoon and get his Christmas out of the way before reporting to work. Tierney showed up at about 1:30.

Tierney removed and hung up the jacket of his Sunday suit.

Shuster filled him in: the medical examiner could find no evidence that either woman had been sexually molested; the fingerprints on the screwdriver were smeared and unidentifiable; no latent prints had been turned up; detectives were canvassing the neighborhood, results negative thus far; the routine et cetera. "From what I gather about Billie, if we wanted a complete list of everybody she was screwing we might as well take down every man's name in the phone book. Do you think Betty is the same kind? I saw she had eyes for you."

This was news to Tierney, to whom the people involved in a crime were almost fictional characters, in no personal relation to himself. He had marked the features of Betty's face, body, speech, and attire and could accurately identify certain unstated predispositions, implications, suggestions on her part so long as they did not apply to him.

Tierney had telephoned Appleton's sister in Winston-Salem, North Carolina, at midnight on Christmas Eve, having come across a letter of hers among the boarder's effects. She turned out to be a Pennsylvanian, married to a Southerner, and was much affected by her brother's death although she had not seen him in eleven years. She knew he had no other living relatives and doubted that, with his equable temperament, he had enemies. His last profession of which she had been aware was that of used-car salesman.

"Lately," said Tierney, "Appleton did some part-time selling for Oppenheimer Creations, costume-jewelry wholesalers . . ."

Shuster listened consciously to very little of Tierney's routine reports. In the same fashion he had received the oral and written material produced by the other officers and the medical examiner. On the other hand, he accepted everything, dumping it, so to speak, in a mental wastebasket into which he might later reach and seize what he needed. He was certain the crimes had been committed by a psycho, for psycho motives, and his investigation would have the strength of this bias, yet he would ultimately reject nothing, not even when the murderer had been found and executed. Five years hence Shuster would still remember that Sol Oppenheimer, say, had some remote connection with the Starr-Appleton murders. Passing Oppenheimer's office building, Shuster would see the brass plate on the façade and recall that the wholesale jeweler had once hired a man who was later to be murdered, and the memory would produce in the lieutenant's soul a little twinge of distaste for Oppenheimer, but also a small thrill as well, as when one comes across the souvenir of an old affair of the heart. Shuster was joined to hundreds, perhaps thousands, of persons by such links.

"What's with old Starr?" asked Tierney, not considering that Shuster, being of similar years, might take offense. It was indeed flattering to Shuster that Tierney did not make the association. The inspector understood that, but therefrom he also identified Tierney's weakness: Tierney thought of himself as youthful, which is another thing than merely being young. Combined with the latter it could be debilitating. Shuster himself had always been in professional matters at the psychic age of forty, from which one can reach out in either direction.

"Going to work him out right now," said the lieutenant. "Come along." But he insisted that Tierney precede him through the doorway, be for a step or two a parody of his superior. The young man stumbled slightly in executing the order, as Shuster knew he would, and performed an awkward shuffle with a uniformed officer who just then passed along the corridor. Shuster flanked them gracefully and left Tierney to his own devices.

Starr had been kept all night in an interrogation room furnished with only a table, two chairs, and an overhead lamp that had never been extinguished. He had not been touched, yet he ached in every articulation. He had now been away from drink so long that he felt unearthly, a state much like that of usually sober persons who get drunk. Starr could walk a straight line only after the alcoholic content of his veins reached a certain degree. It was just as well he did not operate a car, proficiently to drive which he would have had to drink himself into an illegal condition.

He was also lonely, and troubled by memories of the bodies to which he had had such a meager reaction when they lay before his eyes. He was actually yearning for someone to come and beat him, just for the company. But thus far on Christmas Day he had been visited only by the officer who brought his meals, and another had led him twice to the toilet, both of these men remaining silent.

Starr suspected the police had no right under law to hold him in this fashion, but he had not yet asked for counsel. Lawyers frightened him more than cops. He slept sitting upright on a wooden chair, awakening occasionally to shift his bony hams.

On entering the room Shuster took the free chair, and Tierney leaned against a dirty white wall, his shadow lurking towards the corner.

"Andy, Detective Tierney," said Shuster, making ironic gestures of introduction. The quick red eyes in Starr's slow gray face shifted from one man to the other. "Did you have a good night? Sorry we could not find you a bed, but they were all being put to use by criminals. Sometimes it is not comfortable to be an innocent man." His harsh laugh was not echoed by either Starr or Tierney. Indeed, the younger detective looked more melancholy than the suspect.

Shuster released a long, moaning breath. "Andy, Andy, what are we going to do with you? Two neighbors saw you on the block ten minutes before the crimes took place." This was a lie. "The super at your house says you went out just before seven." True. "And we found out some interesting items from the other roomers: seems you invite little girls in from the neighborhood and ask them to do dirty things for a piece of candy." This was also a lie as to fact, but it reverberated with a kind of dream-truth. Shuster could be fiendishly cunning.

As it happened, Starr had enjoyed fantasies in which he lured small girls to a private place, but not for beastly pleasures; rather, to inhale their bouquet, to hear their fluty voices, symbolically to warm his cold bones at their glow, as he had once done with his daughters when they were yet too young to be turned against him by his jealous wife. This was clear love and not clotted sex, the latter being an accumulation, as if of orange peelings, bacon rinds, and eggshells, and he occasionally discharged it, as if carrying rubbish to a dump, on some cheap whore.

However, he knew himself incapable of elucidating these truths for anyone. He believed Shuster's assertion that his fellow roomers had blackened his name, and since he had never given them any reason so to do, he assumed it was merely another example of the motiveless malignancy which other people had directed at him his life long.

"Now, Andy," said Shuster, "it is Christmas Day. When would a better time come to clear your conscience? I'll just ask the stenographer to step in, you dictate a nice straight confession, and then you can go to a real nice cell, with your own bed and crapper. Of course they serve up a real Christmas dinner: turkey, cranberry sauce, and the works. You also will be letting young Tierney here go back to his family for the day. Do the decent thing, Andy. That's all I ask."

"I never did it," Starr replied, his voice froglike.

Shuster failed to acknowledge the statement. He went on in the same manner, intimate without being sympathetic. "Here's the way I see it. You had it in for that boarder a long time. You wouldn't have minded if he just had a once-in-a-while tumble with your old lady, who you were separated from anyway. But you couldn't swallow them openly living together, right? And acting like husband and wife in front of you when you came visiting. On Christmas Eve it was too much. You had been stewing about it for a long time. You had a drink or two in the company of those people, something was said on one side and then on the other, and an argument began to shape up."

Shuster nodded confidently at this point, wiped his mouth, and stared into his hand.

"Billie came in, a little high from a Christmas office party at one of those magazines she modeled for. She took a shower and then joined the rest of you in the living room. She was naked under her bathrobe and crossed her legs sitting on the sofa, giving Appleton an eyeful. You got to thinking maybe he was having his way with her also."

Starr had got genuinely interested in the narrative, in which the character that represented himself had certain attributes for which he had always yearned. The real Starr had been incapable of arguing with his wife and still less with one of her lovers. For years she had humiliated and abused him, and his habitual return was a snivel that looked like a smile, or, when really hounded, a headlong flight. He much preferred Shuster's version.

"The argument grew warmer, and Billie got involved in it. Your wife went to Billie's room. You followed her, killed her, then shoved the body under the bed, hoping at least to get out of the apartment before she was discovered. But Billie entered the room at that point. You had no choice. Unlike your wife, Billie managed to make enough noise so Appleton heard it. He was back in his own room by then, tinkering with a radio.

"As you were leaving Billie's room he rushed out of his, screwdriver in hand. Taking a quick look in, he saw the bodies and pursued you up the hall, through the kitchen, and into the living room, where you and he grappled. He dropped the tool;

you picked it up and killed him with it. You then left the apartment, and lingering nearby in concealment, you waited for the arrival of Betty and Arthur Bayson, after which you returned as if it was your first visit there of the evening."

Shuster interlaced his fingers and made his eyebrows speculative. "The details might have been slightly different, but that's essentially the way it happened. A good counselor might even get you manslaughter. Mrs. Starr might have thrown something at you, attacked you with a nail file. Looks like Billie scratched your face." He nodded towards a tiny cut on Starr's chin, actually the work of a dull razor in a shaky hand the evening before.

"If she did it before you touched her throat, you might even have been defending yourself. In the case of Appleton, of course he approached you with a deadly weapon. I don't think you've got a hope of acquittal, frankly, but you could very well get out in ten years."

Reconstructing the crime for a suspect was one of Shuster's favorite exercises. Snares and booby traps lay concealed within the terrain of such an account. Had Shuster guessed wrongly, the subject would feel superior to him for a moment, and nothing was more dangerous to the guilty than self-congratulation. If on the other hand Starr was innocent—and Shuster believed him so—the more details, the better; and whether or not they corresponded to fact was of no importance. The essential thing was to seem omniscient, and thus to demolish in any person so irresponsible as to be associated with a crime all hope and all pride.

Thus far it had worked otherwise with Starr, who had no hope and little pride to begin, but was developing some of both under Shuster's tutelage. He also wanted to impress Tierney, who was young enough to be his son. Starr had yearned for a son, if

not always then at least since his daughters had grown suffi-
ciently old to turn against him. He noticed, the evening before,
that Tierney had questioned Betty, and he assumed that she had
given the junior detective a very low estimate of her father. Yet
Tierney looked at him not with disgust but with compassion.
Men were much more generous than women, and young men
more so than old. Unlike women, most other men usually wished
you well, perhaps because, as members of the same club, they
had a stake in your fortunes, particularly if they were young and
saw you as a prediction of what they might become.

Listening to Shuster's remarkably consistent account of the
crime committed by the fantasy-Starr, the real one recognized
his obligations to the faith of youth. Tierney believed him
guilty, he could see, believed him capable of that terrible, manly
violence; whereas it was just as clear that Shuster did not and
was tormenting him as his wife always had, so as further to
reduce his self-esteem.

When he understood the situation Starr still feared Shuster
but he no longer believed the lieutenant invincible. After all,
his wife had played that role long before Shuster, and she now
lay in the morgue. Starr survived, and always would. He knew
that. Yet he had never done more than maintain his position,
which was very low indeed; had never improved it, never won
a victory.

His chance had come. Because he had gone so long without
a drink, he was utterly drunk in the only viable meaning of
the word.

Looking at Tierney, conveying love and asking more in return, Starr said: "I did it all right. It happened just like you say.
I was jealous of my old lady and the boarder. I got an ungovernable temper. I used to beat her up a lot, and the girls too,

when I lived there. I always been violent. Guess I lost control, it was Christmas Eve and seeing them sitting there like that. . . ."

While Starr was still talking, Shuster rolled his eyes, got up, and left the room.

Tierney slowly approached the empty chair, put his hands on its back, leaned forward.

"Tell me about it," he asked in a sad, youthful voice.

"It was like he said." Starr faltered, upset by Shuster's sudden departure. He needed both of them, enemy and friend, for satisfaction.

"It took a strong man," Tierney said, helpfully.

"I might not look like I have a lot of strength, I know," Starr answered. "I been in poor health for years. But when I get worked up—I just wanted to slap her face, is how it began. But I couldn't stop, got to punching her. Hit her maybe twenty-thirty times and her head fell back like a doll or dummy. Then Billie came in screaming at me, and the same thing happened again. It was terrible, like watching a picture of it happening and not taking part myself. . . ."

"Beat them both to death," said Tierney, stating and not questioning. His eyes were high on the wall.

Starr nodded. He meant his tone to be contrite, but instead it was eager: "I'm ready to take my medicine."

Tierney continued to look at nothing. "You filthy old man," he said in the same melancholy tenor. "You never touched them. They were strangled."

Starr's swallow was like the rubbing of chapped hands.

Detweiler's work consisted of helping people to make the most of themselves. He believed that the great flaw in the accepted morality was the better-to-give-than-receive principle, as a result of which it was a rare person who knew how to accept a kindness, whereas the world was overrun with donors. So what he did to compensate for the imbalance was to travel about among the public and arrange opportunities for total strangers to befriend him.

In a crowded subway car, for example, he would pretend to be lame. It was gratifying to see the seated passengers as he limped on board, contesting with one another to claim the power he had made available. Detweiler understood that this state of affairs must be depressing to the truly disabled, and therefore he himself made it a practice never to do a favor for a cripple, but rather to ask a kindness. He would collide with a blindman, saying, "Excuse me, I am blind." Always the individual concerned would lead him to a seat, guide him across an intersection, and, of special interest to Detweiler, would often conceal his own disability. That is, would believe he was concealing it, which did him a world of good. For a few moments, anyway, he was not blind, for experience is the interaction of contrasts.

Today, Christmas morning, the car that Detweiler rode was otherwise empty for several stations. Then five persons came on board: two young Puerto Rican men, a middle-aged couple, and an old man who carried a paper bag. Then, just as the doors had begun their closing glide, a nimble-footed Negro girl performed a running entry, breathing through her bright red mouth.

Choosing a subject was sometimes the most difficult phase of Detweiler's work. Who among the present company most needed to be reassured that he, or she, could exert force? Several of these persons no doubt knew social deprivation, but that was of no concern to Detweiler, who was interested solely in fundamentals. He saw the girl, for example, as a lively, attractive young woman. The middle-aged couple were past their prime, no doubt suffered from bad feet and worse digestion, but had each other. The old man might be alone in the world but appeared self-possessed, glanced at no one, put the paper bag against his thigh and opened a tabloid. The young fellows conversed in Spanish, a language to which Detweiler was partial because he could understand nothing said in it, and was therefore not distracted by the arbitrary demands of reason.

He was fascinated by the little crowd. To Detweiler any ride on the subway was a feast. He looked from one passenger to the next, eager but cautious: people were put off by too much enthusiasm. Which would he choose? He read the headlines on the old man's newspaper and saw something there that caused him to cross the aisle, sit down, and look at the profile of bald head and hairy ear.

After a while the old man turned to stare back, prepared to show irritation, but when he saw that Detweiler's interest was in him rather than in stealing a free read of his paper, he was flattered. Embarrassed by the emotion, however, he turned away.

"Excuse me," said Detweiler. "I broke my glasses this morning, and I am very nearsighted. I can't read the station signs." At random he chose a destination and asked if they were near it.

"Fifteen minutes yet," replied the old man, at first politely avoiding Detweiler's eyes. Then he suddenly peered into them with his own rheumy pair. "I don't wear glasses at my age; you are blind without them, too bad. It is dangerous not to see good when even perfect specimens are murdered. If you can't see, then you never read the paper this morning: three slain last night, including a beauty. Anything else you want to know from the paper? Comics or horses?"

"No, thank you kindly," said Detweiler. "The same news will all be there again tomorrow and the next day after that. I am interested only in the things that last."

The old-timer grunted and fell silent for a while, annoyed at such a lofty attitude on the part of a youth with bad eyes, yet also stimulated by it.

"You have got to think of *something*," he said at last in benevolent exasperation. "What else is there but what happens daily? That is life, though I agree the best of it isn't always in the papers. For my money, I would not print so much about mayhem and killing, in order that kids not get influenced in the wrong way. For when they do good, nobody writes of it." He chewed at his blue lip.

"Why," asked Detweiler, squinting through his weak eyes —for he experienced his impostures to the bone; though normally he enjoyed 20-20 vision, he now genuinely saw only a blur beyond the three-foot mark—"why *read* of life? Life is here and now, this train, these wicker seats, this motion. For you and me that murder is a story. We know of it only what we have been told by someone else. Nor was it the personal experience of the newspaper reporter, who is just passing on what he has been told."

The man shook his head, amused by the infantile philosophy. "You'll be nowhere at all unless you believe somebody. You must figure in each case whether the guy telling you has got an interest in lying. When you buy a used car, the salesman's got every reason to lie, O.K. The papers exaggerate to sell more copies, O.K. Maybe the model ain't so hot-looking in reality, who knows? But she was strangled all right. That I believe, and I am interested because she was a person and so am I."

He had never before worked out his motives for so simple and obvious an endeavor as reading the daily news. He had taken it on faith that being old, he was wise. He felt affection for this young man who had given him the opportunity to prove it. His own children never let him say a word. He fished two tangerines from his bag and offered one to Detweiler, who accepted it gratefully.

Detweiler peeled the fruit and reveled in the aroma. Carefully he lifted off the underskin webwork, then pursued the remaining white filaments each by each. The train had gained two stations before he was done, and the old-timer had almost finished eating his own tangerine, having slung the peelings under the seat. Detweiler wished with all his heart that he could convince the man that at the moment these tangerines were life, were quite as consuming, vibrant, and significant as those murders. Every experience was as valid as the next. Nothing was born and nothing died.

But from Detweiler's silence the old man assumed that his own eloquence had triumphed and he moved to consolidate his position.

"Police are questioning the father," he said. "Imagine that, his own wife and daughter. Well, maybe he was provoked."

The first segment of tangerine, to which Detweiler had so looked forward, turned sour in his mouth. He put the rest of the fruit and the peelings into a coat pocket, stood up, and walked along the swaying, clattering coach to the door.

The old man was astonished. He wondered whether he had

said something offensive, decided quickly that he had not, and put the boy down as a nut. As the train stopped and Detweiler stepped out, the old-timer shouted: "This ain't your stop!" Too late: the nearsighted screwball was already running through the turnstile.

Detweiler plunged into a phone booth, found the number of police headquarters in the tattered directory, dialed it, and asked for Homicide. He was still in the station, and the noise was deafening as the train pulled out. When his hearing returned, a voice was saying, "Who is this?" with a hard edge, as if it had already asked the same question more than once.

"I want to talk to the officer in charge of the investigation of those murders."

"What is your name?" the voice asked. It was now definitely an order rather than a request. Detweiler felt his nerve endings tremble with the beginnings of ferocity. He was peculiar in that he could not endure a command. Abuse, derision, contempt could not touch him, but he took orders from no human agency. He prayed now that this voice would not persist.

"Let me talk," he said, "to the officer investigating the Starr murders."

It was Tierney who took the call. "Give me your name and address," he said in answer to Detweiler's question.

"Let me tell you something, sir," he said to Tierney. "I will not acknowledge these impertinent questions at this time. I will not be distracted! Do you understand?"

Tierney said calmly: "All right, sir. Just take it easy. Nobody is going to give you a bad time."

"I realize that you gentlemen are doing as well as you can," said Detweiler, "but if you think Mr. Starr killed those people, you are making a terrible mistake."

Tierney cleared his throat. He knew a crank when he heard one. He was also aware that once in a thousand times a crank could furnish useful information. It was not out of the question that this one might himself have committed the crimes. It was quite as likely, however, that some joker was pulling a hoax. College boys and drunks occasionally tried to delude those who enforced the law. Tierney himself had once on a dare, at the age of fourteen or fifteen, phoned the local precinct station with a bogus complaint to the effect that a gorilla was abroad in his neighborhood. The desk sergeant, an old hand, promptly told him off. Tierney had been impressed, amazed by the instantaneous certainty of the sergeant. Actually, wild animals did now and again escape from zoos and circuses; the story was not preposterous per se.

This experience, so insignificant on the surface, had been one of the most influential factors in Tierney's subsequent decision to join the Force. Assurance meant much more to him than authority. He had no great urge to ferret out, or even to punish. His need was to be right. When he was assigned to Homicide, he found his earliest, naive ideal embodied in Shuster, but by that time his belief in himself had dwindled through some years' duty as a patrolman, during which tour he had often been incorrect in his unspoken judgments. This had not affected his performance, else he would never have been promoted to detective, but it troubled him, made him perhaps too conservative when dealing with the obvious. For example, he assumed Shuster had seriously considered Starr as a suspect. Having discovered this was not so, he was at a loss to explain the event. Then Shuster had sent Starr home. "He'll go to the papers," he said to Tierney, "and tell them we kicked him around all night and we'll deny it, which nobody will believe, and that's exactly what we want."

Tierney had been studying this matter when he received the call from Detweiler, and now believed he got the picture: the police must be made to seem as ruthless as the man who had committed the murders, else the public would have no confidence in the Department. But Tierney had learned that principle as a rookie. The Force *was* force, not justice or understanding or pathos or regret. He should not have felt any personal emotion towards Starr, except perhaps a routine contempt for a man who so obviously gravitated towards the unrespectable.

Now, talking to this crank, who might be killer or joker or nothing, Tierney was suddenly struck by an urge to hang up the telephone. He resisted that, but gave in to a succeeding impulse that was even more reckless.

He asked with genuine anger: "What makes you think your opinion is valuable? Why should I listen to you?"

Shuster's eyes widened at this apparent irregularity. It was not standard to lose patience with an anonymous caller, whatever the provocation. The proper tone was weary, bored, sometimes ironic, always superior.

Detweiler, on the other hand, was cleansed of his own ire by Tierney's show of weakness. He hastened to speak in his most fetching way, his voice like that of a contrite child.

"I'm sorry, I'm sorry. Please forgive me." He felt utterly helpless when faced with disapproval.

"How old are you?" Tierney asked sternly.

Detweiler said: "Sixteen."

"Sonny," said Tierney, "it is a serious thing to try to hoax the police. You could be sent to reform school for not much more than that, but seeing it is Christmas, I'm going to let you off if you promise not to do this again."

"I promise," Detweiler answered and hung up. He went back to the platform and abjectly waited for the next train, with an idea of throwing himself under it, but it was too long in coming and meanwhile he was distracted by a machine that vended tiny chocolate bars. He bought one and let it melt upon his tongue: quite the best candy he had ever eaten, an exquisite experience, purging him of the guilt he had felt at trying to dupe the detective. He had not lied about his age; at that moment he had been a teen-aged prankster. Detweiler could be almost anyone or anything he wished. It was done with the will.

"Some damn kid," Tierney told Shuster. "Tomorrow we'll begin to get the anonymous letters." All the same, he should not have lost his temper. He decided to bluff it out. "He would have gone on for an hour if I hadn't cut him short. When I was a boy we used to call the zoo and ask for Mr. Lyon."

"Could have been a boy," said Shuster, merely to get the knife into Tierney, who was running off at the mouth. "I got a neighbor with a twelve-year-old kid, five foot eight in height and weighs one-sixty." His telephone rang at that point and, grinning, he lifted the instrument.

It was a detective in Narcotics who had just collared a junkie. When interrogated as to where he had spent the night, the addict finally named the street on which the Starr apartment was situated. A dried bloodstain appeared on the toecap of his left sneaker.

Chapter 3

Betty Starr accepted an offer from a morning tabloid to write a series of articles on life with her mother and sister, and she and Arthur had been installed in her choice of midtown hotels, all expenses paid, to facilitate that project: a two-bedroomed suite, with a spacious living room between. Arthur whistled at the price he would not have to pay, and urged on by the attendant reporter, who would do the actual writing while Betty talked, ordered a big steak from room service, but while masticating its bloody segments, worried over the question of who should tip the waiter. For in a place like this, even the gratuities would come to a tidy figure.

Betty was too excited to eat. She had always had an urge to write, had done the humorous "class will" for her high-school yearbook and in succeeding years turned out a few poems and what she called mood pieces. Aware that her work ran counter to the popular vein, she had not sought publication, indeed never showed the product of her pen to anyone except a young artist who had once boarded at her mother's, and to him only because he was hopelessly in love with her.

She took two sips of her maroon manhattan, and turning her chair so that she would not have to watch Arthur devour his meat—he was not the world's most graceful eater—she said, "Where do I start, with being born?"

A tall, loosely dressed man called Alloway, the reporter put down his glass of beer, picked up his pencil, and nodded. He had first to get some example of her talking style before he made specific suggestions.

"I came into the world on a frosty morning in November," Betty began. "Few people can recall any experience from when they were babies, but as it happens, I can with extraordinary vividness, even terror."

Alloway had expected to have his ass bored off by this narrative. The relatives of murderer and victim were usually the most tedious people in the world, could remember only the most commonplace details about the principals, were inarticulate at the outset but before long developed a case of verbal diarrhea. Betty might be simply reversing the process, but he was professionally attracted to her early use of the word "terror."

"Yes," he said, "that's the thing."

"I was laying—lying in my crib, looking at a string of red and blue beads that hung between its bars, when suddenly the horrible face of a monster or animal rose slowly up from the floor in my view, bared its teeth, and leaning over, bit me in the toe. Not for years did I realize it was my sister, the late Wilhelmina Starr."

Betty crossed her legs. Alloway briefly saw the gleam of

garter clips. He was a very carnal man, a bachelor of thirty-two whose natural prey was wives. His peculiarity was fanatical: he could not so much as get it up with an unmarried girl. God knows he had tried. For six months he had gone with a maiden named Sandra, who at last, in no more contempt than pity, told him that with what we nowadays know about the human personality, and with all respect, he might be basically homo, really crave husbands but could not admit that, so went for the thing closest to them.

Alloway had worried about his taste, but Sandra's assessment simply made him laugh. "It's more likely," said he to her, "that I hate other men and want to discredit them, show I can do better." The argument broke up their association, as his failure in bed never had, and Alloway reassumed his old pursuit of married quiff, oddly with a lighter heart than before.

He was getting hot for Betty, and he was grateful she had not been the murdered sister. He had seen the lace-panty, bareknocker shots of Billie and was no more moved than he would have been by photographs of stacked luggage. Betty was his type, with her housewifely Sunday suit of black velvet, white blouse, little black hat with its veil retracted, and underneath it all, white underwear over soft skin. The flesh of wives was softer than that of single girls: Alloway did not know why that was. It couldn't be because they were older; Betty for example was in her early twenties. He would have preferred to work with her in the Bayson house in the suburbs, which surely was decorated with corny little figurines and flowered fabrics. Alloway could get an erection sometimes from one look at such domesticity. It had to be middle-class, though. He was seldom stirred by the wives of the poor; he felt little lust in tenements.

But it was part of the deal with the paper that the Baysons

would stay in a hotel. Betty had insisted on that feature. She had great strength of personality, a trait that made Alloway even hornier.

In his professional role, however, he gave a very low value to the story about Billie's biting her toe in the cradle, especially since Betty went on to characterize that incident as the sole interchange with her sister, during Billie's tragically short life, that reflected aught but mutual love. "We shared our toys as children," Betty said, "as we shared our girlish secrets later on, our joys and heartaches."

Alloway took down little of this, though it was very much like what he would write later on, the reason being that Betty had obviously derived her style from standard tabloid stories— some of them no doubt written by Alloway himself. Instead, he doodled, drew a picture that eventually came to represent a bourgeois living room with flowered curtains, tiny lamp on an endtable, plump couch.

"Between us," Betty went on, "rivalry was unknown. It helped that we were basically such different people. Billie was the gay butterfly, often soaring too near the flame—"

Arthur was startled from his coma of steak. Mouth full, gesturing with a roll, he said: "Muff . . ugh . . . moth, not butterfly." He cleared his throat again. "Moth."

"You may be scientifically correct," Betty responded petulantly, "but can't you see that it would spoil the image? I want something gaudily colored, yet self-destructively attracted to fire."

"Some moths have bright coloration," Alloway offered. As it happened, he was a bit of an amateur lepidopterist, having picked up the hobby from an ax-murderer on whom he had once done a story. He had inherited that unfortunate's collection, occasionally adding to it specimens he came across when assignments took him near greenery. Though he never went out deliberately to collect: he would have thought that queer. "The Cecropia moth is as vivid as any butterfly."

Betty, who had mistakenly imagined that Tierney was attracted to her, had so far been blind to Alloway's genuine interest. Or perhaps her instincts rejected an occupation so narrowly genital. She had seen the reporter as merely a kind of microphone into which she spoke, but on the basis of his latest remark she began to dislike him, believing he took Arthur's side in the argument.

She said: "I can't keep to my train of thought if I am going to be incessantly interrupted. You should have gone down to the restaurant to eat."

Her husband made no answer, no move, chewed on. What a clod he was. Alloway could have pitched him out a window, could sooner have done that than suggest to Betty that he and she adjourn to one of the bedrooms. Alloway had no sexual nerve at all unless he got some sign from the woman.

Arthur swallowed and spoke. "Butterflies go around in the daylight when the sun is out." He stuck to the subject with the same persistence he had applied to his meal: he had at all costs to keep his mind off Billie's murder, for which he felt guilty, having disapproved of her so greatly. Having had a certain fondness for Mrs. Starr, he was not nearly so affected by her death.

"This is impossible!" cried Betty, ejecting herself from the chair. "Come on," she said to Alloway. She marched into the east bedroom and slammed the door.

Alloway was choking on his tongue as he followed her, his knees gone to fluid. He did not look at Arthur, but heard the unconcerned clacking of the silverware.

Reaching the door, Alloway tapped timorously upon it, opened it, and sidled in. Betty stood by the window but looked at nothing outside. She was trying to recapture her mood. Finally she went to the nearer of the twin beds and half reclined upon it, still wearing her little black hat. Alloway saw no way out of sitting down in the only chair, an overstuffed job upholstered in hotel-green synthetic.

Betty resumed her narration. "I was the sister more given to intellectual pursuits, though that is not to say Billie was deficient in brainpower. Far from it. She was shrewder than I in her human relationships. I cared for ideas, beauty in the arts, philosophy. Billie was interested in people, men specifically. She had to try and charm every one, and she succeeded with more than you might think, for though Billie was certainly a pretty girl, in all fairness I must admit that my elder sister would probably not be called truly beautiful by the profounder type of mentality."

Alloway's notetaking continued to be very sketchy. There was nothing for his use in Betty's bitchiness towards her dead sister. Readers did not want to hear of that sort of envy, unless masked by moral disapproval.

Discreetly, cowardly, he had left the door wide open. Glancing into the living room now to check on Arthur, he saw his own abandoned glass of beer, three-quarters full.

"Excuse me," he said, interrupting Betty. "I think I'll just get my drink before we settle down. Would you like yours?"

"Really," she answered. "You're as bad as Arthur."

Alloway however was cheered by this statement, the first evidence that she saw him as a being and not an instrument. He went with a springy step to fetch the potables.

Arthur was staring miserably at what remained of the steak: bloody T-bone, charred fat. To whom it may have concerned, he announced: "I'm going to bed. I couldn't sleep all last night. This thing has really hit me." He rose and plodded to the other bedroom, unfastening his clothes en route. Alloway stood there in awe, watching Arthur disrobe through the open doorway, strip right down to the hairy buff. Then Arthur saw Alloway, narrowed his eyes in indignation, covered his shame with one hand and with the other reached to slam the door. Damn queers, they turned up everywhere. Only two days before, he had noticed a fellow accountant eying him at the office urinal.

Perhaps some fairy had committed the murders. Who else would do in a woman? With that conviction, which strangely comforted him, Arthur climbed into bed and went instantly to sleep.

Alloway wandered back to the east bedroom, carrying the glasses, and as he handed the cocktail to Betty said, with an effort towards joviality, "Drink up."

She astonished him by impatiently upending the vessel and swallowing three-fifths of a manhattan neat. Alloway sat down with some difficulty, owing to a sudden surge of his anticipation. She would soon be drunk: he could hardly bear it.

But as the afternoon slunk along towards the early evening of December, Betty's capacity for strong drink proved as extensive as her narrative. Room service had supplied three or four subsequent rounds, always on Alloway's suggestion, and whereas he had begun to suffer the effects of beer-bloat, Mrs. Bayson's fettle was unaltered. In despair Alloway had even finally got around to taking a few genuine notes, though Betty continued to be eloquent in a subtle manner impossible of reproduction. Insisting on her unalloyed affection for Billie, she yet recalled few instances in which her sister had not exemplified meanness or vulgarity.

And with Betty's thin skin, Alloway felt he must suppress the advice that you cannot print that sort of stuff about a dead person. You can show her as foolish, as immoral, even as depraved, but such must be portrayed as the result of exaggerated generosity, the wearing of the heart on the sleeve, the too-much-too-soon, the overabundance of everything: beauty, lust, ambition. The onanists who bought the paper must not be disabused by an implication that the murderer had performed a public service.

For the third time Alloway excused himself to go to the toilet. A bathroom accompanied each bedchamber, but modesty forbade using the facility the entrance to which lay five feet beyond the bed occupied by Betty. He frequented Arthur's, which, the suite not being symmetrical, could be entered from the living room. Another door connected it with the west bedroom, and it was through this portal that Arthur now roamed, blinking, rubbing the sandman's sprinkle from his eyes, dressed in shrunken underwear.

Unfortunately, Alloway was yet some distance from the can and actually facing Arthur's door. He always prepared himself en route, rather than spend undue time hovering over the water closet, which was usually either repellent or dull of aspect. One hand to his fly, seeing Arthur he smiled wretchedly, guiltily, as was his habit with a man he wished to cuckold.

Arthur's features blurred in disgust; he stalked back into his room and across to Betty's.

"That fellow," he stated, "is really a pervert."

Betty inspected his attire, curled her nose, and said: "Who?"

"The reporter. He was obscene just now, over in the other john."

Betty's laugh was coarse. "You mean, playing with himself?"

Arthur abhorred that sort of loose talk. "No," he frigidly announced. "He's trying to—well, he was gesturing at me, you know. He's apparently queer."

"They make some of the best writers."

"Aw, Betty," Arthur said sorrowfully. He padded back and noisily locked his private door to the toilet. At the same time, however, Alloway left by the other door, came around and stood in the entrance to the bedroom. He had mistaken Arthur's expression. Alloway narcissistically believed himself a massive threat to the institution of marriage. He was sure that Arthur seethed with jealousy, and he intended to try to mollify him.

Standing before the dresser, Arthur spotted in the looking glass what he understood as Alloway's beastly attempt to steal up on him from behind.

Furiously he turned and said—trouble was, he could think of nothing to say that would not compromise himself. To acknowledge a pervert as a threat was to play into his hands. Arthur knew that above all these gentry seek a positive response; had heard of a type who, peculiarly gratified by abuse, would accost with an indecent proposal a normal man in broad daylight on a crowded thoroughfare. Arthur had no impulse to punch Alloway. Not that he dreaded violence: it was simply a mystery to him. Reason held that balling the hand and thrusting it against such an obdurate surface as that of the human jawbone would result primarily in broken fingers.

Within three seconds Arthur arrived at the shrewd decision

to carry it off, rising above squalor. The right and the power were on his side. It was Alloway, not he, who had to measure up to one standard or fall to another.

"Yes?" he asked, loftily prolonging the sibilant.

"We have been hard at work all afternoon," Alloway stated uneasily. "We have really made some progress."

"Splendid," said Arthur.

Alloway added: "I think we're getting there."

"Good," said Arthur. Believing that that ended his responsibility, he looked at the ceiling.

Betty, however, gave Alloway a strange, penetrating, yet amused look when he arrived in the east bedroom.

She had earlier been speaking of Billie's attitude towards men, how her sister rather cruelly toyed with the affections of decent types while invariably falling victim to the destructive charm of bad actors. For example: "One Bobby Cox, a salesman of some kind, we never learned of what. He was a crook if you ask me, and you can print that. Cheap, and I mean also in spirit. Was what people of ordinary taste would call good-looking. Billie thought he was heavenly. He admitted he was married but claimed to be separated from his wife, waiting for the divorce. Which turned out to be a lie. He lived in wedded bliss somewhere and had three kids to whom he was a devoted father when home.

"My sister was helpless against his wiles. He treated her badly, you see, and she never could resist that technique. Stood her up again and again, I guess when he couldn't get out of the house or maybe he also had other girls. Billie finally confronted Bobby with the facts, and he turned livid with rage, stopped the car on a parkway and made her get out on the center island and drove away."

Alloway looked at his watch. He had about an hour and a half to get back to the paper and write the initial installment of Betty's narrative.

Betty said: "You know what I think? I don't say it lightly, and I did not mention it to the detectives. But I seriously believe now that Bobby Cox might have killed my mother and sister. He certainly is capable of violence—to put a girl out onto a crowded highway. A man who would do that would not shrink from murder."

Alloway stood up and put away his notebook. He said: "You have the theater tickets. And all the meals you take at the hotel will go on the tab that the paper will pick up. I'll be back tomorrow morning at eleven or thereabouts."

"You're not interested in my theory about the murders?" Betty asked with ill will.

Alloway said: "I'm not a policeman, Mrs. Bayson. It doesn't matter what I think." He suddenly felt very sorry for himself. He would have liked to lie down with his head in her lap. Murder seemed to him not nearly so terrible as the hopeless procession of moments called daily life. He had to go now and at top speed write page on page of futility, and in one day the story would be obsolete. In two days Betty would return to the suburbs, unravished by him.

The surprising thing was that all at once, in the midst of her annoyance, Betty found herself sympathetic to Alloway: she had detected the sadness in his heart.

She said: "What you think matters to me." Though seldom exercised, Betty's generosity was authentic when it came into play, no counterfeit, not in the least sentimental. Her voice now was neither warm nor soft. Alloway could take or leave the statement that she valued his judgment, man to man.

Alloway felt worse: he wanted pity, not respect. He wished he could get that over to Betty, but she came up to him now, looked him in the eye fair and square, and gave him a ward politician's handshake. She strongly suspected he was a fairy. Arthur was superficially stupid but had reliable instincts, especially when it came to sex.

As soon as Alloway slunk out the door, Arthur appeared in Betty's room, still in his underwear.

"What should I wear tonight?" he asked.

He had really come over to watch her undress. Betty loved Arthur for such attentions. She pretended to ignore him, to be businesslike. She and Arthur had never had intimate relations until they were formally engaged. Because of her sister's example, Betty had long remained a virgin, though she would neck and pet with anybody on a first date, and often took the initiative from the boy. She could be bold because she maintained an absolute command over herself.

Once at the age of fifteen she found herself seated in a movie theater next to a dignified, gray-haired gentleman who smelled of expensive shaving lotion. On a whim Betty let her foot steal across until it touched his oxford. He moved his shoe away, but from the corner of her eye she saw a flicker in the white of his. She sat loosely, right leg at a thirty-degree angle from the left, body softly slumped though standing she was very firm in those days. At last the man's long thigh began to incline towards her knee, touched it lightly, withdrew. She sighed and lowered her head as if falling asleep; her plaid skirt rode three inches higher.

Then a terrible thing happened: the man rose from his seat and walked up the aisle, leaving Betty alone with his clinging scent and a nightmarish suspicion that he had gone to report her to an usher, though she was guilty of nothing. But then her cold fingers, dangling over the armrest, in fright opening and closing like the pincers of a beached and overturned crab, touched wadded fabric. He had left his coat behind. She thought he would not have done that had he gone for authority: the girl who made advances might also steal. It was expensive material, a heavy, silken gabardine. She was still stroking it when he returned from the men's room or wherever. She pulled back, yet he must have seen her white wrist.

He settled in, the coat upon his lap. The picture concerned war; a cannonade was in progress. Betty felt unbearably warm as she watched a nurse move calmly about a field hospital though it was under fire. The thin, cool hand resting on the inside of her thigh felt refreshing. She had no idea of how it got there; the man sat farther away from her than he had previously, seemed remote and rigid. A precise finger began to trace the hem of her pants, climbed to the softness of her lower abdomen and traced a circle, around and around. It was soothing to Betty, who had not known what she wanted, but when nothing further happened for an infinity, she grew bored, even watched the picture, wherein the soldiers had captured a store of enemy wine and sausage and were partaking of it with ingratiating gluttony.

Unobtrusively the man had withdrawn his cool fingers. Betty peeped at his unwavering, aristocratic profile, in the reflected candlelight from the simulated rathskeller. Suddenly his head moved close to her ear.

His voice was low-pitched but thin. "I'll give you five dollars for your briefs," he whispered.

Betty at first assumed this was some jargon way of saying he wanted carnal knowledge of her, and that of course was horrible and perverse because he was old and she was fifteen though mature for a year and a half. Now it was she who must fetch the usher. However, her natural optimism asserted itself at this point. She would call his bluff. A hand at either thigh, a shift of the hips, and her pants were off, an action so deftly managed that it would have seemed only an adolescent squirming to the casual onlooker. Anyway, five seats to her left were unoccupied.

He accepted the balled garment and gave her a note that felt like money though folded into a tiny square.

"O.K.," she said, "I'm leaving now." He stuffed the used pants into a pocket of his lovely gabardine topcoat and made no reply. Betty felt curiously linked to him and was reluctant to go.

She tried again to elicit from him some expression of feeling.

"Will I ever see you again?"

"No." His mouth was stern. She rose and squeezed past his sharp knees.

The bill proved genuine when she later examined it in the Ladies.

She cried herself to sleep that night, and for years all she had to do was think of that pathetic incident to achieve a sense of poignancy. The awakening, confused passions of the pubescent girl versus the jaded appetite of the man past his prime: two kinds of appearance and no reality at all. It was pure poetry and the most beautiful experience Betty had ever known.

She wished she had the nerve to tell Alloway about it, though no doubt such stuff could not be printed. The public had a dirty mind, would accept without protest an account of some loathsome performance on the man's part but never this graceful, hopeless transaction.

Throughout these memories Arthur was making love to her. Betty returned to the present as he disengaged and rolled over on his side, stertorously claiming air.

When Arthur could speak, he asked, wrinkling the little patch of hair which almost joined his eyebrows: "Do you think that's bad taste?"

"What?"

"This, with what happened yesterday."

"No," Betty stated definitely. She left the bed and moved towards the bathroom, collecting from the floor en route the underclothing which, abstracted, she had shed before obliging Arthur. In a surge of self-pity she wondered whether anyone in all the world would now pay five dollars for her pants. She liked being married, but it somehow made her feel obsolescent.

Chapter 4

ANOTHER paper contracted with Betty's father for his life story and assigned two reporters to write it. These men were named, respectively, Roy Dilworth and Harry C. Clegg. They installed Starr in a first-class hotel and then took him to lunch downstairs.

The reporters foolishly allowed Starr to drink three servings of rye with an idea that his tongue would thereby be oiled; but inundating an empty stomach, the spirits rendered him mute. Suddenly the seat of his worn trousers lost its purchase on the banquette, and he slid under the table by three-quarters. In fetching him up, Dill's elbow caught the tablecloth and pulled some crockery to the floor. Nothing broke on the thick carpet, but gravy, ice water, celery, and black olives spattered abroad. Harry apologized to a woman with befouled ankles, and with Dill got the bastard out to the lobby and into an elevator.

Propped against the rear wall, Starr was absolutely silent, with ceramic eyes.

On the seventh floor they maneuvered him into the room, telephoned for gallons of black coffee, and ran the shower, but Starr refused to strip, threatened to vomit, and then passed out. Harry and Dill drank the coffee when it arrived, and Clegg called his city editor.

"You schmucks," he was told. "The competition is already on the street with the first installment of the Bayson woman, by Alloway. Unless we can start ours tomorrow, I'll dump it and bill you two for the hotel tab. The police think they can make a junkie for the murders."

Clegg repeated this intelligence to Dill, then looked at the bundle of refuse upon the bed. "Jesus," he confessed, "I could beat that pig to death. I wonder if the wife and daughter were anything like him."

Dilworth said: "I went out with a girl once who posed for pictures. She was philosophical, full of little sayings like 'Don't try to saw sawdust,' 'Only a balloon profits by hot air.' Nobody would have killed her out of passion."

"Well," said Clegg, "your Uncle Harry isn't going to lose this story because of a lush. Let's drag him into the shower."

So they set about it, an easier task than they had supposed: Starr was skin and bones though he usually had a good appetite for food as well as liquor. Neither could bear to unbutton Starr's foul clothing—he stank enough while fully dressed. They hauled him to the bathroom as he was, Harry at the shoulders and Dill carrying the feet, lowered him into the tub, and turned on the shower again. Watched it splash onto his unshaven visage, darken the suit. The reporters themselves were dampened by the ricochet.

Starr at last opened his mouth and drank as a child might, standing in the rain. Then he began to gurgle, and fearing he would drown, the newsmen hauled him up and over the white incline and onto the bathmat, which he overhung, puddling, at each end. He was heavier to lift when wet, and Dilworth professed to have sprained, or strained, something. A hand to the small of his back, he hurled a large white towel at Starr. Harry Clegg knelt and slapped Starr's face, to and fro.

Dill laughed in a hiss; and Starr opened his eyes, afraid of snakes. He had been aware for some moments that he was being summoned to life, but had remained apathetic: it was their job, not his. He started to shiver as the full import of the cold water reached him, though it was not an altogether unpleasant experience.

Harry watched Starr's eyes revolve ever more slowly, finally clicking into position like cylinders in a pinball machine.

"Here," he said, suffocating him in the towel. "Dry off."

Of course it took several hours to bring Starr around to operational condition. Having to go out and buy the subject new clothing to replace the wet stuff, Dilworth spotted a shop in the hotel lobby which offered resort wardrobes for those visitors en route to Caribbean vacations. As a joke, and also for convenience and simplicity, Dill purchased therein a pair of brick-red cotton slacks, a sport shirt of candy stripes, straw sandals.

Surprisingly enough, for Dill had not taken his sizes, the summery togs fitted Starr very well. He looked like a beachcomber who had been picked up and dressed by wealthy practical jokers in an effort to lift a sagging holiday. The reporters had got several quarts of black coffee into him, then a steak, then peach pie with strawberry ice cream: his own choice of menu. He asked for no more booze. Still he would not talk.

Could not, he claimed; all was blurred: effect of the horrible crimes, police brutality, long-term illness, bad luck. Clegg sat on the hand with which he wanted so much to knock out Starr's rotten teeth, and stared at Dilworth, then gave him the high sign.

They went into the corridor and closed the door.

"It's already running into money," Dill said. "I hope Ed will O.K. the charges for those clothes. You know what a hotel markup is on their shop stuff, but I couldn't take time to look around town for bargains."

Clegg nodded in answer to a portly housekeeper's ritualistic greeting. She walked on, with her eyeglasses and keys. Essentially they were actresses, playing maternal parts, thoroughly unnecessary, since the maids cleaned the rooms. "Come back to us again," she would say when they left, if she could catch them. Contractual friendships made Harry's skin crawl. He loathed telephone operators who said "Good morning" before they identified the firm. "Yeah, we have gotten nothing out of him so far. It's like trying to pick up a dime after you trimmed your fingernails. I know this type. If a man's completely rotten already, he can't be corrupted. He is fearless. He has no needs."

"Who wants to corrupt him?" Dill said. "We just want the story." He habitually rejected Clegg's keen insights.

Clegg frequently suffered from a nervous illusion that a tiny fragment of cigarette paper clung to his underlip, and he would pluck there.

"Thay," he said, his fingers still at his lip, "think he'd talk to a girl?"

"That's more money yet," Dill noted, dropping both shoulders of his drab suit. "Brother!" He took two steps, swung around, returned.

"Look at it this way," said Harry. "So far we got *nada*. I don't understand what he's trying to pull. I figured he would talk his head off; they always do. That's turd about the beating Shuster gave him. He doesn't show a mark, and you do, you know, if hit with anything that's hard enough to hurt, rubber or whatsoever. He's just a rotten wino."

"Then he won't go for a girl," Dilworth said with obvious relief. "Alcoholics can't perform. That's basic. Women mean nothing to them."

"Balls," replied Clegg. "There is no man that a woman doesn't mean something to. I'm serious, Dill. Even a fag responds to a woman: he hates or envies her, she makes him queasy. Same thing's true of a lush who's sexed DC. A woman gets some kind of rise out of him even if it isn't the main event. These killings are involved with sex, even though the women weren't attacked. Starr's wife was sleeping with the boarder, Billie was screwing everybody. Who knocks off two women in a row except for a sex motive?"

Harry was speaking intensely but kept the volume too low to be heard by Starr inside the room. Nevertheless he now steered Dilworth to the end of the corridor. A fire-escape door there looked twenty stories down a wall broken only by the frosted-glass windows of sixty bathrooms. What a quantity of waste that added up to, thought Dill, who had a dirty, as opposed to a sexy, mind.

Clegg resumed: "I'd like to make Starr for the murders." His lifted eyebrows suggested the anticipation of triumph. He dug Dilworth in the ribs. "Huh?"

"Come on, Harry," said Dill. "He's weak as a cat, for one. Then Shuster was at him for hours, whether he beat him or not. Then why would he all of a sudden get worked up to the point of killing by a situation that had existed for years?"

"Dill," said Clegg, "I know you won't go for it, but I'll lay it out for you anyhow. Don't start screaming until I'm done."

Dilworth found that speech invidious. Clegg could be very offensive in such subtle ways, though he never quarreled openly with anybody.

"O.K., here goes." Harry put up both hands and backed off with his trunk and neck, speaking rapidly: all this in preparation for Dill's expected reaction. "I think Starr was screwing Billie."

Dilworth's face became a mask of desolation.

"That's right," Clegg said, going into a scarifying whisper. "His own daughter."

Dill produced a kind of whimper.

"All right, all right," said Harry. "But look how it fits. Mrs. Starr catches them at it, Starr strangles her in a rage. The boarder hears the scuffle, runs in, and Starr kills him too. That leaves Billie, and she has to be knocked off because she has seen it all."

Dill calmed down; it was too ridiculous to take seriously. "If you want to speculate, you could just as well say the boarder was laying both women and Starr killed the whole tribe out of disgust. Except you have seen that drunk in there with his bird chest and chicken arms, and you've looked at the boarder at the morgue and seen he was husky when among the living, and the police so far have so little evidence that they haven't even put a theory together. Why haul in Krafft-Ebing?"

Dilworth would certainly admit that incest existed in the

world. In seven years as a crime reporter he had seen much, and at least heard of more in the way of remarkable combinations. One man had been convicted of obscene acts with a Muscovy duck. Another had allegedly had congress with a fantastic electronic device, though the case was dismissed for insufficient evidence.

Yet the more he saw of human oddity, the firmer Dill's belief that only the normal was operative in significant experience, to the degree of 99 per cent. The man with the electronic apparatus had no effect whatever on life in general.

The way Dill looked at it was that even if Harry's preposterous theory held water, it told nothing of value. Murder was murder irrespective of the motive. Three persons were dead, whether for love, money, power, or something nastier.

He expressed himself to Harry, and Clegg said: "Oh, I agree that interest in the crime for its own sake is ghoulish. But that's what the readers are, Dill, all those hardworking, standard types who wouldn't say it if they had a mouthful. Speaking for myself, I want to see the murderer caught, and speaking as a newspaperman, I'd like to crack the case myself. Nothing wrong with that. I'm just tossing the hat at the wall to see if it will find a hook someplace. I say we should get a girl for Andy. Something might transpire, and Christ knows we aren't getting anywhere as it stands."

Dill grimaced. What bothered him was the idea of calling in a whore as a professional colleague. That would be an admission of failure in one's craft. He was amazingly naive for a veteran reporter, Harry told him. Cops used stoolies all the time. They were themselves, or the paper was, paying Starr to talk in the first place, paying for the hotel. The opposition was paying Betty.

"Come on," said Clegg. "Let's put it to him." He knew Dilworth's trouble was the pretentiousness that so often accompanied supersensitivity. Dill loved to do those over-all surveys of social problems—juvenile delinquency, venereal disease, suburban crime—in which the raw material was hygienically statistical and the conclusions pointlessly universal. He retreated from specific realities; still, after all these years, looked grim on visits to the morgue. On the other hand, that character made him a good partner for Harry, as Harry realized. Clegg himself could have waded nonchalantly through a reservoir of blood, so long as it had not issued from his own veins. This was not callousness but rather health; he was ultimately less egoistic than Dilworth.

They returned to the room and found Starr still sitting in an overstuffed chair, stupefied, drinking coffee.

Dill had another try before Harry could suggest the new plan.

"I figure you for a man who has never got a chance to tell his story," Dilworth said sympathetically. Starr looked at him through eyes that expressed no judgment; they resembled those of a jungle animal long maintained in comfortable captivity: no recognizable friends, really, but no enemies either. "We're going to give you a fair shake," Dill went on, "tell your side of it. A million people will read that tomorrow morning. You're a celebrity."

Starr's viscous eyes swam slowly away like bits of sewage in a sluggish drain.

Standing behind the chair, Harry said: "How about a girl? We'll have a party. A real cute girl I know. Anything goes. She'll like you, Andy. She gets her jollies with mature men."

Starr's eyes floated back and solidified as ball bearings. He twisted inside his resort shirt, some gray chest-hair springing out at the V-neck.

He said very clearly: "You wouldn't crap me?"

"Never," said Clegg. "I'll call her now."

"How far she have to come?" Starr fondled his own unshaven cheek, in as ugly a gesture as Dilworth had ever seen.

"Be here instantaneously."

Starr rose vigorously on his arms. "Tell her to keep it on ice for a half hour. I got to get cleaned up."

Chapter 5

SHUSTER was in possession of the account book in which Mrs. Starr had recorded the names, and subsequently the forwarding addresses, of the persons who had boarded with her. An individual named A. A. Smart had left Mrs. Starr's to move only two blocks south and one east, where according to the phone book he was still in residence.

To interview him, Shuster sent Tierney and another detective, a huge man named Matthias. Matty stood six feet five, weighed two-forty, and therefore had to buy his clothes in those special shops that catered to outsized individuals.

Matthias' presence caused Tierney to feel a physical despair of the type suffered by people who live under a mountain. There was always a shadow in the upper corner of one's eye. Matty also habitually stood too near whomever he engaged in conversation, loneliness being a concomitant of his size. He craved the protection of the standard-made. His head alone must have weighed seventy-five pounds, his ears were like hands, his nose as large as a baby's head and much the same shape.

Shuster liked to believe that Matthias produced the desired effect in interrogations by simply looming over the subject while a smaller man posed the questions, but Tierney was not so sure. Matty had only one style: if the threat posed by his sheer bulk yielded insufficient returns, he tended to assume the burden of proof, in the discharge of which he might throw the subject through a closed door.

Tierney pressed the button under Smart's typewritten name-plate and soon heard the buzzer that opened the door. The elevator seemed even smaller than it was, with Matthias as fellow passenger. He instinctively leaned against Tierney, transferring no weight but maintaining contact. Tierney pushed him away under the guise of searching for a cigarette, kept him so by blowing clouds of uninhaled smoke towards Matty's hat.

They deboarded on the fifth floor and Tierney ground his cigarette against the tile floor. The building had been remodeled from an ancient walk-up. The externals were new—elevator, metal apartment doors, wall-paint of pale blue—but the old fundamentals were in some places evident, in others to be assumed. The window on the landing had a wooden sash, scarred though much painted over. An indifferent craftsman had laid the new tiles over the veteran floor, which undulated slightly. Here and there cement had squeezed above the level, causing an underfoot roughness. Tierney could feel the reluctance of his right shoe to proceed with grace. Lifting it in his hand, he saw the sole had worn through in the superficial layer. Matthias of course bumped into him from behind, too gently to knock him down, but Tierney was thereby thrown into an impatient mood.

Ignoring the bell push, he rapped on the apartment door in a technique designed to threaten him who heard it, and when a small man answered the summons, he stared at him with narrow annoyance.

"Are you Smart?"

The little man gave him eye for eye.

Only after Tierney had repeated the question in a menacing tone did he become aware of the pun. Even so, he chose to turn it the other way, to assume it was he who had been mocked.

"Police officers," he said in rebuke. Matthias bumped him again, with no excuse whatever this time. Tierney thrust his badge forth and quickly brought it back.

"May I see that again?" asked the alleged Smart.

Tierney furiously pushed it at him, and the man said: "Wait." He reappeared with a notepad and pencil and, squinting at the badge in the poor light, apparently wrote down the number, for he asked Tierney to specify whether the last digit was an 8 or a 3.

"May I have your name also?"

Tierney scowled. "Are you being clever?" He avoided the word "smart."

"Sir," said the short man, who wore a cardigan over a checked shirt and a plain blue tie, "you know very well that it is my duty, as well as my right, to demand positive identification of anyone who represents himself as a police officer. The police department themselves regularly warn citizens to do that. There are confidence men who pose as detectives. I must say your reluctance is inclined to make me suspicious."

"Let me give you a piece of advice," Tierney said. "If we

were not officers, you'd be in trouble right now. Your door is already open. If we were imposters, we'd already be inside and working you over. Either don't open your door until you're sure, or if you do, accept the situation and when they are gone, report it to the Department."

He felt better now that he was able to correct a citizen and assume the heavy, paternalistic style in which policemen speak to noncriminals. He knew now that Smart was harmless, it being an absolute rule in his experience that no one who resorts to violence ever questions an officer's purposes.

Smart's quick nose twitched. He cocked his head like a wren.

"That's true," he said, surprising Tierney, who had expected such a punctilious man to give him argument. "Come in, officers. I *am* A. A. Smart."

Tierney gave his own name and introduced Matthias, but no one tried to shake hands. In the living room they took the offered chairs, sitting in their overcoats. They were always careful to remove their hats indoors.

Before Tierney was able to say a word, Smart, perching on an arm of the sofa said: "I would have come forward voluntarily, but I knew you gentlemen work at your own pace. As you are aware, I once rented a room from the Mrs. Andrew Starr who was murdered on Christmas Eve. Therefore I knew both of the deceased women. I merely rented the room at first and did not take any meals in the apartment. Later I went on board also."

Smart described his profession as that of ladies' shoe salesman.

Tierney asked: "Are you married, Mr. Smart?" The room was neuter in furnishings and arrangement: beige rug, light-green upholstery, green ottoman striped like a circus tent, a

glass-topped coffee table on top of which a selection of magazines were neatly shingled so as to display the titles, as if in a
public library. The last could have been women's work, but
Smart himself seemed meticulous enough to have been responsible for it. From where Tierney sat he could see along the
hallway to a closed door, which perhaps concealed a wife, perhaps merely an unmade bed.

"Yes I am," said Smart. "I was between wives when I lived
at Mrs. Starr's. I left there to marry for the second time." Saying which, he looked hypersensitive, perhaps vain, and left the
sofa's arm to sit properly on one of its cushions.

"How did you get along—" Tierney started to ask, but his
voice was obscured by a short question which Matty had already
put.

"Divorced?"

"Yes," said Smart, crossing his legs and picking at his sock
He had child-sized feet.

"Not an annulment but a divorce?"

"Right," said Smart, and seemed to display an air of self-
congratulation. Smart's attitude implied he was proud of what-
even his role had been, adulterer or cuckold: as yet Tierney did
not know enough about him to say which was more likely. The
question had been Matty's and revealed a personal interest:
Matthias was secretly separated from his own Mrs., a fact to
which only Tierney was privy. Matty didn't want it bruited
about the Department that his wife was carrying on with an
ex-juvenile offender whom Matty had befriended and kept out
of reform school. The odd feature was that the lad had really
straightened out, working honestly at the menial job which
Matty had got him. Matty's wife was forty and they had a
daughter of fifteen. This home-wrecking boy was now twenty-

two. Ways to get rid of him were infinite, for a police officer; but Matthias was leery of his wife.

"How did you get along with Mrs. Starr?" Tierney now was able to ask.

"I guess it came out about even," Smart answered with a snicker. "There was nothing we would not have done for one another, and that's what we did: nothing."

To pinch off the wise-guy progression, Tierney asked quickly: "What did you do on Christmas Eve?"

Smart said, earnestly: "Right here."

"Did you ever visit the Starr place again after checking out?"

"Never."

"Are you sure about that? It's just a couple blocks away."

Smart instituted a smug movement of his neck and mouth. "Not likely. I had enough of her."

"What's that supposed to mean?" It was Matthias again, leaning forward with his huge head, like a lion over its meal of red meat.

"All right," Smart said after a long breath. "Wilma slept on the couch out front. So if you came in after midnight you had to go through the living room, and it always woke Wilma up. She complained about it every time, and I got pretty annoyed since I was paying my rent and was entitled to come and go as I pleased.

"After several such occasions I threatened to move out, but she didn't want that either: she wouldn't like to lose a good, respectable roomer of my type, she said, and was sorry to have put me to any trouble, but she was a light sleeper and also worried about this separated husband of hers, who she was afraid would get in some night and beat her up. I said O.K. but I reserve my right to come and go, it was not my responsibility that she had to sleep where she did.

"So we let it go at that, but the very next time I came in late she began to bitch from the darkness over by the couch, and I told her to go to hell, I was leaving in the morning, and went down the hall to my room, got into my pajamas and went to the toilet and brushed my teeth, returned to the room and found it dark as if the bulb or a fuse had burned out, and too tired to investigate, climbed into bed."

Smart had thus far spoken dispassionately, but now he produced a smile in which pride and embarrassment were braided.

"I climbed in right on top of a woman. I don't know if you've had the experience, but it isn't sexy. It's creepy if you don't expect it, especially if the arms and legs start to squirm about like fish or snakes. I froze for a while. It took me a while to realize Wilma—or Mrs. Starr, for we hadn't even got to first names by that stage—had got into my bed. She was in her forties but still set up. A nice-looking woman, a little plump. I hadn't noticed her much in that way, because of that daughter. I don't mean I was horny for the girls, but just that you notice women in their twenties over older ones if they are all in the same household, particularly Billie who was something of a show-off, going in and out of the bathroom a lot with her robe loose or sometimes in just a slip.

"The squirming Wilma did was because I had put my knee into her stomach as I got into bed. When she had moved out of the way she lay silent and heavy, never touching me, and then she finally asked if I was going to say anything. That's how I recognized it was Wilma, from her voice. I guess I had up to now thought it might be Billie, whose room was right across the hall—if I had any idea, that is, being astounded."

Smart now laughed outright. "To tell the truth, what I did then was to get sore. I was still mad about her complaint and since she never figured as sexy in my mind, I had a crazy idea she got into my bed with me to argue some more. I am a man who likes his privacy, which is why I didn't take board there."

Matthias had been scribbling in his notebook. He now interrupted Smart's account, which had been flowing smoothly, to ask the pompous question: "Did you and she have intimate relations?"

Smart was startled, and Tierney was furious with his partner. It was destructive to impede the fluency of an interrogation, so long as the subject did not stray into irrelevance, which Smart had not. It was unusual for a man to reveal this sort of experience without undue prodding, and it signified that Smart, whom Tierney had assessed as brimming with the self-love characteristic of many small persons, tended towards exhibitionism.

Smart appealed to Tierney. "Must I answer that?"

See what you've done, you horse's ass, Tierney silently told Matthias. To Smart he said wearily: "You were going to tell us anyway, weren't you?"

"I didn't intend to relate personal details," Smart said, returning to the prissy manner which was apparently his habitual reaction to what he saw as official duress. He was one of those persons who speak freely if given their own head and allowed to believe they are helping the police voluntarily.

"Before I did anything like that, I'd have to consult a lawyer on my rights," Smart added, with growing rigidity.

"Now, calm down, Mr. Smart," Tierney said in his assuaging tone and dreary rhythm. "We're just doing our job. You can't say we have been impolite to you in any way. We just want to hear the story in your own words. Three human beings have had their lives taken from them. I know you want as much as we do to see the responsible individuals brought to justice."

Smart said warily: "I'm not sure I approve of capital punishment." He glanced towards Matty, who was again writing in the notebook. "I guess that makes me a suspect according to your lights."

"We're not judge or jury," Tierney said. "Please proceed, Mr. Smart."

The small man opened his mouth to do just that when Matty looked up and stated: "I want an answer to my question."

For a moment they stared at each other, and Tierney developed a violent contempt for them both: the inept, stupid, obdurate, cuckolded Matty, but also for Smart, the civilian.

The telephone rang twice before Smart rose and walked stiffly to its wrought-iron stand beside the entrance to the hallway.

It was for Tierney. Having announced that, Smart laid down the instrument and went to the bathroom, halfway down the hall. Matty lumbered to his feet.

"I'm getting it," Tierney said.

"Where's he going?"

"The crapper," Tierney said in a low voice. "Let him alone, will you?"

Matty looked hurt.

It was Shuster: "The junkie was a waste of time." He cursed in lieu of an explanation. "How does Smart look?"

"Who knows?" said Tierney. "We just got here." He counted on Smart's hearing that through the bathroom door, but the toilet began to flush before he finished.

"Listen," said Shuster. "I might as well tell you now that

Matthias has got some trouble."

"I know."

"No you don't. The precinct men up in his home district have just picked up that kid that Matty supposedly straightened out. He held up a candy store, using Matty's extra revolver."

"Uh-huh," Tierney responded. Matthias had gone back to his chair.

"Don't say anything to him now," said Shuster, wheezing slightly. "I'll catch him when you come in. I'll shove it up his ass, I can tell you that. If Smart is clean you want to go for what's-his-name—" Shuster rattled a paper—"Detweiler, Joseph Detweiler. You got the address."

Tierney grunted and hung up. "Nothing on the junkie," he told Matthias, who had put away his notebook and was toying with the brim of his hat.

They looked at each other in mutual apology. Matty spoke first. "I been nervous lately," he said, smiling almost paralytically.

"You and me both," Tierney admitted in something more than sympathy. Smart *was* a little smart-ass. Tierney saw that now in retrospect, and when Smart emerged from the bathroom with an air of gratification, Tierney laid it on the line for him: no more pissing around would be tolerated. The change of tone caught the little man off guard. He showed bewilderment and sat down.

"I was trying," he stated, "to show some respect for the dead. . . . All right, Wilma moved in with me. It was very homey, and she prevailed upon me to eat with the family, too, it being ridiculous in my position to go out for dinner, she said. So I went on full board finally, except for lunch on my own, of course, near work. Billie was around a lot, usually half dressed. She was always taking baths and leaving her underwear on the bathroom floor. More than that once she was totally stripped when I passed her door, which she seldom closed, and looking at herself in a full-length mirror. Yet I will say this: she was not sexy. It was kind of innocent the way she displayed herself. I mean it. I remember my brother Charlie, who was a health nut and lifted weights as a boy: he used to stand in front of a mirror in only his jockstrap and study his build. He wasn't admiring himself, but merely checking his development like a carpenter might look over something he had put together."

Smart raised his eyebrows at Tierney, pushing his point.

"I had got myself into a peculiar position there. Guys that came to call on Billie thought I was her father or stepfather. I was treated very respectfully. Sometimes this gave me a kick, for I couldn't be more than ten years older than Billie. But the mistake was understandable since I'd be sitting around the living room in my shirtsleeves or maybe still at the kitchen table."

Tierney asked him to name some of these guys, but Smart said he could remember only first names for the most part: Al and Ralph and Maury or Murray, all of whom came for Billie; and the descriptions he furnished were undistinguished. Al was tall, Ralph was probably Irish, Maury once got a parking ticket and claimed he could get it fixed. "They were generally a lot older than she," said Smart. "You might have thought they were coming for Wilma."

He looked significantly towards Matty, who had remained silent, on his good behavior. "I don't know whether they were intimate with her or not," Smart said. "She was a model. They might have been associated with her in business."

For the hell of it, Tierney asked him what Billie had modeled. Dresses, hats?

Smart didn't know that either.

"Oh, come *on*," Tierney said. "You're beginning to break our balls again." He glanced at Matthias in affinity, but Matty made no return, looked barren.

Smart winced. "I wish I could get my position over to you. I realize it sounds fishy. But I never wanted to get in with them. Wilma made the play. It was easy for me, simple. I didn't have to do anything. My first wife was conceited and selfish and lazy. Her idea of a meal was to warm up something frozen. I had to darn my socks myself."

A keenness refined his features, as of cruelty, but in view of his statement, rather that received than dealt out.

"I didn't want to get involved with the Starrs," Smart protested. "Wilma tried to suck me into her affairs just because she was sleeping with me. Her husband would come around to get money out of her, I guess. He was harmless, some old drunk. She talked about him trying to beat her up, but that was nonsense. He was scared of me, and I am five-four. 'Kick him out,' she said. I refused to get involved. Anyway, all he'd need to do was know I was in the apartment and he wouldn't stay.

"I always figured Wilma would say anything to get me, suck me in, wrap me up, and not for marriage because she claimed she would never divorce Starr. Though she wasn't religious, either. I believe she liked to hook men in one way or another. She'd do all types of favors which you never asked, like washing and ironing shirts. She was motherly, if you like that. Frankly, I don't. I got stuck there for a while and then pulled loose."

Tierney had gone over the list of boarders and verified his memory, letting Smart run on in his characterization of the late Mrs. Starr though it was not likely to be useful. What people thought, or believed they thought, generally was worthless in the investigation of a homicide. Smart may have been quite right in his theory that Wilma Starr tried, morally speaking, to suffocate a man, but that opinion, like all such, was a dead end. The next boarder, of another make-up than Smart, might analyze her personality to an altogether different conclusion. Or if he and ten more agreed, it might still suggest nothing as to the identification of the person who committed the murders.

Matty came to life. "You resented Wilma Starr's ways? Did you argue with her, maybe lose your temper? Why did you move out if you had it made?"

Smart took no offense. He shook his head sadly. "She was really kind to me. I am sorry she had to die like that."

"Where'd you say you spent Christmas Eve?" Matty asked, as though he expected the man to change his story for no reason at all.

Smart answered as he had earlier: here, here at home. Tierney had of course noticed on entering the apartment that no Christmas decorations were displayed, not even a jarful of colored balls or a pyramid of silvered pine cones. Yet Smart did not seem to be Jewish.

Tierney asked: "You and your wife?"

Smart made a funny, defenseless, ducking movement of the head. "I don't get out much. She's sick, and it costs all I've got to have a nurse here while I'm at work. I'm home today because they are taking inventory at the store and don't start the after-Christmas sale until tomorrow." He rose without using his arms; strong in the legs, like many small guys. "You can come see her if you want."

It was Matty who said decently: "We won't disturb her?"

"Not at all," said Smart, smiling. "It gets pretty lonely back there."

He led them along the hall, a veritable child or midget ahead of the elephantine Matthias. He opened the door after a courtesy-knock, stood aside for Tierney to pass through, but in view of Matty's bulk, himself went second. A woman lay in bed. She was probably about thirty years of age in standard time, but ancient in illness: yellow within the sheets, her eye sockets as dark as her hair, hands and wrists gone skeletal. She was indeed dying.

Tierney had once worked on a case in which the female corpus delicti had been butchered into sixteen parts with a rusty implement and wrapped in as many separate sheets of newspaper, then packed into two valises and deposited in the main checkroom at Grand Central Station. The victim had probably been quite dead before the dismemberment commenced. Thus a particular sympathy was beside the point. By aesthetic definition it was a horror, but in human terms was perhaps not so bad as it looked: suffering may not have been an issue. And in fact, when the killer had been apprehended, he claimed, if he could be believed, to have crushed the woman's skull while she lay sleeping.

On the other hand, a divine sadist was devouring Mrs. Smart, one corpuscle at a time, and this shook Tierney, who, though he had been reared as a Catholic, never thought about God unless he could lay some criminal act at His door: the Omnipotent Malefactor, exempt from punishment.

In a corner, on top of a television set now dumb and blind, was a small Christmas tree, bedecked, entinseled, and a little bell of red foil terminated the pullstring of the window shade. Through the sickroom odors came the aroma of spruce.

Matty spoke graciously to the patient on commonplaces of the season. Tierney had never seen this side of his giant partner.

"The long needles last longest," Matthias was saying. "It's the short ones that fall out creating a mess."

Smart, kneeling, unwound the cotton sheeting that swathed the base of the tree. "Have to add a lot of water," said he, peering into the container between the legs of the supporting tripod. "It evaporates in the heat of this room." He topped up the level from a long-spouted, miniature sprinkling can, the indoor-garden model.

Mrs. Smart worked at a response to Matty: froglike sounds issued from the waste of her throat. Tierney could not begin to understand the words, which seemed to be of the vocabulary one hears in dreams, recognizable as English yet incomprehensible to the dreamer, to whom only pictures speak. Her eyes, though, were jewels.

Tierney smiled and mumbled, standing stockstill with all his musculature in contraction; he was a kind of human projectile and could have been shot from a cannon.

In a moment Smart showed them out, of the sickroom and the apartment. "Thank you," he said in the hallway, summoning the elevator with his small thumb. "Being absolutely hopeless, it is not as hard to take as you might think."

"Except for her," said Matty from high above, as if pronouncing divine judgment.

"I was quoting her," Smart said, crossing his arms over the cardigan like a woman. It was drafty in the hall and someone shouted metallically on another floor. Smart said: "Let me know if I can help you further. I'm not going anywhere."

In the down elevator Matty kept his distance, remaining silent except for a little breathy whistle emanating from the forefront of his mouth, to no tune: *pippeesh, pip-peesh,* like radiator steam.

In the car Matty observed the human beings they passed, pedestrians and the occupants of other vehicles, on the off chance he might recognize a wanted person or even spot a crime in progress. In his time he had done both: three years before, while waiting for a traffic light he had seen upon a corner a man resembling the mug shot of the professional gunman Stanislaus Witchek, circulated by the Detroit police. Having been seized without warning and slammed against the wall, the suspect admitted immediately that he was indeed Witchek and was taken into custody without resistance. At another time Matthias had watched a man run from a jeweler's with a bag in one hand and a pistol in the other. From the window of the car Matty fired five shots, killing the robber and superficially wounding a passerby, who subsequently sued the city.

Tierney said: "My aunt died of stomach cancer, but she was sixty-eight."

An unshaven man in his fifties, wearing a dirty plaid tie, answered their knock on the basement door. He asked them inside before they could state their business, and addressed them as "Officers" before they identified themselves. From this behavior Tierney inferred that the super either had a record himself or was in some other role a veteran of encounters with the police: perhaps his tenants were often criminals.

Tierney therefore wasted on him none of the courtesy and patience that had been shown to A. A. Smart, and in possession of his name, Moran, was conscious of no fellow-Irish affinity. In the current situation Matty was not a detriment. The superintendent was a tall man and heavy, but Matty was bigger than anyone.

Backed against the dank basement wall, though he was not touched by either officer, Moran remembered a tenant named Joseph Detweiler, a blond kid, short, skinny, nuts. He wasn't here no more, and didn't leave a forwarding address.

But Moran would check anyway, so they let him by and followed his dramatically cooperative stride, shoulders swaying loosely in exaggerated professionalism, past an open closet full of brooms and pails, into a living room that would not have been really squalid in better light. A small artificial Christmas tree stood on the mantle above a blocked-up fireplace. The TV was half alive with some murky representation; the sound was off. From his angle Tierney noticed only frantic shadows, which swooped towards an intense but transitory point of light as Moran extinguished the set.

Moran plucked through a little file of the kind housewives use for recipes, and withdrew an exceptionally clean three-by-five index card. It had not seen much traffic. He prepared to read its legend aloud, having ostentatiously placed a pair of glasses on his head, but Matty's great hand descended on him like the ax of an executioner and took the card away.

"What do you mean he was nuts?" Tierney asked.

Moran winced in thought. "He was a nut about noise. My wife goes through the rooms with a vacuum every Friday. He said the sound drove him out of his skull."

"He around all day?"

"Sure," said Moran, "molding these statuary heads. He was a sculpture, artist. Once I told him if he wanted to do one on the subject of myself, he could forget about a week's rent, so he did it and there it is."

He pointed to an object alone on the top shelf of a bookcase otherwise the repository of stacked newspapers, then asked Tierney if he would mind stepping across for an examination, for it was fragile and shouldn't be carried or handled.

Tierney of course picked up the head straightaway, so as not to show respect to Moran, but he was secretly careful with it. His hands got the impression of weight, crudeness; no pleasure to his tactile tastes, which ran to precision mechanisms: watches, locks, jointed and wheeled devices. Art seldom was complete in itself and asked too much of him; in its presence he grew peevish.

The head did resemble Moran's own, which being bald was easy to simulate in the top third. In the rest, the sculpture was less coarse than the original, as it were smoothing Moran off, further cheapening a visage which in life displayed little probity. Tierney, though, was insensitive to its testimony, thought it badly executed. What he saw in the living Moran were the eyes, compounded of guile and cowardice, whereas of course only two holes appeared in the representation.

"It's just cooked clay," Moran whimpered nervously, watching Tierney weigh the piece in two hands as if he might toss it into the air.

"He told me I could of got it made into bronze if I could of got the money for it, though pretty expensive, he said. But I ain't got no money for that." Moran produced a horrible, wheedling smile.

Tierney asked: "You don't own this house, do you?"

"Nah," affirmed Moran, still grinning through moistened lips.

"Then I take it you paid the landlord out of your own pocket for the week's rent you told Detweiler to keep."

The super sucked back his smile, and said: "Sure."

"And didn't report the room empty for that week."

Moran said hoarsely: "I am one-hundred percent square with the boss, Officer. You can run a check on that."

Tierney said: "I'm not going to, Moran. I'm going to ask your precinct captain to do it, O.K.? You won't be disappointed?"

Moran nodded, and wrinkled his nose so as to show he appreciated Tierney's wit, and said: "O.K., I haven't nothing to hide."

"You're shit, too," Tierney said. "Detweiler never came around here again?"

"No," said Moran, still shaky. "He knew better than that. I would have called you guys."

Tierney still held the clay head, the broad nose pointing upwards.

"He owe rent? Did he steal something?"

"No," Moran said, "oh no. He was the perfect tenant, paid me a week in advance every Saturday morning at ten A.M. Could set my clock by him. Clean, too. No parties, no breakage."

Tierney sneered at the blinded fireplace and left it to Matty to ask: "What you mean then, you would of called us?"

"Sure," said Moran, instantly going beyond recovery into the beginning of a swagger: he knew something the cops did not.

The head had no pedestal. Tierney erected it again on the bookshelf, resting it on the smoothed end of the raw neck.

"Fella," said Matty, "are you going to tell us about it without more cute farting around?" He swung his trunk left, then right, rubbing each elbow against his belt, as if to warm the grease.

Moran hastened to say: "He almost killed another roomer."

Chapter 6

DETWEILER never dreamed, yet he often awakened in the morning with a piece of intelligence he had not possessed on retiring the night before.

So it happened this morning. There seemed to be another thickness of curtain across the window, but walking there, which tickled as his bare feet met the floor between the rugs, he saw a wealthy descent of snow outside the pane, a collection of it on the sill and in the street below, parked cars already enmired. A fat man plodded along the opposite sidewalk, ankle-deep. Detweiler noted with relief that this pedestrian was wearing artics. Joyfully he then determined to pelt him with a snowball, raised the window for that purpose, was flushed by the pure, cold, serene air; all sounds were muffled, distant, lovely; a truck rolled ahead of long furrows, as if on silent runners. Detweitler, chortling, tried to roll a ball of the cold fluff—then all at once he received a dispatch, or rather accepted that which had been delivered during his sleep and lay in its yellow envelope, unopened, on the night table of his mind.

They were after him. He must elude them.

He lowered the window, repaired to the closet, and got from its top shelf his old rucksack. His extra pair of socks, washed the night before at the basin and hung across the radiator, were almost dry. He owned two sets of underwear, two shirts, a few ties and handkerchiefs and socks, one sweater, a suit. When fully dressed, he had very little to pack. He possessed no books, having not for years engaged in what was for him the utter futility of reading: Detweiler was innocent of a sense of humor, never got the joke implicit in imaginative writing, but on the other hand had too hopeful a temperament to appreciate philosophy and found exposition too abstract for his practical senses: he never, for example, read the instructions as to how to reclose a cracker box so as to keep the contents bakery-fresh, but either figured it out on his own or ate soggy saltines. It was offensive to him to trace out Flap A, Slit B, and effect their junction. He would not subordinate himself to tiny inkmarks on paper.

Detweiler looked forward to a time when he could Realize the packing of his clothes, Realize himself upon a train, every detail precise and perfect—fellow passengers, passing landscape, meals in the diner, braking into stations, accelerating out, noises and smells—Realize his arrival at the destination. He would be *there,* without having physically left *here.* Yet if sought here, he would be there in body as well. He would be able to translate himself into a new context, using only the mind.

Everybody would be capable of this technique in time to come, outmoding cars, railroads, aircraft, with their racket and dirt and dizzying motion. Detweiler knew he was merely the forerunner and therefore had no cause to be arrogant. Indeed, did he not know that God was omniscient, he would have believed himself a poor choice for the role, he who was so liable to distraction. As yet he could Realize not so much as his neckties into the haversack. He stood in the center of the room, staring at them as they hung upon a string stretched between two thumbtacks on the inner surface of the open closet door. Perhaps the striped one trembled; perhaps it was only the draft. Anyway, he was distracted, unable to bring 100 per cent of his force into play. They were after him.

He had never been pursued in this fashion before, but he had many times run afoul of those who were hostile to Realization. Usually these persons were stupid rather than malignant, captives of erroneous assumptions about reality.

For example, he had gone to several private doctors and a number of public clinics, with a simple request: that his penis be amputated. His motive was not perverse. Of the basic pleasures he enjoyed nothing more than making love to women. Indeed, he liked it too much. Sex was a major distraction. How often had his labors been interrupted by no more than the sound of a woman's shoes on the distant pavement. Realization was possible only in a state of utter serenity, desires purged, the mind unresponsive to contemporary phenomena. But heel-clicks on the sidewalk, a girl's high laughter, a filament of perfume in the sea of air—a suggestion of femininity, however slight and remote was enough to divert Detweiler from the most elaborate project, turn him from Realizing to mere dreaming, imagining, conjuring up nipples and the warm inner surfaces of thighs.

Elimination of the obstructive member would take care of the problem. He had explained as much to the various physicians to whom he applied for relief. It was anyway his own organ, to dispose of as he saw fit. Were not sex maniacs sometimes emasculated by law? But his appeals were unavailing. One doctor advised frequent warm baths; another prescribed two aspirins every four hours. At last, in a public clinic, he was referred to a psychiatrist, who questioned him on a host of subjects that had only their irrelevance in common: his parents, masturbation, attraction to other men, and whether he had ever yearned to be a girl. However, Detweiler found these questions more amusing than objectionable, and he liked the doctor, who though childish, perhaps even weak-minded, seemed sympathetic and made a genuine effort to understand. Detweiler talked to him at length about Realization. How much got through was another matter, but at least the man listened.

Perhaps he was being merely polite. Detweiler loved good manners. When the doc offered to treat him, he accepted, though he recognized in himself no illness that needed care. However, it would certainly have been rude and mean to turn down the invitation. So to be obliging he went occasionally to the psychiatrist's private office for an hour's talk. He was never asked for a fee, and considered that what he told the doctor about Realization was adequate payment for whatever was being done for him.

Now, as he fastened the straps of the rucksack, Detweiler remembered that doc, that really nice guy, recalled he had neglected to see him for ever so long. He should at least have sent the doctor a Christmas card. Detweiler made his own cards, drawing each one freehand in India ink and adding the tint in water colors: his favorite subject was a big, roly-poly Santa Claus, with one boot in the chimney, one on the roof. It was full of good feeling. He had forgotten to make any this year, owing to his preoccupation with Betty, and nothing had come of that, and now he was being pursued. God, the distractions! He had tried once to amputate his penis himself, using a razor blade, but hadn't the nerve to go through with it. The pain, so simple a thing, was unbearable after the edge penetrated the skin jacket and sank into the red core of nerve and muscle.

He was frequently hindered by natural, basic processes. Sometimes, poised on the very threshold of a Realization, he felt ungovernable hunger, had to forsake hours of work to go eat a bowl of vegetable soup. But Detweiler never surrendered to despair. He found joy even in losing, through his conviction that at any time he could see only a portion of the sphere of maximum being, in which an apparent reverse might be really an advance from another direction: as in terrestrial travel you may go either east or west and eventually reach China. And it was with ecstasy that he thought of himself as an average person. What he could do, could be done by any other normal person with similarly routine gifts. And ultimately he could do anything, after having overcome certain massive resistances.

He swung the haversack onto his shoulders, buttoned his wool-lined raincoat, and went from the room, leaving the key in the lock. Rent was paid up to next weekend. Detweiler understood that the super was entitled to keep the surplus in lieu of notice. Along the hall and descending the stairway to the ground floor, he looked for his friend the house cat, a very interesting animal of the tough city breed. Detweiler had invited it into his room one night early in his residence. After cautious investigations it lapped up the saucer of condensed milk he had provided. But when he sought amiably to scratch the cat's head, indignant claws opened furrows on the back of his hand.

Dispassionately, Detweiler got into a pair of leather gloves and batted Cat's head around. It did not run away, but stood and fought back, though ineffectively, against the drubbing. Noble animal. This cleared the air between them. From then on, the cat would rub its length along Detweiler's shins whenever they met. And for his part, he was always good for a handout. If he had the money he might even buy thick cream for his pal.

At the moment Cat remained somewhere else, and Detweiler opened the street door and departed from that address forever. He had lived in many places, liked most of them, forgot them all when he left except those in which he had made some enduring human contact. He remembered the Starrs' because of Betty.

Taking the snow in his face as he came down the stoop, Detweiler decided to walk to the railroad station. His shoes were rubber-soled and sound, and he wore a good warm stocking cap. He found this type of weather refreshing. He strode so rapidly that he began to perspire after three blocks, and he breathed through his mouth, thereby catching snowflakes that dissolved in little peppery flashes on the tongue. The snow stuck to the sidewalks and streets, however, insulating the city. Detweiler sensed that it was going to be a fall of some proportions: his nostrils picked up a gunpowdery smell, and the atmosphere was growing ever more opaque and yet whitening as well, providing illumination in and of itself while denying access to the sun. It might snow for days and arrest all movement.

Excited by his thoughts, Detweiler plodded northwards. He was disappointed to see the station suddenly appear across the street. He could make it disappear through Realization, replace it with Valley Forge as of winter 1777 with Washington striding grimly about in his greatcoat and boots, soldiers warming their hands over campfires, horses stamping and steaming.

Inside the station he bought a paper headlined ARTIST SOUGHT and with tepid interest but no surprise read his name in the story that followed. Having turned the page, he saw the first installment of Betty Starr's narrative. Overwrought, he quickly discarded the paper into the nearest trash container. He bought a chocolate bar full of almonds, usually a favorite treat, but could hardly swallow it for the lump in his throat. Betty provided the great disappointment in his life. He had loved her on the very highest level, where the passions gave precedence to spirit and mind.

He did not wonder that she had turned to professional writing: her intelligence was radiant. She was the only other person who grasped the theory and practice of Realization. In her presence and aided by her moral strength, he had conducted his most successful experiments. Certainly he never touched her, and she made no sound except an occasional murmur as they sat side by side, sometimes in the dark, often on his bed, to which she tiptoed after lights out. In another kind of association Detweiler would no doubt have been attracted to Betty: he could admit that academically. But by contrast to this enterprise, sex was pathetically fragmentary. You had it and it was done for the moment; you waited for the reservoirs to refill. It was not truth-retaining, not durable. You were incapable of it until puberty and after a certain age, whereas Detweiler had begun to practice Realization when he was ten years old, and he expected to work at it until he died, which would be ever so long because he planned to live a lengthy span. His will armored him against physical ailments. Detweiler was never under the weather, nor even got cavities in his teeth.

He had met Arthur Bayson once or twice in the Starr living room, was technically aware that Arthur came to take Betty out, and could even remember, when he made the effort, that Arthur had given Betty an engagement ring. Detweiler took none of this seriously. Therefore he was dumbstruck when Betty married Arthur and left home to live with him in the suburbs. He could not understand that Realization meant so little to her. Together they had attempted to Realize Cleopatra drifting down the Nile on her gaudy barge, being fanned by giant blue-black eunuchs. Little handmaidens offered grapes in silver dishes. Brawny slaves strained at the oars when the rectangular sail fell slack. Old Antony stood at the rail, a weak but pitiable character. There you had the limits of lust. To see him there, his lackluster eye, his used face, his skinny shanks, varicosed, was to apprehend historical truth.

Nothing that happened ever passed out of reality: all was still in existence, every image, every voice, all occurrences, filed away as it were, on cosmic film if you like to call it that, so long as you understood that it was in no way a representation, a re-creation, but rather actual and eternal, its temporal divisions being merely a human argument. That was to say, Time, though often seemingly important, inconvenient, even dangerous, was not ultimately serious.

Realization could be only approximated in language, *talked about*, but not *experienced*. Betty had understood this from the first. Though normally loquacious enough—Detweiler loved to hear her bright chatter—when they were Realizing together she silently took her cue from him. This sympathy had been essential to his efforts. Never before and not since had he approached so closely to an Absolute Realization: the first AR, which would be known in the records as AR^1, for this was a science, and Detweiler knew he was only a forerunner, a kind of Archimedes, of the great Realizers to come.

He had almost no money left after buying his ticket, so he stopped a passerby and asked him for a dollar. His victim was a dark-skinned person wearing long sideburns and a hairline mustache. At first he took it as a joke that a sober, clean, blond individual would ask him for aid, but no one who looked at Detweiler's committed face could mistake what he saw there as wit.

Detweiler explained: "I haven't eaten anything today. I'd like to get a decent breakfast before I board the train."

The young man solemnly forced a slender hand into the pocket of his tight trousers and came out with two dollar bills. They were in fact his last two, though he would rather have died than let that on to Detweiler, and presented them with an air of casual munificence, then waved, saying nothing.

Detweiler ate a plate of scrambled eggs which to anyone else might have resembled a boiled pigskin glove, and a cairn of french fries more grease than potato, but he thought them very good indeed, and said as much to the girl cashier as he paid the check. In his habitual enjoyment of the moment, Detweiler had forgotten again about Betty. He had also momentarily forgotten about Realization. When he noticed the cashier's full breasts, however, and was conscious of an acute urge to take one in each hand with the nipples between index and third fingers, he remembered why he was going to another town: to find a doctor who would mutilate him. He assumed it would be easy to arrange that elsewhere, in a city with different customs.

But he was weak, so terribly weak. He could not help himself. He accepted his change and leaning towards the cashier, he said fervently: "I would like to make love to you."

A sullen, stupid, white-faced, black-haired, urban girl, she short-circuited her change machine and an avalanche of quarters clattered down the chute, overrunning the collection basin. With the fence of his hands Detweiler stopped those coins which would otherwise have rolled off the counter. He returned them to the girl, who gazed tenderly at him in total acquiescence. She astonished herself; she generally reacted with pseudo-hatred to any evidence of male admiration.

Detweiler, however, seemed genuinely to need her: she was urgently required!

But then for him a sense of duty intervened. Detweiler reached across and touched her wrist, applying no pressure, yet it seemed as though she were in the grip of high authority, a principal in affairs of magnitude.

"However," he said, "I have to go away."

Dumbly she nodded, nobly restraining her grief though the loss was major. No sooner had Detweiler vanished, however, than she took him as the product of a hallucination. A short blond man had stood there all right, and said something, but not that.

The girl hired by Harry Clegg to ingratiate herself with Andrew Starr looked incessantly for work in the theater, but when unemployed as a Thespian she would for payment allow a man, often a total stranger, to caress her intimately and eventually thrust himself inside one of her body openings. Her ego was of sufficient strength to admit that this behavior added up to prostitution.

Clegg now and again called her number when he wanted to oblige someone so as to get a story out of him, as now. Which made Harry as much of a pimp as it made Lois a whore. There was no sexual attraction on either side.

Dilworth, however, was new to Lois; and as she arrived at

the room the reporters had taken just across the hallway from Starr's, she assumed Dill was the trick and showed him the smile that would have been commonplace and unevocative in any other context. This is all Lois ever did by way of initiative. She would not voluntarily touch a customer in or out of bed. And if a man took her hand and put it on him, she withdrew; a second time, and she threatened to call off the game. Oddly, this treatment usually seemed to aggravate·the man's passion, sometimes to the point of prematurity. Which was all to be desired by Lois. Whatever the nature of the discharge, her obligation ended with it.

Harry said: "Our guy's across in four-twelve." Generally he preferred to tell Lois as little as possible about the client, but in this case he believed she would recognize Starr, whose picture had been run in every paper with the first story on the murders.

" 'Old man Starr?' " repeated Lois with a wince of non-recognition. "Who is that supposed to be?"

Lois always managed to amuse Harry. "You don't read the paper you free-lance for?" he asked, almost affectionately.

Dilworth was intrigued by hookers, with whom however he did not consort. From boyhood to the present day, he had never lost his capacity to be enchanted by a reminder of the existence of women to whom one could do anything with impunity. It was wrong for a man to force his attentions on a respectable woman, but if she was a whore, no holds were barred. She was as a criminal to a cop, or public buildings to a revolutionary, or a fire-ravaged department store to a mob of looters. Anything went. Absolute freedom. Dill's fascination was philosophical, not physical.

"All right," Lois said wearily. "I give up." She had ignored Dilworth after learning he was not the customer. She listened·

languidly to Harry, and said: "Murders? I glanced at the headlines, but I never read that sort of story. I suppose something is lacking in me. If a fire truck rushes by, siren wailing, I never have the impulse to turn around and watch where it goes."

Dilworth was interested: a reflective tart—though perhaps they all were.

Lois went on: "I feel instinctively apart from the herd. It is a constitutional thing."

Dill spoke: "You abhor violence?"

She turned suspiciously to Clegg. "Does this Starr want to be dumped? I don't do that, and you know it."

Dilworth couldn't get over how banally Lois was dressed: a black suit, with some lint on it; white beads like blanched almonds; small hat. Perhaps she was striking when naked.

Harry laughed again, exposing his carnivorous front teeth. "No, he won't want to be whipped. Mr. Starr is a distinguished gentleman of the old school. You can certainly handle him."

Lois hated Clegg's entrails for always going out of his way to treat her as a prostitute—for example, not introducing this other man—but until she became better established as an actress she could not afford to lose the work he got her. He had also promised to introduce her one day to his colleague on the paper, the drama critic C. John Blackmeyer.

"Don't worry," said Harry, still laughing hatefully. "He's a physical wreck. . . . Now, here's what we want you to do—"

"We?" Lois asked stubbornly.

"Dill and I."

Lois shook hands with the surprised Dilworth. "How do you do, Mr. Dill. I am Lois Fern."

Her hand felt like a lettuce leaf: so cool, crisp, weightless, nonfleshly. Unwhorelike, she had given her last name.

Dill pronounced the full version of his own.

"I'm sorry."

"Not at all," said he. "You didn't know it." They both stared contemptuously at Harry, and Dill felt himself falling in love.

Harry was oblivious to all of this, saying: "Get him to talk, get him to boast. Men sometimes let things out in intimate moments with women that they wouldn't otherwise."

"What kind of things?" asked Lois, wondering whether she needed the money this badly.

It then occurred to Harry, as it had not before, that to tell Lois of his theory that Starr was the murderer might not be the best preparation for her encounter with the slob.

So he said merely: "We think he has some connection with the crime, though he himself is a harmless old codger. Knows more than he has told the police. His wife was screwing the boarder, and God knows who was shoving it to Billie Starr—"

Lois turned towards the door. "I don't have to listen to your foul mouth," she said. "This is a business arrangement and if you can't conduct yourself in a gentlemanly manner . . ." She was authentically offended, almost to the point of tears.

This uppity demonstration by a hooker infuriated Harry, but in the interests of the project he held his peace. He said harshly: "Try to get him to talk about the case. That's your job. Remember anything he says, no matter if it seems insignificant to you. As incentive I'll double the fee if you come up with anything useful."

"O.K.," said Lois, "but in case I don't, I want my usual right now." She reached. To avoid the wretched scene, Dilworth looked at the hotel-painting over the nearest lamp: of course a sailboat in white water, broad mat, silver frame.

Lois counted the money, found it five short; some acrimony ensued, and Harry finally handed her another bill.

"Did you say four-twelve?" Lois asked Harry.

"He's expecting you." As she opened the door Harry looked as if he might shout something rottenly ironic like "Have fun," but in fact he turned and went into the toilet.

Dilworth sat down at the writing table and through its glass top read room service's catalogue of light provender and beverages.

When Harry came out, Dill expected him to abuse Lois after their obviously abrasive encounter, but Clegg did not.

"She's a reliable kid," Harry said instead, grunting in satisfaction. "She'll get something out of him, you'll see." His head was soaked; he had water-combed it in the bathroom, and it was the kind of fair hair that turned green when wet. He suggested they call room service for beer and club sandwiches, or, for that matter, complete dinner: it was getting on to that time of day.

So Dill did as much and hardly had he lowered the telephone than a rap sounded upon the door. Nearer it than Harry, he went to answer and found Lois upon the threshold. She seemed dazed.

Harry cried: "Didn't he let you in? Sure you tried the right door? Four-twelve. Maybe he's in the crapper."

Choosing the chair Dill had vacated, Lois sat down precisely, like a little old lady.

"Hey-hey-hey!" protested Harry.

She said slowly, gravely: "I have seen some weirdies, but nothing to compare."

It was Dilworth who asked: "What did he want you to do?" He spoke without thinking; he did not wish to hear; he was prepared to shout hysterically to drown her out.

Lois said: "I'd almost rather do it than tell you about it." Her face was bland as nougat.

Harry had blood in his eye. "God damn you," he said. "You don't perform, you return the money. Who's a whore to get high and mighty? How many ways are there to take a dick?" He revolved once in pure rage, necktie flying, then advanced on her.

Dill said: "Hold it, Harry."

Harry glared at him in astonishment, not anger.

Behind this confrontation, Lois said: "He wanted me to pee on him." She then put the unearned money on the writing table. When, looking over Dill's shoulder, Harry saw that, he instantly lost all hostility and became simply bored. "Get the hell out of here," said he.

Dill offered to take Lois home.

Harry paid no further attention to either of them. He thought vigorously for a moment, then crossed the hall to 412, the door of which was ajar.

Fully dressed, Starr sat on the far bed in the same benumbed state as Lois. He blinked wistfully at Harry's greeting.

Harry said: "Look, Andy, I know you've been under pressure."

"Sright," Starr answered hoarsely.

"So let's have a few drinks and hit the sack early. We'll get a fresh start tomorrow. O.K.?"

Starr nodded as if in the grip of palsy, squeaked gratefully, and Harry called room service to send up a couple of quarts of rye. His plan was this: to encourage Starr to drink himself into insensibility again, and then to interrogate him, to say certain provocative things into his ear that might touch off, as under hypnosis, some drunken, sleep-talking response.

Harry by now had not the slightest interest in the series of articles he and Dilworth were supposed to write: he wanted only to get a confession out of Starr. Yet he was still a responsible newspaperman. He made the reverse trip across the hall, to ask Dill to go ahead and fake the first installment. They just might be able to get away with it: an overblown description of what met the father's eyes as he arrived at the apartment on Christmas Eve, maudlin reminiscences of how he had held Billie in his arms as a baby, et bullshit cetera, a kind of introduction to gain time.

But Dilworth was no longer in the room; he had been in earnest, then, about taking the whore home. Harry could not figure him out. He was fairly certain Dill did not want to lay her, which surely he could have done more conveniently in the hotel room than anywhere else, unless he would have been embarrassed to have Harry know. But if that were his concern he would not openly have gone off with her now. Harry could see no professional reason for Dill's further association with Lois, and still less any personal motive. After all, he had been opposed to calling her in the first place.

The room-service waiter showed up with the beer and club sandwiches. Being in good appetite and thirst, Harry engorged Dill's share as well as his own.

Chapter 7

"YES," SAID BETTY. She had changed from the bereaved daughter and sister Tierney had interviewed on Christmas Eve. Something had been done to her hair, by a professional in those matters, that tended to rigidify her head by exposing the ears. She had also developed a cynicism, an edge to her voice.

"Yes," she said, using the word as a negative, "I saw in the paper that you were looking for Joe."

They were in the sitting room of the hotel suite. Arthur had gone down to the barbershop. Betty had thought Tierney attractive on Christmas Eve, but it was true she had then been distraught. She could see now that he had no expanse of heart or mind: detectives after all were merely a sort of policemen.

Tierney observed that she had not mentioned Detweiler when he asked her about the other boarders.

"Which should prove something," said Betty. "He's the last

person I would think of in connection with anything horrible."
She gave Tierney a keen, poignant look; that is, she produced
such a look for whoever was there to witness it, and it happened to be he; it was not *for* him in any personal sense.

Betty wanted to talk about knowing Detweiler, how he
was in love with her, how she had broken his heart. Yet her
taste told her to suppress these data, and that decision was confirmed by her intelligence. She did not want to get Joe into
trouble. He could not have committed the crimes, but he was a
weak and confused person and, if badgered by policemen with
their routine theories about rejected lovers, might strike a self-
damaging attitude. He was sensitive to a fault. Betty liked him
a lot, but as a type of brother.

"Do you know where Detweiler is at the present time?"

"No."

"Where he might be?"

"No."

"Has he got in touch with you recently?"

"Huh-uh."

"When was the last time?"

Betty was most reluctant to break the negative progression;
it gratified her to deny Tierney. "Oh I don't recall," she said
almost spitefully. "Joe didn't do anything. He's a dreamer."

"Seen him since you were married?"

"Definitely no."

Tierney asked: "Were you lovers?"

To an American cop this meant did they hold hands and go
to the movies together. To Betty, who read certain novels, the
term signified a couple whose sexual organs regularly met.
Once more she was entitled to say no.

Arthur returned from the barbershop, smelling of talc and lotion but looking the same: he had merely a light trim, costing him plenty nevertheless, and he did not have the nerve to put it on the tab that the newspaper would pay. It bothered him that the paper should provide his room and board; Betty's, all right, but he was doing nothing for his. He was a moralist of the old school.

He greeted Tierney, and the detective responded by asking about Joseph Detweiler.

"A nice guy," Arthur said. "An awfully nice guy."

"Did either of you," Tierney asked, "ever see Detweiler do anything violent or show any tendency toward violence?"

Arthur was flattered by being included in, but he had to admit that he had really seen so little of Det——

"Certainly not," Betty said with some heat. "You're completely on the wrong track. I don't think Joe would slap a mosquito that was sucking his blood."

"How did he get along with your mother?"

"I'll just say this," said Betty, "with all it implies: he called her Mom. He was a real member of the family."

"The brother that you never had," Arthur added helpfully, unconscious of the double entendre.

Betty's trouble had always been that when she found a man with whom she felt intellectual affinity, he did not appeal to her physically, and vice versa. She could hardly bear to be alone in Arthur's presence unless he was pawing her.

"And your sister?" asked Tierney.

Betty passed a hand across her high forehead. "You are being rather inconsiderate, you know. The funeral is this morning."

Tierney made the usual catch-all excuse, that he was merely doing his job. Then: "If Detweiler is as harmless as you say, then he has nothing to fear. But you know, various people see various sides of a given individual. We have heard that Detweiler could be a crank about noise. At another place where he lived for a while, he assaulted a fellow roomer because he was annoyed by his radio."

"Whose radio?" Betty pointed her nose at Tierney's scalp. "I don't believe a detective should be ambiguous. Do you realize from what you said it could be Joe almost killed the roomer because the *roomer* was peeved at *Joe's* radio?"

Tierney replied with sarcasm. "Lady, I'm not a writer like you. I'm just a simple-minded police officer, stupidly looking for the practical joker who choked your family to death so you could stay in a luxury hotel for the holiday season."

Arthur had been standing at the window, watching the fall of snow. Then it dawned on him that the detective was being rude.

"Officer," he turned gravely and said, "you are coming perilously close to slander. More of that and you'll find yourself in a very awkward situation." Arthur was rather formidable when his rights were threatened: he often predicted lawsuits against double-parkers who obstructed his car, neighborhood hi-fi owners whose apparatus smote his nervous system.

Tierney stared sardonically at his own shoes, which happened at the moment to be damp from melted snow. He refused to wear rubbers, but he was always touched by his wife's urging them on him.

"Well, you just do that, Mr. Bayson," he said, though Arthur had not specified any form of action, "but meanwhile I have to find a murderer. You fight the police; that's real smart."

Arthur failed to get out an answer before his indignation evaporated. Obviously Tierney was a decent individual and an efficient practitioner; no doubt he had his reasons for this provocation. Like that of many high-spirited women, Betty's energy occasionally focused on meaningless targets.

Arthur mentally threw up his hands and turned again to look out the window. He might take a walk in the afternoon, if the snow had not got too deep. On the other hand, the worse the weather, the less likelihood one would be mugged. He must ask Tierney whether it was true that, as he had heard, fewer crimes were committed in inclement seasons: if so, it indicated that criminals were normal in at least that respect.

With the supreme effort of an aircraft leaving the clutch of earth, Tierney climbed above the situation, and asked impersonally: "Does Detweiler make a living with his art?"

Bored by Arthur's intervention, Betty suddenly reversed her style.

"I don't know," she said. "I suppose nobody ever knows what anybody else might do." Her smile expressed pathos. "We are all basically strangers. Perhaps back of his façade Joe is a monster. There's no guarantee. I am conscious of odd impulses in myself that scare me, from time to time. I believe I could kill, having the opportunity."

Tierney disregarded this useless confession but of course did not let on to Betty, rather stared narrowly at her as if considering seriously whether she might be the murderer, which he divined was what her ego demanded. He saw that heretofore he had been far too impersonal with her.

"I suppose you could. A lovely face can conceal a black heart." This was certainly a purple passage in Tierney's idiom, and ordinarily he could not have pronounced its like except in temporary irony. But now his attitude towards Betty was becoming wholly ironical, a definitive role. Years before, Tierney had played the part of a girl in a class play at his all-male high school. In the street-clothes rehearsals he could not bring himself to mimic feminine attitudes: his soul dropped a portcullis against that distortion. But once in full disguise, frock and flowered hat and high heels (feet killing him), he was oddly free to bend his wrist, switch his hips, and vainly touch his wig with two sets of fingertips when under observation by a boy playing a boy; that is, when the entire context was make-believe, so was the code. No one could say that in real life Tierney displayed an iota of swishiness, but in this single case of dramatic invention his imposture was pronounced superb by a guffawing audience who knew him otherwise as the football team's high scorer—precisely the point of the joke.

So he glanced now at Betty's shiny knees before coolly meeting her eye, acknowledging her body on the way up, as it had not really occurred to him to do earlier because both he and she were married. As it was an aspect of his professional performance, he made no attempt to conceal this from Arthur, who had heard the speech flattering Betty and turned to watch him.

Arthur usually felt only pride when his wife's person evoked admiration from other males, did not even take umbrage at teen-age catcalls towards the concentrically globed seat of Betty's slacks. But Tierney represented the Law. To detect evidences of lasciviousness, or indeed any personal appetite, in him was to fear for the future of the common weal. Arthur plodded across and put his hand on Betty's shoulder, announcing stiffly: "I think that's enough questions for today."

Having at last and by accident established a rapport with Betty, Tierney disposed of her husband. He said, flagrantly staring at her body, "Let's let Mrs. Bayson decide for herself. She looks very healthy and self-reliant to me."

The wind up was in Betty. Her head, in the new hairdo, felt helmeted. Whereas with the queer reporter she had resisted Arthur's interference, she now intertwined her fingers with his, compounding her strength vis-à-vis the aggressive maleness of Tierney, who was one of the policemen who had beaten her father, whose statements she had jealously read in the rival newspaper. Tierney had a granite jaw; a short but jutting nose; a hard crewcut head. His left breast, over the heart, bulged with his concealed revolver—or so it seemed to Betty. (It was the way Tierney sat, his jacket bunching out; actually the .38 rode in a clip-holster at the side of his belt; nor had he ever taken a life with it.)

"That's all right," she said, and each man supposed she was addressing him. "Things begin to come back to me when I think of Joe, since you insist," she told Tierney. "You ask about his art work. He modeled a head of me once, laboring over it for weeks. It was not a photographic-type resemblance, of course. Mother never liked it, and Billie thought it was funny; it was bald, you see. Joe said hair was not basic to the structure, being arranged by what he called accident: you have it cut and set, and so on. But your basic bones don't change."

Arthur continued in the jealous vein now, though when he had called upon Betty in the old days and met Detweiler as a resident of the same apartment, he had had no qualms about him.

Accusingly he said: "I never saw that."

"No," Betty answered, still speaking to Tierney, Arthur after all being mostly behind her chair. "He called me into his room. There it sat, on the desk before him, my head, bald and cold but it was spiritually me all right: I always thought he had real talent. Then he said, handing me a little tack hammer, 'It's your right,' he said, 'to destroy this miserable image.' He meant that in a flattering way; it couldn't do justice, he said, to the living original. But I refused: 'Oh no, Joe. Oh no.' He said, 'Then it's my right.' And with true zeal he struck it once in the center of my skull and a lot of cracks appeared, then slowly the fragments parted and fell. I felt very queasy."

Betty waited. Tierney glanced at Arthur hulking above her in his sack suit. Detweiler was wrong in the theory that only the fundamental structure mattered. Human beings were of a piece, including their attire. A skeleton was not necessarily basic.

Look at Tierney being intellectual! thought Tierney, catching himself up. There was something corrupting in the subject of Detweiler. God damn him. Tierney began to hope he would prove innocent, but he wanted to find him first.

Betty got tired of waiting. " 'Right' was the word he used."

Arthur made a blurred noise and dropped her hand. "Aw, Betty, I don't think it's wise to take that pretentious talk seriously." He was still jealous but saw his motive as rather a concern that if Betty made too much of this nonsense she might get Detweiler into hot water. He wondered whether she realized she had changed her tack and was being damaging to the guy and for what? Vanity. Ordinarily Arthur saw that quality as an aspect of his wife's hearty response to life. But Tierney wanted someone for Murder. That tended to be forgotten in a rush of hotel suites, newspaper articles, steaks, snowfall, the posing of a would-be artist: let's, Arthur said silently, get back to the law of gravity.

" 'Right,' " Betty repeated, unmoved by the plea. She kept staring ever more brightly at Tierney, but he refused to crack.

Choosing to pretend the whole performance was in answer to the question he had asked at the outset, he instead asked: "Then how did he make a living?"

Snorting in laughter, Arthur came back into play. "Stuffing animals!" He walked self-consciously away from Betty's chair, shoulders high as if he were cold: he was dramatizing the absurdity of the information. He shot himself onto the far end of the sofa of which Tierney occupied the cushion nearest Betty, threw out his heels, punched together his large white hands.

Tierney: "Huh?"

"Taxidermist," said Arthur.

"Where?"

Arthur splayed his feet, rolling them on the heel-backs; then he made pigeon-toes. "Don't know," he said shyly. "Betty?"

But his wife, holding her ground, said: "He wanted to make something *real,* not reproduce or imitate what already existed. The original is always perfect because it is original. Which is not the easiest concept to grasp."

"Very interesting," murmured Tierney, telling the truth; he had heard and even, despite Betty's implication, understood: he had been obliged at college to study Aquinas and other thinkers. But his clear and pressing duty was to establish in space and time the taxidermy shop, leaving metaphysics to those professional at it.

"Was this his own business or did he work for someone else?"

Suddenly Betty showed enthusiasm. "I went there with him once. We walked from home. I don't know the name or address, but I could take you there probably."

Tierney rose and found a classified telephone book, as he knew he would, in the middle drawer of the table-desk. The book was in mint condition: a beautiful virgin directory, and Tierney fingered it with reverence and a concomitant pleasure.

Having located the rubric "Taxidermists," he carried the book to Betty, who smoothed her lap to accept it, but he tarried until her hands reluctantly came up. He was all business.

Head down, pink nail quickly exhausting the possibilities, too quickly, she soon said: "I don't recognize any of these names. Never knew the right one."

"Then look at the addresses," said Tierney, standing away.

"No," Betty said for each entry, "no, no, no. Don't see any that could possibly be, unless he moved."

Arthur, resting or thinking under a visor of hand, heard a knock at the door, went to answer, and saw Alloway's dung-eating grin on the threshold.

"It is eleven already?"

"Ten or so past," the reporter said conscientiously through chapped lips. "Hard to get a cab in the snow. If it keeps up they'll all go home, as they do when it rains."

Arthur nodded almost affably, discovering in himself a novel tolerance towards Alloway as a result of a new suspicion of Tierney. He gestured at the reporter's coat, the snowflakes on which were hard to see, melted or whole, in the black-and-white houndstooth. "Better hang it in the bathroom." Then pointed imperiously, so there could be no doubt, at Betty's.

Alloway colored slightly at this acknowledgment that Betty's quarters were the peculiar locus of his needs, but he was getting anxious now to find out what Tierney was up to, had been trying with the other part of his attention to hear the detective over Arthur's and his own commonplaces. He flopped his coat across the seat of the nearest straightback chair and, in distinction to the sidling movement in which he entered the suite, he stalked forthrightly at the detective, as the newsman that he was.

"What's the latest on Detweiler?" he asked, even ignoring Betty for the moment.

Tierney gave him a tile-glazed eye, said: "Call the Department."

"And ask for Matthias, huh?" Alloway returned, brandishing his needle.

Quick to sniff the bouquet of ill will, Betty asked: "Who's that?"

"One of the real brains at Homicide," said Alloway. "Taught Tierney everything he knows." Alloway didn't give a crap about maintaining good relations with the police. As a pro of the written word, he always had one up on the cops, who were almost obliged to be inarticulate, and nowadays he anyway usually did feature stuff, often exposés of city departments, for which he got little official cooperation. He preferred to work with social reformers and critics, for whom he had contempt but who spoke in platitudes which were easily quoted, and criminals, whom he admired because they frightened him.

Had he absolute power, Tierney's first act would have been to abolish the freedom of the press. He had read Alloway's initial installments of Betty's story: swill. Future segments, now, no doubt would present a perverted image of Detweiler. Shuster had expressed his usual amoral satisfaction at that likelihood: "Might goose him into coming in." Which was highly unlikely and still no excuse. Tierney could have bought his wife a new winter coat with what Alloway's paper paid the hotel per diem to accommodate this vain bitch and her blockhead husband.

He stood up and said commandingly: "I want a private word with you, Mrs. Bayson."

"Surely." Betty loved this. She led Tierney to her bedroom while Arthur watched with little, angry bear-eyes, and Alloway stepped rapidly in their wake, calling to Tierney: "What are you trying to pull?" Betty slammed the door on him, leaned against its inside surface, knee bent, foot lifted, as in the outmoded response to a kiss.

Tierney gestured to her to come over by the window: the reporter might listen at the door. He said in an undertone: "You think you can find the taxidermy shop?"

Standing so close to him, Betty detected Tierney's odd smell, neither pleasing nor repugnant in the standard sense: perhaps cleaning fluid or some Irish-Catholic incense. For her part Betty and also her room reeked of a costly scent she had obtained in the hotel drugstore and put on the tab. Tierney pretended to himself that he was suffocating. He disliked overdone women as well as spicy foods. He remembered what he had not noticed when it was current: that Betty had been attractive in a straight, clean, girlish way before she mucked herself up with hard hair and burnt eyes.

Betty answered in a whisper, conspiring: "I said I could take you there."

Tierney felt foolish. He moved about, saw through the open bathroom door a set of beige underwear drying on the shower rod.

"How soon can you shake off that reporter?"

Newspapermen often talked piously of keeping a confidence if so requested by the police, but invariably proved treacherous in practice. It was like getting a hungry shark's promise to ignore a bleeding swimmer.

"He'll be here all day," said Betty, still whispering. Then, louder, she blurted: "Oh, I forgot the funeral."

The cheap little cunt, with no respect for the dead. And thinking that, Tierney knew his first faint desire for her.

Like the banging of conscience, Arthur's thumps sounded upon the door. He cried: "Betty, we better get started." Alloway could be heard urgently querying: "Where? Where?"

"When will you be back?" asked Tierney.

Betty replied, figuring: "There's the service, then the trip to the cemetery, the burial, then the ride back. Maybe by four, four-thirty to be on the safe side. You pick me up here?"

As if she were making a date. But what Tierney found much more appalling was a tendency in himself to assume the same style: indeed, he identified hers by means of his own.

"All right," he said harshly, policing himself. "And don't tell the reporter." He hated having to explain. "Whatever your opinion, Detweiler is shaping up as a psycho. They are harder to trace than normal people, and we haven't got a line on him so far. If you can think of anything else about him it might help. But the reporter will blow it." He saw her back in the dressing-table mirror, across the room, and beyond it his own still-collegiate face looking solemn, his newfound irony against her ebbing, or perhaps altering to mere cruelty. "And hire the taxidermist to write *his* series. They don't care, you see? A few years ago reporters like Alloway found out the place and pickup time for the ransom of a little boy, went there in a crowd with camera trucks and radio cars parked all down the block, and scared off the kidnaper. He strangled the child and buried it in a marsh."

In the mirror Tierney saw the tips of his fingers appear over one of her shoulders, like an epaulet. He gripped her in the clutch of moral ardor, not animal lust. His hand did not seek to palpitate or warm or even feel; else Betty would have cried out for Arthur and subsequently reported the incident to the police department. She would not suffer herself to be caressed extramaritally. But Tierney was stating a principle, and besides, was hurting her. She would show a bruise there tomorrow, a kind of insigne of office: Betty Bayson, honorary policewoman.

"They have no, no—" Tierney struggled for an idiom, his iron claw deep into her tender shoulder muscles. In a second she would scream, not for help, not to bring about cessation, but rather to celebrate her enduring the unendurable: she, the frailest Starr, the one who so far had eluded wounding.

"They have no *decency*," said Tierney, his eyes charred, features drawn, like some fanatical, ascetic priest.

Betty nodded dumbly, nostalgic for his torturer's hand soon as he withdrew it, though her shoulder still chanted with pain. Tierney rapidly left the bedroom and then the suite.

When Betty emerged Alloway was still complaining. "You didn't tell me about the funeral." He stood there tall and limp, his lower lip dangling.

"Come along then and we can talk in the limousine," Betty said, efficient again. "I don't see any disrespect in that. After all, it's an appropriate occasion for the subject matter. I sincerely believe my mother and Billie would approve. They never liked Joe Detweiler from the beginning. Now it turns out, in the irony of fate, that they had to die to confirm their intuition."

Alloway jotted this down while Arthur tried to clear an obstruction that blocked his throat, barricaded his eyes, and corrupted his breathing. He did not soon succeed: he understood for the first time that Betty was utterly wanting in a sense of justice. As fair play was at the essence of Arthur's mystique, on the one hand, and his life was unconditionally coexistent with Betty's, on the other, he must part company with himself or rub elbows with a madman. Therefore he relinquished his integrity and said nothing. Detweiler would presumably not be framed. Whatever Betty said, the police and the courts must establish evidence of his guilt before they could execute the poor devil. Public justice still prevails, whatever the private arrangements under which we labor, all of us who live with women.

"I foolishly defended him," Betty went on, not to Alloway but to her readers. "Certainly he was strange, but frankly I never saw the violence in him. The sensitive hands that worked so delicately in clay, that they might be lethal instruments . . ."

Alloway requested her to slow down so he could get it word for word.

"You ought to get a tape recorder," Betty said. "I'm misquoted repeatedly in the first installment and you added things of your own. I certainly don't mind cuts, because I understand the space problem, but to see material printed under my name that I did not utter—"

Alloway felt it politic to caution her. "Of course, we can't print prejudicial statements against Detweiler until the police find him, and maybe not then unless he confesses immediately. If he does, of course we can go whole hog."

"That I know," Betty said. " 'His hands might be *lethal* instruments.' I'm not saying they *were*. Yours or mine *might* be."

Or mine, thought Arthur, enjoying the newfound freedom of a fragmented personality.

"Well, anyway," said Betty, "he will confess when they

get him. I know Joe Detweiler. He may be a murderer, but he's not a liar. As for me, I feel only pity for him, not revenge."

Chapter 8

DETWEILER had a gratifying journey, though many of the other passengers groused about the degeneration of the railroads; the aisle was ankle-high in litter; a half-dozen seats were broken; the water tank was soon dry and never replenished; the conductor materialized only to take tickets, smile at the complaints, and vanish. But, insofar as he had any sense of privation, Detweiler enjoyed roughing it. He thought of the oldtime travelers in their coaches, bumping along behind foam-flecked horses where these twin bands of shining steel now ran: incredible, what time had wrought. Earlier, a trackless waste; and much, much earlier, acres of primeval slime in which dinosaurs wallowed, mastodons trumpeted; preceding all that, the earth had been an undifferentiated, infinitesimal piece of the sun, a whiff of burning gas that had spun off the parent body, cooled, and solidified. A splendid mystery, a source of joy.

Detweiler put his head against the cushion, his ankles on the opposite seat—one of the broken ones, so that he was denying nobody—and occupied with his universal reflections, in no time at all he had completed his journey. Fellow passengers had come and gone, he spoke to none. He was anonymous, pale and fair, almost invisible.

In the middle of the night, lamps extinguished, a drunken sailor en route to the toilet fell on him when the train lurched. Awake but quiescent as a bundle of old clothes, Detweiler let the man collect himself and wander on, leaving behind a sour odor, the stench of life unrealized: poor devil, groping through the night, benumbed, forsaking his instinctive strengths. Detweiler found it hard to understand such a person, easier to forgive him; obviously he was the passive type, did not knowingly seek to obstruct the flow of transcendental energy, just occasionally tripped and fell in its way, could be stepped over.

But next morning, having arrived at his destination, and taken a quick, refreshing wash-up in the station, Detweiler went out into the breath-catching cold of the yet snowless street, found a lunch counter, and there came across another kind of human being, that specimen who embodied negative principles with positive force.

It took Detweiler a while to understand, sitting there on the stool, facing the chromium-plated napkin container, that he was being ignored by the individual who should have taken his order: a white-capped man, fully mature, knobby-faced, to whom Detweiler was initially of course sympathetic, looking forward as he was to a cup of steaming coffee milked down to a chocolate tan, and two doughnuts virginally dressed in sugar. He inhaled the perfume of the fried bacon, the bouquet of toast, thrilled to the yellow flow of egg on the plate of his right-hand neighbor. Though he could not himself afford such luxuries, he venerated all those who trafficked in them.

Therefore he tolerated the counterman, who was deliberately tidying up around the coffee urn with a stained rag, and called to him in a friendly voice. No response. Five other customers applied themselves to their cups and dishes; some were friends and conversed in an amiable hum. Someone departed, squeezing along the narrow aisle behind Detweiler in a bulky coat, pleasantly brushing his back, blowing cigarette smoke over him, which, though he did not himself use tobacco, had an interesting, pungent, stimulating aroma.

Again he called out, no less genially should the man be deaf, and the subject slowly turned, stared at him briefly in unspecified, neutral hatred, turned back, filled a coffee cup sloppily so that the saucer ran with liquid, served it up.

"And two sugar doughnuts, please," Detweiler said for the third time, as he saw the man act as if the exchange were closed.

Again he was ignored. The counterman as of old worked with his brown rag. Detweiler lifted the napkin dispenser, found it of suitable weight—for he knew what he was doing and though enraged was not the victim of a feckless impulse— and with ardent force and commanding accuracy threw it into the counterman's head.

The target jerked with the impact, white cap flying off as though winged. He fell forward into the coffee urn, cut his mouth or nose on a gleaming tap, folded, and dropped to the floor behind the counter, bleeding fore and aft. The other eaters froze in their respective positions, one with fork in the air; another averted his eyes for a long moment.

Detweiler left the stool, put on his coat, lifted his pack

from the wall-hook, and since he had not partaken of the fare, walked past the front counterman, the one who doubled as cashier, without paying. "Hey," said this person, torn between the cash register and his colleague on the floor, but not at all sure of which represented his principal responsibility, if either. Detweiler was only vaguely conscious of the iterated "Hey's" as he went through the door, taking the cold air in his face, and having turned the corner, forgot the incident utterly. He was not followed.

By means of public conveyance Detweiler reached an area which he recognized through elapsed time rather than its name —he had no quarrel with Time in such practical applications, used it without thought—walked three blocks still guided by his instinct, entered a shabby building through a rank of ash-cans, climbed three dark, odorous flights of stair, and knocked upon a twilit door.

He heard someone shuffle up on the other side and throw the latch. It opened not cautiously but all the way, swinging back. There stood a woman, gray-haired, eyeglassed, medium-stout, but resembling him all the same, so much so that he got a queer catch in his throat when he looked into the eyes so companion to his own.

"Hello, Mother," said he.

Mrs. Detweiler answered: "Hi, Joey." She stepped aside for his entrance, scrubbing her hands on her print apron of blue and white. She said: "I bet you never had your breakfast."

" 'Bet'?" said Detweiler in ironic amusement, of which he was capable only with his mother, because in all the world she was for him the only eccentric. A spiritualist, she got most of her information from the other world; hence Detweiler's question: she seldom "bet," being usually certain.

In a certain defiance she said: "Wasn't I right?"

He grinned and nodded. He was greatly fond of her.

"Then come on," she said. "I knew you would be showing up sometime today, so I got ready with all your favorites, made applesauce and a devil's food cake and bought some of that rattrap cheese you like to melt and everything."

He followed her into the redolent kitchen, remembering that each time he came to visit she supplied a new list of his favorite foods, presumably obtained through spiritual channels —and never accurate, except in the sense that he was omnivorous and devoured everything with zest. But the few dishes that stood above the rest in his estimation—hot dogs covered with both chili con carne and sauerkraut; very hard to obtain at lunch counters or street stalls, where it was usually either-or; cherry Jello, rice pudding with raisins—she never seemed to hit upon. But then Detweiler had never thought spiritualism held water; his mother was a real crank, though lovable.

For breakfast he ate three wedges of chocolate cake, a bowl of applesauce, and over his mother's protests, a cold, not melted, cheese sandwich.

"Joey," she said while he was thus occupied, sipping the Postum she favored as an evasion of coffee-nerves, ulcers, and cancer, "Joey, I hear you are getting along very well out there, making progress in every way, and you sure look good. You must be eating well."

"Yes, Mother," Detweiler answered quite seriously. Though he might question the source of her information, which had probably come from some séance, he would not mock her. And anyway, he always told the truth, just as he invariably accepted as truth all that was stated to him. "Yes, I'm doing fine."

"Just where is it you are located now?" His mother dipped

a crust of bread into the Postum and ate it neatly. Apparently her otherworldly data on him was none too specific.

He told her, and added: "Everybody is real nice."

"Treat someone nice and he'll be nice," said Detweiler's mother. "It runs in a great current, like electricity, around the world. I met a Hindu from India the other day. He said, 'Hello, sister, we met once in another life'."

His mother often encountered Asiatics in her circles and believed they saw farther than Occidentals, using the inner eye.

She said: "Mr. Lall. He gave me a reading on you, Joey. It seems you are overcoming resistances and are going to make out well in the end if you stay patient. For you, animals represent a positive value. Do you still work with animals, Joey?"

Detweiler finished his second glass of milk. "Oh, I am always somewhere near animals, Mother. You can bank on that."

Beside the plate he found the napkin in his old napkin ring, which had obviously been polished for his homecoming: his mother did give such demonstrations of clairvoyance. Detweiler never denied her gift; it was just that predictions of the future had no utility for him. The central problem remained eternal: how a man might realize his force. All animals did, with no reflection, no doubt, and no apology. A tiger killed, a rabbit ran, an owl sat motionless in daylight, a snake flowed along the ground; and these were not murder, cowardice, sloth, and guile, but rather respective expressions of peculiar truths.

"Ah!" said Detweiler, slapping the napkin against the tabletop. "I forgot, I have a Christmas present for you, Mother." He went to his haversack and brought from it a bundle wrapped in a maroon sweater. "Sorry I didn't have gift paper, but it would have been difficult to make a decent package of it anyway, because of the awkward shape. I hope you like it."

He wound off the sweater, being careful because the object within caught here and there on the weave, and at last revealed a common gray squirrel, stuffed and mounted on a base of varnished walnut. The small animal sat on its haunches and held a beechnut between two paws, not yet nibbling but about to: you could almost see the tiny mouth twitch, so true it was.

Mrs. Detweiler took it reverently into her broad-fingered hands, peered into the bright-button eyes, stroked the fur.

"I like it, Joey. It is swell. If you don't mind me saying so, it is more real-life than them clay images you used to make, and represents an advance in thought and mind."

Detweiler cocked his head against his right shoulder, an attitude in which he was usually photographed as a boy, an expression not of appeal, which is how it was often interpreted, but rather of contemplation.

"It *isn't* bad," he had to admit. "Of course you must understand it is dead, Mother, an attempt to preserve or to remember what was once perfect. This is no longer a squirrel, and for that reason there is a sadness about it. But sculpture starts as nothing, and thus if anything results from it, it is a triumph."

Mrs. Detweiler got her eyeglasses out of a frayed leather case she carried in an apron pocket, put them on, and further inspected the stuffed animal, from time to time looking benignly over it at her son. "You are reaching out, Joey. You are crossing the barrier."

Detweiler stubbornly shook his head, not at her but at a thought of how little he had achieved. "I don't do sculpture any more. It doesn't go far enough." A constriction developed in his throat, a weight fell behind his forehead. He sat down again. "Nor taxidermy. I quit my job with that guy. I worked for a while at a zoo, cleaning out cages and feeding animals so I could be near them, study their methods. But they don't have *methods,* Mother, but *ways,* which are hard to understand if you are a human being, though we are also basically animals."

"With spirits, son," his mother said gently, placing the squirrel alongside her cup. "Why don't you come and lay down now awhile, and if you want I'll find the old book, which I always kept, and I'll read you about Peter Rabbit and Reddy Fox, like I used to and what started you out on animals in the beginning."

Though a crackpot perhaps, his mother was one of the finest people in the world and Detweiler tried always to please her, so he followed along patiently into the bedroom. Then, having removed his shoes, he lay down on the crazy quilt. His mother soon found the childish book, drew her chair from the sewing machine to the bedside, and in the light that penetrated the sooty curtains began to read.

Before long Detweiler fell asleep. His mother continued to read aloud, simulating the various voices, Peter Rabbit in a high yet robust tone, Reddy Fox with a sinister half-lisp. The pages opened easily and lay quite limp; years ago the binding had been cracked when Detweiler's father threw it at her.

Clegg had a big mother of a hangover in the morning, owing not so much to his own drinking as to being all night at close quarters with Starr. When he raised the window for a clean breath, Starr woke up howling about the cold, predicting pneumonia. So down it came again, and Clegg returned to the twin bed alongside his subject's, where he sat, too warm in shirtsleeves, in near asphyxiation from the sweetish rye-fumes emanating from Starr's open mouth and the glassful on the night table between them.

Soon as Starr's breathing again indicated somnolence, Clegg began his crafty appeals to the man's subliminal self.

The first pitch, put in a soft, crooning voice, was: "I don't blame you for doing it, Andy. They had it coming if anybody ever did."

Starr breathed on; it was still too soon after the extinguishing of the lamp to get any optical intelligence of him. But even when Clegg's night-vision was fully instituted, the room proved too dark to see much. He put on the bathroom light, leaving the door ajar, but shortly Starr cried out. So it was utter darkness and foul air: Clegg's image of hell.

"How did you do it?" he said next, after an appropriate interval and in a voice of wonder. "That's what I can't understand. A slender, sick man like yourself. Appleton outweighed you by forty pounds."

Starr turned over. Clegg persisted: "Tell me, Andy. I admire you, a man who defends his home!" Starr murmured into the pillow. Clegg stole across and put his ear close: "Beg pardon?" He stopped off his inhalation, to defend himself against Starr's noxious exhale. Silence. "Billie was some piece," Clegg whispered. "I envy the man who had her. She'd be worth killing for."

Starr stirred. Clegg trembled, had to turn his head away to catch a breath. When he came back, Starr said in a dreamy mutter: "Shur off at fockin radio, lemme shleep."

Clegg withdrew, still far from discouraged. He had got a response that indicated he had been at least heard. Having planted the seeds, he would stay awake all night to listen for the bloom. After some hours, however, the warm air and the darkness degenerated his will; he fell into a coma, starting awake from time to time at the sound of human speech, but was too groggy to comprehend it: he seemed to be capped in foam rubber.

When he at last came fully to, his watch put the time at 10 A.M. The drapes were pulled wide, and a snowy, eye-hurting light was extant. Starr sat eating breakfast from a wheeled tray of silver-domed dishes. He was dressed again in the resort clothing.

Turning his skinny neck in the Hawaiian shirt, he said to Clegg: "You know you talk in your sleep? Kept me awake half the night. I almost walked out on you, and then where would your story be? I want a private room from now on, get me? I ain't anybody you can push around. I can sell my story to any paper in town, and don't forget it."

He used Clegg's desolate look to flog himself into further indignation, strutting with his head and shoulders, though seated, spitting out little fragments of toast. "I ought to call your boss."

Clegg hauled up from the bed, swallowing with a tongue of suede. He stumbled to the bathroom and took a drink through his hand from the ice-water tap. Then he returned to the bedroom and heard Starr say: "What do you think about that?"

Clegg walked across the room, thrust the breakfast table aside, lifted Starr by the collar with his left fist, and hit him in the mouth with the right. He saw blood on his hand: his own. He had cut his knuckle on one of Starr's rotten teeth.

By afternoon he was out of a job; he was also codefendant, with his paper, in a suit for assault and battery. The paper's big-time attorneys eventually battered Starr's sleezy lawyer, by a combination of veiled money and open threats, into a more tolerant position, and the suit was dropped. Starr's fee for the series was increased, and Dilworth took over the writing thereof.

Betty Bayson endured the funeral in a type of trance, though no one knew that to see her: she cried at the undertaker's and again at the graveside, and at the latter was observed so doing by a crowd of those ghouls who manage to discover the loci of such events despite official secrecy. There were only about thirty of them, but most were hard-core, standing in shank-deep snow, passive except for one woman with milky blue eyes, who slipped past the guarding cop and asked Betty for an autograph, saying: "I'm glad you done it, dear. God bless you." Betty sniffled and sighed.

Technically the burial was inconvenient owing to the snowfall. Snow was several inches deep in the open grave and still descended. Functionaries dusted it off the coffin-tops now and again, which appeared pathetic because pointless, since both receptacles would shortly go below ground and there lie unprotected throughout eternity against ravages worse than crystals of frozen water. This thought occurred to the Presbyterian minister who had been drafted into service though none of the Starrs, dead or alive, had been his parishioner. But he went where called by the mortician. A veteran of his trade, he had a kit, as it were, of phrases that would fit any mortal: of daughters, of mothers, of the bereaved; and it was in no way disrespectful or false that he used them in his valediction on the murdered Starrs. They were, or had been, human; as was he; as were all.

Perhaps his remarks were more eloquent when applied generically than when he had known the deceased and could speak of particularities, death being the only truly universal event. He did his job at both mortuary and cemetery, and Arthur for one thought it very good indeed but avoided thanking him because of an embarrassing puzzlement as to whether or not a preacher should be tipped after a funeral as after a marriage.

Alloway accompanied the Baysons throughout, but got little from Betty in her present state, into which she had fallen by surprise in the cab en route to the funeral parlor: it was not so much depression or despair or melancholy or sorrow as total nullity: suddenly everything, including herself, seemed to be made of frosted glass. Externally this was due to the falling snow through which one must needs peer in such weather. Within, however, it unaccountably contradicted her habitual sense of lucidity, which had if anything grown more assured in the days since the murders. Betty had always felt she immediately understood anything of an emotional or moral or intellectual nature. All at once, she did not. And did not care to, had no interest.

She sat—or, at the graveside, stood—contemplating the absolute void, multiplying zeroes. It was neither a pleasant nor an unpleasant situation; it was nothing at all, nonexistence.

Her father did not show up for either part of the ceremony. Only Arthur had thought of notifying him, but didn't know where to look.

Afterwards, when the undertaker's limousine had delivered the three of them to the hotel, Alloway made his congé, hot-footed it down to the paper, and wrote for tomorrow's edition an account of Betty's alleged reflections while viewing the obsequies: "As the caskets slowly sank from sight into the cold ground, I murmured a final farewell to my loved ones. Theirs would be the peace which passeth. . . ."

Tierney appeared promptly at four. While he had talked to Betty that morning, his ex-partner Matthias had shot himself. Shuster had taken Matty off active service pending a departmental hearing that would consider whether he had been negligent in leaving his extra pistol where the punk could lay hands on it. Only Matty knew, and Tierney suspected, that the punk had been given it by Mrs. Matthias.

To safeguard what he was old-fashioned enough to regard as his honor, Matty had tried to blow his brains out. But from professional experience he knew that a suicide in which the subject discharges a firearm into the mouth is a nasty affair for those first to discover his remains: like a watermelon smashed against the wall. He did not wish to impose that unpleasantness on his wife, to whom he bore no ill will. So he got himself a room in a cheap hotel, a hot-bed establishment used by streetwalkers, a lair for petty criminals and junkies, and too quickly—because the mise en scène was unendurably degrading —he whipped his revolver towards his lips, pulled the trigger, and blew off the top of his face, but remained quite alive, even conscious until doped at the hospital. The doctors predicted he would survive, though naturally with only one eye.

Tierney spent the early afternoon hanging around the hospital though he was useless there, Matthias continuing under heavy sedation. Weirdly, Tierney lingered in hopes that Matty's wife, whom he had never seen, would show up, and he suspected every forty-year-old woman in the visitors' lounge of being she. What he had in mind was not clear to himself; he could not imagine such a confrontation—which is why he stayed there for two hours; he, a police officer, killing time.

However, Mrs. Matthias did not appear, or if she did he could not identify her in the despondently furnished hall into which various folk trudged to sit somber-faced—though a few were merry: had either got the good news their loved ones were recovering or were malicious, sadistic types or perhaps merely heirs of someone whose condition had lately been pronounced hopeless.

At last Tierney left the hospital and went to Betty's hotel.

"Where's the reporter?" he asked.

"Gone," said she in a flat voice and with no special expression. "My husband is downstairs eating. He missed lunch and—"

"All right," Tierney broke in as if he were questioning a suspect given to ungermane ramblings.

"Are you allowed to have a drink?"

"No," Tierney said. "Get your coat."

Betty carried out the order, brought the garment into the living room and struggled girlishly to thread her arms through the sleeves, with Tierney maintaining his obdurate stand in the corridor.

Downstairs they left the elevator and passed the otherwise unoccupied restaurant in which Arthur partook of an extraordinarily late lunch or early dinner. Tierney could see him through glass doors, raising a fork laden with something soft and white, a mess of the melted cheese and cream with which that sort of place habitually masked honest meat.

Actually Arthur was eating mashed potatoes: he shared Tierney's distaste for luxury; had sent away the unctuous wine steward and drank ice water. He failed to see the departure of his wife and the policeman, of which, however, he had received foreknowledge from Betty.

The afternoon whiteness had turned dirty above and underfoot, the guttered snow crusting with intermixed filth, though not so durably as to bear weight, as Betty discovered when she waded to Tierney's automobile.

Betty observed nothing coplike in the car except the two-way radio and a certain metallic odor. Tierney drove east and then south, and when Betty first registered their situation she saw the familiar block, and then the very house in which her kin had lately been done to death. She was disturbed by her refusal to be disturbed by the recognition, but this she forgot as Tierney ground the car in hub-deep at the left curb, next to a fireplug, and got himself onto the sidewalk, leaving her again with the unpleasant pedestrian chore.

Owing to the inclement weather, the cop on house-guard no longer stood before the door; he sat, with a colleague, in a police car parked just ahead of Tierney's. Tierney exchanged nods with them. He had keys to the doors of house and apartment, went first through both, and not until Betty was well through the latter, stood in the known living room the carpet of which showed a fresh-washed area, a blond pool amid dirty beige, marking where the boarder had bled his last, did Tierney look at her. And when he did, it was queer.

Queer to be here at all, queer to notice that the capricious heating system had for once overreacted to the challenge of the outside weather. It was rotten hot, tropical, breath-denying, and dim, with a smell of dust.

"Now," Tierney said, queerly it seemed to Betty because of the spite in his voice, "I want you to look around carefully and see if anything's missing or out of place. I know you did that once, but I want you to do it again."

Betty at last understood what was queer about the place: its irrelevancy, her absolute lack of association with it. Their coming here now was an exercise in fantasy: pretend familiarity, pretend you care, when the real thing is melting snow in your boots, wet fabric at the instep, a nasty, crawling clingyness. Betty loathed being damp in any particular: it was as if one had been flayed and reinserted in the reversed skin. She shivered.

Interpreting this manifestation as evidence that she was moved by a poignancy of place, Tierney became less spiteful: she was not, then, as callous as he had supposed; she was capable of sorrowful recollection, of family loyalty, had not sold out. He was somewhat ashamed of himself for bringing her here for a personal motive, to rub her nose in it. He felt shame because it had been unprofessional: he had nothing more to learn from the physical disposition of the apartment. His job was to find Detweiler. Yet he malingered in this living room, which was dull and characterless like all scenes of murder when the humanity had been removed. Ghosts never walk where life has been taken illegally: the cop's superstition.

He gave her a kind glance. To which she crinkled her nose and whined, an adolescent: "My feet are sopping!" She stamped them, which worsened the condition, the captive moisture having no exit. "Can I go and get a towel?"

Taken by surprise, Tierney said rhetorically: "Why not?"

Betty insisted on answering. "Don't you have to keep it all as is?"

"No," Tierney said abruptly. "We know what's here." He turned away in embarrassment at the personal note. His own feet were also wet. When dry his shoes would show a waterline:

a thing he wouldn't want his wife to see, with her obsession about rubbers. She never seemed to worry that he might get shot or knifed in his line of work, having a Catholic girl's fatalism in that regard, but a cold fell within her area of command, too petty for God yet all the same sometimes lethal. Her Uncle Jack sneezed one day, died a week later.

Betty went through the kitchen and along the hall, which was dark but to her unspooky. She threw the bathroom switch. No towels hung on the racks: the laboratory men had taken all away. Spares were in the cabinet below the washstand, stacked on the left, well separated from scouring powder and cellulose sponge. She fetched one, sat on the closed toilet, removed her boots, and having undone the garter clips, peeled off her stockings and hung them over the lip of the tub. Her feet were excessively pink.

Tierney appeared in the doorway. He said: "Are you all right? You were gone a long time."

"These boots," said she, "have a flannel lining. It'll take a long while to dry."

She rose and went towards him, he backing considerately away, still in his overcoat in the unbearable heat. She had left her coat across a kitchen chair.

In the hall, walking barefoot on the worn runner, she approached Billie's door, stopped there and asked plaintively: "Is this where? Did she meet him face to face?" Betty was not thinking of Joe Detweiler at this moment, nor of Billie, but rather constructing an ideal crime, with ideal murderer and victim, ideal violence devoid of pain or even motion, silent.

She stepped inside the room. The police had taken away the bedclothes, leaving the striped mattress.

Tierney reluctantly moved out of the spill of light from

the bathroom. Being decent, he muttered: "That's it."

"What?"

"About it," he said, reaching the entrance of the room.

"Oh." She turned and met his eye.

He said: "If your boots are dry, we better go on our way."

"Give them a few minutes."

He nodded and retreated to the living room.

Betty lowered herself slowly onto the bare bed, taking care her skirt was modestly arranged lest Tierney come back. She was a virtuous woman, unlike her late sister.

Chapter 9

AFTER HIS NAP Detweiler set about finding a doctor. His mother would have been no help in this regard, because she believed all physicians were charlatans and, when ill, a rare situation for her, doctored herself with herb teas, compounds of charcoal and honey, pulverized roots, and the like, and was soon fit. Detweiler himself felt that doctors had their place in the scheme of things for those who needed the services they supplied. Most people if sick beyond a certain degree required *someone else*. It was the otherness that did the trick: being ill was essentially being lonely.

Detweiler walked several miles so as to get out of the neighborhood though he was utterly unknown there, had not been raised locally, but he was well aware that someplace police were searching for him and had undoubtedly sent his name and description around the country. He did not wish to expose himself publicly in the immediate environs of his mother's home, on the chance that some busybody would notice that she and the wanted man had the same surname, and that her son had suddenly turned up.

Over lunch he had taken the simple precaution to say: "Mother, I wonder if on this visit you would call me, to my face and when speaking to your friends, something other than Joe?"

"Sure," answered his mother, gathering up several wedges of a fried round of baloney onto her fork. "How would you like 'Ernest Blue,' or 'Randolph Binocular'?"

Detweiler laughed his head off. His mother certainly amused him. "What a name!" he cried. "Where did you get that one?"

"Made it up," said she. "I know a lot of things." She narrowed her eyes and nodded wisely.

"I'll take Ernest Blue," Detweiler said soberly. "And not be your son but your nephew. O.K.?"

"All right." His mother was very good at this sort of game and would never slip up, even if awakened suddenly in the middle of the night, until he called it off. She doted on make-believe and novelty.

So off he went. The weather had held clear and cold, too cold to snow, as he was assured by two of the several persons with whom he exchanged greetings on the walk: a candy-store proprietor and a policeman.

The latter had looked uncomfortable though buttoned up in his greatcoat, and Detweiler expressed sympathy: "You have a chilly job."

The officer quickly inspected him, found no reason for action, and amiably made the observation on the unlikelihood of snow.

Before entering the candy shop Detweiler unobtrusively took out a penknife and cut his thumb, wrapped a handkerchief around the wound, and went inside.

"Too cold to snow," said the man behind the counter.

Detweiler said: "Say, I just cut my hand while sharpening a pencil. It's not deep, but the knife was kind of rusty. Maybe I ought to see a doctor so I don't get blood poisoning."

This went over big with the man, whose mother, he said, had wanted him to be a doctor. He had not had the brain, patience, or money to go in for med school, but had retained an inclination towards therapeutic pursuits.

"Let's see the wound," he cried, hurling himself halfway across the counter. Detweiler had no choice but to unwind the handkerchief and display his bloody thumb.

"Not so bad," said the man. "I'll take care of it forthwith," using a consciously comic pomposity of idiom as part of his bedside manner. He insisted that Detweiler come along to the tiny lavatory let into the rear wall, where he cleansed the cut with soap and water, dried it on toilet paper, applied hydrogen peroxide "which won't smart," and finally fought an adhesive bandage free and plastered it around the decommissioned thumb.

Thus Detweiler was frustrated in his initial attempt to reach a physician in this town, although he had a valuable experience which was not to be sneezed at. He wandered on throughout the day, mostly by foot, for he had little money and he was also leery of the distractions available on public transport. No doubt by striking up an acquaintance with a fellow passenger he could eventually be directed to that person's family doctor, but he was aware that the operation he sought fell out of the ordinary range, that the doctor might believe him a kind of nut and mention the incident, with raised brow, to the patient who sent him, and the latter might feel ill-used by the anonymous fellow who had once shared his bus seat, truth being the loser.

The alternative was to move slowly and carefully, making a long-term friend rather than a transient acquaintance, and then, when one could rely on informed sympathy, to put the question. The trouble with this was that Detweiler could make a true friend only of a member of the opposite sex. With men there was always an instinctive rivalry, as much, he was ready to admit, on his part as on the other fellow's. It was the meeting of protuberances, of like configurations that would not mesh. As much as he liked most other men, he hated them fundamentally.

Betty Starr had been his friend from the moment he took the room. It was she who served him the largest portion of meat at table, who listened intently if he spoke, who offered him first choice of the newspaper. Without announcement she began to wash and iron his clothes, not part of his deal with Mrs. Starr, and cleaned his room, which was, but she did it with a care no boarder could expect. She had even once left behind a blue cornflower in a crystal bud-vase. There could be no doubt these were marks of special favor, for she was not an agreeable girl in general. She made caustic remarks to her mother and often quarreled so loudly with Billie that Detweiler, separated from them by two doors and the hallway's width, had to cover his ears.

He could not endure the display of violent emotion. It was as if the earth revolved in a blur, growing ever larger, while he stood motionless but dwindled. This terrified him, and if it continued he sobbed in a miniature voice commensurate with his size.

On one such occasion, head buried in a pillow, face down, minuscule, he felt a touch upon his tiny shoulder.

"Are you O.K.?"

He turned quickly, instantly magnifying, for only when others engaged in it did violence disturb him, and said, truthfully, "Sure."

Betty stood at the bedside, a sad-sweet moonface. "I thought you were feeling badly."

"And I thought you were," Detweiler said.

"Me?" She winced as if trying to remember, then shook her head vigorously, hair swinging.

He did not want to bring up a painful incident. He shrugged and lifted himself to a sitting position.

"Oh," Betty said, "you mean our fight. Billie and I are always at one another's throats. That's normal."

Detweiler listened carefully. "It is?"

"Really," Betty assured him. "Don't you have any brothers or sisters?"

"I don't think so."

"What's that mean?"

"I'm sorry. . . . When I was little I had a baby sister for a while, but she died. What I meant was, I don't know what it is like to grow up alongside a brother or sister and whether it is usual to quarrel with them." What a nice girl Betty was, her face so yielding and blurred.

He asked: "Do you have any pictures of yourself as a baby?"

She joked: "Bare skin on a bearskin? I don't know if I am safe, alone in this room with you."

Detweiler failed to answer. His little sister had died badly. Alongside the kitchen stove in her highchair, she had clambered up on rubbery feet, reached with infant fingers at the glass coffeemaker from the lower globe of which boiling water was surging into the upper through the hollow crystal column; a stimulating event to Detweiler himself, aged seven, who watched from across the room, milk-mug lowered. For a breathless moment all water bubbled and danced in the superior sphere, the lower was magically void; then it would, descend, transformed to another liquid, leveling up as black, then brown, then amber. It always had. But this time his sister's stubby, groping fingers had sent the wondrous progression awry. The topheavy device leaned towards her, soon crashed in a boiling sheet of deadly transparency, beautiful but killing, and scalded her out of life.

Detweiler explained: "I believe that life is never destroyed but transformed. However, I don't think my sister is living in any kind of heaven and looking down in an anthropomorphic shape." That had to be said because his mother very much did hold such a belief and talked, in séances and dreams, with a host of the deceased.

Betty sat delicately upon the foot of the bed, laid her head on a shoulder, and squinted at him, saying: "That's intriguing."

"But I am convinced that life or energy or spirit exists forever as a sort of current or fluid—the trouble is that when you try to express it in words you run into the problems of language. Words have traditions and histories of their own." Detweiler said, grinning: "So you are talking about something that cannot be talked about. Odd, eh? Paradoxical."

Betty's eyes narrowed. She asked: "Were you having some sort of fit before?" She touched his forearm quickly and withdrew. "You don't mind me prying? Tell me to go away anytime."

"Why?" Detweiler meant: about the "fit," having no memory of such. But Betty took it as a reference to her leaving.

"Because it's your room."

Matters of possession made him uneasy. He traveled light so as to escape the despair of ownership, the tyranny of material. He left his seat on the bed that was no more his property than the other: a demonstration of the difficulties you got into when the subject of belonging arose.

"I can take a hint," said Betty, rising too but moving little.

"No," said Detweiler. "You have a lovely apartment. It's the nicest room I have ever had. I hope I can continue on. I won't make a mess. I have given up sculpture, so there won't be any clay around to get on the carpet."

"Sculpture?" Betty said.

Detweiler repeated that he no longer practiced the craft, but to no avail; she kept after him, she loved all manifestations of the urge to create, and at length, because she was a girl with a woman's natural sympathy, he finally agreed to do her head. Thus he was led, through his inability to refuse a plea, by his wretched vanity, to commit another crime: to represent life and so to despise the actuality which sat as his model. But Betty was so innocent as to believe she was being celebrated.

"I'm thrilled at the prospect," she said. "And wait until I tell Billie."

"Will you quarrel with her again?" Detweiler asked in trepidation.

"Probably." She smiled carelessly. Detweiler was amazed: he saw nothing to be lighthearted about in bad feeling. He hated so much to quarrel that, simply to settle the matter, he would try to kill his opponent.

Walking the streets of the city, Detweiler summoned up this memory. Of course, such reminiscence was a kind of Realization, but of a low order, being part of his own history, brought back from only a few years before. But in a modest way it suggested what could be done even amid the distractions of a public thoroughfare. At the moment he was in a business district. Evening had come; office workers were homeward bound, moving along under clouds of steaming breath. Detweiler had exhausted the day but not himself, in miles of wander. He had not yet come up with a feasible means of locating a doctor, but he did not regard time as a material that could be wasted or expended: it was ever there and he was in it, as a fish is in the water.

He dined on, and shared with purple-gray pigeons, a loaf of day-old bread purchased at small expenditure from a bin of stale products in a supermarket. He had seen the late-afternoon sun of winter celebrate the windows of high buildings. He had watched a man change a flat tire on a busy avenue, deftly work the well-oiled jack and spin off the precise wheel-bolts, at the curb opposite a shopwindow exquisite with eggshell china.

"Do you want any help?" he asked the laboring motorist, merely as a courtesy, for he could see the man exerted perfect control over his devices and was furthermore a quick, coordinated, sandy-haired individual with a natural high temperature of personality and hence immune to cold, working indeed with bare, freckled hands.

"Thanks no!" the man chirped brightly, between the windrush of passing vehicles.

Obviously it was not the time or place, nor the person, to ask for a doctor.

Detweiler had also ambled through an enormous department store. He assumed such a large establishment, dealing with the public, would keep a dispensary, complete with physician, to attend to the customer who fainted or suffered a heart attack or epileptic seizure while on the premises. But, attracted by the acres of colorful merchandise, he roamed throughout as if in a spring meadow, feeding his senses, touching the toecaps of display-shoes, fingering silks, smelling woolens. Never did he pretend intent to purchase, and never was he regarded with anything but consideration by the salespeople. However, he understood that he was in a potentially commercial relation to them. Any attempt to introduce personal particularities would alter the equilibrium. It could not be done unobtrusively. People were sympathetic. Were he to simulate sudden illness and be conducted to the house doctor by the salesclerk who at the moment had amiably accepted the statement that he was "only looking" at the neckties, Detweiler would have established a peculiar identity.

"What was wrong with the guy I sent up yesterday?" the clerk would ask the physician, and perhaps receive an incredible answer.

Anyway, here was Detweiler, walking along later in the evening, past shadowy bars and small hotels. He had recently had a cup of coffee and a doughnut, but their warmth soon leaked off in the intense cold, and his extremities felt brittle as twigs.

It took severe conditions to make him uncomfortable, but once in that state he was no masochist: he tried to change it. He now, though not a drinker, stepped into a corner tavern and bathed with pleasure in the heated, though smelly, atmosphere. Contrary to his practice elsewhere, he took a stool as far away from the other customers as could be managed. Detweiler was leery of drunks: they were often so touchy, and tended to respond perversely to the friendliness which most sober persons were glad to accept from him.

A beer was probably the least offensive beverage he could get away with, and he ordered one, thereafter taking an occasional mouthful of its soury chill and ignoring the circumvolution of foam which stayed behind in a sort of bathtub-ring as the level descended. The occupants of the nearest stools were two elderly men who muttered towards, but did not look at, each other. Then in louder tones the one on the left reviled the man on the right, in unspeakably foul epithets, his ancient, transparent ears quivering under a hatbrim stiff with dried rain. An old speckled fist trembled under an old purple nose. The men wore like overcoats, black, heavy, and both hung similar pairs of cracked shoes, with diagonaled heels, from the lowest rung of the stools.

There you had the sort of inebriate situation that Detweiler was always at pains to avoid. In haste he signaled the bartender to come collect for the beer. He would have left the money and fled, but had only a dollar bill to his name.

"Buy me one?" said a woman behind his left shoulder, where the bar met the wall. He was startled out of the fear engendered by the old-men's quarrel; he had not looked for a human intervention from that locality, where there was scarcely room for a person to stand. But he had underjudged the space. Not only had a woman slipped therein, but a substantial woman and vivid even in the dim barlight.

Her face showed up as almost-orange beige; her hair, done in a big hedge-ball, of the next tone of the spectrum, almost-red orange, her lips vermilion. Detweiler was taken by her appearance. She also smelled sweetly. She looked about forty, with the deluxe figure of that age though hesitating at the margin of what could be called weightiness: rather, solid; ample.

Detweiler was conscious of a sudden appetite to have sexual knowledge of her: she seemed to exist for the purpose. For that reason he turned away, hard as it was for him to be rude: it was his peculiar torment that, in search of mutilation, he found but another argument in its favor.

She said reproachfully: "I was only looking for company. You could just say yes or no."

Detweiler turned back and replied as earnestly as he could, as usual. "It isn't that easy," he said. "You don't understand. I would like very much to go to bed with you right now. But it would take me away from my work, you see."

"Aw hell, honey. Aw hell," said this large fruit of a woman, pushing him with her hip, from which he assumed she wanted the stool, so he slid over to the next one and was thereby closer to the old men and their burgeoning altercation. He was now under greater pressure than before, but felt less desperation: such was the effect on him of comfortable women.

"I'm Rose," the woman told him, still leaning flagrantly against the stool he had vacated. "Who're you?"

"Joe," he replied, and put out his hand. She accepted it and tickled the palm.

Seriously he asked her: "Isn't that a funny handshake?"

"It's supposed to be sexy, dear. Didn't you do that when you were a kid?"

"Never."

"Didn't you play 'show me yours and I'll show you mine'?" She shook all of hers in robust merriment.

Detweiler had spent most of his childhood by himself. If he approached other children he was extremely cautious: they often kicked, punched, and bit, girls as well as boys. It was true that a little girl had once proposed such an exchange and, when he asked for clarification, explained: "The secret thing." So Detweiler reached into his jacket pocket and brought out to deposit on the grass the coil of his garter snake, a beautiful, gentle, trusting creature whose pleasure was to flow up his sleeve and peep out the vee of the shirt. The girl screamed and ran away to fetch a brother bigger than either Detweiler or she. Before Detweiler could ascertain his intent this lad had pounded the snake into a writhing foam.

The memory made Detweiler feel awful, but it served to water down his lust. It also revived his painful awareness of the quarrel beyond his right shoulder: the furious old man was now threatening to disembowl the other with the point of his shoe. Detweiler began to gulp air into the back of his throat.

"Won't talk, hey?" said the woman with the red-gold hair. "Playing it safe." She mounted the seat, put her left elbow onto the bar and her right hand, large and strong, into the descent of his lap and massaged him there.

His attention returned to her. For the first time he appreciated that she was drunk, much of her high color taking its source in that condition, though her speech had clarity.

"Excuse me," Detweiler replied. "I did play that game once, and it ended badly." An image of a coconut came to him briefly: the boy's cropped head, which he had cracked with the baseball bat that killed his snake. The boy collapsed, weeping and bleeding—Detweiler was too small to have killed him—and the little sister looked at the snake's remains, looked at her brother, threw her dress up and her drawers down, and said: "O.K., here it is. . . . Now I better go get him some iodine."

The woman's hand persisted, as if she were diligently sifting sand in search of a lost gem. Detweiler said in regret, referring to the dollar bill which the bartender had not yet taken: "I can't pay you anything. This is all the money I got to my name."

At once her hand flew away. "You shit," she cried. "What do you—Who do you—Are you calling me whore?"

In amazement Detweiler stared into his amber beer.

"You little fart," said the woman. "My husband will destroy you." She snatched his glass away and took a prodigious draught. Something struck Detweiler on the shoulder. It felt like a loosely wadded piece of newspaper, no bulk but thrown hard. The one old man had finally assaulted the other, hurling him against Detweiler.

Detweiler left the stool, left the woman, left his last dollar. Before he reached the door, however, a man of about his own size though thinner, dark, saturnine, even sick-looking around the green-ringed eyes and pinched nose, stepped into his path and struck him in the mouth. It smarted rather than hurt. Detweiler covered up with crossed arms. His assailant continued to flail away. From the utterances shouted simultaneously, Detweiler gathered his attacker was the woman's husband. He doubted that the man was in a state to listen to an oral self-defense, so he said nothing. Nor did he fight back: having naught to fight for, no anger and, since he understood that the man labored under a misapprehension, no resentment. He certainly was not being hurt by the ineffectual blows against his forearms.

At last the assailant lowered his fists and, gasping from the exertion, said: "Will you apologize?"

Detweiler wondered where the husband had been while his

wife stood at the bar. It was an odd situation. But he saw no reason why he should withhold that which this gallant individual sought so ardently.

"Of course," he said.

And the man seized his hand, saying: "No hard feelings?"

Detweiler shook his smiling head, though his upper lip, where he had been struck before he put up his guard, had now begun to ache.

"I'll buy you one," said the other. He retained Detweiler's hand and with it pulled him to a table in the front corner of the room. "I have to sit down. I'm not well. Tubercular."

Hopefully, Detweiler asked: "Are you under a doctor's care?"

The husband proceeded to disappoint him: "Not me. Oh, I tried them, went to hundreds, but they're all crooks and quacks and phonies, taking money unearned by the production of results. You can't get away with that in any other line of work. Be in jail if you tried." He chewed a mottled lip with yellow teeth, giving off an odor similar to that of the stale bread on which Detweiler had dined.

"My real trouble," the husband went on, "is my temper. It drains my strength. I didn't have no quarrel with you just now. I saw her handle you. I got the right picture, but a man hasn't any call to strike a woman, correct me if I'm wrong? But pride, my friend, you have got to serve pride and decency everywhere. What's your line?"

"Taxidermy," Detweiler said, "preserving animals."

"I know what that is exactly," the husband answered quickly, proudly. "Skin them and stuff 'em! I used to be a rabbit hunter. Kill one and you should gut him on the spot, rip up from asshole to breastbone, take him by the two front legs, bend over and whip him between your legs and out fly the guts. I'm going to like you. What's your name?"

"Joe."

"Walt here. What's your pleasure in the drinking line? I myself am beer all the way." He put a bony finger towards Detweiler's lip. "I connected there, Jesus, did I connect. Puffy, and also cut. Must have been this ring: cheap but cute." He showed Detweiler a death's-head on his knuckle, polished brass with red-glass eyes. "Serves to remind you nothing will last forever, not Mr. Money nor Mrs. Cunt, nobody and nothing. I find it healthy."

Detweiler flinched at the dirty words. He found this person unrewarding, but he did not know how he could get away from him without once again challenging the man's pride.

Then the wife appeared and put a half-filled glass of beer before him. "You forgot this," she said, grimacing neutrally. She decorously sat down at the table, across from him.

Walt told her: "You had too much."

"All right," said she.

"Well," Walt informed Detweiler, "you got your beer. Drink up." He poured himself a glassful from a bottle that had apparently just been opened, it being yet misted with cold. He seemed to be turning disagreeable once more. He said, with a melancholy stare into the middle murk of the room, "Oh, I got my principles, but what have I ever got *for* them?"

It occurred to Detweiler to ask: "What do you want?"

"Look at those two old killers," said Mrs. Walt, nodding her orange cocoon towards the ancient combatants at the bar, one of whom was still pushing the other, who accepted it doggedly while trying to return to his original position: both were now afoot, but had not moved far. The bartender stayed distant, deftly rinsing glasses. He had not collected Detweiler's dollar.

Walt answered gravely, meeting Detweiler's eye: "The impossible. My youth."

"In my opinion," said Detweiler, "if you don't mind me saying so, 'impossible' is not the right word, but rather 'irrelevant.' Time can only get to you if you let it. Don't you sense that whatever your body is or does, and your mind too, for that matter, you, the essential you, stays the same? Did you ever hear of an old soul or a young one?"

Walt looked from Detweiler to his wife and back.

"I'm using the word 'soul' because it's convenient," Detweiler explained. "What I mean is a sort of energy of awareness, a definite conviction that you exist. Do you feel that you exist any less than when you were younger?" He nodded brightly at Walt disregarding physical intelligence from his groin, into which, across and under the table, Mrs. Walt had insinuated her stockinged foot. She had apparently slipped her shoe off.

Walt stared disagreeably at Detweiler's right earlobe and corrugated his own upper lip.

"Well," Detweiler asked heartily, "are we here or not? You can begin basically. Where is your youth? Where is your old age? One was once here and the other will come. But where are they now? Where do they come from and where do they go? No place. But *you* are always here, right? Where is here? Wherever you are: that's how you tell. It's certainly not noplace. And if you are here, then it must be worthwhile."

Walt shifted his eyes to Detweiler's chin and mumbled sourly.

Undeterred, Detweiler said: "So youth and age are not things to be taken seriously. They are not to be gained or lost, except in a mechanical way: Einstein says if you go fast enough, time stops. Therefore how can it be important?"

Mrs. Walt suddenly wiggled her toes vigorously. He pulled his chair back several inches and her foot fell audibly to the floor.

Walt crowed in triumph, spearing with forked fingers an imaginary olive from the air between him and Detweiler. "If you say it don't all go up in shit when you die, you are a dirty liar."

Detweiler reflected that it had been an error to get involved in a consideration of Walt's dead-end mystique. This was the kind of wasteful distraction he could avoid were he to find a surgeon to stem the leakage of vital force. There would then be nothing for Mrs. Walt to probe towards, she who, in maximum stretch was now sitting on the small of her back, red head hooked onto the top of the chair, scarcely above table level. She looked like a midget from Detweiler's perspective. He could feel her toes once more. He could also sense, and even see from the bottom of his eye, his inflated lip, which now felt more like a growth than a pain.

"You're a rumdum slob," Walt said ferociously and left the table, in a limp that Detweiler had not hitherto noticed. He took two steps and then returned and without warning hit Detweiler in the right eye. Detweiler of course closed it and caged it in his fingers, and watched from the good one Mrs. Walt squeeze wincingly into her shoe and follow Walt to the door, through which, both waving goodbye to the bartender, they exited.

Soon thereafter the aggressor of the two old men hit the other with a beer bottle. Without examining the fallen, the bartender got a dime from the till, entered the public telephone booth next to a door marked "Toilet," and placed a call.

Detweiler watched the proceedings through his good eye, serenely. He no longer found the violence infectious. He was still sitting there when the police arrived, two of them, large men in blue. They burst in as if propelled by some source of energy on the sidewalk, but collected themselves quickly and stared at the recumbent old-timer whose head lay in blood. He who had committed the assault raved through a toothless mouth, to them but more to the world at large, that the victim had made indecent advances to him, which was a crime. The police took him away. He announced he would go "under protest," and showed as much by his indignant, foot-slapping march.

Detweiler sometimes felt sorry for other people; so much of life seemed loathsome to them. He waited until the ambulance came for the old man who had been wounded or killed, and after the accompanying interne, dressed in soiled ducks, had sent the victim out upon a litter borne by attendants in impeccable whites, Detweiler waylaid the doctor, displaying his puffed lip and sore eye.

He said, craftily: "May I come along and get treatment?"

"Put cold compresses on those and get some rest," the interne answered and departed.

Detweiler's dollar lay yet where he had left it, anchored by some spilled beer so as to go unstirred by the commotion of the battle. He waved it at the bartender.

Who, back at his glass-washing sink, called pleasantly: "Walt took care of that."

"But I had my beer before I met him," Detweiler stated.

"No, he caught it."

The other persons at the bar showed no curiosity about this exchange. Detweiler, however, found it remarkable. Had Walt, then, directed Mrs. Walt to make his acquaintance? And if so, why? In generosity or meanness? To whom?

As always Detweiler had had an interesting day. When he arrived at his mother's apartment, standing in the interior hall he could hear her speaking in falsetto behind the closed door of the living room. She was holding a séance. From the hatrack hung the outer garments of her co-participants, the deceased loved ones of whom would speak through her if she made successful contact. They would all be holding hands so as to make a human circuit. What they were after was a kind of Realization, but too simple-minded to appeal to Detweiler, who repaired to the kitchen and ate a peanut butter and jelly sandwich. He then went to bed and fell asleep while pulling the blanket towards his chin.

Chapter 10

TIERNEY darkened the doorway.

Betty said: "I thought of something else in connection with Joe Detweiler. He once gave Billie a mounted squirrel. It stood on the dresser the last time I was in here before the murders."

She wanted encouragement, but Tierney seemed strangely indifferent, saying merely that he would go over the inventory: perhaps the technicians had taken it to the lab. He admitted he had not seen it.

He asked: "Are you ready to go?"

Betty preceded him into the hall, and he waited until she had turned through the kitchen door before he extinguished the bathroom light. She lingered at the stove, where on entry he could have collided with her, but his reflexes were astonishing. The illumination rippled smoothly across the linoleum from a floor lamp in the living room beyond.

"You're sure it's Joe."

"No," Tierney answered literally.

"But you will get him."

Tierney shrugged, a movement she more heard than saw.

Betty said: "You have guns and radios and labs and the power to take away somebody's freedom for parking next to a fireplug. Joe is one man, or boy really, skinny little fellow and soft in the head. He might not even know you're looking for him: I don't think he ever reads the papers. He wouldn't have the faintest idea where or how to hide out."

She was ready now to go on into the living room, but Tierney, it seemed to her, was reluctant to move. Or to speak. His physical effect was bulky in the half light: he still wore his overcoat.

The slick chill of the linoleum reminded her she was barefoot.

"My boots and stockings."

"I dried them out," said Tierney.

Betty wandered from the kitchen into the light and saw her boots standing erect on the shallow sheet-metal cap of the radiator between the front windows. She crossed the pale area of carpet where Appleton had died.

"Where are my stockings?"

"Here." Tierney took them from the pocket of his overcoat. It seemed odder to her that he surrendered them with no embarrassment, than that he had carried them so. He next denied her the opportunity to ask him to turn aside while she put them on: ostentatiously he retired to a far corner, stooped, gathering the skirts of his coat, and peered at the baseboard.

She was shod when he returned.

"Find something?"

"Old scar, varnished over," said he. "Caught the light."

"These old apartments," she stated.

Tierney helped her into her coat, though not considerately, holding it too high. She went up on her toes. "You must have a tall wife."

"No," Tierney said obtusely. "She is about your size."

"And blonde," Betty guessed, having penetrated the sleeves at last, keeping her back to him while she fastened the three big wooden buttons. He made no answer.

She turned and said: "I'm trying to regard you as a person."

Tierney raised the obscure brows over his clear blue eyes. He had a facility for maintaining himself in a neutral equilibrium while others moved futilely and aged.

He smiled without amusement. "Brunette."

"And detectives always have children."

"Just like people." Tierney knew as he said it that he had now willfully disarmed himself. He had as much self-pity as the next man, was underpaid and overworked, unloved and mistrusted by everybody and respected only by criminals, yet never before had he found it necessary to snivel to a woman.

Quick to seize her advantage, Betty yet spoke slowly and as if in discomfort: "Well, I didn't mean that, and you know it." She was now in a position from which she could taunt him endlessly. In a merciless calling, he could expect no mercy: that was the clear morality of it.

She looked at his right ear, which lay efficiently close against his head: he was built for action. She put her hands against the several layers of clothing between the air and his hard chest, and groped.

"Leave your gun at home?"

Boyishly he opened his coat and jacket and displayed the little clip-holster at the turn of his left hip. As he reached for it he caught her hand, but held it flabbily: she squeezed through and clasped the butt once, then withdrew.

She said, grinning: "I thought about it for a long time, and did it."

He considered her eyes for a moment and then laboriously unfastened the strap and removed the pistol, opened the cylinder, ejected the shells, and presented the weapon to her.

Now Betty kept her hands to herself, saying: "Actually, I've always been afraid of guns."

"Go ahead," Tierney said, swaggering somewhat. "It's unloaded." The weapon was smooth and hard and smelled of oil: a man's device in extremis, nothing in it for doubt or wonder, utterly predictable. "The way to get over a fear of something," he sententiously went on, "is to know it. A firearm is just an instrument, with no power in itself." He demonstrated the technique of cocking and firing, but with a thumb restrained the hammer so the trigger would not snap against space; which was bad for the firing pin.

He dropped a bullet, bent to fetch it, saying: "We have to pay for these ourselves." Again the note of self-pity. The shell bounced to rest between Betty's feet. She refused to move as Tierney knelt there. He tapped her boot as a signal she should shift it.

The doorbell rang then. Tierney let the shell go and leaped erect, stowing away his revolver in one neat motion. But before he answered the summons he did a strange thing: pushed Betty at the couch, made it clear she should lie there. As she submitted, he lifted her legs by the ankles, swung them up and on.

Then he went into the hallway and admitted a patrolman through the street door.

The cop said: "I am going for coffee. You folks want any?"

"Oh," said Tierney. "Well, we're leaving soon. I don't guess so."

The officer's chill-flushed face nodded between his cap and high-button collar.

"Thanks, Minelli." Tierney instantly remembered he had got Spinelli's name wrong, an unprecedented mistake; he had known the man for several years. No fitting apology occurred to him, so he asked: "Shuster hasn't been looking for me on the radio?"

"You'll know it if he does," Spinelli said as he left.

Tierney called after him, at the closing door, in the empty hall under the yellow ceiling fixture: "Mrs. Bayson is resting. She doesn't feel well."

Betty of course could hear this. He must go now and face her hard upon a lie, the motive for which was not obvious to him.

She was waiting, but oddly enough showed none of the ugly triumph he expected, appeared instead as sweet and shy. She had taken off her coat and sat demurely on the couch, hair back of one ear. The bullet rested where it had been dropped. He intended to get it, was on the way, but she put out both arms.

He knelt before her, and her legs opened to admit him in his overcoat. He had a sense only of clothing, wadded wool of his and her various nonfrictional stuffs. She avoided his mouth. Her hand once reached his groin as if by accident, drawing quickly away thereafter. Had he ceased to struggle, they would have been lying there in a heap, as though in the aftermath of an accidental collision. He tried then to pull away; even now he was not of a single mind. But she had been working unobtrusively at his belt buckle, and the zipper, and the snap fasteners of his drawers, and suddenly his shame was bare. She remained fully dressed, her skirt no higher than the lower garter clips. He alone was indecent, exposed, in violation of the ordinances, and firmly she took him into custody.

Betty had been thirteen when Billie had told her: "Get hold of it and you can do anything with them." Billie was fifteen and Betty assumed she was merely being dirty, theoretical, speculative. Billie in those days talked of much that she did not do: brushing cornstarch into the pubic hair to give it sheen, firming the breasts with egg-white massages, various self-manipulations as training for the control of passion and the increase of pleasure, how to belly-rub a boy hard while dancing or brush him with a knocker at the drinking fountain. In practice, to Betty's observation, which was close, Billie realized none of these projects. She was actually very modest with boys; and as to her body, treated it as an athlete's, showering and exercising daily, and walking on the balls of her feet so that her calves were in tension and her buttocks under strict management. She neither smoked nor drank and could not suffer the company of those who did. The boys who frequented her had like interests, were gymnasts and weightlifters, with guileless eyes and short hair. Billie in fact remained a virgin throughout high school.

Having always believed that wrongdoing took conscious effort, Tierney was delighted to find himself now relieved of moral weight. He had a pleasant sense that time had stopped, that his capacities were therefore infinite. In apprehending the malefactor, the police take responsibility for his crimes: he who is powerless can no longer be evil. He was not troubled that Betty wished him ill. He was happily married and in no need of comfort.

Betty began to tire but not to weaken. Here in her house she would give all and take nothing. Having caused Tierney to secrete his venom, she would drain it. Her concern was that he not interpret her intent as loving.

All at once Tierney took charge. He was finally no pervert. He fingered aside her straining interstitial strap of pants, like a spring or rubber band, and made gliding entry, constricting as though through a ring, expanding thereafter in yielding yet close imprisonment: he could go anywhere but not unaccompanied. She would even follow him out, as retiring from one statement he prepared the next. His wife lay inert, whores drily thrusted: Tierney had not known of a third style, and was momentarily appalled. Yet the fleshly argument was overwhelming.

Betty recognized in horror that her treasonous body was making love with his, engrossing, devouring that which it could never retain, breaking its heart, though morally she had vanquished him: proof there was no justice in creation. And now Tierney had claimed her mouth and she was gulping his, and his hands had penetrated her clothing, defiling her everywhere as he could not have done were she stark naked. She was in the most calamitous, obscene disorder, and he was her master.

It was as if she were acting as accessory to her own murder.

The doorbell rang. Tierney hesitated for a microsecond, then pushed himself off her and retracted his trousers. It was an extraordinary moment for Betty: she was still enthralled. He closed his coat, and was whole. This seemed to take no more time than if he had not touched her. He vanished into the hallway. She kept nothing of him.

Tierney was still open under the coat, trousers clipped at the top, but the fly gaped and his belt buckle dangled, and he knew from the absence of a certain weight that his gun had slipped from the holster he had not restrapped. Nevertheless, it was with a sense of self-possession that he again opened the street door to find Spinelli.

The officer exhaled a burst of steam. He looked as though he had run up the stoop.

"That was Shuster," he said, referring to the police radio. Cold wind blew up Tierney's overcoat and toyed intimately with him. He received the subsequent message without comment on it, but asked Spinelli to call in that he was on his way.

Spinelli wanted to talk. "You can't ever tell with a psycho, huh?" He erected, and gestured with, a gloved thumb. "The lady O.K. now?"

Tierney nodded heavily. He reflected that he must be smeared with lipstick and wondered why Spinelli failed to notice.

But Spinelli continued jovially: "Too bad the prick didn't come in in Florida." He steamed again and thudded his hands against his heavy blue coat.

Tierney laughed in a kind of wheeze and closed the door. Betty was precisely where, and as, he had left her, with one exception. She held his pistol. Oddly enough, throughout the interruption he had maintained himself, or was maintained, in a state in which he could have returned and finished with her, and so preserve the order of things.

Now his blood receded swiftly. A firearm was most deadly in the hands of the unpracticed. Any policeman would rather face a veteran gunman than an amateur.

He had begun to stalk her when she said, wistfully: "You forgot this," and laid the weapon beside her on the couch. Her lipstick seemed intact: therefore he must not have been defaced. He had got away with it, probably; could not recall any irony in Spinelli's manner.

He strapped the .38 into the holster. It had been a close call, all around, but he had emerged without damage. With his back to her he fastened his fly.

Then he turned and told her that, and where, Joseph Detweiler had given himself up.

Betty gasped.

Tierney was touched. He wanted to help her from the couch, or something, but was certain she would reject any offer. So he just stood there and tried to smile.

He said: "I have to go along now."

"Poor Joe," said Betty. "Will you hurt him?"

She seemed genuinely worried. Tierney believed this was the first evidence he had ever seen in her of authentic emotion. Perhaps it was not that she never had such, but rather that he had not detected it. But he was a detective of facts and not suppositions; else he was doing a job other than that for which he had been hired. No one would pay a nickel for him as a person, at the mercy of normal human weaknesses. He worked on call, like a device; and like a mechanism he did not understand regret.

"*I* won't have responsibility for him," he said, with some amazement at her plea.

She searched his face. "He might say funny things, but it won't be defiance. He looks at things differently than most people. He expects more of people than they do of themselves."

Tierney found himself oddly embarrassed. He said: "Who doesn't?"

"You don't," Betty replied with bitterness.

Jesus Christ, thought Tierney, so we're back to that. All the same, he was impressed by her consistency. She was quite a woman. He could fall in love with her if he wished, but it would be too much trouble.

"That's how you can tell you are sane," Betty added.

Tierney drove her to the hotel in a slow crosstown passage through rush-hour traffic and snow-wet streets. The curious episode at the apartment had lasted only about ninety minutes. He had gone there to lay her, and succeeded: he decided this in retrospect. With Detweiler in custody, Tierney would have no further reason to see Betty. He seemed to suffer no ill effects from coitus interruptus; he kept his mind off the subject, though maintaining a surveillance on his body. In his profession health was a major concern.

Tierney pulled into a snowdrift some distance from the entrance to the hotel.

"Would you mind?" Betty asked derisively. "Would you mind letting me out up where it's clear?"

They had said nothing on the journey.

She went on: "What I have always heard about a cop's manners is true: they are nonexistent."

Before complying, Tierney took her gloved hand. He said with awkward evidence of despair: "Can I see you again?"

Betty had known all along that she could make him fall in love with her.

She asked: "What for?"

He drove to the main entrance, and the uniformed functionary opened the door.

As Betty swung her boots out, Tierney said softly but distinctly: "Ah, to hell with you."

Chapter 11

DETWEILER got out of bed and saw a white angle across the sash of the window. The snow had followed him cross country. He turned his back to it as he performed his exercises. He squatted, spread one hand against the floor between his knees, and lifting himself upon it, legs drawn up, sat like a frog upon a toadstool. This took strength and more than strength, balance, and more than either, will.

Usually when in this position he meditated on that which was inexpressible, his faculties in suspension. There were yogis who claimed that in its ultimate refinement the exercise could be done without the supporting hand, but Detweiler did not believe such was possible except by some kind of self-delusion: that is, the practitioner deceived himself into thinking he sat on air. For the physical laws were absolute, made sense. The earth was a magnet that attracted anything which had weight. It was a marvelous principle, and Detweiler had no interest in trying to defy it. He was no enemy of the natural.

Today, various practical considerations addressed him as he aligned his forces along that rigid arm growing from the root-like fingers. Perhaps he would not succeed in getting himself mutilated. Certainly his efforts of the day before had been fruitless. He knew he tended towards the idealistic. What he really wanted was for a doctor to seek him out, to suggest the operation as if it were a surprise: "Say, I specialize in amputations. Sell you one?" Casual, breezy, but not vulgar. Detweiler could then accept tentatively, as if it were not of enormous importance to him; or maybe initially resist, ask for a prediction of the advantages thereof. "Come on," the doc would say. "What the devil."

A thin but assertive pain began to insinuate itself through the tendons of his wrist. This was not right: his breathing must be off. That snow was getting to him. It was certainly distracting to think of the mess he had left behind. Detweiler began to lose confidence in the arm on which he was supported; his body started to sway as if atop a high pole in a breeze. There was this to say about concealment: it led to misconceptions. Suppose a man performed an act which had another appearance than the one intended, or perhaps its significance was that it had no significance: driving to an urgent appointment, he ran down and killed a pedestrian, but kept on going because he was already late. Thus he became a criminal in the eyes of the law, though he had had nothing to gain from destroying the victim and, in fact, no interest in him. Indeed, he could have remained wholly legal if he had only stopped and displayed some concern for the fallen. His crime was one of omission. However, were the pedestrian already dead, whatever the driver did subsequently would be relevant only in a social way, only to satisfy the Law. There were reasons why the Law had to be absolute and not allow for exceptions. Otherwise it would be preposterous to punish a motorist for not stopping to minister to a man well dead.

There was knocking upon the door of his room. Detweiler said, "Come in," and his mother did. He performed a headstand and, seeing her upside down, said: "Good morning."

"Good morning, Ernest," replied his mother. "Did you sleep well?"

"As a matter of fact, I did. But I got up on the wrong side of the bed. I'm trying to figure out something about the Law, at the moment."

"Of course I can't see you properly in that position," said Mrs. Detweiler, "but your nose looks swollen and your one eye seems to be black. I wonder if you fell out of bed."

"No," Detweiler answered, "a drunken man hit me twice last night. In the mood he was in he had to hit somebody, so it was just as well it was me rather than someone who would have been hurt."

"And you're feeding the areas with a fresh flow of blood now," said his mother.

"I suppose I am, but not intentionally. I'm really thinking about the Law, as I said."

"Manmade or natural?"

"Their connection, if any."

"How so?"

"I was wondering whether I ought to go and report something I did that was against the Law."

"Report to whom, Ernest?"

"The police," said Detweiler. "I don't imagine anyone else would be interested. But the police are probably puzzled about it, and they work pretty darn hard. It makes me feel lousy to keep them in suspense, taking up their time with a problem I could very easily settle."

"But would they be any better off?" asked his mother. "The police always have lots of work. Any job you take off their hands will be replaced with another. It reminds me of that time you worked as a postal clerk, sorting mail. You would dispose of a great stack of letters, all in the proper pigeonholes, and it was a real satisfying feeling to have everything managed so nicely, but then, you remember?, a fellow would wheel up a cart and line up another three hundred letters in front of you. Took away your incentive, you said. At the end of your shift there remained as much mail as at the start, and it would go on so forth throughout the night, and no doubt unto this very day."

"Yes," said Detweiler. "But if one letter went astray it would mean something to the person who mailed it. That I am sure of. Just because there are a lot of people in existence does not lessen the value of particulars."

"What was it you were thinking over reporting?"

"I'll remember in a minute. I had a reason for doing it, and so the whole thing was canceled out. You know how you will add up how much money you owe and then match it against what you have, pay the bill, and then forget the specific figures?"

"Sure," she said. "I've never had a head for figures. Which is why I couldn't ever be a numerologist, though having known some lovely people in that field. The great composer Johann Sebastian Bach wouldn't take a step, couldn't write a note without determining its numerological significance. I reached him once, asking for help with a numerical situation in which a friend was involved, but for the most natural reason it came to nothing."

"He spoke in German," said Detweiler, from under his chest. "Exactly."

"I hope you had a good séance last night," Detweiler said.

His mother answered: "We had one doubter, and that can often be disruptive because doubters want blowing winds and floating trumpets and the claptrap. They are dumbfounded when you tell them that matter obeys its own laws; and so with the spirit; sometimes the two are combined, as in human and animal life, contained in physical bodies but animated by spirit. But the purely physical does not have a life of its own, and no spiritualist ever claims it does."

"I disagree with you there, Mother, I must say. I think if you kick a table leg the table feels it."

"All right, Ernest, that is its nature. But a table won't ever fly."

Detweiler let himself down and lay on his back.

"I was just thinking, in connection with calling you 'Ernest'," said his mother. "If you keep calling me 'Mother,' anybody would know you were my son no matter what I call you, wouldn't they?"

"Oh yeah," Detweiler replied, snapping his fingers. "That's right."

"Of course I am at an age where you get addressed as mother by total strangers," said Mrs. Detweiler.

Detweiler began to laugh. He said: "I can't keep it up, this false-identity stuff. You don't have to pretend any more. Guess I wouldn't have made much of an actor. But you really keep the professional touch."

The reference was to Mrs. Detweiler's early days as partner in a mental act with Detweiler's father. They played little clubs, theaters, county fairs, trade conventions, his father in a turban out among the audience, his mother blindfolded upon the stage. They were supposed to work by means of a code: in Mr. Detweiler's phrasing was the clue to the object he asked her to identify. "What have I here?" perhaps signified a gentleman's watch. "Can you tell me what this is?" a lady's comb. And so on for two dozen common articles found in pockets and purses. Rarer items were dealt with by a laborious system which secretly spelled out key words.

In fact Mrs. Detweiler never learned even the simple phase of the code; she had no head for that type of symbolism. And no need for it, being naturally able to see through faculties other than the physiological eye. Thus when her husband was not able discreetly to ignore some member of the audience who handed him a small jar of calf's-foot jelly; said: "Well, well, ah yes," the signal for the institution of the difficult code; and began to spell "jam" with the first letter of the first word in the first sentence, the second letter of the second word, etc. ("Just a moment, please. My partner is concentrating. She uses memory, introspection, clairvoyance. . . .")

Mrs. Detweiler did not count efficiently or spell with any conviction. She had tried, though, and would try again, for her husband strongly disapproved of her using techniques other than his. Any suggestion of the supernatural made him furious, and he might punch her face if aroused. Still, she often took a chance on his being so distracted by showmanship as to overlook her defection from the modes of reason. Calf's-foot jelly was a case in point. She got "jam," but "calf" was taking so

long to announce, though her husband was glib, and she soon
lost count, and it was foolish anyway to make so arduous what
was no task at all: in her mind's eye she could see very clearly
the little jar, ex-commercial peanut butter; the label, hand-
lettered in pen and ink; the paraffin disk that topped off the
jelly; the screw-on lid.

She interrupted her husband to make the identification.
After the act was finished and they were back in the dressing
room, he struck her with the old one-two. Her husband was
show-business all the way: he never gave her a beating the
effects of which could not be concealed by make-up or costume.
He never caused her to limp. Nor did he make a commotion
which would wake young Detweiler, a baby in this era, asleep
in his portable crib. Mrs. Detweiler did not protest against
these well-deserved punishments.

When Mr. Detweiler passed on she was free to take up
spiritualism. By the time she got through to him he had calmed
down. Life in the otherworld was such as to extinguish high
emotion. All there was serene, truly superior, and beautiful.
You could choose your age and remain in it: Mr. Detweiler
decided on twelve and wore knickers above high stockings, and
a billed cap. He remained an entertainer, amusing the Elysians
with sleight-of-hand and jokes, for fun was the rule Over There,
where no one worked or needed an income.

Of Joseph, he often told her: "We don't have to worry
about him. He'll make his way. He's no fool." But, like her
husband, Joseph had a temper. He disliked noise, rudeness, and
cruelty unless it was the natural type displayed by animals.
Mrs. Detweiler could not endure watching a cat stalk a robin,
but as quite a young child Joseph assured her this was as it

should be in the great circuit of existence. But he half-killed a neighbor boy who plinked at birds with an air rifle. They, Joseph and she, had to leave town. They left many towns, and his formal education had been catch-can, but he seemed to turn out well nevertheless, and philosophically he was developed far beyond the standards of the schooled. He also had this artistic talent from an early age, could make likenesses of anybody in any medium, and was therefore popular though quiet.

Mrs. Detweiler found it easy to gather about her a little circle of spiritualists wherever she was: they recognized one another on sight. Nose around a local grocery or bus stop and you would find a kindred soul. This elite was never numerous, but international, of all races and levels of income. The more prosperous communicants provided her rent- and food-money; give what you can, she levied no charges and used her gift as strenuously for those who had no money to spare.

Since Joseph had grown up and gone away to follow his own bent she had lived in the same place. He had occasionally visited her in the years since, without incident. But now he was apparently involved in some difficulty, his nose enlarged and his eye ripe, and she suspected she might have to move soon again.

"I had better go pack the suitcase," she said.

Detweiler shook his bruised face. "No, I don't think that's necessary, Mother, I really don't. Nobody knows me here, and this trouble may not turn out to be serious. I just wish I could remember. At the moment I just have this sense of something wrong at the back of my head. He might have been deaf."

"Who?"

"This guy."

"The fellow who hit you?"

"No," Detweiler said. "The fellow I think I killed."

His mother shook her head: too deep for her. Joseph had his own doings. If he wanted to elucidate, he would in his own time. Now she had to get some breakfast for both of them, went and fried some cornmeal mush and served it with Karo syrup, and Detweiler spooned up most and then, scraping his fork across the plate, collected the sweet film between the tines and licked them clean.

What had previously been inchoate now fell into place. Detweiler shaved himself again though he had done so only yesterday and his beard was very light, and put on a necktie and a suit of his father's that his mother had kept for twenty years—still in good condition, moth-free, and better than the one he had worn on the trip out. The pants were somewhat large but supported by suspenders. Detweiler had been fond of his father but never missed him. He had not seen it as a pity that his father had done away with himself, given his rationale. His father had always lusted to make it big in the entertainment profession: next season, next year; he had been a slave of time. But the intervals of experience measured by clocks and calendars were arbitrary creations.

When a boy Detweiler had been amazed by the people who had no sense of reality, who rejected the here and now in the quest for the other, like the boys who wanted to "be" something when they grew up. With the same idea, his father wanted to "be" a headliner, as if that were a type of existence which differed altogether from the kind in which he presently lived.

To Detweiler this was an extraordinary misapprehension, especially in view of the fact that an entertainer's audience had no face at all, and his father had a thorough disregard of even the identities of its individual members as he circulated among them and chose their personal possessions for use in his act, held up a comb with no acknowledgment of the living hair through which its teeth had swept.

Detweiler's father had therefore hanged himself. It had been Detweiler, who was seven, who found him: like a side of meat or a big bunch of bananas, leaving no note. The mise en scène was a room in a small hotel in Denver, Colo. The immediate cause, Mr. Detweiler's chagrin that he could not afford the inexpensive suite the Detweilers had occupied the last time an engagement brought them to Denver. This occurred on a day in late summer, warm in town, but if you looked across into the western distances, the vast reaches, the mounting, aspiring thrusts, you saw the first cap of snow on the Rockies.

In his father's suit Detweiler sat down now on the narrow bed and began to Realize the experiences of a party of westward emigrants lashing their ox-pulled covered wagons up the slopes, winter on its way, biscuit and water running low, no game sighted in days, but ahead the awesome echoes, the blue and white infinity, a high-wheeling eagle: grand, splendid, unconditioned. But Detweiler did not like the wagonmaster's curses, though he loved his blue-ginghamed daughter with her cornsilk hair.

Today was blue for Detweiler. When he had put aside his Realization, the falling snow against the window looked blue. His father's suit was navy, the necktie royal; even his shirt had a thin blue stripe. An enchanting color, deriving, like all hues, from the sun: there was an opinion that called it cold: not so, sparks were often blue, and very hot skies.

"What else is blue?" he asked his mother, who was at that moment passing through the hallway.

"The false name you selected," she answered.

"Oh yes."

"Joseph," said she, "it just occurred to me: could I check into the matter for you?"

Detweiler understood the reference and all its implications. She was offering by spiritual means to determine whether the man was dead, the man he had spoken of earlier.

"I'd rather you did not, Mother. I better handle this myself."

Detweiler put on his coat. His haversack was packed and ready to go.

Said his mother: "You certainly look fine in that suit. I was talking to your father yesterday and he hoped you would wear it sometime."

Detweiler neither believed nor disbelieved in his mother's traffic with the otherworld. He saw no reason why he had to take a definitive position on it.

He said: "How is he?"

"Fine. Though of course it is a mistake to think they don't have problems Over There, little annoyances, difficulties. It is of course Perfect, but not perfect in our sense. And there is one very, very unusual circumstance that the living never think of."

Detweiler raised his brows.

His mother said: "Over There you cannot die to escape your troubles."

Cap in hand, pack on back, Detweiler kissed his mother and said: "Thanks for everything. I'll send you some money if I get some."

"I know you will. God bless you, Joseph." She went with

him to the door and stood within its frame as he descended the stairway.

When he reached the first landing, he stopped and, reflecting that he might not see her again in this life, he called up: "I really enjoyed breakfast."

She waved and he went down and out into the snow.

The receptionist in the lobby of the newspaper building looked suspiciously at Detweiler's haversack but sympathetically at his eyes. He had first asked for the managing editor but then turned his attention to her earrings, saying: "Aren't they pretty!"

Ever on guard against attempts to butter her up, she yet could not believe that his purpose was damaging to her, professionally, economically, sexually. Therefore she identified them as coral.

"From the bottom of the sea," Detweiler said in wonder. "To your ear." She had a greatly attractive ear, too, pink as a shell.

The young woman sensed in herself a tendency to relinquish her spirit to him. Still, she had a job to do.

She asked: "Could I request the nature of your business? Won't someone else do? The managing editor is terribly busy. You understand."

Detweiler was still looking at her ear.

She felt the need to apologize, but he suddenly gazed into her eyes with profound grace.

"Anybody who is aware of events, I guess, would be appropriate. I asked for the editor rather than a reporter because I figured he would be here, working at a desk. Whereas reporters are always out around town, aren't they?"

"Do you have a story?" the receptionist asked very seriously, for oftentimes unusual people came in off the street with such. In journalism you could not disallow a person on his appearance or manner.

Detweiler thought for a moment, and then he nodded soberly. "It well may be. That's what I have to find out."

The receptionist was all at once too shy to ask him more. She called a city reporter down on the intercom.

When the newsman arrived Detweiler asked: "Are you on the Crime Desk?"

"What's that?" the man coldly replied, but Detweiler's face showed a generosity he could not long withstand, and the reporter said amiably: "Well, I write about crime if it is a story." He laughed and said: "Have you committed one?"

"I might have. I thought maybe you could check for me."

The reporter sucked back his smile. He suddenly had a feeling about Detweiler and stared plaintively at him: he feared ingenuousness.

Detweiler said: "I didn't want to go to the police because they would be annoyed if it turned out not to be a crime."

"They would?" The reporter found himself at the mercy of this small, odd individual. For one thing he had difficulty in assessing Detweiler's age, seeing him, absurdly, as a kind of adolescent old man.

"Oh sure. I don't want to make fun of the cops," Detweiler explained. "That is pretty rotten, considering the risks they take to protect us all from violence. I wouldn't want to turn out to be a crank, like those people who call up the police and say, 'I put a bomb in the so-and-so hotel lobby.' Then they clear the place and search and it turns out to be not true: the caller's threat was empty, and he had misused the considerable power of a citizen in this day and age. That couldn't be done in the eras before the invention of the telephone. The crank would have had to send a note and then wait until delivery had been made: too long, and he wouldn't be sure the proper authority had got it."

Detweiler was talking a lot because he had a great sense of well-being from having the ear of a gentleman of the press, a person with the means of vast communication at his fingertips. For himself, Detweiler disapproved of writing. Words were elements of another kind of reality than that which claimed his primary attention. He would have written things if by so doing he could create actual states or situations, if by writing "John is happy," John would indeed be rendered happy. But if John was already blissful, to write that would be solely to describe. If John was unhappy, it would be a lie.

However, writing was a reporter's business, and Detweiler did not feel it corrupting to be written about. Indeed, he relished telling his story through another person. Newspapermen always said what they wished anyway: the guilt would not be on his own head. A clever person could fish out the truth. The main thing was to get it told. For example, there might be great value in publishing an explanation of why he wanted his penis to be amputated. Perhaps others had the same aim and had been frustrated as he had been. There was no limit to what men, any man, could do. Detweiler wondered whether the reporter had any sense of his own potential.

The reporter said, timidly: "Would you like to come up to the city room? Would you rather talk there?" He glanced about at the people moving through the lobby, suggesting that Detweiler found them distracting or at least craved privacy.

"Sure," said Detweiler. "Any place where you would feel at ease."

The floor they got off on was the scene of much activity and businesslike clamor: vital machines and talking men. Detweiler nodded here and there, but most people were too involved in newspaper matters to respond. In the center of all this the reporter claimed a desk as his own and got Detweiler an extra chair.

"Now," he said, "I don't know your name."

Detweiler answered expansively: "That is beside the point for the moment. What I had in mind is if you could determine whether recently a man was killed in a lunch counter."

"Where?" The reporter looked quickly at Detweiler's hands. It was instinctive, murder being usually a labor of the fingers: on a trigger, a knife, even around a vial of poison. Detweiler's were small and boyish, even to the scab over a minor cut he might have got from playing mumbletypeg. His eye, however, was black, had been from the beginning of the interview. The reporter had of course registered that but not noticed it until now.

"You should see the other guy, huh?" he essayed to joke, but Detweiler showed polite quizzicality.

"Could you find out?"

He was a stubborn little guy, had a moral force to him. The reporter was amused by his arrogance, but nevertheless called the police.

"Results nil," he said as he broke the connection some moments later. "No killings. No luncheonette fights you could fit in have been reported, anyway. Why don't you just forget about it?"

"I don't like rudeness," Detweiler said. "But the counterman I hit might have been deaf, you see? He might not have heard me. If so, I was wrong. I should have been more patient, maybe." He winced. "But he did hear me when I ordered coffee, so why not when I asked for sugar doughnuts?"

The reporter could not understand what was interesting about this inconsequential affair, but he found himself caught up in it. Detweiler's earnestness was irresistible.

"Hell," he said, "we all have moments when we are not at the top of our form, but then time passes."

Detweiler regarded this statement with care as a young fellow quietly but rapidly took away some papers from the desk. The place was only superficially in confusion: actually there was a scheme. The newspaper would appear on schedule, assembled, organized from all this movement and noise. It was a marvel of directed energy, that's what Detweiler liked about it. He had no interest in news in any particular sense, except now to wonder how these purposeful people were able to choose from all that happened incessantly, those relatively few items which they felt were worth writing about.

"Yes," he said, "it's not easy to pierce the illusion that Time goes somewhere from which it cannot be recovered except in the counterfeit form of history, the representation or reproduction but not the actuality."

"Pardon?" asked the newspaperman. He had not really suspected that Detweiler was a nut, for all the apparent evidence of nonconformity in the lad. He was briefly desperate: he should have brushed him off downstairs.

But Detweiler was no boor. He knew the man had work to do and was not likely to be in a contemplative mood amid the jangle of a hundred telephones.

Therefore he got to his feet and said: "I want to thank you for your kindness. Perhaps we can work together again when

I have refined my techniques of Realization. You might be interested if you are a student of Time. Meanwhile, God bless you."

The reporter rose involuntarily, as he did only for men of the cloth. "All right," he said, "do that. Good luck to you." He suddenly gave his name, from a motive no more clear than the others of which he had been recent victim. So close did he come to letting Detweiler walk out of there to vanish, perhaps forever.

He said: "Pat Allen."

"Glad to have met you, Mr. Allen. I'm Joseph Detweiler."

The Starr case was national news. Allen kept smiling idiotically as Detweiler backed politely away for a step or two and then turned to leave. Oh Christ, oh Christ.

Allen finally managed to call out in a queer voice: "Let me walk you to the elevator." He caught up, and with all his heart and soul could barely squeak: "Detweiler . . . know the name . . . from somewhere."

Detweiler answered with a sweetness that exceeded belief. "I guess it's even got out here. The police are looking for me."

"They are?" Allen felt as though he were floating, experienced an odd lack of care. He bit his lip so as to get a purchase on something. "They are?" he compulsively asked again.

"Sure," Detweiler cheerfully confirmed. "That's their job."

Allen suddenly remembered his own, losing all sense of Detweiler as a possible murderer, a menace, and transforming him into a commodity.

He said: "Listen, let's go and see the managing editor."

"Now, isn't that funny," Detweiler responded, stopping near a desk where a young woman was applying herself furiously to a typewriter. "That's who I asked to see in the first place." He looked at the woman and said to Allen: "It's marvelous how you people can work in all this noise."

Allen said passionately: "You can make a lot of money out of this."

Now it was Detweiler who said: "Pardon?"

"For exclusive rights to your story," said Allen. "For turning yourself in to us rather than the police."

"Oh, I wasn't thinking of doing that." Detweiler was amused. He had been carrying his haversack and now swung it about as he chuckled. Had that happened before Allen had conceived his idea, the reporter would have seen the pack as a weapon. But now he was fearless.

"Come on," he said. "You knew what you were doing when you walked in here. I never took that lunch-counter stuff seriously."

Detweiler was hurt. His lower lip came out. They had continued to walk and were presently at the elevators. He didn't like anyone to believe him dishonest.

He said: "Well, I'm not crazy. What would I get from handing myself over to the police?"

Allen naturally supposed Detweiler was being coy so as to build up his price, and told him that for sums of this nature only the managing editor could negotiate. He pressed the Up button.

"Why do you keep talking about money?" Detweiler asked in annoyance. He saw, despairingly, that the reporter's impression of him was getting ever more mean. He went along helplessly as the elevator climbed, stopped, and Allen led him hastily past a protesting secretary into a large, handsome room full of wooden furniture, bookshelves, and a decisive man who listened to Allen's identification of them both. The managing editor, for so he was, also harped on money.

At last Detweiler put up his hands. It was getting too noisy. He said: "With all respect, the only thing you have said that interests me is about the syndication. If I tell my story for you, you can get it published all over the country?"

Of this he received vociferous confirmation from a roomful of those who should know. The editor had sent out the summons. The publisher himself, and all his executives, were now there and listening to Detweiler. It was pretty nice to have such attention, and though importunate, they were all mannerly.

"Well, O.K.," Detweiler agreed. "Then I'll do it. Can you get me a lawyer?"

The publisher said: "I'll get you Melrose."

"Is he good?"

The publisher laughed in affirmation, and the managing editor, who had turned paternal, said: "Son, he is the best. He has never lost a murder case."

Detweiler felt misunderstood. "Oh," he said, "if you're going to call it murder, I might as well have gone to the police."

The others fell silent, and the managing editor said: "Son, you want to tell us about it?"

"Sure," said Detweiler and began to talk about Realization into the microphone of a recording machine they hooked up for him: it was marvelous to know one's expression was being preserved indefinitely: in itself, an aid, like photography, to a kind of mechanical Realization. Useful, though not the real thing: only a machine, condemned to the monotonous inanimate circuits, producing not the voice but an electronic imitation. Still, it was a handsome, precision device, and Detweiler enjoyed his association with it.

They let him talk on uninterruptedly until a secretary brought in a handful of contracts for him to sign. Having done so, he was about to resume when the managing editor said: "Son, we are paying you a lot of money and we don't consider that your philosophy is worth that. We haven't heard you say yet how you will plead. Did you murder those people?"

Detweiler kept control of himself, no easy task, but he understood that attacking this man would only be detrimental to his aim. He thought again of the possibly deaf counterman. It might be that the editor was deaf, if not physically, then morally: so many people were. Which was why Detweiler had decided to tell his story through the news medium: everybody read the papers. So he held on, gripping the arms of the leather chair in which he sat.

He said carefully: "I never murdered anybody in my life. The money means very little to me except insofar as I can use it to further my work. And my sole purpose in talking to you gentlemen of the press is to disseminate knowledge of my work. Realization means not only recovering the past, making it current and thus ending the bondage of Time. It also means realization of the potential of the human race.

"I don't want to insult you fellows, but have you ever thought of the futility of what you do? There is another newspaper every single day: all those that have gone before are dead. All you powerful, clever, and wealthy men are slaves to that rhythm. Do you seriously believe that the quality of existence would be changed if you suddenly one day failed to bring out an issue? Would life stop because you did not write about it? Or do you write about life at all? I mean the fundamental kind of life that a snake lives, or a fish in the sea, or a bird.

"Cannot what you do be seen as a game or even a dream? Does it matter? Won't there always be another inning even if any one or all of you have quit? Your own time runs out, but Time continues. Yet human beings usually fancy themselves as superior to animals. Animals don't have newspapers or policemen or clocks, that is, unless they are domesticated. Mind you, I'm not saying that men should or can live like animals. Too much has happened—"

"Joseph." It was the publisher who now broke in. Had the editor spoken at that point, Detweiler would probably have tried to eliminate him. He had gripped the chair so tightly that four fingers of each hand had penetrated the leather, broken through into the stuffing. But the publisher was someone new. Also he had promised to get this splendid lawyer Melrose, and Detweiler was counting on that: he needed an eloquent advocate to say what he wanted said, before he went to the electric chair.

"Joseph, you say you are not a murderer, is that right? But did you have anything to do with the Starr women and the boarder on Christmas Eve? Did you see them, did you talk to them? If not, how did you spend your time that evening?"

Detweiler nodded. "There you have it—'time' again." He shook his head. "Frustrating, isn't it? But far from hopeless!" Then he said: "Oh, I killed them all right. But it wasn't murder, because I had nothing to gain."

Chapter 12

THE LOCAL OFFICERS who came to the paper to take Detweiler
into custody began by squinting hostilely at him and certainly
did not shake the hand he offered. There were five of them,
two of high rank with extra insignia, and to each Detweiler
introduced himself, saying "Joe Detweiler," and putting his
hand out five times. Nobody took it, but the lowest-ranking
policeman, a detective in mufti, could not help murmuring
something in return: not actually his name, but a pleasant mutter, then glanced fearfully at the leading inspector, who ignored him.

The inspector had been instructed by his superiors to register a protest against the publisher's having kept Detweiler
under wraps for six hours, but once within the paneled office,
up to his shins in the moss-green carpet, facing the self-reliant

man who had the ear of millions of readers locally, not to mention those reached by his syndicate, the inspector merely gave his own name much as Detweiler had done to him, though with less assurance. He did not seek to shake hands.

The publisher disregarded the police. Instead he was reading the statement that Detweiler had dictated; trying to, anyway. Trying to see how something readable could be made from it. As it stood it comprised thousands of words of insane rubbish, with no further reference to the homicides after the first sentence: "I killed them, but that is not important. Time is the sole essential. Can we free ourselves from its bondage? That is the question. Professor Einstein says that time slows down as speed increases, referring to physical motion. But what of mental motion? Can the mind move at a speed that will kill Time? Can a moment be stopped, suspended, frozen, as light can in a motion-picture projector; and reversed, relived? This is worth consideration. . . ."

Detweiler was an insane killer. Thus the rules applying to his and the publisher's relationship were quite different from those for which there was precedent. The paper had run the memoirs of heads of state and five-star generals: the publisher's friends, neither homicides nor maniacs. Men of power, like himself only more so; therefore the publisher neither really liked nor trusted them. Detweiler was actually a powerless nonentity in the usual sense of the term. The publisher felt paternal towards him, if anything; even fond of this boy, who had yet murdered three persons with his bare hands.

Savagery did not frighten the publisher, at least not at his habitual remove from it. He had nothing to fear from Detweiler in a physical way. Yet, though his soul shriveled as the killer talked on hour after hour about Time and Realization and Mind and Will, he was ever more disinclined to interrupt. There was that about an obsession, even a lunatic's, which commanded respect. Indeed, all successful men were obsessed: the publisher himself, who had begun life as a rich boy but refused to accept the cretinism which so often accompanies inherited wealth; labored in his father's warehouses without privilege, sold want-ads, battered his way to the top while a weaker character might have sauntered there, the result being that though not every President had kissed his hindquarters, none had kicked them with impunity. Therefore he felt a certain organic affinity with Detweiler, even with Detweiler, crazy killer, who was prepared to die to get his message across.

The message, of course, was impossible. Naturally he could not honor his promise to Detweiler to print it as is. Indeed, it was not even accessible to revision. The managing editor had already assigned a deft reporter to prepare a new version. Detweiler would have been extradited by the time the first installment appeared, under close guard. He was, after all, a homicidal maniac, with no rights.

The local police were an awfully nice bunch. Detweiler thought that now he had confessed to breaking the law, he would be mistreated, because he knew that cops hated criminals, and he had begun, already in the publisher's office, to make his body hard, impervious to torture. In such a state he could have been beaten for hours without feeling pain or showing a bruise: like a rod made of vanadium steel. However, the process of transformation took a lot out of him, annealing his mind as well: he was good for little else than endurance, so ordered. Therefore he was relieved when the plainsclothesman dispassionately hooked the claw of the handcuffs on his wrist and made it snug through the ratchet, secure but not painful. It actually felt good to Detweiler. The detective himself wore the other manacle; they were linked in the Law. It was the first time Detweiler had ever had an official connection.

Photographers kept taking pictures. "Just one more, Joe. . . . Joe, this way. . . . Inspector, move in close, please. Take him by the arm." Busy, lively fellows, with winking lights. The publisher at last ordered them off and came to shake his hand.

"Good luck, Joseph."

"Good luck to you," said Detweiler. "That lawyer hasn't called back yet, has he?"

"Don't worry," the publisher said. "A message is at the pier. He'll get it the moment he steps ashore." Melrose, the criminal attorney he had promised to get for Detweiler, was fishing for tarpon off Fort Lauderdale.

Detweiler said: "I want to thank that reporter, Pat Allen, whose idea this was in the first place."

"He's back at work." The publisher laughed. "We have to get a paper out, you know. But I'll have someone tell him."

Detweiler suddenly twisted himself in pride, jerking the attached detective. "I wish you would tell him yourself. It *was* his idea."

Now the publisher's laugh was somewhat hateful. He said: "You have my word."

The police took Detweiler for a ride through city traffic and then gave him a sparkling clean cell, equipped with a toilet and washstand and a bed. He would have liked to use the first, but people kept passing the door and privacy was unobtainable, so he lay down on the bed and went to sleep. Later they woke him for an excellent meal: meat loaf, stewed tomatoes, peas, and raspberry Jello. It was so delicious that tears came to Detweiler's eyes. He took tiny mouthfuls so as to prolong the pleasure. The only thing missing was A-1 Sauce.

He called the guard. "You wouldn't happen to have any A-1 Sauce?"

The guard was about to respond with leaden irony (ain't no hotel), but looking at Detweiler's face, he checked the impulse. He felt as if he had but narrowly avoided committing a breach of manners; had been on the point of breaking wind before one of his own offspring.

Instead he said gravely: "I'll see." He went into the room in which a delegation of officers awaited the out-of-town detectives, expected to arrive by air within the hour. Reporters were also in attendance.

Many murderers had passed through this functionary's care in his term of service, and they never bored him, though his strategy was often to pretend otherwise. He was always interested to hear of their subsequent disposal whether by electrocution, gas chamber, or lifelong immurement; whatever, he had if only in a small way participated, and a man's work is peculiarly associated with his being. For some he even felt pity. He was, however, not sorry for Detweiler. He took him seriously.

He went to the chief of detectives, who was just finishing a one-word, yet long-drawn-out response to the comment of a subordinate: "Yeahh"—a sour, negative sort of affirmation. When he finished he retained enough of the accompanying facial expression to turn it on the guard.

"*He* wants some sauce for his meat." It was already the custom not to sound Detweiler's name.

"He can go fuck himself." It was not the chief who answered, but the subordinate, a young detective endeavoring by various devices to appear more seasoned, among them a willed slackness of jaw.

But the chief said to the guard: "I guess we wouldn't want them to say we can't take care of their prisoners." To the young detective: "Go down to the delicatessen."

"Which one?"

"Oh shit," said the chief. "Where they have the policy game, on the corner. Unless you want to pay for it yourself."

"A-1 Sauce," said the guard.

Shuster decided to go himself to extradite Detweiler, and took Tierney as his partner. Tierney was in trouble. Shuster first accepted that as a fact when the man ahead of Tierney shoved a briefcase too far under the seat and it emerged behind, encroaching on the detective's foot room. Tierney kicked it back viciously, but as the aircraft took off the case returned, like a bad conscience. The owner seemed already asleep. Tierney unbuckled his own belt and hurled the case into the overhead rack. Of course the stewardess appeared on the instant, stretched to retrieve the case and in so doing showed an inch of sexless white slip between navy-blue jacket and skirt. As always with them, she was so girdled as seemingly to have but one buttock.

She gave the case to Tierney. "Please put this under your seat, sir. And please fasten your belt."

Tierney went into an inarticulate rage. He tried to buckle his belt while holding the case. His coat gaped open, revealing the pistol at his left waist. Seeing it, the stewardess lost the spuriously sweet, falsely committed expression she had been trained to show even during outright disaster. Her trace of mouth disappeared, she turned her putty-face towards the cockpit and began to walk in that direction.

Shuster climbed over Tierney. Without apparent haste he caught her at the cockpit door. "Miss," he said, "we're police officers. That's why the gun."

"I know," she said, "Are you following someone on board?"

Shuster said no.

"I still have to tell the pilot."

"Why?" Shuster on general principles disliked any publicity whatever. It was never to a detective's advantage to be recognized by anybody.

"Because he's in authority." She opened the door, giving Shuster a brief glimpse of that seat of power, all switches, from which he was excluded, and closed it behind her.

Depressed by the exchange, he returned to find Tierney had apparently dumped the case in the owner's lap, a tight-assed midtown type, and was glaring at the back of his short haircut.

"You need a drink," Shuster told his subordinate. "Move over and take the window seat."

Tierney's state was altered by what he interpreted as generosity, though Shuster's motive was rather in the interests of convenience. But then when Shuster attempted something genuinely kind, Tierney froze.

Shuster said: "I don't know what you're doing with Betty Bayson, and I don't want to, but in the end you're not going to like yourself."

Tierney asked, "May I have permission to go to the toilet?" He scrambled out over Shuster's legs, so that the point in changing seats was lost.

If an officer wanted a piece he could always get it from a female less troublesome than Betty Bayson: the women relatives of offenders were always better game than witnesses.

Detweiler was sleeping again when the extraditing detectives arrived, but woke up as they stood outside the bars with their local colleagues and looked at him. He gazed drowsily at them and then his eyes drifted away in indifference, like those of a lion in a zoo.

Tierney was in a strange state of mind. He despised criminals in an impersonal way, more so when they had been apprehended than while the pursuit continued: in captivity they bore the additional stench of failure. Psychotics of course were another matter: the first problem was to determine whether a given example was genuinely a psycho or faking. That determination was not legally a policeman's business, yet try to find the officer who would not make it. You had to. You were only human.

But at the first sight of Detweiler, Tierney experienced the onset of two convictions. One, that Detweiler was crazy and thus necessarily beyond moral judgment. Tierney could not have explained this decision. Nothing in Detweiler's appearance was even eccentric—except perhaps his suit.

The second feature of Tierney's reaction was that he hated Detweiler immediately, desperately, savagely. He would have liked to beat him to death and beyond: to pulp him, as it were, trampling his vital organs. This passion was unprecedented; he had felt nothing like it when, the year before, he had collared the pimpled wretch who sodomized and mutilated a two-year-old or the apish truck driver who killed his sick wife with repeated blows to the head.

Tierney did not disclose these feelings to anyone else either by deed, word, or implication. He apparently looked at Detweiler with the same indifference as that with which the killer gazed at him. Eventually he was coupled to Detweiler by the handcuff's other claw, and the three of them, Shuster and the Siamese twins, caught a return flight.

Detweiler's mother, who never read the newspapers, might very well never know precisely of his disposition. If a fellow communicant in spiritualism brought up the matter, she could be relied on to dismiss it neatly. Such money as remained after paying the lawyer he would have forwarded to her. She might through extrasensory means get some sense of him, but since he was not in trouble—trouble to Detweiler being when things did not add up, which was scarcely the case now he was on his way towards execution—she would not know pain. He soon fell asleep once more; it was serene to float upon an ocean of cloud.

Tierney avoided looking at Detweiler, but felt his attached arm grow slack. Shuster sat behind them, alone in that row, whether by arrangement or merely because of a shortage of passengers, Tierney did not know. In Shuster's company he was nowadays a flunky. Shuster knew nothing of the actual relations between him and Betty: the man was bluffing, as he so often did in the interrogation of criminals. Tierney had reported only that he and Mrs. Bayson had revisited the Starr apartment on her suggestion. Her memory of the missing stuffed animal might have proved valuable had not Detweiler come in of his own volition. It was all reasonable. Unless that patrolman, Spinelli, was one of Shuster's informants. The lieutenant had various spies throughout the Force, though he complained himself of being spied on by his departmental enemies.

For his part, Shuster did not believe in criminal insanity. That was a defense lawyer's tripe or, worse, a psychiatrist's. Detweiler, he thought, might beat the rap. He was light-complexioned. He had turned himself in, and he had confessed in a style used by those who intended to plead insanity. Shuster disliked the interrogation of psychos. You had to listen to a lot of malarkey, and then their lawyers always managed to suggest to the jury that you abused them. His heart fell as he perused the typescript of Detweiler's interminable composition for the newspaper. He kept getting lost on the third page.

On landing the airplane was met by a delegation of policemen and an entourage of official cars. Shuster's schedule was to wait until the other passengers had struggled into their coats and exited, before he rose and signaled to Tierney that they should haul Detweiler out.

A reporter and photographer came aboard. Disregarding the stewardesses, Tierney threatened to shove the camera up someone's rectum, and Shuster, agreeing with him for once, vowed silently to take the badge of the officer who had let them by, but was forced to abolish that resolution when he reached the open hatch and recognized the police commissioner standing at the bottom of the mobile stair.

The press and TV had their way for the next quarter-hour. Detweiler cooperated with the cameramen, looking this way and that on command, but he said nothing in answer to the shouted questions, which were hardly serious. Anyway, he had signed a contract giving exclusive rights to his utterances to the newspaper and its syndicate, and he was not the one to go back on his word.

Eventually he was led into the rear seat of a police car and sat, like the filling of a sandwich, between the two detectives who had accompanied him on the airplane.

For the first time he spoke to the man to whom he was handcuffed.

"Will I be fed again?"

Tierney did not answer. He continued to repeat his fantasy concerning Detweiler's activities as a resident of the Starr apartment. Betty denied that her relations with the killer had been intimate, but Tierney took this rather as circumstantial evidence that they had been at it like rabbits. She was hateful and vicious and cunning enough to know she could hurt him, Tierney, more by maintaining this fiction than by admitting what was obvious to reason.

Shuster said: "You cooperate with us, son, and we'll cooperate with you." The old bastard never forgot his job.

Detweiler noticed from his limited view of the world outside that every trace of snow had already vanished from the city streets, and he found it interesting to think that if he had scooped a cupful of it the other day and preserved it in the ice-cube compartment of a refrigerator he would by now have a rare substance, indeed probably unique: old snow. Frozen time.

At police headquarters he was conducted into the midst of more newspapermen, and the commissioner was there again, and also, finally, the man whose responsibility it was to see him condemned to death. Detweiler therefore was interested in him. He was in somewhat the same relation to Detweiler as Detweiler had been to the Starr woman and the boarder.

This man, wearing a suit of beautiful brown flannel, approached him and said, "Joseph Detweiler, did you—"

"Excuse me," Detweiler interrupted, firmly though not in the slightest degree insolent.

Nor did the man take it so, being in no doubt of his authority.

He said, below his long nose and short lip: "I am the district attorney of this county." He peered for a moment at Detweiler and added patiently: "My name is Crews."

Detweiler said: "You can beat me if you want, but I will not break my contract."

The district attorney's heavy eyebrows crawled up his steep forehead. "We don't do that sort of thing." Then he gazed abstractly at everyone and no one, and asked: "Contract?"

Tierney was still there, behind the principals, no longer manacled to the killer. He waited respectfully until it was apparent no one else would speak, then elucidated: "Sir, I think he believes his agreement to give the exclusive story to the newspaper means he can't talk to anybody."

Crews said: "Will you take my word for it that your contract does not apply to what you tell us?"

"I certainly will, Mr. Crews," Detweiler replied. That was a weight off him.

The district attorney's brows had not yet come down. "Well then," he said, "did you murder Mrs. Wilma Starr, Miss Wilhelmina Starr, and Mr. E. C. Appleton on Christmas Eve last?"

"No!" Detweiler said with force. "I did not murder them. I killed them."

"All right, all right," said the police commissioner, who on arriving at headquarters had lost the gladhanded politician's charm he had shown at the airport. "We want to hear **exactly** what you did and how."

"I'm sorry," said Detweiler. "I don't want this distorted. I think I better wait until my attorney arrives."

Once again the D.A. addressed the room at large. "Who is his counsel?"

Shuster answered in the anonymous voice he reserved for such occasions: "Henry Webster Melrose."

"I have heard of him," responded the D.A., and everyone but Detweiler smirked painfully.

Chapter 13

MELROSE did not like to defend madmen. Otherwise he had few prejudices as to clients. He had represented so many professional killers that his enemies had success in labeling him as a gangsters' counsel, with the implication that he was therefore himself a criminal. This reputation proved of great value, bringing him not only more business from the mobs, but also from little helpless people who had got into trouble: and if condemned for taking an enormous fee from the employers of one Joe Guglielmo, accused of murdering one Vito Marino with a sawed-off shotgun and sinking the corpse, weighted with a cargo of cast-iron objects, into a body of water, Melrose could always point to his subsequent defense of some penniless Negro charged with breaking his wife's neck in a family quarrel.

Melrose could have done so if he wished, but as it happened he never defended himself: he had too much contempt for others. In return, except by the disreputable elements, he was universally feared and detested, for his associations, for his arrogance, but mostly for his habitual courtroom victories. He had served as defense counsel in eighty-two capital cases and had never yet lost a client to the executioner.

As to the moral guilt of his clients, Melrose had no interest whatever. If they confessed to him, as they sometimes did, his immediate and only concern was as to whether they had also done so to anyone available to the prosecution. Not that he was discouraged even though the district attorney possessed a detailed statement admitting all and signed by the creature Melrose must defend, along with eight eyeball witnesses. Melrose preferred hopeless cases and preposterously unfavorable odds. He loathed criminals and, as a man who lived by his wits, despised violence. Had he been a police officer, no lawbreaker would have received his mercy. As a judge he would have been implacable—and furthermore would never have tolerated a Melrose in his court.

But as it stood he was neither more nor less than an attorney at law, and his opponents must encounter him on that ground or void the field. In any trial that which was tried was the prosecution's case. According to the great and fundamental principle of Anglo-Saxon jurisprudence, the accuser bore the burden of proof. Not even the massive power of the state could penetrate this armor into which Melrose had buckled himself at the beginning of his career and in which he expected to be buried, like Frederick the Great in his impregnable Prussian uniform. Therefore Melrose could afford to be otherwise disaffected from his fellows. He had no political ambitions, no social or ethnic identifications, and secretly, and contrary to the charges of his enemies, he was essentially modest. His opinion of himself was not so high as his assessment of others was low. He existed in a time and place in which, it seemed to him, only relative judgments were feasible: he perhaps came off better than most because he was almost alone in wanting to practice his profession: to do the job, and not to gain love or power or the approbation of anonymous hordes living or dead.

The Detweiler case had every recommendation but one. It was certainly hopeless enough at first glance. The killer had not only confessed, but to a sensational newspaper for a large fee. The crime was gaudy and peculiarly outrageous to the layman: female victims, one a mother, and on Christmas Eve. Detweiler had been billed by the papers, pejoratively, as an artist; a jury's unfavorable bias might be assumed. If the public could be said to have moods, its current one had been conditioned by other mass murders of the year; six victims of a berserk gunman in Oakland, California; four, including the suicide of the perpetrator, his entire family, in Battle Creek, Michigan; and the work of a killer-rapist in St. Louis. Detweiler's achievement might be seen as the continuation of a trend, which if not stopped by the stern hand of justice might, etc., etc. And that he had not attacked his female victims sexually or committed theft might be to his disadvantage: Melrose could sometimes lead a jury into a curious sympathy for the perpetrator of a crime-for-gain: who among humankind felt no lust or cupidity?

Furthermore, Melrose was hungry for battle. It had been a good fourteen months since the last trial which quickened his blood. Like a Don Juan who surfeited with easy conquests could feel desire only in the pursuit of very special prey—novice nuns, frigid princesses—he gained no sustenance from the routine diet. In the Guglielmo case, more than a year before, he had won an acquittal for the gang-hired hatchetman by exploiting an idiosyncrasy of the killer's weapon, a shortened twelve-gauge shotgun with a quirk in its sear which permitted the arm to fire only when held at a downward angle from the horizontal. As only Melrose and the defendant knew, Guglielmo had first to knock his victim to the ground before discharging into him the double load.

In court Melrose opened a fresh box of Super-X shells, chose two of the blunt red cylinders, and having passed them among the jurors for examination, dropped them into the breech.

He presented the weapon to his assistant counsel. "The safety, Mr. Willingham, is *not* on."

Much of Melrose's pleasure owed to his awareness that both the judge and the prosecutor would have been peculiarly gratified to see his head blown off. The jury of course were enthralled, except for Number Three, a sardonic-looking man in whose countenance Melrose had watched unsympathy grow throughout the trial.

"Now, Mr. Willingham, would you please place the barrels at my chin." His assistant took care to keep the breech ever lower than the muzzle while Melrose pressed against the twin openings of barrel.

"Now, Mr. Willingham." His voice was necessarily distorted. "Will you be so good as to squeeze the triggers."

The cynical juror stared aloft in disgust. He was very dear to Melrose at this moment.

"Squeeze, Mr. Willingham, squee-ee-eeze."

The sear held, refused to release the hammers. Melrose called for greater force of finger, he was in a seizure of ecstasy, only the external symptoms of which were for display: at such a

196

moment, only at such a moment, did he experience a maximum sense of life. The judge soon called an end to the demonstration; the prosecutor inveighed against the courtroom circus; the jury subsequently acquitted Guglielmo.

Melrose waited for the discharge of the jury, so as to thank its members as was his custom, and his warmest reception came from Number Three, who in the world to which he was returning, that bleak world outside the courtroom, worked as an alteration tailor.

"Mr. Melrose, it wasn't easy. You had the other eleven more or less against you when we went out. They took the shotgun thing as a trick, Mr. Melrose."

Melrose smiled within while showing aggrieved astonishment without: nothing gave him more gratification than a favorable verdict returned by a jury who knew it had been hoaxed.

"One man, he knew guns, says you rigged it," the tailor went on. "I say nobody can fix an exhibit. He says Melrose can get to anybody or thing. I says, if he had the judge in his pocket why did the judge never sustain an objection of his while always for the prosecution? I says why did the judge threaten him many times with contempt. He says to make it look good."

"You must be an eloquent man, Mr. Kleinsinger," Melrose said. He was still pleasantly astounded in particular but not in general at the revelation that Kleinsinger, his supposed enemy, had been his actual friend. In a murder trial there were no absolute surprises, because there were no true precedents. A unique life had been lost, and another was at stake. Every soul involved was under the mortal pressure of the grand hazard. Melrose disapproved of capital punishment, but without it his profession would be but a game and humanity thereby devalued.

He had never sought a license to practice in any jurisdiction in which execution was not the ultimate penalty.

What Kleinsinger had done was to mask a marked bias in his favor. This juror's tactic was not unknown to Melrose, but he had misjudged Kleinsinger's appearance, which as seen from the defense table had not suggested sentimentality.

Kleinsinger said: "No, I can't take such credit. I held out for a point. I says your client was a hood and he might have shot the other one, but the prosecution never proved it in this courtroom beyond a reasonable doubt. Isn't that the idea of justice? If the state wants to take a life, even of an evil person, they got to have a hundred per cent excuse. We are not talking of how God would do it."

"Do you believe in God, Mr. Kleinsinger?" Melrose asked.

Kleinsinger replied proudly: "In fact I do not. I believe in being a *Mensch*."

Melrose thanked him and, without irony and though he had already lost interest in the tailor, who had not proved as subtle as he first supposed, said: "God bless you."

In trials as in sex, the more glorious the moment, the more deathlike the succeeding quiescence. If only Detweiler were not a psychopath.

But the newspaper publisher, when Melrose returned his call, said of that there could be no doubt, and was cheerfully positive on this matter owing to his vulgar misapprehension Melrose would find it attractive.

"I'm sorry," Melrose replied: "I cannot take the case."

The publisher said: "This means a great deal to me personally."

"Why?"

"I gave my word to him that I would get you."

"I don't accept that as placing me under an obligation," Melrose said. "Your arrogance aside, I am on general principles disinclined to place any great value on the 'word' of the press."

"All right," the publisher said in a jollying tone. "I'll play along with you and your reputation for giving a hard time to respectable elements." He raised the offered fee.

"No," said Melrose.

"Look, Melrose, I don't want to be gross, but you are getting to be known by the public in recent years as almost exclusively a hoodlums' lawyer. I personally don't like to see this happen. You are a man of extraordinary talents—"

"I merely practice my profession, sir. I am not a moralist."

"But here's my point," said the publisher. "This boy is crazy as a bedbug, yet that in itself won't save him. We just can't take a chance on some inferior defense lawyer. Crews had blood in his eye and is no idiot whatever else you can say about him. He wants the next gubernatorial nomination. He may be approaching desperation: I don't have to tell you that his last term as D.A. has not been distinguished. He will be out to fry this boy. Now, I have spent an afternoon with Detweiler. At first he was merely a story to me. I had never before sat in a room with a murderer—"

"I know," Melrose broke in, "and you discovered to your surprise that he was human. Again and again over the years your trashy papers have editorially called for vengeance against the so-called enemies of society, and this is the first one you have ever laid eyes on."

"Now you are being moralistic," said the publisher. "I think I have you there. And uninformed, as well. Some of those editorials have been written by former police reporters who have seen as many criminals as you."

"But not in the same way," Melrose said soberly. Nevertheless, the man had scored a point off him.

"Detweiler is not an enemy of society. He is sick."

"You are qualified to make that diagnosis?"

"I am not on the stand, Mr. Melrose," the publisher said waspishly. "I know something about men. I know Detweiler is mad." He paused. "He has no malice in him."

Melrose was suddenly embarrassed. He found he could not explain his prejudice against maniacs without revealing more of himself than he could afford to do. Surely one of the reasons for which a man becomes an attorney at law is to evade the law as applied to himself, to be an officer of the court of life and not a defendant, to speak always for others, the state or the accused, and never oneself; and yet so to celebrate the self. Else the Law was unbearable.

In self-protection, then, Melrose felt compelled to take the case. But he could not let this pretentious ass think he had been won over by the argument. Until he accepted Detweiler as client, Melrose would not care whether the killer lived or died, sane or crazy.

So what he did was to demand a fee precisely twice as large as that which he had been offered. The publisher agreed, but whether Melrose had deceived him could not be determined at this time. Powerful men, Melrose knew, could often be manipulated more easily than janitors, but they were more skilled in concealment.

It had been a defeat for Melrose nevertheless. Finally it was he who had been manipulated by his own vanity. His clients were all the same to him; whether innocent men or rogues, he shared with them a community of interest. Their motives had been rational. If killers, they had murdered for a reason: money or hatred or jealousy. If wrongfully accused, they had yet been arrested in a situation or condition which suggested to rational men—the police and the district attorney—that they had committed the crime for rational motives. There were rules to the ensuing battle, and Melrose's joy was to exploit the possibilities within the discipline, as a poet uses the constricting form of the sonnet. That he was often misidentified as a maverick or even an anarchist testified rather to the quality of his enemies than his own.

But a madman was something other, a resident of a different universe of discourse, with no neighbors, feeling no affinity even with other maniacs; by his very existence derisive of Melrose's art, wit, life. And that Detweiler was psychotic, Melrose had been certain from his first perusal of the newspaper stories, he who was famous for objecting to any qualitative description of a client's manner by a nonprofessional witness.

> Q. Please describe the defendant as you saw him on the morning of the twenty-ninth.
> A. He seemed nervous.
> MR. MELROSE. Objection, Witness is not a psychiatrist.

If the witness *were* an alienist Melrose went at him as a ferret at a rabbit: Had not all psychoanalysts themselves been psychoanalyzed? This question reminded jurors of the folk wisdom, immanent in most allegedly normal men, which held that he who trafficked in derangement was himself perhaps deranged—and served to distract them from a similar suspicion that a criminal lawyer was touched with crime. . . . Were there not many different schools of thought in psychiatry? Was the witness a member of such a school? If he was, Melrose managed to suggest organizational rigidity and bias; if not, his subsequent questions tended to reflect on the possible irresponsibility of the free-lance, the eclectic, the practitioner who could not make up his mind. Of course the prosecutor objected all along the line, which served, whether or not he was sustained, in fixing the matter ever more firmly in the jurors' minds.

Melrose was no less zealous in the protection and enhancement of psychiatric testimony for the defense. He kept available at least two professionals who would fearlessly state that theirs was an exact science, reliable as physics: one with a German accent, another as American-looking as a highway patrolman.

A sane man, greatly exercised because of drink, passion, anger, might strangle a woman. As means of murder went, strangulation was really one of the kinder forms: the victim soon became unconscious for want of air. In taste it was more palatable than a man's discharging a firearm into the flesh of another human being or drawing a blade across a throat. It was intimate, an extension of an embrace; human, not mechanized or chemical.

But to strangle two women in succession, neither for love nor money, was for Melrose conclusive evidence of madness. He did not in such a personal judgment think legally. He who lived to practice his trade never confused it with life, and thus remained its master and not a servant. What he believed privately of Detweiler would have no influence on the representation he would make in public, in court, according to the Law which neither he nor Detweiler had made.

Therefore he should now not be disturbed. He despised such clients as Guglielmo, the killer-for-hire, stupid and brutish, and yet with a clear conscience freed them to murder again. But it was clean work, a man's job, a fair contest between himself and the prosecution. With a psycho, however, whatever the outcome, no one triumphed, all were somehow dirtied except the defendant, whose peculiarity was that he could not be

202

touched by other human beings, not even by the man who had saved his life.

Melrose recognized that he was jealous of Detweiler.

He packed his suitcase and drove the rented car from Fort Lauderdale to Miami Airport, at one point, near Dania, crushing a host of the land crabs who suicidally frequent the highway after dark. He disliked the sound, but knew no other route. He was something of a gastronome, but according to the natives these crustaceans were inedible, unlike their marine cousins, the famous Floridian stone crabs of which he was fond. Melrose stood five feet nine and a half inches and weighed 196 pounds. At forty-nine he was a bachelor. Over the years his sexual tastes had grown so special that he was hardly ever nowadays gratified, and had all but forsaken the quest for women who were elegant but not so much so as to lack sympathy, were aware of his career but never asked about it, were bright of body but melancholy of spirit and in their early thirties without having been married and yet not noticeably neurotic about their situation, above all not bitter.

Melrose had actually never met a woman who filled the bill in every particular and was also tall and wan-complexioned, his physical requirements. And while in earlier days he might find a certain amusement with those who missed perfection by as much as half, from forty-five on he tended to accept his lonely lot. He could not imagine not living alone. When he had had love affairs he never spent the night with the girl, always climbed out of bed to go, or to drive her, home. This distaste to share his private life extended also to friends. He had been invited to Lauderdale by a prosperous old Army buddy and wife, who lived in luxurious vulgarity on one of the canals. But Melrose would not stay in the guest room though it had its own bath.

"Who is he hiding in that beach apartment he rented?" the wife asked her husband.

"He just has to have his own place," replied Melrose's erstwhile comrade-in-arms. "He would never sit on anybody else's bunk. I can still remember that. Or borrow money. But I guess he likes us or he wouldn't come at all?"

"I suppose he'll eat here once or twice anyway," the wife said stubbornly. "I'll find those Frenchy recipes for the cook, which he seemed to like last time, and you better check your wine cellar and have the right years." Despite her air of annoyance on the subject of Melrose, she was partial to him. He was the only male friend of her husband's who commented on her clothes. And if she expressed opinions, he listened and did not pick out little flaws in her logic, smiled in the right places, in others waited for elucidations with shrewd eyes. His reputation for barracuda tactics in the courtroom saved him, for her, from being hypocritical; he could cut her to ribbons if he wished, but was too gallant.

Still, there was something wrong with him, of which she was always reminded after Melrose had left and the nervousness she felt in his presence had been replaced by despondency. He had been visiting them for years, and yet she felt he did not know her at all.

Melrose was fond of these people, who were like a family to him, too fond to call them from the airport. He would instead write when he got home. He had his sentimental side.

For some hours after Detweiler announced his firm intention not to speak further in the absence of his lawyer, they continued to question him anyway. He supposed they could not be blamed for this persistence though it was foolhardy to try to get him to break his word. But policemen work with so many criminals that they find it difficult to understand the motives of a man of honor who happens to run afoul of the law. He listened with alternative indignation and amusement, both concealed, to questions based on an assumption that, because Mrs. Starr and Billie were women, something dirty was involved in his killing them. Betty could testify he was no sex fiend.

Betty. But Betty was an angel. He could not bring her into this wordly business of cops and courts and lawyers, this man's affair. He would instead, now that he looked forward to imprisonment for a certain period—because he knew trials were not quick to start and subsequent executions not immediate—he would resume his work on Realization, jail being the perfect laboratory for such an endeavor. Odd that this had not occurred to him before, but one sometimes searches endlessly for what lies at hand. If he Realized Mrs. Starr and Billie, and the boarder as well, they could certify that he definitely had done nothing filthy to the women.

However, he was distracted at the moment, not by the questions of the important officials, but by the presence, in the back of the room, of the detective to whom he had been handcuffed on the returning airplane. This man had avoided looking at him during the flight, but now that they were no longer joined in steel, were a dozen feet apart and separated by the intervening persons, he was aware of the detective's close watch on his countenance. The man had a peculiar interest in him, beyond the superficialities of police work. It was personal, not organizational, and expressive of a genuine human requirement. Detweiler had sensed his distress across the manacles, but at the time it would have been out of order, bad taste, to breach the association of captor and captive, to sully the dignity and equilibrium of this traditional arrangement, by word or deed.

Now, however, they were in another situation. One which, furthermore, the detective understood, as revealed by his explanation to the district attorney of Detweiler's agreement with the newspaper, his admirable disposal of the misapprehensions on both sides. He was in a unique sympathy with Detweiler, though he himself might very well be unaware of it.

It was Detweiler's observation that so many people failed to understand where their interests lie and thus are self-resistant.

Detweiler sat at the head of a plain wooden table. The room was brightly, even harshly illuminated, but no more so over his chair than any other. None of his interrogators struck matches slowly or turned a spotlight on his face or threatened him. It was cosy, the collective body-heat all to the good, for the room had been cool on entry.

The district attorney was saying: ". . . anything to the women after you strangled them?"

Detweiler said: "They promised me, in the car coming here from the airport, that I would be fed again."

"How about it, Joe? You'll have to tell it sooner or later." Crews chuckled, reached over and playfully slapped Detweiler's forearm. "Now, I would say you were pretty clever to stay silent —if you hadn't already admitted these killings. I think you would have been so hard to crack, frankly, that I am certainly grateful you confessed. You have really helped us, but why stop there? Unless you give us more of the particulars, we will probably assume the worst. Now, I don't consider myself your enemy. I'll have to bring you to trial because that's my job, but I can do it gently or I can do it in a pretty unfriendly way, because I figure the man who doesn't cooperate with me is no friend of mine, so why should I help him? I just don't know yet about this case. You surely had a good reason for killing three people. I'd like to hear whether it's good or bad."

"What about that promise to feed me?" asked Detweiler.

The D.A.'s eyes roamed for a while as if he were tracking a bird through the sky. Then he said quietly: "Who made it?"

Detweiler pointed over Mr. Crews's head to the older detective, standing behind, and he was interested to hear that the D.A. knew who it was without turning.

"Shuster," said Crews.

"Yes sir."

"Get him something to eat."

"Yes sir."

"Shuster?"

"Sir?"

"I don't mean you. Send What's-his-name."

"Tierney," said Shuster.

So that was it: Tierney. Detweiler thought it a very good name, and was annoyed that the district attorney had not known it. Mr. Crews went down several degrees in Detweiler's estimation: not to know the name of one of the men he sent to fetch a fugitive seemed irresponsible.

Detweiler still did not feel it was his own place to use the name, so he spoke to Tierney informally, as the detective moved towards the door.

"What I would like is a tunafish-salad sandwich on white bread without mayo, and a chocolate milk shake."

Tierney stopped and looked at him silently.

Mr. Crews helpfully told Detweiler: "He is waiting because you have not said whether you want lettuce."

"Oh," said Detweiler. "Well, what do you think? By this time of night the lettuce is likely to be wilted."

Just as this care for detail was causing Detweiler to think better of the D.A., Mr. Crews barked nastily: "Get going, Tierney!"

Tierney did as told. As it happened, he was not nearly so upset as Detweiler by the D.A.'s failure to know his name. Nor was he outraged by having to act as errand boy or waiter for a murderer. Tierney seldom allowed himself to be victimized by false pride. In the case of Betty Bayson the issues of pride were real. Had she gone to bed with Detweiler?

He had concentrated his personality on this one question, like a monster. Yet as he took a devious exit from the building in order to elude the newspapermen who infested the main passages, and went out through the streets, Tierney was an efficient officer, alert, *semper paratus,* suspicious of current phenomena. He saw two punks straining to jump a light, gave them a hard look; which they returned too idly to suggest the car was stolen.

Then he passed a polo-coated man who breathed stertorously and moved in a slightly eccentric stride. Tierney stopped to consider a delicatessen window. The place was closed, the glass, with no light behind it, reflecting the far side of the street and the pedestrians thereon. Before Tierney acted on what he saw, a patrolman came along testing doors.

Tierney said, giving unobtrusive directional signals: "Black coat, brown hat, carrying something in the folded newspaper. His mark's the drunk in the polo coat."

The patrolman said: "Shit, he's made us!" Tierney turned quickly to watch the potential mugger drop the paper, and whatever was inside, in a litter basket and walk smartly westward. They did the same, the beat cop snatching up the discarded tabloid without breaking stride: it contained a length of iron pipe. They fell in beside the suspect, Tierney inside and the patrolman on the curb.

The man was fair-complexioned, in his middle twenties, and still retained some acne. They walked him to a darkened block and around the corner, the uniformed officer inquiring as to name, address, and profession, and enumerating the disadvantages of appearing again on his beat.

The suspect's name was Horace Manners. He said, respectfully: "It isn't illegal to carry a piece of pipe if you're a plumber's assistant."

"No, it isn't, Horace," said the patrolman. He shoved Manners, face-forward, against the wall of a building, frisked him, then pounded him to the ground with the pipe. He helped Manners up, and said: "I'll call you when my toilet is busted, Horace." He began to work him over again and seemed to have the situation in hand, so Tierney left them and went to the Chinese restaurant he had originally been heading for. He ordered egg rolls and chicken chow mein to go, and while he waited he watched the pimps and their whores having a late dinner before the girls went on their tours of duty.

Tierney had once brought his wife to this restaurant, on a rare occasion when they could afford to eat out; but early in the evening, long before whore-time. His wife's idea of a prostitute, like her image of any other kind of lowlifer, had its source in the movies: a busty redhead who swayed along the street swinging a beaded purse. A hood was a pockmarked guy who talked from the side of the mouth. A rapist was a big Negro, and so on. His wife stayed altogether innocent of evil, and it was to Tierney's taste to keep her so, his home being his castle, though his work permitted him to return there only intermittently.

He had seen his wife only once, briefly, since the strange episode with Betty Bayson. Tierney lived in a two-bedroom apartment, and was father to two young children and a baby. Before taking the flight, he had gone home to change his shirt and underwear and collect his toilet articles. He could have used a shave at the moment: his chin felt grainy from the inside. Tierney dreaded being soiled in any fashion.

He decided to call his wife, which was not necessarily considerate in view of the late hour, and anyway she was trained not to hear from him for extended periods. She would not be worrying now; undoubtedly she was asleep. It was therefore not a kind impulse that took him to the wall phone in the grimy passage between dining room and kitchen. No booth: the instrument hung unprotected and the caller rather more so in the traffic of rice bowls.

Katherine answered in the middle of the second ring. The home phone stood at bedside.

"Sorry, Kath, if you were sleeping. Just letting you know I'm back." Tierney pressed himself against the wall to avoid a passing tray.

She said: "No, somebody called about midnight and woke me up. And woke up the kids. And we all got settled when now—"

"I'll be down here all night," Tierney said. "Who called?"

"An informant."

Crime being an exclusively human enterprise, when criminals were apprehended it was usually because of information received by the police from other human beings. More often than not, these useful people were themselves criminals, than whom no one could speak with more authority on the subject. Every detective had his own collection of stool pigeons, known to himself alone. These relationships were characterized by a peculiar mutual loyalty, much more reliable than any association based on sex or even money, though the officer usually paid the informant a small sum for each item. The stoolie's real satisfaction came from betraying more successful criminals than himself, and in his clandestine but substantive connection with the law: he was in effect the detective's detective, the fingernail at the end of the long arm.

As to Tierney, he would sooner have sold his wife on the street than to reveal the identity of one of his stoolies even to Shuster. That simply was not done.

Several of his informants preferred to call him at home, so that if they were under observation or spoke on a tapped phone, the number would not signify police headquarters. But this call was unlikely to refer to the Detweiler case. Stoolies, like everybody else, were out of touch with psychos.

"Because," his wife went on, "she didn't leave a name or number."

He did not ask Katherine to repeat the pronoun, though he had no female informants. He said: "I guess that was one of my girl friends."

Katherine's habitual laugh was a tone lower than her speech; it was sometimes called "dirty" by her old school pal, Margaret Walsh, with whom she drank coffee almost every afternoon. She laughed now and said, with the stage Irish accent she often assumed for purposes of levity, and which Tierney hated, hated with all his heart, for in neither of their families had there been in living memory anyone with a genuine brogue and besides hers sounded nothing like an Ireland Irishman's, but rather like a Jewish comedian doing a Gaelic imposture; but which Tierney found it impossible to protest again in view of the profound meaning it obviously had for Katherine, who might, in bed, as his hand traveled downwards across her navel, murmur: "Ah, me boy, me boy."

She currently was saying: "Tell me what kind of girl would be so shtoopid as to call a man at his marriage bed, now?"

A smiling Chinese gestured at Tierney with a paper bag. Tierney said: "That's the only kind I can get."

He had been at first shocked, then furious: who did that rotten bitch Betty think she was, calling his home. He controlled himself briefly, so as to tell Kath, as usual, he would see her when he saw her, hung up, grabbed the bag, paid the Chink, and left. Lucky for the pimps that they were seated well off his route, or perhaps unlucky: some were faggots, with a taste for brutality administered by attractive young policemen.

Back at headquarters, Tierney received another surprise. Shuster stood outside the closed door of the interrogation room.

"Here's one for you, kid," said the lieutenant. "He says he'll talk now, but only to you. He says you're the only one he feels is attuned to him, and a whole lot of other baloney." Shuster ha-ha'd: the reverse of Katherine's, his laugh did not sound dirty but usually was. "Let me tell you this: when an alleged psycho starts talking you would wish he was back strangling women. That little prick will keep you up all night."

Tierney went inside. The district attorney and the others were on their feet, and Detweiler sat where he had been.

"All right, then," said the D.A., apparently to both Tierney and Detweiler, as if they were in a conspiracy. Then to Tierney: "He doesn't want a stenographer yet, though I told him he will have to go all through it again so it can be taken down."

"No problem, Mr. Crews," Detweiler said brightly. "Tierney, won't you sit down?"

The police commissioner asked for Tierney's gun. Tierney

understood the precautionary measure: he was to be locked up with a homicidal maniac. Yet it reinforced his feeling that his colleagues were abandoning him morally.

Chapter 14

DETWEILER opened the bag and carefully withdrew the cardboard containers. He looked at the egg rolls, the rice, the chicken chow mein, the fried noodles.

He said to Tierney: "This is quite a provocation."

Tierney lifted his expressionless eyes and said "O.K., you wanted to talk."

Detweiler stated: "Nobody provokes anyone else unless he has some special interest in him. The others have done what I asked. But not because they like me, or hate me. They are just doing their jobs, and they figure that it's a kind of trade: I'll do what they want if they do what I want. I am really learning something. I thought the police used force pure and simple. I expected to get beaten up, whereas I have never been treated more nicely. I will certainly tell that to the press."

"You love publicity, don't you?" Tierney asked.

"That's fascinating," said Detweiler. "Why do you say that?"

"You turned yourself in to a newspaper."

"I see. . . . Well, maybe it's not right to ask you this, Tierney, because doing a particular job well requires a narrowness of focus, I believe, but I wonder if you ever, in your off-duty life anyway, considered the multitude of interpretations that can be made of a single phenomenon?"

He paused, but Tierney remained silent. Detweiler continued: "I never went to the paper with an idea of doing what turned out to be the case. But accidents occurred: at least, they seemed like accidents, though perhaps they were opportunities." He closed the containers and pushed them across the table, saying: "I don't eat Chinese food unless my stomach is upset. Anyway, you didn't bring implements to eat it with."

Tierney took from his breast pocket a pair of plastic chopsticks encased in cellophane. He had forgotten them, but one never apologizes to a suspect. He pitched them onto the table.

Detweiler said: "Would you like to know why I picked you?"

"I'd rather hear about the homicides," Tierney said, in a gritty voice, but as if to himself.

"Did you expect to bend me to your will?" asked Detweiler. "Was this a kind of test, whether or not I would eat something as different as could be from what I ordered?"

Tierney answered levelly: "You have admitted killing three persons. Now I understand that you are ready to explain how and why these crimes were perpetrated. I don't know why you want me in particular to hear the explanation, and I don't care. As for the food, you are in the custody of the police, and you will eat what you are given or go without eating. It doesn't matter to me. There's nothing special about you, once you are here. You are a lousy little runt who flopped at everything you ever tried except the strangling of two helpless women. You couldn't make it in art, couldn't hold a job, you go into tantrums because a harmless guy next door plays his radio. But you're a genius, aren't you? A philosopher. You don't have to observe the rules of decent, ordinary slobs. If they get in your way, and they are women, or their backs are turned, you assault them."

Tierney leaned across the table. "To me you are yellow and phony and a pervert, a stinking little rat. You pull any more of that philosopher shit on me and you'll go out tomorrow with the garbage collection."

When a suspect is eager to talk, as Detweiler had announced he was, his interrogator is properly at great pains to do nothing which might impede the flow; rather, to encourage, to affirm, to reward; to repress that which suggests punishment or a division of the common interest. This is the time of conversion, when with the sanction of all authority, criminals serve the law and lawmen participate in crimes, walk along as accessories, supplying mislaid items. There is extant, on both sides, good will, a feeling of accomplishment in cohesion, a sense of history. What can man not achieve when he joins hands with his fellows and forsakes destructive individuality. The criminal who reaches his unique pleasure during the act of confession is a type well known to students, amateur and professional, of the human personality. Crime may be his only means of expressing affinity with, love of, the race. The police are ever eager to collaborate in such an effort, not being a punitive agency. The police apprehend, catch, seize, arrest; they do not keep; and only the courts may punish.

Tierney reminded himself of these truths, for he suffered much from a memory of his irresponsibility with Betty. But now his seemingly uncontrolled outburst had been preceded by deliberation. He resented being selected to hear Detweiler's confession; that the killer's request had been honored by the D.A. was unbearable. Tierney had not captured Detweiler. If anything it had been the other way around, and now he, Tierney, was the prisoner of a politician and a murderer.

He must show Detweiler that any further display of vanity was out of the question.

Detweiler said: "I knew you were the only one with guts or pride. But I don't know whether those who don't have it can be condemned. It may be essentially the ability to resist distractions, and speaking for myself, I am so easily distracted that I have achieved very little. Listening to your estimate of me, I had to agree with you. Except that I have assaulted lots of people, not just women or men who I caught unawares. I fight a lot, but there's nothing personal in it. Of course, that may be even less admirable than your idea, but I did want to point it out."

"Have you killed anybody else?"

"I don't know," Detweiler said. "I certainly don't fight people with the plan of killing them. I can tell you that. Yet I suppose there isn't much point in fighting unless somewhere in the back of your mind is a knowledge that life is always at stake. But the other person, being human, knows that too, so it is fair." He thought a moment and added: "Of course, you will find people who pretend otherwise."

"Fight?" said Tierney. "Is that your name for it? When the other person is a woman? Why don't you admit you like to beat up girls, to hurt them: the more pain they have, the more your kicks. They are soft and you are hard. You can prove you're a man then, striking something stiff against something that gives. Otherwise you wouldn't know."

"I don't fight with the other person in mind at all," Detweiler answered. "That's what I mean by its being impersonal. I'm thinking exclusively of myself at such times, and they get in the way. You may be correct when you say I am a pervert, because of my tendency to get trapped in details though my aim is universality. But so far as sex goes, I am so normal in that area I have tried repeatedly to get rid of my penis."

Tierney tried to ignore the statement; he had no use for it; but Detweiler persisted. "I have never been able to accomplish that. So you are right about my being yellow. I took a razor blade in my right hand, and my organ in the left, and I started to make a cut down at the root. Puncturing the skin wasn't painful, a razor blade is so sharp, so I got it inserted all right, but when I reached—"

Tierney shoved his chair back and walked rapidly to the barred window. Because of his work many men must have stood, must be standing, in a similar attitude in various places of confinement. Necessarily he always minimized the discomforts of prisons, doubted their adequacy as punishment—if that Chinatown mugger had, in the course of robbing him, killed the man in the polo coat he might have got as little as twenty years of three nourishing meals per day, Saturday night movies, Sunday baseball games, payment for making license plates in the prison factory, not to mention training by masters in his true vocation, against the day he would escape or be paroled. But now Tierney understood that if he himself ever committed a punishable crime he must lose his life before capture: he could not endure constraint. Detweiler, however, seemed not to mind; he was insane. He was not faking in his description of the attempted mutilation. Tierney could feel its authenticity in his own groin, he who sometimes came naked from the shower to lather his face over the basin, to wet the razor, but never to lift it before he had hung a towel from his waist.

Detweiler was saying, with his boyish grimace: "Gee, it really *hurt!* So I stopped. Believe me, it is an awful thing to try to cut off your penis. It is *terrible.*" He sounded like an adolescent registering an extravagant complaint against a minor catastrophe: flat soda, term paper.

If degeneration this was, it must be a subtle form, too fine for Tierney to distinguish. He could see that Detweiler was serious, and as a fellow man, even one who had never attempted it, he must affirm that self-mutilation would be painful. One knew that as a basic truth. Being mad, Detweiler had to test it for himself. Tierney formulated a definition for a maniac: he who accepts nothing on faith, a kind of scientist of the soul.

But an obvious question remained.

"Why?" Detweiler repeated, but not rhetorically. He seemed to do nothing for effect. He was the only suspect Tierney had ever interrogated whose response could not be called a performance. "I suppose more vital energy is lost by that route than by any of the other orifices, certainly any but the mouth.

"Now, I am aware of the theory that sexuality is initiated in the mind, and not the organs, but remove the organs and the mind will adjust to the new situation. Take a bull and make him an ox and you will see he loses his aggressive character but none of his strength.

"So the idea was far from ridiculous. What was lacking was courage on my part. I really don't like pain, and it seems pointless to inflict it on oneself in this day and age when anesthetic surgery is practiced everywhere. So I got into the habit if I would pass a municipal clinic of going in and making my request. But I'll tell you this: I never found a doctor who would do it. So I continued to lose a lot of force constantly. You know how you often wake up in the morning with a physical craving for sex which has come from nowhere, or riding a subway, not even looking at women, and your organ is suddenly in a ready state, intruding into your thoughts, which may be of an entirely abstract nature. This has led me to consider whether sex really has anything to do with people, oneself included. It so often seems inanimate.

"Did you know that the common ant experiences sexual desire only once in a lifetime? That bears some thought, especially since like human beings ants are social creatures and build great cities, structures, roads, fight wars, and there is reason to believe even have a sort of politics. I don't care much for those ant colonies that you can buy already made up, though: encased in glass and with tiny manmade buildings labeled 'School' and 'Church' and 'Town Hall.' "

Tierney had once as a boy read a science-fiction story in which the entire world as we know it was but a drop of water on the slide of a colossal microscope. Hurricanes and earthquakes were caused by the probing of the massive personage who operated the instrument. His eye was the sun.

Tierney still stood at the barred window, looking through which he now saw, across the areaway, a lighted office, a detective he knew on the Safe & Loft Squad. They were always busiest at night, obviously the optimum time for a hired arsonist to burn the warehouse of a businessman in trouble. Tierney had no difficulty in making the immediate transition from fantasy to such a routine recognition. Lawrenson, the Safe & Loft man, had just made first-grade detective. Tierney was not up for promotion, had been only nine months in second-grade. Lawrenson had been on the Force for years and years and was at least a decade older than Tierney; his upgrading had been long overdue. Tierney did not feel any sense of injustice, but Shuster would have.

Shuster had been a lieutenant since Christ was a patrolman —an expression of his own. He resented every promotion, even Tierney's though he had recommended Tierney for it, and he had some dirt on everybody. Shuster would know for example that Lawrenson had, two years before, bought an eight-room house costing much more than he could afford, both in down payment and monthly installments. Shuster knew all the grafters, the sadists, the adulterers; undoubtedly he had a thing or two on the D.A., and perhaps even the mayor. Yet none of this knowledge represented power—that was the interesting thing to Tierney. Shuster stayed a lieutenant.

Meanwhile there sat Detweiler, the ultimate criminal, the man who Tierney was willing to believe had murdered for no motive at all. And Tierney had his back turned to him. It had been preposterous for the commissioner to take away his gun. Tierney was certain that lethal instruments were irrelevant, in Detweiler's view.

He turned and asked: "How did you happen to use a screwdriver on Appleton?"

"Isn't that something?" said Detweiler. "I never knew what his name was until you people here began to use it. To me he was just a man. I had left Mrs. Starr and Billie in the bedroom and was walking slowly along the hall towards the living room when his radio suddenly stopped playing. I guess it was his radio, because it had been playing in the room I used to rent when I lived there and the door had been ajar all the while, though I didn't know who was in there because you couldn't see from the hallway. And I didn't want to know, because it was deafening and loud noise always makes me want to kill the person who is making it, and I didn't go there to get into a fight.

"So by the time I reached the living room the effect of the beautiful stillness came over me, and I stopped to enjoy it. I didn't have any place to go and so was in no hurry. You have no idea how sweet it was there in the absolute quiet: inanimate objects are at their best in the silence. There was one lamp on a table near the windows and its soft light made the fabric of the sofa look like velvet, and I had never before noticed that the shadows made a pattern on the carpet that undoubtedly had a significant meaning could one have read it. When you speak of nothingness in any area it is often only because of insufficient knowledge. Everything is teeming with life. I'm convinced of that."

In the harsh light Detweiler seemed almost translucent, and if he cast a shadow, he contained or consumed it. He was portable in every sense of the word, with no excess, leaving no mark. He was almost nothing but mind or spirit, and that was warped. He was worthless.

Yet Tierney listened with a peculiar sympathy. Detweiler's view of things had a logic of its own: if you accepted a loud radio as sufficient motive for killing, then you must also admit the sense in enjoying the shadows on a carpet. Consistency is a value which the sane must support in ordinary circumstances; all the more so when consorting with the disorderly. But Tierney, who had seen those blue-faced, tongue-biting, distended-eyed corpses of Mrs. Starr and Billie, the worst of murders, far worse than when the mortifying body is broken and can shed its blood—in gunshot and knife murders, the victim loses some of his corporeality; strangled, his gain is horrible—Tierney also marveled at Detweiler's facility in making transitions.

"How long did you stand there?"

Detweiler said happily: "I don't know! Time did not apply. Funny, I had been trying for years to bring time to a stop and never succeeded. Oh, I could slow it up some. Everybody knows that time goes fast when you eat delicious food or make love or engage in any entertaining or attractive pastime. And slowly if you don't care for what you are doing. But take a swallow of strawberry milk shake and try to hold it—I don't mean the actual fluid but the exquisite sensation of sweet and fruit and smooth and mellow and slippery and cool in one instant retained infinitely, or let go and then summoned back next day or week or year." Detweiler was radiant. "My God, wouldn't that be *wonderful?*" He fell back into the chair. "We have it all, but lose it, let it go, proceed to the next phenomenon, distracted by what seem to be successive promises."

"Appleton entered the room while you were looking at the carpet," said Tierney, who had a job to do.

"Obviously he did," said Detweiler, shrugging. "I was aware that he was saying something, perhaps not words but sounds. I suppose now that he had seen Billie, anyway, whom I had left on the bed. I had put Mrs. Starr underneath, because I didn't want Billie to be upset by the sight when she came in, and—"

"Where was Billie while you were strangling Mrs. Starr?"

Detweiler said: "I want to follow the line I'm on at the moment. Can't you see I am developing a point, and furthermore, one which you got me started on by asking about Appleton?"

Tierney, pulling at his lips, accepted the rebuke and, his

claustrophobia was thereby diminished. Detweiler's insistence on arranging his own kind of order made him more feasible as a companion in a locked room. Tierney returned to the chair opposite the murderer, turned it back to front, and straddled the seat, folding his arms along the top rail.

Detweiler nodded smartly and proceeded. "It gradually dawned on me that someone else was in the room and not in sympathy with me, so that time was starting up again, slowly and uncertainly at first, as when you pick up a clock that has wound down and begin to tighten the mainspring, tock . . . tick . . . tock-tick, tock, tick, ticktock, *ticktockticktockticktock!* I turned around and saw this man, rather large and baldheaded. He was making sounds that I could not distinguish, and they did not seem to be synchronized with the movements of his lips.

"Well, it was rather embarrassing. I said, 'I'm Joe Detweiler. I used to live here, in the same room that you have.' I walked towards him and put out my right hand. He was trembling but looked friendly. He put his hand out, but as I was about to shake it, I saw he was holding a screwdriver in it. I said, 'What's this?' He spoke at last, thickly as if he had a cold but understandably: 'Fiddling with the radio. Station knob loose; tiny screw.' He said pathetically: 'This screwdriver has too big a blade.'

"I thought what he needed was one of those screwdriver sets in which ever smaller blades are fitted one into the next, and all nestle in the handle of the biggest, underneath a metal cap. You unfasten the cap and shake out one after the other until finally you can go no farther and you have a delicate little blade that will fit even the tiny screws in a wristwatch.

"However, I didn't tell him that. I remembered how loudly he had been playing the radio while I was talking to Mrs. Starr.

I said: 'You should have consideration for other people. Don't you know that sound can kill?' This is true, and has been done in laboratories with white rats and guinea pigs, and isn't it terrible that living animals should be destroyed to prove what everybody knows in his heart? People who have to prove things are either crazy or immoral, but people who make noise are insensitive, deadened by the repeated impact of molecules of sound."

"So," said Tierney, "you had given your name to Appleton, and realizing he would identify you, you killed him with his own screwdriver."

"Not quite," said Detweiler. "You know how different actual experience is from any speculation about it, and even a description by a participant, for that matter. That is what makes Realization difficult: it is definitely not memory. In fact, memory obstructs and perverts the process, for we all have our selfish interests to serve in the ordinary recollection. For example, I am trying now with the best of my ability to remember what happened with Appleton."

Tierney of course was trying to get Detweiler to admit that the murder of Appleton had been premeditated, even if for half a minute.

He said: "But you did tell him your name."

"Yes, I am positive of that," Detweiler answered, "at least, as positive as one can be of anything of a phenomenal nature."

"And he found the bodies. Did he accuse you of killing the women?"

"That he had seen Billie is really speculation on my part. I don't know that he did, nor do I know that if he saw her lying on the bed he would recognize that the life had gone out of her. He might think she was sleeping."

"Naked?" asked Tierney.

"Oh, Billie was frequently naked. She was a great one for forgetting to close doors. She was a lot like an animal in having no sense of shame about her body. If you lived there you certainly had lots of opportunities to see everything she had, but speaking of myself, I have never been terribly interested in ogling from the sexual point of view. In sex I want to get as close as possible to the center. Looking keeps you outside, confines you to yourself.

"But supposing he did get the correct picture, he seemed bewildered. I asked him what his own name was and he didn't answer. He did not accuse me of anything. He just stood there. I said: 'Merry Christmas, then.' He nodded, smiling slightly, I thought. I turned to leave and he jumped me. But I don't think he was a treacherous man. I believe that it had taken him that long to move into action, and that he would have attacked at that moment regardless of whether my back was turned or anything else. He was strong and brave, but I think confused.

"I would not say he was trying to kill me."

"So," said Tierney, "then it was not self-defense." He was obliged as a police officer to seek out the truth as to an alleged breach of the law. Whether a suspect was legally guilty or innocent was not his affair. Yet in practice, which is to say morality, he was gratified only by what tended to incriminate. This was quite impersonal. Tierney had by now lost the initial animosity he had felt towards Detweiler. You cannot hate a man who has no pride—no, that was imprecise: rather who has another kind of pride. Detweiler was mad, but not without a method.

Detweiler shook his head. "I would say he wanted to detain me. He did not understand what had happened, and it is almost impossible to kill a human being—always excepting the case of pure accident—when you are confused as to your motive and theirs."

"And that also applies to you," said Tierney. "You were not confused when you killed these three persons. You knew what you wanted to do, had thought it out, planned it, and did it. Now all you have to tell me is your motive, and we can get a good night's sleep."

Detweiler answered sadly: "I asked to talk to you because I believed that alone among the people with whom I have come into contact since entering the newspaper office, you would listen, not, frankly, because I thought you were terribly intelligent, but mind, in itself, is inconsequential. But now you are willfully placing yourself in obstruction, to the end that, if you had your way, I would confess to murder, pointlessly.

"Now, I will do that for you, if you truly want it and it is not merely a nervous reflex. All I ask is that you be *serious*—I don't mean solemn, you can laugh or joke, but for God's sake accept responsibility."

Tierney was not caught off guard by this impassioned statement. He had expected it, had indeed tried to provoke it, and now believed he had scored another gain. He had got Detweiler to come out of moral hiding, to acknowledge if only in a negative way the crime of which he was accused. Detweiler understood the charge against him, could differentiate between right and wrong. Whatever the features of his madness, no other issue was germane to this inquiry.

"Do you confess to the premeditated murders of these three people, or to any one of them?" Tierney asked compulsively.

Detweiler said, in a rush of anger: "Do you want me to?"

"I don't come into this," Tierney said. Then he heard himself add, inappropriately: "I am not charged with anything." The personal pronoun disturbed him.

"That's right," Detweiler said. *"I'm* certainly not accusing you."

"Why did you do that?" cried Tierney.

Detweiler looked alarmed and puzzled. "Excuse me?"

"Put that funny twist on the word *I.* Are you getting cute with me?" Tierney was jumping with nerves.

Without any adjustment, Detweiler resumed: "The reason I believe he wanted to detain or retain me was: he grabbed my shoulder. If he had wanted to kill me he obviously could have done so with most hope of success when my back was turned.

"He grabbed my shoulder and pulled me around. I tried to put him at ease about one thing, if that was the trouble.

"I said, 'Yes, I killed them, if that is what you are in doubt about.' "

Detweiler shrugged. "Then we began to wrestle. The reason I don't say we fought, at that point, is that there seemed to be more the spirit of a game about it than a life-and-death struggle. You know, each was trying to best the other, not to destroy him, for there would be no contest if either were eliminated from the competition. He would get a hammerlock on me, I would finally break it. I would have him in a sort of half-nelson, he would struggle free, and so on. Though we were not wrestling in any formal sense, so the holds were far from classic. . . . I can demonstrate, if you like."

Detweiler started up, but Tierney, his defenses rising more swiftly, ordered him back. It would be no game were he to touch Detweiler.

"O.K.," Detweiler said goodnaturedly, and slumped in the wooden chair until his shoulders touched his ears. But it was not an insolent movement, and Tierney took no offense.

He said: "But all during this game, this sport, you were trying to get hold of the screwdriver."

"Nope," said Detweiler. "The screwdriver had fallen to the floor and was just lying there. Neither one of us was interested in it: we could not have cared less about it!"

"Then how did it end up in Appleton?"

"Ah yes," said Detweiler. "Obligations come with knowledge. Had I not known Appleton was alive and present in that apartment, I would have left. But in possession of the facts, I had no alternative but to finish out the pattern. Having killed the other two residents, I could not abandon him to loneliness. I had to clean it up. Otherwise it would have been a disgusting mess for him. On Christmas Eve. I never could have forgiven myself for leaving him with that.

"So I snatched the screwdriver from the floor, and caught him with it as he lunged. I used both hands, plus his momentum, and the combination was enough to penetrate his temple, but that is solid bone there, seizing the blade and tearing it from my hands as he fell. In telling you this for your purposes, I am compressing the experience. In your irritable mood, your nervous chronological captivity, I am really reluctant to mention the extraordinary feature."

Tierney gave a cop's shrug. "Rely on me," he said.

"For what?"

"Oh, for Christ's sake." Tierney swiveled his head about.

"It strikes me," said Detweiler, "that the standard interrogation is designed to conceal or suppress the truth."

"Believe me when I say this isn't the standard type, but

you may be right anyway," Tierney said literally, patiently, as if he were speaking to Mr. Average Citizen, whose taxes paid his salary. Occasionally, for relief he had to pretend Detweiler was sane.

"A suspect naturally tries to make you believe he is innocent. Or if he has confessed he tries to explain why he committed the crime. He tries to associate himself, as best he can, with normal behavior. Everybody gets mad, everybody has moments when he is out of control, everybody at times breaks the law."

"They do?" asked Detweiler, marvelously, and Tierney could see he was not faking. "You're not saying that to trick me, are you?"

"I wouldn't lie to you, Joseph."

"I'm sorry I was difficult about the chop suey," Detweiler said. "It was nothing personal. I got to thinking it over, and it just didn't seem right to eat if we were having this talk. I should have explained that, but you were posing as unfriendly at the appropriate moment."

"That's right, it was just a pretense," said Tierney. "You tell me anything you want. I won't make fun of it."

"I wasn't worried about that. I don't mind being ridiculed; I just can't stand not being listened to."

"That's why you killed Mrs. Starr, wasn't it?"

Detweiler struck his hands together. "I told you that we, you and I, had an affinity, did I not! This is great! . . . Of course, of course, you understand perfectly." Detweiler put his hands on the edge of the table. "Do you mind if I get up?"

"Go ahead."

Detweiler began to stride about in the suit that was too large for him. Yet to Tierney he did not look pathetic.

Reaching the window and reversing, his wide cuffs sweeping the floor, Detweiler said: "I am excited by the possibilities of our association. Since we're both men, sex isn't a factor. That was the trouble with Betty as a partner. She was a woman, and that could not be ignored altogether."

"You went there on Christmas Eve to kill her, didn't you?"

"Certainly. But you know it all now that we are in alignment, so let's not waste any more energy on the matter. We have a job to do which, accomplished, will place these things in perspective."

"What is that?" Tierney asked in earnest, for despite his apparent disingenuousness, his sudden assumption of the familiar, avuncular style of the routine interrogator who has won a suspect's confidence, he was authentically naive now, else he could not have produced involuntarily the accurate statement of Detweiler's motive. He could not explain his clairvoyance except by use of Detweiler's theory: they had some profound though unreasonable link.

Detweiler said: "To kill Time."

Chapter 15

DETWEILER continued: "People use that expression negligently, in reference to the interval between what they believe to be important phases of experience. Between the end of the workday and dinner, they kill time. Sunday is ideal for killing time in this sense, which signifies idleness, quiescence, the mind a blank, the body either limp or, if active, engaged perhaps in a game the outcome of which is inconsequential: solitaire, for example, the winner and loser of which are both yourself.

"A waste of time, in the conscious opinion of most, who would not be so occupied if they had a task, but they do not say 'waste': they say 'kill.' Very interesting. The alternative to killing is using. Time is used to arrest criminals, to print newspapers, and so on. Time is killed by playing games, but not if the players are professionals; or gazing at trees, but not if the observer is a botanist.

"I did not use Mrs. Starr or Billie or Appleton. I killed them. As I am not a professional killer, I was also killing Time."

"Then killing them was a game?" asked Tierney.

"Yes, but one like solitaire or ticktacktoe if played by yourself: there was no personal winning or losing."

"By you," Tierney felt he must point out in all justice. "They lost their lives."

"Certainly it must seem that way to someone who believes life can be won or lost," Detweiler said, leaning on two hands at the end of the table. "Like the district attorney, and the commissioner of police, and the older man who accompanied us on the flight. But not to you and me, and not to Mrs. Starr, Billie, and Mr. Appleton."

"You can speak for them?" Tierney terminated this with the accent of interrogation, though he knew there was no question in Detweiler's mind.

"Because, having killed them, I possess them," said Detweiler. "And they me. They are in me and with me, and I of them and with them. And now I shall be executed because of you, and we all shall be part of you."

Tierney apologized. He said: "I do not understand."

Detweiler smiled helpfully. "I'm going to confess to premeditated murder in the first degree."

"You will do that for me?"

"Not for you," said Detweiler. "You will see that it is not exactly a reward, though to superficial minds like those of your superiors it may seem an accomplishment. I say because of you, because you are capable, because you will accept responsibility for the lives you incorporate. You are not a frivolous individual by any means."

Tierney said softly: "Forget about that, Joseph."

"The advantage is that you have a profession," Detweiler said, "and a special kind: you regulate and control. Exactly what is needed, lacking which I have not made the progress I should have."

"Joseph, I am not your partner or collaborator in anything. You must understand that. I am not, believe me for your own sake. Do you understand? I am a police officer, and what you tell me can be used against you, so you want to be very sure it is the truth. All these speculations and thoughts of yours, however interesting and maybe even brilliant at times—they are not appropriate here. I am not a priest. I do not have the right nor, to be frank, the competence to deal with these other matters. You'll get the opportunity to speak with a spiritual adviser, a minister or priest. Save your ideas for him." Tierney paused, then added bluffly, to take the pressure off: "Hell, I'm not worthy of these high-powered concepts. I am just a cop."

"If you want to be simplistic," said Detweiler, "then I am just a killer, and Billie and her mother and Appleton are just corpses and already rotting, and God is just a despot."

"God?" asked Tierney. "That's the first time you have mentioned God."

"It could be the last," Detweiler said matter-of-factly. He rolled his head about and, lowering his chest to touch the end of the table, did a few standing pushups. He said: "That's one subject on which I try to keep from being vulgar. Suffice it to say that you and I can do without the name, so long as we have the power."

Tierney was embarrassed, and asked a sophomoric question. "Do you believe in God?"

Detweiler did a pushup. He looked at Tierney with what

seemed to be amusement, and said: "You can be pretty crafty. I'd certainly hate to be interrogated by you if I were a criminal."

Tierney sighed and collected himself. He said: "Joseph, do you really think we're getting anywhere? I put it to you. You're an intelligent fellow. Aren't we wasting our time? Now, you told Mr. Crews you were ready to make a statement, so we co-operated with you. But it's getting later and later, and the rest of us haven't had any sleep since last night. Frankly, I don't think you're being considerate."

"More than once you have used the word 'frankly' or a form of it. I just want to tell you," said Detweiler, "that I never doubt your sincerity. No need to reassure me. I trust you completely, no matter what it seems you are doing at the moment."

There was an implication here that Tierney did not like. Before he could protest, however, Detweiler had intuited his reaction.

"I mean," said Detweiler, "that though it might *seem* as if you are trying to distract me right now, I'm ignoring it. I know you are testing me."

"For what?"

"To see whether I'll break under the strain. One has to be careful when choosing an associate for dangerous work. Think of the mountain climber who must trust the comrades who share his lifeline. One cannot survive if the other is capricious or forgetful or has an uncontrollably humorous turn of mind, though a direct sense of enjoyment is all to the good. I can assure you that I am seldom very witty."

"Oh, that I can believe," Tierney said seriously. "But supposing I promise to talk over these philosophical or religious problems with you at a later time. Can we make a deal? Right now you will stick to the facts about what happened on Christmas Eve at the Starr apartment. No interpretations or abstract stuff, O.K.?"

"That," said Detweiler, "is a distinction I find hard to make. Between 'fact' and 'idea.' But I will do my best, and if I get off the track, please let me know."

"Another thing: shouldn't we get a stenographer in here so this can be taken down and you won't have to go through it again for the record?"

"Matter and mind," Detweiler went on. "Their connection is Time."

"Joseph," said Tierney, "you are off the track."

Detweiler shook his head. "You know," he said, "it's a funny thing, but the rare occasion on which I am *not* distracted, when I am on the track, the world invariably pulls me away. Even you do it, with the best of intentions. Betty always did, too. I would simply give up but for one thing: I know I'm right. I cannot be that all experience passes away forever, beyond recall." He struck the tabletop. "That is unthinkable. If it is so, then there goes your law, Tierney. Your profession is meaningless, then, and you are an idiot."

At the moment it seemed to Tierney a realistic appraisal of himself and his job. What point would be served by aiding in Detweiler's conviction? If he were so disposed of that he could not kill again, there would yet be other murderers, rational or insane—another meaningless distinction, along with life or death, fact or idea. Since all men would die anyway, a murderer took nothing essential from his victim but time. If Detweiler believed he could stop time, he must believe he was God. This little, skinny, pale criminal dressed in a baggy suit.

Tierney asked him: "Joseph, are you God?"

"Yes," said Detweiler. Then: "But that shouldn't bother you. You are too, if you want to be."

"And Mrs. Starr and Billie and Appleton?"

"Certainly."

"Then how could you have killed them?"

"Exactly," said Detweiler. He returned to his chair. "You understand thoroughly."

Detweiler believed everybody was God, but Tierney had had too much of religion in his schooling to be anything but a practical atheist. Tierney recognized that this distinction was much greater than that between criminal and cop. Under the appropriate conditions he could see himself strangling Betty, but he could never accept a connection between humanity and divinity.

"Well," said Detweiler, "now that we've got that settled, why don't you call in the stenographer?"

Tierney opened the door and asked the uniformed men to come in. Without looking again at Detweiler he went along the corridor to the room where the D.A. and the others waited amid clouds of cigarette and pipe smoke. Mr. Crews held a blond briar between his incisors. He had taken off his jacket, exposing the embroidered initials on the breast pocket of the white shirt and the full length of his blue-figured tie.

He looked at Tierney. He wasted no show on subordinates; it was self-evident that the occasion was momentous, else he would not have been there at all. He was unassailable; Detweiler would not have chosen him as confidant.

Tierney was aware of many pairs of eyes as he spoke to Crews, belonging to as many superiors; the commissioner, a few captains, Shuster, detectives on the D.A.'s staff. It was his moment.

"Sir," he stated to Crews, "I'm afraid I can't come up with anything. He might want to talk, but what he says is psycho malarkey, like the stuff he gave the newspaper."

Crews sucked his pipe, which was either empty or not alight, looking cross-eyed towards the bowl; he could manage such an expression without being absurd. Yet he was not a genuine pipe smoker: the pipe was much too blond.

He said: "Tierney, I wish you would not use the word 'psycho,' or any similar terms, in referring to this individual. I intend to have him indicted, and to try him for, Murder One. I don't care whether he gibbers like an ape or eats his own excrement. I don't care how many noted alienists Melrose brings into court to assure us that the defendant is as incapable of moral decision as a chipmunk. I am going to hold him legally responsible for his actions, and I am going to get a conviction. We all have our quirks. You overlook mine as I overlook yours, and as we will all overlook Joseph Detweiler's."

"Yes sir," said Tierney. "I suppose he is trying to make fools of us." He did not feel he was selling Detweiler out. What kind of contract could be made with a maniac?

"A routine type," drawled Crews, around the hard-rubber bit between his teeth. "Thank you, Tierney." He spoke to two of his own men, Detectives Hatfield and Speyer, as Tierney faded away into the corner where Shuster stood.

"Well," said Tierney, "I tried."

"Did you touch him?" Shuster asked.

"No."

"You are a stupid son of a bitch," Shuster whispered.

Hatfield and Speyer went to the interrogation room. They were not huge men, yet both were fit and larger than Detweiler. Tierney believed that the killer would hold out more stubbornly with every blow he received.

Tierney was wrong. By morning the D.A. had a complete statement of the approved type, in which Detweiler confessed to the premeditated murder of not only Billie Starr, but Appleton as well. Tierney assumed that Detweiler had broken under the punishment; that the prior symptoms of madness with which he, Tierney, had been confronted had been faked or at any rate exaggerated: Detweiler knuckled under when he faced the D.A.'s men, who were efficient and unreflective. Tierney made this assumption because it was his duty so to do, and it did not alter his private judgment that Detweiler was insane. Tierney saw no conflict here: he was very normal.

It never for a moment occurred to him that Detweiler assumed he had sent Hatfield and Speyer to take the confession which Detweiler understood he and Tierney had agreed on; just as to Detweiler the thought did not occur that Tierney had betrayed him. Detweiler rarely thought the worst of anybody. He felt no animosity towards Hatfield and Speyer for punching him around some before it became clear he was not resisting them.

The D.A.'s men of course shared Tierney's belief that they had beaten a statement out of Detweiler, and felt a sense of achievement. Detweiler did not know about this; but it is probable that if he had known, he would have done nothing to set them straight, interested as he was in the rewarding of purpose by accomplishment.

On the following morning Detweiler was taken to the line-up:

a brightly lighted stage at the end of a room that resembled a gymnasium, a man on a nearby platform, an audience. A number of other persons were assembled behind the stage, but Detweiler was sent out first.

He had had some sleep after giving and signing his statement, in a neat little cell furnished with all that a man might need: bunk, toilet, washstand. He had eaten quite a nice breakfast of oatmeal and coffee with sugar and milk, and there was plentiful hot water, soap and a clean towel. He understood he was supposed to get a uniform, but had not received it so far, and his shirt being soiled around the neckband, he washed only the collar and squeezed it in the towel, then smoothed and stretched it in his fingers. It was still damp and felt cool, refreshing, around his throat, which was still somewhat sore at the adam's apple from having been seized by one of the men who took his statement: "Is this how you did it, Joe?" But he no longer remembered the bruises he had sustained in the saloon encounter with Walt.

On the stage his situation was noteworthy. Because of the lights he seemed utterly alone, that is, though he knew the room was thronged he could see no one. The joke was on him, who during one phase had experimented with processes for making himself invisible, which he had proved was impossible unless everyone else was blinded, but of course here was the secret: concentrated light. If one could travel within an incandescence. . . .

The man on the platform read aloud a brief account of how Detweiler happened to be there, and then he said, kindly: "Turn around, Joe." Detweiler did so and studied the horizontal lines on the wall, which demarcated certain heights, and then the man said: "O.K., Joe, you can face front again."

Detweiler came around, smiling at the thought of his super-visibility in the brilliant lights, against a white wall graduated like a laboratory vessel. The police certainly did a thorough job; they were specialists in recognition and identification; in their hands one felt established, on record, in place.

"Think this is funny, do you, Joe? Joe strangles women, but when the boys come to play, little Joey runs away," said the platform man.

Detweiler had no idea why this man was perverting the facts, but since his voice was kind, malice was out of the question. "No," he said, "I also killed Appleton, though he was neither a boy nor came out to play, exactly."

"And you are proud of it, right, Joe? Is your face somewhat bruised, Joe? Look over this way. How'd that happen?"

"A fellow in a bar, a couple of nights ago, hit me."

"Uh-huh," said the platform man. "How have you been treated in police custody?"

"Fine," said Detweiler. "Swell."

"No complaints, huh Joe? Nobody gave you a bad time?"

"Certainly not." Detweiler saw no reason to get those fellows who succeeded Tierney in trouble, though they had struck him a few times, but in the middle of the body and not the face, and probably through misunderstanding; and besides, his questioner, being a policeman, would know of this and not have to ask him.

"Joe has made a statement to the district attorney," said his questioner to the invisible audience. "All right, Joe. That's all."

"Thank you," said Detweiler.

"Don't mention it."

Next Detweiler was taken to be arraigned, which was to say, formally charged with having committed certain actions which were criminal according to the laws of the state. Everything having to do with Law was carefully managed, he could see. After experiencing this at close hand, Detweiler doubted that justice often miscarried. He had by now repeated several times an admission of responsibility for the three deaths, but apparently his obligations were not yet discharged. The newspaper, the police, the district attorney, and Homicide Court, where he was at present, with the grand jury, he had been told, yet to come. In the house of exterior reality were many mansions to occupy, categories to satisfy, persons with a job to do. Man had made a remarkable structure of mechanical morality. Detweiler however could not let himself get too involved in these matters. Thus he was happy to meet the square-built, well-dressed individual who approached him in a hallway of the court.

"Are you Joseph Detweiler? My name is Melrose."

"Really delighted to meet you," Detweiler said, eagerly lifting his right hand but, inhibited by the quick restraint of the handcuff around that wrist joined to Tierney, who as the arresting officer was obliged to accompany Detweiler on all formal occasions, dropped it and put out the other. Melrose made no attempt to take it, from which Detweiler could see immediately that he was a man of propriety and spurned the unnatural: he would not shake a left hand, unless perhaps his vis-à-vis were one-armed, perhaps not even then! Detweiler liked such classic ways. He also noticed that Melrose failed to acknowledge Tierney at all.

Detweiler said no more to the attorney until Tierney unlocked him from the cuff and left him and Melrose in a little interrogation-cell behind the courtroom.

Detweiler said: "The newspaper publisher told me you were

the best defense counsel in the country. Would you mind telling me how old you are?"

"I'll be fifty in June."

"You may think this is an impertinent question," said Detweiler, "but I wonder if you'd mind telling me how long you think you'll live, until what age, I mean."

"I don't mind the question," Melrose answered, "but I don't have a response to it, because I have never thought about the matter—no, that's not precisely true. Of course I have, but not in that way."

"Then I guess you and I will get along all right, because neither have I," said Detweiler. "Frankly, I wouldn't trust you if you got statistical on me."

"Frankly," said Melrose, "I don't care whether you trust me or not."

Detweiler had difficulty in ascertaining the spirit in which the lawyer had made the statement, Melrose's expression being impenetrable.

He said: "Could you clarify that?"

"Surely. I am your counsel. I am not you. I will speak *for* you and not *of* you. I am accused of no crime, and I will not be on trial. You are, and will be. That is the difference between us, and it is important to remember at all times. If I take the case—as I am apparently doing, because I am here—we will share a common interest: you want to live and I want to win. Neither of us can do damage to the other without harming his own cause. Trust plays no part at all."

Detweiler listened carefully to this, but he was also observing Melrose's person and attire. The lawyer wore a medium-gray suit, pin-striped in a darker gray. On sitting down he had unfastened the middle button of his jacket and plucked up his trousers at both knees. His cufflinks were large, flat ovals of silver, engraved in an exotic design; his collar pin a narrow silver bar. His pocket handkerchief was a cloudlike puff of linen. The vest was a surprise: dove-gray, unstriped, with opalescent buttons, and of a fabric somewhere between felt and velvet. A tie of silver grillwork over an intense blue, rising to a huge knot at the white collar of the silken shirt whose body was, however, pink, an effect which Detweiler could see on closer inspection was due to the tight intermixture of red threads with white.

"Is there egg on my vest?" asked Melrose.

"I was just interested in your shirt," said Detweiler. "I imagine it was special-made, for you alone."

"That is true." Melrose slowly lowered the eyebrow he had raised. "O.K.? Do I pass?"

"Sorry," said Detweiler. "I did not mean to imply I was giving you a test. I admire your taste in clothing as well as your brilliance in argument. I am beginning to appreciate your gifts."

Melrose showed the saddest smile Detweiler had even seen. He said: "I haven't finished on the subject of trust."

"Quite all right," Detweiler said. "I know that in your profession you have to protect yourself with cynicism, being the middleman between crime and punishment. Your clients are by definition morally inferior to the rest of humanity, and are on trial for doing things that you, yourself, would never even be suspected of. To speak for them requires great irony on your part, but there must be an even greater irony that nobody understands but yourself. I mean, I suppose people tend to think of you as something of a criminal if you defend criminals, and those you defend think of you as being ultimately on the side of the law. As for yourself, you must wonder whether you chose the profession because of compassion or cruelty."

Melrose stayed sad. He said: "You have not retained me to study my motives, Joseph, however more valuable that may be than any jurisprudence. My sole importance to you is that perhaps I can save your life."

Detweiler was astonished that even such a man as Melrose could be utterly naive.

"But I don't want to save my life!" he exclaimed. "That's not the point at all. I have killed three persons, and I must pay for the crime."

An unprecedented animation showed in Melrose, whom, until this moment, Detweiler would have described as merely bland, impeccable. Now his face began to take on the hue of his rosy shirt.

"Pay whom?" he cried.

"I don't know!" Detweiler shouted back. "You tell me. You're a lawyer."

"I'm *your* lawyer."

Melrose shrugged in an odd way, and Detweiler sensed he had hurt him somehow and had a feeling that to apologize would make it worse.

"Listen here," he said, "I don't mean to diminish your role in my trial. I just wanted to be honest and let you know that I don't have any quarrel with the Law. If you can find any legal justification for my having killed those people, more power to you. I can't see any, but then I am not a lawyer."

Melrose said: "Will you let me worry about that? Now we must go into court for your arraignment, and a statement of charges against you will be read, and then you must plead either one way or the other."

"Guilty or not? Which do you think I am, Mr. Melrose?"

The attorney shook his heavy head. "Joe, what you are is not relevant. What concerns us is what you can be proved to be in a court of law. That is a highly technical matter in application, though in essence it is very simple: in bringing a charge against you, your accuser takes on the burden of proof. You may accept this silently and make no defense whatever—which is in itself a defense."

"I have considered doing just that," said Detweiler, "but it doesn't seem right. I don't think the State would spend all their time and money and the energy of their employes if there wasn't a good reason. And in this case, we know the accusation is justified. I certainly killed three people. The only doubt is whether it was murder. I think I should explain it was not, from my point of view, because the difference between killing and murder is that malice is present in the latter. I have previously spoken of 'gain,' in the sense that I got none from these killings, having in mind robbery, vengeance, and so on. But I have to admit I was being deceitful, even to myself, when I made that assertion."

Melrose leaned forward, apparently fascinated, though Detweiler could not have said what if anything in his counsel's attitudes was genuine and what was lawyerly craft. To be another man's advocate required a peculiar type of personality. He had been amazed by Melrose's professed lack of interest in the real, as opposed to the legal, issues in the killings, yet now, only a moment later, the lawyer seemed intent. Detweiler had been much more at ease with Tierney.

"Do you really want to hear this?" he asked.

"Of course," said Melrose.

"Your mention of silence—how the accused can defend

himself silently—suggested this new interpretation, and the more I think about it, the more likely it sounds. You see, Mrs. Starr was making noise. The shouting did not bother me because at least it was personal. She wanted me to leave and not to wait for Betty to arrive. She made that clear. I tried to explain, but she wouldn't listen. She went into the kitchen and began to stack plates, banging them together with that special sound of crockery, unlike any other in the world, piercing, jagged, white, searing, the noise of almost-breakage, never-quite, a cold sound, icy, ice sheets pounding together in the Bering Sea—"

"Joe," said Melrose. "We must get into court."

"I went into the kitchen and begged her to put those plates down. She was banging them so loudly she could not hear me. Those plates were driving her crazy; they were getting their chance at long last to get revenge for years of abuse. Don't kid yourself," Detweiler told Melrose as if confidentially, "material objects are aware of us at all times, rocks and stumps as well as sophisticated devices, but luckily they are all at odds with one another or people would long since be overwhelmed."

Melrose said: "Come on, Joe. Your ideas are not terribly original. The revolt of the machines against their human masters is one of the oldest clichés in science-fiction writing."

"That's not exactly what I am saying, is it?" said Detweiler. "Anyway, I'm not trying to be creative, I'm telling you what happened. I expect most of it will be an old story to a man in your job, defending killers as you do."

"You killed Mrs. Starr to stop the noise?"

"Yes, so you see, I did gain. I gained silence."

"Joe, it takes a while to strangle a person. She would have stopped making noise as soon as your hands closed around her neck. Yet you continued to squeeze and squeeze and squeeze, did you not? Once your hands were at her throat you could not control yourself, isn't that so? You forgot all about Mrs. Starr as a person, a living human being of flesh and blood. She was now not *she,* but *it.* It opposed you, you must remove it from your path—"

"Oh no!" cried Detweiler. "What you are describing is a confusion of persons and things, namely murder: removal of the person who obstructs you from a desired end, as if he were a piece of furniture. When I said that material objects have an awareness, I don't mean they are not to be distinguished from living organisms. Certainly she stopped making noise. I had gained that, without killing her. Thus far it was like shutting off a radio, and I was about to take my hands away when I saw it. I was startled, to see it there, to recognize it!

"Mr. Melrose, you don't know what this moment meant to me after my years of searching. Sculpture, a reproduction of the form of life. Taxidermy, closer insofar as it used that which remained after life had gone: something at least that had once contained life, unlike art. I had wondered what came next: embalming? I thought about taking a course in an undertakers' school.

"All the same, I knew it was one absurdity after another, for life is not form but Time. A dummy could no doubt be constructed to meet every chemical and physical test, plastic skin, eye-lenses ground to specification, vacuum tubes and wires conducting electrical impulses the equivalent of human energy. As to the moral qualities, they would be easiest of all to establish: you merely arrange the switches according to a scheme furnished by such a person as my friend Tierney, who being a policeman is an authority on right and wrong.

"But though you'll have something fine, you won't have life, because the one thing that cannot be simulated is time. And time is what I saw in Mrs. Starr's eyes, behind the superficial pain and fear—genuine but superficial because pain and fear, no matter how intense, pass away in *time*. And *if Time is stopped*—well, you cannot do it by holding back the hands of a watch with a needle—I have done that—any more than you can alter spatial measurements by cutting an inch off the end of a yardstick.

"So I squeezed her throat and as I did so I looked into her eyes, which were hazel and beautiful and sympathetic though the rest of her face showed anguish, for it is terrible to be killed, but at least she was not alone. I could hardly bear her pain at second hand. I know I could not have strangled myself while looking in a mirror: I hadn't had the courage even to emasculate myself.

"So in her eyes I watched Time move, flow, continue, and it did not slow down or speed up, because in real time there are no intervals as in the running of a watch, no tick-tock, and it is not like a river with here and there a ripple, a floating leaf or twig, a random current. It *was,* and then suddenly, it *was not.* Time had gone out of her and thus life. I had not caught it, arrested it as a policeman apprehends a lawbreaker, locks him up and can at will go to see him, feed him, consult him, beat him or whatnot—"

Melrose quickened and asked: "Did the police beat you?"

"It was nothing personal," Detweiler said impatiently. "Never mind about that. I've been treated a lot better than I expected. . . . I released my hands and her body sank to the floor. I was depressed. So I have failed, I thought. I have brought pain and terror and taken a life. Tierney had pointed out that I have been a flop at various endeavors, and in general the police tend to emphasize that two of my victims were women and suggest that I was trying to rape the Starr ladies or something, which is ironic when you consider that Billie, at least, begged me to. She was naked, you see, having come from the shower. . . . But at the moment—I use the terminology because though I had watched Time stop in Mrs. Starr, it continued in me.

"I heard a noise at the door, not loud but penetrating because metallic: a key probing the lock. I picked up Mrs. Starr, carried her down the hall to the girls' room, now Billie's alone since Betty had left, as it turned out: there was only one bed. At the end of the hall was the closed door of what used to be my room, light showing in a half-inch strip along the threshold, the violent sound of a radio within: a boarder. There was always one, though I had not seen him. Back there, because of this radio I could not hear what happened out front, but I assumed someone was entering the apartment. Betty, could it be Betty? The dresser lamp was lighted. Hastily I put Mrs. Starr under the bed and extinguished the lamp. I stood in the middle of the room. I had no plan. All was now dark, and I could hear nothing but the radio behind the boarder's door, music, a Christmas carol, oddly enough 'Silent Night,' loud as could be. This served to remind me of two things: one, that no Christmas decorations had been put around the apartment. Mrs. Starr always did that on Christmas Eve with the help of the girls: a small, artificial tree, Santa Claus beneath it, made of colored cotton, riding a sleigh along a strip of white cotton; wreaths. The other thing that was in my quick glance at Billie's dresser, I did not see the mounted squirrel I had given her for Christmas the year before. Had she destroyed

it? I wondered about that, and it was an important consideration owing to the fact that I had brought along with me this
year another very much like it, for Betty; in case Betty showed
up; I did not intend to leave it there for her. I had carried it
under my arm while hauling Mrs. Starr's body into the bedroom. I was still holding it: I certainly took care of that
squirrel.

"There was someone in the room with me, other than Mrs.
Starr. Someone alive. I could smell her perfume, and she was
humming 'Silent Night.' I felt a rush of air as cloth passed
me: she was removing her clothing and tossing it onto the bed.
I stood right there, but it was dark, so neither of us could see
the other; and we were each ignorant of the significance of
the situation, she not aware of my presence, I not knowing
what she intended to do.

"Another important feature: I thought it was Betty, I really
did. I had a choice, either one or the other, so naturally I chose
the one I preferred. The quality of a voice is difficult to judge
if it is heard only humming, and I could tell nothing from
the perfume.

"As to why Betty would come into the apartment in such
an assured way though she no longer lived there, did not occur
to me. I had hoped she might leave her husband and return,
and then I could get my old room back, and we could take up
where we left off. She would make hot chocolate and little
saltine sandwiches with peanut butter, and put a marshmallow
in the cup, which the best technique was to leave until the last
swallow, maybe only a drop or two of cocoa left and the slow-
moving, melted lump of white sweetness—it was agonizing
to wait for it to slide towards your tongue. Betty was a marvelous cook and did things of genius with peanut butter alone:

with pickles, with fried bananas, though her mother didn't like her to be in the kitchen, wanted her to improve her mind. Well, I used to talk philosophy and religion with Betty, but her mother didn't like that either. I suppose she was afraid of sex cropping up: misconceptions in the opinion people have of others are often sexual in their content. You take the district attorney and the police: they were seriously inquiring whether—well, I have already said that.

"Sex is important, like food, but at the same time very simple. It can be pursued by just two people, a man and a woman, alone on a desert island, or alone in all the world. You can't get much simpler than that, if you think about it, when it comes to human relations. Of course, when it comes to larger populations, then you get tastes, jealousies, and various diversions of energy, organizational matters, laws. I noticed in your list of whom you defend, Mr. Melrose, that no mention was made of sex criminals."

"You have an eye for particulars, Joe. I believe sex is the concern of medicine and not law. But perhaps I am just a coward. Nobody wins a sex case."

"Winning is important to you, I haven't forgotten that," Detweiler said. "And I don't condemn you, but maybe the greatest trial of this whole affair will be between you and me. Look, I don't *want* to be executed, because I don't like pain, and surely there must be some involved though electrocution is supposed to be very fast indeed, but I am not bothered by the prospect of being dead. I don't believe that except in particulars (for which you say I have so good an eye) it is different from being alive: mind and will still exist, and matter is merely converted into something else."

"Joe," said Melrose, "I swear to you that though like all

men you will one day inevitably die, you will not be executed as a result of the charges now against you. It is not my habit to make predictions, and I have never before given such an assurance to a client, but this I swear to you."

"But what about my obligation to society?" asked Detweiler. "People can't be allowed to go around killing others if things are ordered rationally."

Melrose spoke quickly and harshly, as if to prove Detweiler's theory that they were antagonists. "If you want to be rational, there is of course no proof that society exists, except as a meaningless term signifying the human beings who live in a certain place and time. Society is merely everybody else, and it is impossible to owe everybody anything. Secondly, people *do* go around killing others, although things are presumably ordered rationally."

Detweiler said: "I suppose you could owe them common decency."

"Whatever that is," Melrose answered sardonically. "It would be common decency for a doctor a kill a patient suffering from a painful, hopeless illness. Decent persons commonly do that to injured animals. But according to 'society' that is unjustifiable homicide, at least so says the Law."

"You may not be able to prove the existence of society, but you can see its power, anyway. We wear suits and ties, you and I, like most everybody else around us. We disapprove of murder, like most everybody else. Obviously there are various motives for taking human life and various means of committing the deed: these must be examined, in order to determine whether there was justification. I myself do not approve of mercy-killing."

Melrose asked sharply: "Why?"

"Because it denies the possibility of a miracle," Detweiler said.

"Joe, I don't care whether you had good reasons or bad for what you did, or no reason at all. I want you to plead not guilty."

"I guess my argument is full of holes," Detweiler admitted. "I don't know much about the Law, but I don't welsh on a promise, and I promised Tierney I would plead guilty."

"Did Tierney beat you?"

Detweiler laughed. "Far from having struck me, he never even asked me to confess. In fact—and this will go to show you something about the man's quality—he told me not to confess to that unless it was the truth!"

"Joe," said Melrose, "you are an interesting man to talk to, but I don't know whether I can afford the luxury of it, and I doubt that Tierney can either. You seem persistently to maneuver the other fellow into taking what should be your side of the argument, and you take his. Generally if I have to warn a client, it is against overoptimism. I have acquired a reputation for keeping people out of the death house, but it is a dangerous game. At any time a jury might decide to break my perfect record, and when I lose in a capital case my client may lose his life. I therefore must warn him at the outset to expect the worst.

"With you I am in the unique situation of insisting that you accept the best. There is the distinct possibility that Tierney was tricking you, that having assessed your character as the sort that works against the grain, he induced you to condemn yourself. When I was a child in grade school, underweight and puny—unlikely as that seems today—I was often the target for the bullying of a certain large and muscular boy. It would have been hopeless to try to fight him, so I employed guile. On an occasion when I was in his presence and he did not strike me, I demanded an explanation for the failure. 'I like to be punched,' I said. He was dumbfounded. I insisted. He reluctantly knocked me down. It hurt, and I don't like pain any more than you do, but I had far rather suffer physical pain than moral. I insisted he do it again. The second time, his blows lacked half the force he was capable of delivering. 'You are getting weak,' I said. 'Again.'

" 'You are crazy,' said he.

" 'And you are a yellow son of a bitch,' I replied.

" 'Well, I'm not crazy anyway.' He balled his fist to strike me, but I had him now.

"I cried: 'You are a weak, yellow son of a bitch.' I said this from a bloody mouth.

"At that point the lout burst into tears and blubbered: 'You leave me alone!'

"My point is," said Melrose, "that in human relations there are many different types of power, but the aim is always to get the other fellow to do what you want."

"That is the most extraordinary story," said Detweiler. "Almost unbearably ruthless. Did you have no pity for your victim?"

Melrose answered softly: "None whatever."

Detweiler was terrified. If only Tierney were there to help him—or even the district attorney, who sought only his execution. Melrose was out to save his body and destroy his soul. Obviously, since he had committed the killings, and since there was no legal excuse for them but one, if he were to plead not guilty Melrose intended to represent him as insane.

Then Melrose made a final, crushing statement: "I didn't ask you to be my client, Joe. If you remember, you came to me."

Detweiler traced this out in his mind. True. He had a prior obligation to Melrose: it was a matter of time.

"There is a practical difficulty," he said. "I signed a confession."

"Under duress," Melrose replied. "They beat it out of you."

Detweiler began: "Oh, no—"

Melrose cut him off. "Joe, you have your own theories of reality, and they are interesting, challenging, serious, so serious that you took human lives in their pursuit, and are willing to lay down your own life as well. My own philosophy does not have the magnitude of yours. I practice a profession of particulars, and I tell you that in a courtroom, reality is what the jury believes."

Melrose was a guileful man, as a lawyer should be in view of the imprecision of the law. To Detweiler, and he knew Tierney agreed with him, the punishment for killing was death. But he was now in the hands of this devilishly shrewd fellow, and no longer under the control of the straightforward, benevolent police. Melrose would have his way, had been practicing prevalence since childhood, according to his remarkable anecdote.

Cunning was something new to Detweiler. It apparently consisted of pretending to do one thing while preparing to do another, like a cat crouching near a mousehole, simulating animation.

"All right," he said. "I will go along with you. I will plead not guilty, and may God have mercy on my soul."

He had decided to strangle Melrose, premeditated, malice

aforethought. No one could deny this would be absolute murder.

But as luck would have it, at just that moment Tierney came to take him into court.

"You will visit me soon at the jail?" Detweiler asked Melrose.

"Inevitably," his counsel promised and then gave Detweiler a hearty handshake with every evidence of honest feeling. "Thank you, Joe. Now let's go in to face the bench." He picked up a beautiful briefcase made of lizard skin. Once he got his way Melrose was not devious about showing his pleasure.

Chapter 16

TIERNEY asked his wife to return the fried eggs to the pan for a once over lightly to coagulate their mucosity. She was relentless about not doing this till requested: it was her quirk. But very little irritated Tierney when he was home. His profession drained him of spleen.

When Kath returned the eggs to his plate the yellows were quite hard, and as was his practice with solid yolks, he chopped up the eggs, added catsup, and stirred up the lot into a pink puree, which he spread on his toast. He would have preferred standard sunny-side-ups, firm whites, running yellows into which the toast might be dipped. But he made do. He was not Detweiler, with finicky tastes.

Katharine had got up earlier than he, to give Dennis and Mary breakfast and send them off to some church thing. John Michael, the baby, was still snoozing in his crib, in his parents' bedroom. They needed a larger apartment. Dennis' quarters were in what was supposed to be the dining room. The Tierneys therefore were not equipped to entertain. On holidays they went to Katharine's family, who now had retired to the suburbs. Except New Year's Eve, when Kath's brother James and wife held a regular get-together with relatives and friends.

Katharine had already eaten her breakfast, but had a cup of tea with Tierney while he chewed his. She had very dark hair but very white skin, was slender in outline but giving the impression of pudginess when touched. She had fat, motherly hands. Tierney reached across and patted the one not holding the teacup.

He said: "We'll see Jimmy tomorrow night, huh?" Kath was fond of all four of her brothers, but James, the oldest, was her favorite: he guyed her a lot, slapped her behind, made her blush: "Still pee in bed, kid?" Tierney didn't mind him, Jim being a goodnatured slob. Tierney's sister-in-law, however, made him nervous. Everybody got a little high at these New Year's functions, and men and women exchanged the ritual kisses at midnight; first, solemnly with their mates and then in a jokey manner with the others. Phyllis, Jim's wife, once stuck her tongue into Tierney's mouth, offending, frightening, and exciting him. She was the mother of two. This happened only once, but Tierney remained leery of her. Two nights afterward he had had a dream in which he watched Katharine French-kiss her brother.

Kath said now: "But tonight is New Year's Eve."

"Is it?" Tierney looked at the top of the newspaper. "I lost a day. I could have sworn—"

"Where does Time go?" Katharine asked idly.

"Why'd you ask that?"

Tierney's question had a violence to it, and Katharine showed surprise. She rose to fetch the coffee pot, not answering until she had filled his cup, one hand on the glass cap of the percolator, which was habitually loose.

"Another year will go down the drain," she said. "I hate the thought."

Tierney winced. "We brought in this psycho, you know." He took some coffee into his mouth and let it disappear.

"I saw the pictures this morning." Katharine pointed a spoon at the paper. "You won't like the one of you."

Tierney turned to the centerfold and saw his white face between black overcoat and gray hat. His eyes were caught at half-closure, and the caption of course did not identify him by name. The press generally respected the Department's wish to keep detectives anonymous, save the occasional publicity hound whose awesome reputation was supposed to discourage would-be wrongdoers and capture the imagination of the taxpayer: like Roughhouse Riordan, the Terror of the Underworld, who worked on special assignments. When thirty precinct officers trapped two punks in a cheap hotel and filled the premises with tear gas, Riordan might show up to make the arrest.

Shuster, if you already knew him, could also be made out in the upper left of the same photo, but the focus was on Detweiler and the police commissioner.

"Detweeler," said Katharine. "What kind of man would kill on Christmas Eve? He looks proud of himself, doesn't he?" She was being experimental, giving Tierney the opportunity to talk about the case if he wished. She was superstitious about his work because it was so exclusively masculine; she would have been the same if married to an airline pilot or a Marine.

Tierney had told her very little about the Starr murders, and the paper they took at home was not the one that printed Betty's story, but rather that of old Starr, which furthermore Katharine had not read, as, in loyalty, she never read any special newspaper series that pertained to police affairs.

She was really all wife and mother and gave Tierney no trouble whatever: he didn't mind the quirk about fried eggs and other minor matters.

He said: "He isn't proud. He's nuts."

Katharine answered quickly: "Is he actually, or is he just pretending?" Tierney was astonished to see that for once she opposed him, and in his own work.

He said: "Oh, you know all about it, do you, Kath?"

"I know I hate sex maniacs." Her face colored in anger. "And this town is crawling with them. You ride the subway and someone in the crowd pushes his lump into your backside. A man in a car showed his filthy thing to Dennis last week in the next block, in broad daylight last week."

"You didn't tell me."

"I never knew about it till yesterday."

"Had he seen him before? What kind of car? I don't suppose he got the number."

Kath waved her hands. "I know, a cop's son. . . . But do you realize why? He might have been scared, but he was also impressed, and I find out about it only because I caught him, himself, showing his little whatzis to Mary."

"Oh for Christ's sake," Tierney exclaimed. "I'll tan that little fart's behind for him. I'll teach him to be so fresh. His own sister."

"You maybe are missing the point," Katharine said. "His sister or someone else's. What is so spectacular in a man's anatomy that we all are supposed to be worshipful? Why are sex fiends permitted to roam the streets and even enter private houses and murder women?"

Tierney didn't like to hear that kind of talk from a cop's wife. For one thing, it lacked precision.

"Well, Kath," he said, "I have seldom seen you so worked up. You'd think they were your relatives. As it happens, if you like to know, Detweiler is not a sex fiend. He's even a bit of a Puritan. He didn't have relations with those women: he strangled them and that was that. He's crazy. And it might surprise you but he's quite religious."

"Don't tell me he's Catholic," Katharine stated spitefully, "because never have I made a claim that—"

"No," Tierney interrupted, "he's all by himself in faith, but as to his moral principles, I'll tell you something funny, he has a way about him—you might find this hard to accept, and I wouldn't mention it to anybody else; Shuster for example—"

"I never thought I would hear you defending a criminal."

"You haven't heard what I was going to say."

"But he killed *women,* did he not? The dirty pervert."

"Kath, I have been on this case for a week now and I didn't hear you say a word till the present."

"You never caught him till now," said Katharine. "I never saw him until the picture this morning. Look at him, little washed-out piece of nothing. I've seen them on the subways, squeezing up against you, knee between your legs." She pushed her saucer so that the cup wobbled within it, and said: "Sex criminals are always men. You cannot deny it."

"Not true," said Tierney. "There was a woman in the Tenth Precinct two years ago who molested her own children."

"The exception that proves the rule," Katharine said.

"Women," Tierney said passionately, "rape men in a different, deceitful way, and no amount of bodily exposure is ever considered indecent by them. There are women in this city who wear gray-flannel suits and smoke cigars; they neck in public with their girl friends. Anybody from the Vice Squad can tell you enough about female offenders to raise your hair. You don't know these things, Kath. You've lived a protected life."

Katharine gave a dirty laugh, strangely reminiscent of Shuster's. "No woman who lives in this hell-hole of a city is protected."

In view of Tierney's calling, this was a real provocation. They hardly ever quarreled, and never before on a matter which referred to law enforcement. It was also a revelation to Tierney, after years of marriage, that Katharine, sister of four men, daughter of one, wife of one, mother of two, could level a charge against the breed. And how easily she had dismissed the incestuous feature of Denny's displaying himself to his own sister. Brother Jim slapped her butt, joked intimately of her childhood bed-wetting: these things could be given a sinister interpretation were Tierney as rash as she. But he of course was not. Whatever their flaws as individuals, as a race men were peculiarly committed to justice. You could see this even in professional hoods, who defied the law but understood it.

Tierney now had to consider whether he did not feel more at ease with a male criminal than with any woman. He had never had a sister; his parents were killed in a railway accident when he was a child, and he had been raised by an aunt and uncle, whom he nowadays rarely saw. He hardly remembered his mother.

Without warning Katharine returned to her old role. She covered her mouth to yawn. Through her fingers she said: "Well, it's none of my affair. It's your job."

And as suddenly, Tierney felt an unbearable desolation. "I wonder if it's a job for a man," meaning in this sense a human being and not a sexual differentiation. The weird feature was that a moment later he did not know whether he had spoken aloud or expressed it to himself. No response came from Katharine, who collected their cups and delivered them to the sink. It was all the worse if he had thought, and not said, it.

He went into the bedroom, fetched his pistol from under the pillow on his side of the bed, collected the handcuffs and leather-braided sap from the dresser, leaned over the crib and kissed the baby's translucent forehead. John Michael as yet had very pale hair, even more fair than Detweiler's.

Tierney took his overcoat and hat from a shallow closet in the hall. From there he had a direct view to the kitchen and the back of Katharine's cardigan and bowtied apron strings. It was superstition with him never to kiss her goodbye when he went to work: his was one of those trades, like auto racing, in which it is bad luck to wish good.

He called: "So long, Kath."

She turned and said: "Oh, that informant phoned again last night, real late. I just remembered."

Tierney asked: "The woman?"

"Yeah," Katharine said. She waved a dishcloth at him. "O.K., I'll see you when I see you. If you're on late, you can come right to Jimmy's."

"Sure," said Tierney. "I'll be talking to you."

He drove south for a few blocks through a gray morning with a low, oppressive ceiling that would soon release either a cold rain or a tepid snow, the temperature being definitely above 32° F. His hands were too warm in his Christmas gloves, gift of Katharine, and he unsheathed them after he parked the car, tossing the pigskin gloves, still bright orange on the backs but already palm-blackened, onto the passenger's seat.

He went into a drugstore and entered a phone booth. A deskman at Betty's hotel told him the Baysons had checked out the day before. The forwarding address was that of their home, in the near suburbs. Tierney already had that, and the home phone number, in his notebook, dating from his first interview with her on Christmas Eve.

The line came alive after half a ring, and a weighty voice said: "This is the police."

"What?" asked Tierney. "Who's talking?" He gave his name.

"It's about damn time," the voice responded, as heavy but less ominously.

"Who is this?"

"Arthur Bayson. What kind of protection do you people provide, anyway? All night we've been trying to reach you. We have been enduring a reign of terror."

Tierney had been apprehensive until now, fearing Betty had been trying to invade his home by telephone, on some private matter: this was the only sort of menace that scared him. However, the word "terror" in Arthur's use surely signified that which in Tierney's job was routine. Therefore he was back at work again, investigating the irregularities of others, his own superseded.

Arthur proceeded to explain, and as usual with civilians, he had exaggerated: the "reign of terror" consisted of some crank phone calls. The Baysons were of course listed in the phone book, and now famous. "A target," said Arthur. "This is our home. We have no place to hide."

Tierney said: "The telephone company will give you a new number."

"Absolutely no," Arthur answered indignantly. "I refuse to run, to be run out of my own home. It's up to you to take measures."

Tierney had a feeling he would say, "You got us into this," but Arthur merely created the implication, then said: "Where were you all night? I don't keep guns around the house—I don't hunt or anything. We've got oil heat here, don't even have a poker. I sat up till dawn with a butcher knife."

Tierney said: "Generally speaking, the type of person who makes threatening calls doesn't carry through. Usually he's yellow, which is why he phones. If he was serious he wouldn't tip you off."

"I don't want to hear rationalizations," Arthur said in the kind of voice that might be accompanied by a stamping foot: his tone was deep but his rhythm almost girlish. "I don't intend to argue the matter, mister. You're a public servant, and you can damn well do your duty for a change. Or are you looking for a handout?"

"I'll tell you one thing, Mr. Bayson. Nothing in the city ordinances calls for me to listen to that kind of talk. You should have called your local police last night. That's not my jurisdiction, and I'm not your private bodyguard."

"But this man," Arthur shouted, "this anonymous caller says he committed the murders, that Detweiler is the wrong one, that he will get us next. My wife is sick with fear, in bed, incapacitated. We feel trapped here, under observation from hidden eyes. There's a vacant lot in back. I see a glint there, movement: he could be in that old shed. A high-powered rifle, telescopic sights: he could get us at a window. I'm unarmed. I'm an office worker. I'm not trained for violence."

"Now calm down," Tierney said mechanically. "It's probably your imagination."

Arthur shouted: "Are you prepared to guarantee that?"

"Well, naturally I can't—"

"You're not God, are you, Tierney?"

This seemed to Tierney a very strange query, in view of his recent dialogue with Detweiler, though of course Arthur would not have had that in view: it was a common enough expression of democratic reminder, signifying "Who do you think you are?", the basic city question, leadenly secular, bleakly atheist though as often asked by churchgoers as any other. Tierney had himself asked it of Detweiler. Only now did he appreciate its meanness, its total denial of possibility, its frightened envy, its loser's idiom. For the first time he considered whether Detweiler might not be a better man than his victims, not only the dead but the living; this insane murderer, this generous wretch.

The thought made him more tolerant of Bayson, who after all was a civilian and under pressure. He was also thinking of Betty: in bed, prostrate with fear? Tierney found it unlikely, but attractive.

He said: "All right. I'll come over. If you get any more calls, try to keep him on the phone."

Arthur gave a nervous laugh, then seemed immediately to relax.

"You're probably right," he said. "Imagination. But the calls were real enough. . . . There is somebody in the vacant lot: a kid, playing. I see him now."

"You still want me to come over?"

"Of course," said Bayson. "I think you owe it to Betty."

A cryptic remark if he ever heard one. Tierney called headquarters and left word for Shuster where he would be. Then he returned to his car and saw that his gloves had been stolen. Naturally he had not locked the doors. The vehicle was his own property and bore no special markings, but thieves could generally tell a detective's car from the aura or aroma. No likely prospect was in view. The shop nearest the car was a barber's, two-chair but, early as it was, only one man in attendance. He was of course Italian; answered "Nuh" to Tierney's questions, saw nobody near the automobile.

Bastard, thought Tierney, meaning the barber, who had probably watched the theft with pleasure, recognizing Tierney as an officer; small shopkeepers often had a grudge against the Force during the holidays, when the beat cops shook them down for Xmas remembrances.

Tierney drove away. He would not report this petty larceny to the precinct. He passed a park, the locus, in better weather, of crimes of violence; but now not only the season but the time of day maintained the peace. Felonies were fairly rare from dawn to about 10:30-11 A.M. Even criminals took a while to warm up, wipe the sand from their eyes. Parks held little interest for Tierney in whatever weather except insofar as who might be lurking therein, though he approved of trees and birds: he might take the family on a picnic next spring.

Thirty-odd minutes later he found the Bayson residence on a street that was rural to his eyes: little houses, the vacant lot that Arthur had mentioned, the old shed or garage, and likewise the kid.

This punk, eleven or twelve, had a rifle. Tierney left the car and advanced, opening his overcoat and suit jacket; he did not expect to need his pistol, but there was a cardinal rule that anyone holding a firearm, be they babies, little old ladies, or orangutans, should be approached with caution.

The weapon turned out to be a BB gun.

"What are you doing out of school, son?" Tierney asked sternly.

The boy wore a knitted wool cap with a pompom at the summit. A scarf was wound many times around his throat. Near his mouth it was wettened. His eyes had difficulty in maintaining a consistent direction.

He said thickly, and with no evidence of feeling: "I'll kill you. I'll burn down the shed." He was an idiot.

Tierney disarmed him easily, but finding where he lived was a problem. "Come on," he said, "let's go home and have some milk and cookies."

"You motherfucker," said the boy, again without feeling, and his nose began to run. Tierney fetched out his own handkerchief and applied it. The boy blew his nose, then seized the handkerchief and kept it. The second personal article lost by Tierney within the hour.

Tierney took the boy's hand and led him out to the sidewalk. Presumably he lived down the street, the Bayson house being the last on the block. As they passed he saw Arthur peeping through the closed drapes.

"I'm going to eat some dogshit," the boy said.

"I'll bet this is your house," said Tierney, choosing one at random so as to provoke the child into a confession. By chance it was the right one.

The boy said: "My cat," pointing to a tiger-striped animal rubbing its ribs on a porch pillar.

But the woman who answered the door directed Tierney

three houses down. The boy suddenly spoke with clarity: "Stupid! My cat, not my house."

"No, it isn't your cat either," the woman said sweetly.

"Cock and balls," chirped the boy, and Tierney pulled him down the steps.

At the correct door at last, Tierney was greeted by a youngish woman: "Hi! He get in trouble?"

"No," said Tierney, "but I don't think you should let this boy play with an air rifle."

"Why not? All the boys have them." The woman cocked her head and stared suspiciously, though also with humor, at him. "Who are you?"

"A police officer."

"I wasn't doing anything at all, Momma," the boy said self-reliantly. "He just came and bothered me." He was no longer glassy-eyed and wet-mouthed.

Tierney got the picture: he had been hoaxed. He moved quickly to say—but not before the woman lost the last suggestion of amusement and clutched her son indignantly—"Why isn't he in school?"

She sent her boy into the house. "I sure find something funny about a policeman who hasn't heard of Christmas vacation."

Then where were Dennis and Mary? Oh yeah, something at the church, rehearsal for some pageant or the like. Catholic kids always had obligations. Father Healey would catch him after the show and remind him of the masses he had missed. Healey was a former police chaplain and knew few homicides were committed on Sunday before noon.

When Tierney was young he had thought about going into the priesthood. What decided him against it was his disbelief in divinity. The nearest secular institution was the police force. "You are terribly naive," he was told by an old boyhood pal who had become a cleric after an early term as precocious cocksman, drunk, delinquent. "It's the doubters who do best. Anyway, if you don't believe in God how can you enforce the law?" He was one of those cheerful bastards, spouting paradoxes, teaching at some Jesuit academy for the sons of the rich. Tierney wondered if he had turned queer: it was a useful switch for philosophers, enabling them to reverse meanings at will, to be provocative, amusing, and aesthetic, like old Socrates, turning everybody else's remarks inside out and then going to bed with a boy.

When the real question was: How could you respect the law if you believed in God? Unless, like Detweiler, you also believed yourself divine. Tell me that.

"Tell you what?" the woman asked shrilly.

He must have spoken aloud. He was cracking up, on the last day of the old vear. He shook himself together.

"Tell me why he was lurking in that vacant lot. This is serious, lady. We have reports of a prowler around the Bayson house last night. Was your boy out after dark?"

Then the woman said a curious thing, in the light of Tierney's own earlier thought at the breakfast table.

"Why don't you get a man's job? Meanwhile, if you want to grill my son, come back with a warrant." She snatched up the air rifle and marched inside, slamming the door.

There was no way to handle a woman if you ran out of bluff. A policewoman was always present at the interrogation of a female suspect, to protect the male officers. Tierney dreaded seeing Betty again; unreflectively he had been postponing the confrontation. It would not have been so bad if he had really made love to her, with her; or simply but genuinely screwed her. As it was, he didn't know what he had done except briefly to lose possession of his .38.

The bell button was behind the screen door, and not only was the screen door in place on 31 December, but it was locked fast. Arthur finally peeped through the drapes again, like a neighborhood snoop. Tierney gestured impatiently and was let in.

He had forgotten Arthur was larger than he by several inches and at least twenty pounds: a big, soft but not fat man. Not that Tierney was all muscle, but he was organized. But this was Bayson's home and Tierney a kind of interloper. Tierney removed his hat and tried to breathe the superheated air. He could smell but not see cigarette smoke, and it was the more nauseating for the mystery of its source, which was not a mystery at all. Betty was lurking somewhere within. Arthur did not smoke.

Arthur said: "I saw you with that kid. Do you suppose the anonymous caller could have been him, changing his voice?"

"What did the voice sound like?"

"Gravel-throated, according to Betty," said Arthur. "I never talked to him, actually." He hastened to add: "She insisted, wouldn't let me. She was the one who knew Detweiler, she said. It was her mother and sister who were murdered. I haven't had much of a part in this whole thing!"

Arthur had ended on a whine, and looked very much as if he would burst into tears. His style disgusted Tierney, yet Tierney felt a sympathy for him. It was easy to say that Arthur should give Betty a swift kick in the ass, but if he were that sort he would not have married her in the first place.

At that point Arthur struck Tierney in the jaw. Either Arthur was even weaker than Tierney had thought, or the blow was intended to be but symbolic, for it had no effect on Tierney's physical attitude, except to produce a faint grin. Spiritually Tierney was shocked, astounded that he did not in reflex hit Arthur back. Instead he sat down passively in a bright green armchair. Everything in the room was new and in solid colors. The rug was a light tan, unfigured, almost blond, the kind that would show anything tracked in from outdoors, and Tierney's shoes were filthy from the vacant lot. He had left a trail of mud or maybe even excrement, though he would have smelled that in this stifling atmosphere. He began to wonder whether Arthur had really hit him, or if so, perhaps in accident, developing a gesture. He was in the man's house, and the man was a respectable citizen. In a dark alley, in a tenement hallway, Tierney might already have blown out his assailant's navel. Detweiler was wrong about time: it was *place* that mattered.

Arthur suddenly trembled.

He said: "I apologize. You are a guest in my home. That was unforgivable. We should have stepped outside. . . . I, I don't have experience in these matters."

"You don't?" Tierney asked numbly.

"Well, that's a pretty cynical question," Arthur said, regaining self-possession. "You better get up. I'm going to have to hit you again." He walked arrogantly towards Tierney's chair.

But now Tierney was prepared. He rose and seizing Arthur's right wrist whipped it behind the man's back and jerked it upwards. Then he tripped Arthur and fell with him, on him, knelt on him, knee against his sacroiliac.

"Now what have you got to say for yourself?" asked Tierney.

Arthur spoke with difficulty, into the carpet.

Tierney said: "Huh?" He kept his knee against Arthur's spine, but he took some tension off the bent arm.

Arthur said: ". . . defend my honor."

Tierney sensed Arthur was using the term in a fantasy or literary way, playing a role—which of course did not mean he wasn't sincere. But to talk of honor as being personal was highly unrealistic. Honor for Tierney had no meaning when so disembodied, though he could well understand the honor of the school, the honor of the Department, and so on, something beyond the limitations of the individual, who will die; but institutions are immortal.

Arthur might be another psychopath, but he was probably harmless. Tierney frisked him as long as he was down, of course found no weapons, climbed off him, and Arthur got up.

Arthur said: "That wasn't easy for me to do. It may sound odd to you, in your line, but I have never before in my life hit another person except in fun—you know, with an old pal, you give him a poke. I have a temper. I can quarrel vocally, but—"

The effort seemed to have taxed Tierney more than it did Arthur. Tierney was breathing hard and he had a soreness of nerves.

He gulped a mouthful of air and said: "Are you crazy? What in hell was the idea of that?"

"Just to let you know you can't make a fool of me and get away with it," Arthur said almost buoyantly. He rubbed the fist that had struck Tierney, ignoring the adjoining arm which Tierney had twisted. He remembered only his own assertion of force, and Tierney found that hard to take.

Arthur proudly went on: "If you love my wife, stand up like a man and admit it to my face. Don't sneak around like a common cur."

"Oh Christ," said Tierney. "Did you get me over here for that?" He was stunned. He sat down again in the pea-green chair.

Arthur professed shock: "Certainly not! Those calls were real."

"How do you know?" asked Tierney. "You didn't take them. You said that. Maybe your wife was lying to you."

"But the phone rang. I heard it."

Tierney looked at the ceiling.

Arthur said: "I get your drift. You think Betty told me something about you, and you are trying to destroy her credibility. . . . That's even cheaper than I suspected you would be. I even feel sorry for you: you're at a complete loss in the respectable world. I am trying to understand your attraction for Betty. I have heard that women often like crudeness, brutality, bad manners. But I don't think that's the explanation in this case: I think she feels sorry for you."

All at once Arthur lost the confidence he had gained in striking a detective for a morals offense. Pain suffused his face. He fell into the rust-colored sofa and propped up the heels of his large shoes in the piling of the rug.

He said pitifully: "Can we talk man to man?"

"No," said Tierney. "I'm not going to let you make any more of an ass of yourself. I haven't touched your wife. We were together the other day on official police business. I make out a report on everything I do and every place I go, according to departmental regulations. Those reports are on file at headquarters. While Mrs. Bayson and I were in the Starr apartment, a uniformed patrolman was present at all times, Officer Spinelli. I am married and have a fine wife and family, Mr. Bayson." Tierney got his wallet out. Had he not been guilty he would certainly not have gone to this trouble, but Arthur couldn't know that. He was not certain of what Arthur did know, of what Betty might have told him, but he found the snapshot of his wife and children and held it up, intending merely to flash it as if it were his badge, but Arthur claimed it with outstretched hand.

Arthur studied the photograph. At last he returned it. He seemed none the worse for having been thrown to the floor.

Contritely he said: "Forget everything I mentioned. Forgive me if you can. I should have known it was a nervous reaction. The effects of violence radiate out from the act itself, in ever-widening circles like a stone thrown into a pond. Someone is killed, but a score of other people are poisoned by the vibrations."

In relief Tierney chose to take this seriously, this pompous crap. He smiled, and said: "If that is true, then we're all in trouble, because the homicide rate in the city is two per day."

"Maybe we all died long ago and don't know it," Arthur stated gloomily. But then vigorously he rose from the couch, fetched from the hall closet, and donned, his hat and coat.

He said: "Well, I have to get to work. I have to get back to normal. They'll have an office party this afternoon, but I'll find a quiet corner. Work: that's the answer."

Tierney went into the hall. "Give you a ride downtown," he said.

Arthur looked at him narrowly. "No. You must see Betty." He pointed up the staircase.

Tierney felt as if once again he had been stripped of his pants by a Bayson.

Arthur went on. "I can't leave her here alone in view of those calls. All right, you and I know it's some harmless crank. But doesn't Detweiler seem harmless? In the papers he looks like some kid caught stealing apples. What's he like in the flesh?" He did not wait for Tierney's answer, which was just as well. "God, the people you have to deal with in your work. How can you stand it day in and day out? But then how can doctors stand blood and pus."

"It's the contrast," said Tierney.

Arthur exclaimed: "Oh?" Just that. He did not ask between what and what, so Tierney did not tell him. Besides, Tierney did not know. Actuality and appearance? Respectability versus disorder? Realism as opposed to idealism? Perhaps merely the contrast between home and the world outside: each gave one, if one was a man, a taste for the other. This feeling was also no doubt common to pilots, deep-sea divers, and soldiers. Peculiar to Tierney's profession was the enemy: one's fellow townsfolk.

But it was not peculiar; that was also true of the profession of crime.

Tierney said to Arthur as the latter's hand groped for the doorknob: "I can't stay here. I'll call the police."

Arthur seemed desperate to get away. "All right, all right," he said. "I know you're a responsible individual." Descending the porch steps, he shouted: "I have to get back to normal!" In a moment he shot out of the driveway in his small car; probably would drive as near as he could to the subway station and park there all day, and if he got a ticket he would return to his paranoia about the police force.

But Tierney was no longer contemptuous of Arthur. It took guts for an accountant to hit a cop whatever the reason: few hoods had the stomach for it. As a precinct detective Tierney had once singlehandedly apprehended a gang of four armed robbers burgling a pawnshop. Of course he was holding a gun on them and would have shot at the first surly look. But they were spreadeagled against the wall and trembling, and he was the Law.

Betty's voice was very clear as it came down the stairwell: "Tierney, is that you?"

He climbed the stairs and found her room, which was probably also Arthur's though little could be seen of his property. Nevertheless the bedchamber was not markedly feminine: for example, there were no little bedside lamps shaped like bonnets, nothing colored pink. Betty was sitting up in bed. Maybe she really was frightened: her hair was not arranged and she wore no make-up. Without artifice she looked both plainer and younger. Her night clothes were modest pajamas.

Tierney asked: "Have you got any calls yet today?"

"Not since dawn," she said. "Are you sure Joe Detweiler is the right one?"

"He confessed. There isn't any doubt. You always get these cranks after a murder. Somebody else spills the blood and then they come around like flies. Every time they turn out to be people who would not walk against a red light. They are the people who get their sex from dirty pictures, filthy talk, and daydreams, their violence from the newspaper."

"Has Arthur gone?"

"Yes," Tierney said. As always when intimately quartered with Betty, he wore his overcoat. But he was always on the point of leaving her presence, or so it seemed; the moment took forever to arrive, the suspense built. "You should have let him answer the phone. A man's voice might have scared the pervert off."

"The calls were for me," said Betty. "It was my responsibility. He read my articles, you see. I was taken in at first. He described himself as a book publisher. He flattered me, said maybe I could do a full-length book on the basis of the newspaper stuff. Naturally, I was excited. We made an appointment—"

"Specific time and place?"

"Noon today, at a restaurant in midtown. I wrote it down somewhere. He said his name was Chester Cookson."

"That would be a phony and he won't show up," Tierney said. "But we'll check it out anyway. There might just be a real Chester Cookson who is a publisher, and this guy once worked for him or something and developed a grudge and is using his name for revenge."

"Well, anyway I broke the date," Betty said with what Tierney suddenly recognized as pride rather than indignation, and he confirmed this feeling as she went on. "The thing that took me in was he had really read the articles. Talked about them in detail. He must be educated. His accent was cultivated; you might almost say English. He said, 'Well, then, I look forward to meeting you, Mrs. Bayson. I think this will result in a profit for both of us.' 'Thank you,' I said, 'and goodbye,' and was in the act of hanging up when—had the phone away from my ear when I heard his voice still crackling in it. I brought it up again and said: 'Oh, excuse me, I was just—' and he said: 'We'll have a delicious lunch and then we'll—' "

Betty had stopped and was looking suspensefully at Tierney. Who said: "And then came the indecent proposal."

"Yes. I suppose I should tell you exactly what was said."

Tierney felt himself blush; at least his face rushed with warmth. He said: "No, that's not necessary except if the guy is caught and you have to testify against him."

"It was something abnormal," said Betty. "He would do it to me, then I would do it to him, and then he said he would strangle me for being so nasty. I couldn't believe my ears. I guess I got hysterical. I just kept asking: 'Mr. Cookson? Mr. Cookson?'

"He said: 'I strangled your mother and your sister. I'll get you next. I hate whores.'"

It was Tierney, and not Betty, who could not stand her going on. "All right, all right," he said, putting up his hand. "I take it he called several times again throughout the night. I'm going to contact the telephone company and get you an unlisted number. If this guy quits there might be others. It will all die down in a week or two, but there may be a recurrence when the Detweiler trial comes up. If you get any obscene or threatening mail, be sure to turn it in to the Department." He looked around the room. "Where is your phone?"

"In the dining room downstairs."

"No extensions up here?"

She shook her head.

"You've been running downstairs all night?"

"Oh no. I sat up."

Tierney shrugged. "Never thought of taking the phone off the hook?"

It was her turn to look embarrassed, which she did by pretending Tierney's question was irrelevant. She went back of her head with both hands to adjust the pillow.

"Never occurred to you?" he asked.

Her exhausted eyes were all at once spirited and then hard. She said: "Don't ride me, Tierney."

Until this moment it had all been legitimate police business. He said: "I don't want you calling my home."

"Why not?" she responded. "*He* calls mine. Why should you get off scot-free?"

"I have the damnedest feeling about you," said Tierney. "You seem to be jealous of me. Far more so than your husband is. Why don't you take the examination for policewoman?"

She stared at him for a while, and then asked: "How is Joe?"

Tierney said brutally: "He went to the apartment on Christmas Eve to kill you."

She smiled. "Don't try to provoke me, Tierney. Just be your own sweet, considerate self. Nothing could be more tiresome than that."

She did not believe him. At last Tierney had discovered the breech in her defenses.

He said: "I'm giving it to you straight. Detweiler went there expecting to find you and kill you. You weren't there, so he strangled Mrs. Starr, and then Billie came home and he had to kill her so she would not be upset by her mother's death."

Betty cocked her head, and Tierney explained that this was the situation from Detweiler's point of view. He omitted mention of the subsequent version, taken down by the D.A.'s staff detectives.

She said: "If you listen to a psychopath you might hear anything."

Tierney laughed sourly. "He confessed to the murders, so he has no reason to lie about the rest—unless it would be to find some mitigating circumstances, but this is hardly that. He admits he went there intending to commit a homicide."

Betty said smugly: "Me? But he loves me."

"That's as good a reason as any." Tierney was no longer under the pressure of captivity. He now felt a freedom to come and go as he liked, and decided, freely, to stay awhile. He took off his coat and threw it across a chair.

He asked: "Did you really get those anonymous calls?"

"Of course," said Betty incredulously. And then: "I gather Joe made a favorable impression on you. He's craftier than I thought. And I was feeling sorry for him!"

Tierney said: "There is something likable about him. I've been trying to figure out what. I've dealt with psychos before. They're no novelty. They're always people who don't want to pay the price for services rendered, spiritual deadbeats. 'Give me love, give me understanding and tolerance, forgive me because I can't help it, I'm warped.'

"But Detweiler doesn't ask for anything—except special orders of food. He manages to believe he already has the approval of everybody. He has no sense of shame. He was trying to convince *me* that he should plead guilty to first-degree homicide. For *my* sake. As if I was the one who needed help." It was reasonable that Tierney could talk to Betty on this subject, as he could not with his own wife. Betty was involved.

"Maybe you are," Betty said now. "Aren't you afraid to be anything but a policeman?"

So Tierney got into bed with her, and really had her this time, but it seemed a type of duty and he could not have said it gave him pleasure or a sense of accomplishment.

The pervert never called again, or if he did Betty failed to report it.

Chapter 17

EARLY IN the new year Detweiler was indicted by the grand jury for murder in the first degree, and Melrose and the district attorney began opposing efforts concerning the state of Detweiler's mind insofar as it was germane to the issues. What both sides had in common was their exclusive interest in the law. Religious and metaphysical aspects were beside the point, though the D.A. was an agnostic who regularly attended Episcopalian services and Melrose was a nonchurchgoing believer. Medical judgment, however, would be appropriate, but only as to whether Detweiler was capable of distinguishing right from wrong: so this inquiry, too, had limitations of legality.

Melrose explained the situation to Detweiler on one of his visits to the city jail.

Detweiler said: "Looking at life in terms of the law is rather narrow, isn't it?"

"Of course," Melrose answered. "Life is so various, has so many phases that to cope with it we must divide it up into limited, manageable segments." He had sworn to himself not to get involved in philosophical discussion with Detweiler, but in a very basic way the lawyer's profession was pedagogical: he taught the jury, who were presumed to be in a state of pure ignorance. Altogether to resist Detweiler's infantile quest for knowledge Melrose would have had to be another man.

Melrose said: "Now let's get down to business. You are interested in time, and law is nothing if not temporal. By which I don't mean it's up to the minute, however. What concerns us in this case is a precedent set in the year 1843 and in another country."

"Historical, then," said Detweiler.

"With a vengeance. In that year, in England, a man named Daniel M'Naghten, who is said to have had the paranoid delusion that a conspiracy of persons headed by Sir Robert Peel, the prime minister, were out to do him harm, shot and killed Peel's secretary—apparently by mistake, his intended victim being Sir Robert. M'Naghten entered a plea of insanity. He was tried and acquitted on that ground."

Detweiler said: "He sounds crazy, to get the wrong man that way."

Melrose felt the huge, triangular knot of his golden tie. "You always have a novel perspective," he said. "My own tendency would be to say that whether or not he was mentally deranged would have to do with his belief in the hostile conspiracy against him, led by the head of state. M'Naghten was a rather obscure individual."

"Yet you remember his name."

Melrose admitted that fact to be incontestable. "But not primarily because he was defendant in this trial. M'Naghten himself is historically of little importance. His name merely provides the designation for the formula subsequently drawn up to define legal insanity, 'To establish a defense on the ground of insanity, it must be clearly proved that, at the time of committing the act, the party accused was laboring under such a defect of reason, from disease of the mind, as not to know the nature and quality of the act he was doing, or if he did know it, that he did not know he was doing what was wrong.' "

"That is certainly clear," said Detweiler. "And obviously M'Naghten did not know what he was doing if he shot the wrong man."

"I wonder if you get the point," asked Melrose.

"There's no question about the morality: it is wrong to kill, but I was thinking of M Naghten, the man and not the Rule. How strange it must have seemed to him. Whether he was right about the conspiracy turned out to be irrelevant in the light of Time. He set out to achieve a certain end, failed, and became a historical principle."

"No," Melrose said relentlessly, "you haven't got it. The law in this state is still based on the M'Naghten Rule."

"You know," Detweiler said, "it strikes me that the Law is pretty fair. It punishes only those people who agree with it and doesn't waste its time on the fellow who is thoroughly independent. Rather goodhumoredly it calls him crazy and excuses what he does."

"On the assumption that he cannot help himself," said Melrose. "Punishment is supposed to deter other people from committing the same crime, but presumably it would not deter such a man as M'Naghten, who cannot control himself. To punish him for committing an act which he doesn't understand is criminal would be merely vengeance."

"Call it what you will," Detweiler said. "If he were executed, he could not kill again in this life. I think in that respect the law is tolerant to the point of irresponsibility. The alternative isn't vengeance; it's simply common sense; it's order, and if the Law doesn't provide that, what good is it?"

Melrose said, "I tell you frankly, Joe, whether you like it or not I'm going to prove to the satisfaction of the jury that you are legally insane."

They were sitting at a little table in a counselor's room, or cell. Detweiler could not get at him in that situation, so the killer stood up. However, he decided to make one last plea to Melrose.

"Look," he said, "if I am judged to be crazy, then everything I believe in, all my work, will be thought insane too. I can't let that happen and become just another maniac like M'Naghten, maybe giving my name to another Rule that is as nutty as the first one. Why is not knowing the difference between right and wrong an excuse? Nature gives no such immunity. You will be killed by a hungry man-eating tiger irrespective of whether you know he is harmless. Killing as such is neither here nor there; it is a natural function. But if you start to arrange it rationally, then you should be consistent. If it is wrong for one citizen, then it is wrong for the next. No wonder there is a lack of respect for the Law among certain elements. If it is to be interpreted by means of tricks and illusions, then the clever will have the edge, and by that I specifically mean you, Mr. Melrose, men who deal in language.

"But killing is not a word. It is an act. It has nothing to do with speech; it is more like running or swimming. It is pure motion, and then a halt. There is little in common to saying the word 'light' and then looking at the sun.

"I'm not disparaging language, though. Beautiful things can be done with it, points can be made."

"In fact, said Melrose laconically, "you're using it now, aren't you."

"Well, I tried," Detweiler said, "but to outdo you in the area of your specialty is not likely even for another lawyer: your record proves that. I can only put the argument in my own way. Unfortunately, there will be some pain, but I guess hurting is always part of learning."

He seized Melrose's thick neck, just above the lovely lemon-yellow shirt collar. His fingers were too short to meet around the stout pillar, but they dug in at the sides, and his thumbs pressed together against the windpipe. Every strangulation was different and revealed certain qualities of the victim hitherto unnoticed: Mrs. Starr had a finer throat than Billie despite the disparity in age; Melrose's had looked fat, but proved solid, massive, with great tendons and robust musculature, owing probably to all his speaking. His eyes were of rich amber-brown. He had profound jaws, with the beginnings of dewlaps like some noble dog. His color, normally high, was darkening interestingly against his crown of white hair. He was shaven immaculately, no stubble under the nose or at the lip-ends. Detweiler was really fascinated.

Melrose had never been seized by the throat his life long. He had not engaged in physical violence since boyhood, and then, undersized, he did not favor it as a mode of intercourse with his fellow creatures, as he had implied in the story he told Detweiler on their first meeting. Later he had fleshed out, but from his early twenties onward he had rarely taken any exercise worth the name. He habitually ate rich foods and drank hearty wines. In the bathtub he was not as sleek as when buttoned into his English suits. He was corpulent, his blood pressure ran high, and any quickening of foot pace cost him an effort in breath. He had never received instruction in techniques of self-defense.

Added to these disadvantages, his present role as victim of an attack was an absolute reversal of values to him and hence severely shocking; his profession was to be above the battle.

Nonetheless, no sooner had Detweiler's fingertips made contact with his neck than Melrose was at work, formulating new arguments, considering how best to use this latest evidence that Detweiler was mad, so mad he would assault his own lawyer for trying to save his life, a fact that would impress any jury, all the more so because it was inadmissible. One of Melrose's great specialties was fixing in the minds of jurors that which was stricken from the record. In consequence the transcripts of his victories were often lifeless. His was an evanescent art. Future generations of law students, poring over the records, would get little sense of his quality: tone, attire, attitude of body, inclination of head, response to the very temperature of the courtroom—he could perspire at will, if in so doing he might establish an affinity with the inhabitants of an overheated jury box; though when under the incendiary attack by a prosecutor who was roasting a defense witness, Melrose could sit cool as a gray rock splashed by white surf. All this was lost to Time, like the sound of Paganini's violin.

But he who could not accept transience was mad. Had not Melrose possessed an absolute command of his faculties, he, a man of the moment, might have been rendered timeless thereupon. But a maniac could not cope; and if he seemed to be doing so, he should be thwarted. This was Melrose's thesis, and he would live to prove it.

He rose against the pressure, and with difficulty, because his suit had not been cut to facilitate that type of action, he raised both arms, joined his hands to form a large, compound fist, and brought this natural weapon down with great force upon the crown of Detweiler's pale head.

Immediately Detweiler lost his grasp and stood stunned, like a bird who had crashed into a window, blinking, motionless. Now that the clutching fingers had gone, Melrose could feel their ten discrete points of place, as if his neck were serrated. He adjusted his collar. Detweiler remained in the condition of a toy man that does something at the touch of a button and ceases on a similar signal. Melrose pushed him into a chair.

This had all been quietly managed from the beginning. The guard was out of sight beyond the door, to ensure the privacy of lawyer-client relations. He would have heard not even a grunt or gasp.

Detweiler finally raised his guileless eyes to Melrose's and said, sleepily: "Wow. Have I got a headache."

Melrose said: "I've got a sore throat."

Detweiler closed his eyes and breathed ten or twelve times and appeared to be exerting a tension on the muscles of his thorax. Then he lowered himself to the floor and proceeded to stand on his head.

"O.K.," he said, springing up. "It might interest you to know that I am training for the electric chair. You see, it is my theory that what kills is the shock of thousands of volts suddenly introduced into the body—not the electricity itself, not the flow, but the initial impact. If one could survive that, the body would serve as a conductor, and the current would circulate through it and return to the chair. But you probably believe that that sort of opinion makes me crazy."

Melrose gingerly touched his own neck, found a polka dot of pain and winced. "As if I needed any further evidence! First, you have stated you had no real motive for killing Mrs. Starr or Billie. Next you say: but it wasn't murder. Then you want to plead guilty to first-degree homicide and be executed. Finally, you say you can short-circuit the electric chair and render it harmless."

"I don't know," Detweiler said, "I have to keep in motion, to meet various challenges as they appear, changing conditions. Time is ever on the move. Try to catch it in one place, it flees to another. I know I ought to be despondent, but usually I can't overwhelm my joy."

"At what?"

"At things the way they are, were, and will be," Detweiler said. "At the profusion of life and its persistence. At Time, bitter adversary and yet much beloved."

Melrose offered to shake his hand, saying: "My congratulations."

Detweiler noted: "I hope there's no hard feelings because I tried to kill you. It was just an idea."

Melrose said: "I find your attempt on my life easiest of all to forgive. What I hold against you is your lack of discrimination."

"You mean, I might do the same for anybody?"

"Exactly."

"So," said Detweiler, "that's really why you think I'm crazy."

Melrose was still shaking Detweiler's hand. He now returned it to him, having no reason to believe the killer would ever retract it on his own. Detweiler specialized in making himself available.

Melrose said: "The astonishing thing is that we somehow do end up in agreement. . . . I'm going to send some psychiatrists down to see you, Joe, and I want you to cooperate with them because we will need their testimony in court. Now, at the same time, I suspect the state will set up their own inquiry, a so-called lunacy commission, the purpose of which will be to prove your legal sanity."

Detweiler chuckled and said: "It's quite a contest."

"I have no intention of letting the state commission get hold of you," Melrose assured him, and then, because this statement seemed to disturb the killer, he explained the Constitutional guarantee that no man could be compelled to be a witness against himself.

"And *I'm* crazy," said Detweiler. "Who would be better able to testify than the man himself? Somebody else?"

"We'll talk about that some other time."

"When you say cooperate with the doctors, what do you mean?"

"Just act natural," said Melrose.

"Whew!" Detweiler exclaimed. "That's a relief."

Melrose was good as his word. He brought around a psychiatrist and introduced him as Dr. Brixton. Detweiler remembered him immediately.

"Doctor," he said, "I suppose you don't recall, but some

time ago I came into the outpatient clinic of the hospital where you work, with the purpose of getting my penis amputated, and I was referred to you."

Brixton was gray all over, hair, mustache, suit, tie. He looked sternly at Detweiler and said: "I'm not likely to forget that. You came thereafter for a few appointments and then you never returned."

"That is true," said Detweiler. "I didn't want to take up any more of your time. I couldn't forgive myself for sitting around chewing the fat when there were patients who needed you, and you were too polite to remind me of it."

Brixton was so generous of spirit as now to assure Detweiler that this interpretation was in error, that Detweiler had indeed been one of his patients who needed him most, that he only regretted having lost sight of him. But he couldn't fool Detweiler.

"You are too kind, Doctor. I'll bet a lot of people try to take advantage of you."

Melrose said: "I must be going now. Are you O.K., Joe? May I bring you anything?"

"I was never better," Detweiler said. "You know, it's funny, for years I wandered around seeking peace and quiet in which to work and could seldom find it. Instead I was distracted by sex, or somebody's radio in the next room, or right in the middle of something important I would get hungry. Then jobs. I've had all sorts. The last work I did was dishwashing in a restaurant. The trouble was, I'd always get too fascinated in what I was doing. Do you realize that every dirty dish has its own identity? One has the stain of fried eggs, another the green streak of peas, a white trace of mashed potatoes with a tiny rivulet of pork gravy. Each is like a road map, and then you lift the little soapy dish-mop and run it around and you obliterate the cartography. What speculations this gives rise to! I used to play a game. There was a window by the sink, and some of the diners would go past it if they proceeded west after leaving the restaurant. I would try to guess who had eaten what, on the basis of their appearance and the dishes that had just come in."

Melrose said: "That must have been fun. Well, now you tell Dr. Brixton what he wants to know."

"Sure," said Detweiler. "But wait a moment. I won once! I saw a man coming by, vigorously picking his teeth. The window was always open because the hot dishwater kept it warm in there. I shouted: 'I bet you had the corned-beef hash with a poached egg.' 'Right you are!' he said. Reason I knew that is they didn't use the canned stuff there, but made hash from what was left over from the whole corned beef of the day before, and that meat is always stringy so that it sticks in the teeth."

Melrose nodded.

Detweiler said sharply: "Are you listening?"

"I know better than that."

"What I am leading up to is that on the outside I was always being distracted. But it is perfect here: bed and board and extended periods of the most fruitful solitude. . . . What do you mean, you 'know better'?"

"Than to get involved in an argument with you," said Melrose. "Unfortunately, you and I begin with such divergent viewpoints that I cannot merely listen without responding. That's more than a lawyer can bear."

Detweiler shrugged and looked pleasantly at Dr. Brixton.

"Mr. Melrose is a terrific guy. Last time he was here he hit me so hard in the head that it still aches. He and I are friendly opponents."

"A mutual admiration society," said Melrose, "to coin a phrase. But don't let that fool you. We're out to do each other in, right, Joe?"

Brixton was soberly watching Detweiler all the while.

"Wrong!" said Detweiler, though he knew Melrose was kidding and bore him no ill will. However Detweiler himself never joked, unless you could call strangulation a comic device. He said: "I must admit I am coming around to your way of thinking, at least insofar as the electric chair is concerned. But I'll tell you this: I don't want to go free. Can you promise you won't do anything clever that will make me leave jail?"

Melrose said: "I can't promise anything of the kind. The world might come to an end tomorrow and then I'd look like a fool. You'll have to take your chances with the rest of us, Joe. Meanwhile, I wish you'd talk to Dr. Brixton." The guard let him out.

Detweiler stated to the doctor: "For some reason he is getting very witty these days. Mr. Melrose is ostensibly an exceedingly complex man, with a very subtle mind."

The doctor sat down across the table from the killer. "What is he really, in your opinion?"

"Very simple, actually. I don't mean simple-minded in the sense of idiocy. I mean that his basic proposition is not at all complicated. He believes in right and wrong."

"Do you?"

"Of course. But he doesn't believe I do, or that anyone else does, for that matter. He has no faith that justice will be done. That's why he is a lawyer. Pretty arrogant of him, wouldn't you say? Yet he's the kindest man I have ever known. But he's not as fair as Tierney, and that's why I don't trust him."

"Who is Tierney?"

"Well, he never comes around to see me, but—"

"Joe," said Dr. Brixton, "do you remember our talks of two years ago? I was just rereading my files last night—"

"Excuse me," said Detweiler. "Tierney is a policeman, a detective."

"You like him, do you?"

"It's not a matter of liking. I just think he does a good job."

"Has he hurt you? Beat you or slapped you around?"

"What a question!"

"Well, has he?"

"If he had done that, I would hardly think he was doing a good job."

"Oh?" Brixton said, brow-lines appearing in the grayness of his countenance. Detweiler doubted he was as old as he looked, and he looked exactly as you would expect a doctor to.

"I recall our talks very well," said Detweiler. "You were intrigued by my sex life. I wish I could have remembered more of it for you, but if anything is a victim of Time, that's it. Here today, gone tomorrow: that's sex."

"Joe, your victims were female. Why women?"

"Pure chance. Because they were there."

"Sure about that? Would you have strangled Tierney if he had been there?"

Detweiler laughed. "I wouldn't have got far. He carries a gun."

"Joe, have you ever had sexual relations with another man?"

"You asked me that one other time," said Detweiler. "I remember."

"Do you recall your answer?"

"I can't say I do."

"It was 'no.' "

"Well, there you are," Detweiler said. "I can't improve on it."

"What interests me," said Dr. Brixton, "is that you couldn't remember."

"Since I saw you last, Doctor, so many things have happened that others slip my mind. It all comes back to me now. It may interest you to know I never did succeed in getting an amputation. I suppose it was fate. Jail has done the job better and with no pain. . . . If I can't remember past answers, it goes to demonstrate how much we lose to Time. For all I know, I might have been a raving homosexual at some past time and have forgotten about it."

"You might have been? Why do you say that?"

"I purposely picked the most unlikely situation I could think of," said Detweiler, "to demonstrate my point."

"I find that significant."

"I hoped you would. Anything is possible, Doctor. You are interested in what is probable, according to your interpretation of what a person remembers, but memory is faulty and partial at best."

"Granted," replied Brixton. "But what we remember and what we forget is most meaningful."

Detweiler agreed, but he said: "Think if we could Realize exactly what happened, without distortion of wish and will and the other filters of time lost, relive the event itself, see back over the centuries, focusing in on a chosen moment. For example, I will relate an occurrence that took place some years back that should be of especial interest to you if you are a homosexual."

Brixton suddenly lost his grayness. His features took form in a curious way.

"Wait a minute, Joe. I am not homosexual, if that's what you are saying. I seem to have touched a nerve, to make you strike back that way. Let's get this straight. I am a physician. Because a policeman investigates a murder, does that make him a murderer?"

Detweiler said: "You are the one who insists that any personal reaction is significant, Doctor. Why does a man become a policeman if he does not have an attraction to crime? You see, you cannot stand apart that way if you are human. You must take responsibility for your interests."

"I find it absurd that you, who are sick, should instruct me as to reality," said the doctor, who sank slowly back into his dispassion.

"That's what I mean," Detweiler said. "Your profession is illness, Tierney's is crime, and Mr. Melrose's is injustice. You would all have a hard time proving you are not absolutely dependent on the negative phenomena, not simply passively waiting around for something to go wrong. If, that is, proof were necessary. It isn't for me.

"But I don't want to dwell on that subject. I am not the advocate of anything. It's perfectly all right with me if you are a homosexual. There is this incident I wanted to tell you about. I was in one of those lunch-counter bars eating a knackwurst on rye and drinking a glass of beer, and a girl came up alongside me and asked if I'd like to have a good time with her, and I said just a minute till I finish my sandwich, so I did, and then we went to her room around the corner and I said I should warn you I don't have much money and she said just give me what you can afford and I did, and I thought it was funny she didn't take off anything but her skirt and underpants and lay down with her behind towards me, and since I don't care for anything strange I asked her to turn over, and you won't believe this, but she was a man!"

"What did you do then?" asked Dr. Brixton. "Beat him up?"

"I just gave an embarrassed laugh and got out of there fast," Detweiler said. "But not before one more thing occurred which makes me feel bad, which is probably why I forgot the whole incident for a long time. As I was getting back into my pants, he said: 'Can't you give me just one little kiss?' "

"Why does that make you feel bad?"

"Because maybe I should have tried to overcome my repugnance and grant his plea," said Detweiler. "He was, after all, a human being in need. What did his perversion matter, in view of that misery?"

Brixton's mouth appeared in the aridity of his lower face, a widening crack, slowly upturning at the corners, as he showed a bleak, regretful amusement. "You seem to feel more contrition for rejecting an invert's indecent advances than you do for murdering three persons."

"Because I did not turn away from them. It is better to kill than to ignore."

"You should have submitted to his desires?"

"Definitely not. I try to answer needs, not cater to boundless appetites. Desires are treacherous and insatiable, and any attempt to satisfy them increases their intensity. It is a marvelous experience to be useful to somebody, but lending oneself to certain pseudo uses is to be finally absolutely useless."

300

"You should have embraced him then, at least?"

"I should have killed him," said Detweiler. "Put him out of Time, given him a new start."

"As you did later with the Starr women?"

"Yes," Detweiler said. "They didn't want me, personally. They would have settled for a dummy, except that any person has as much power over a dummy as the next. Life makes all the difference: to claim the attention, the energy of a living being. Attract him, divert him, distract him. I suppose I could have filled their void in a mechanical fashion, but it would not have helped. Betty protected me, while she lived there. She was interested in my work, and that interest was my armor—because it wasn't always easy to resist temptation.

"Billie was gorgeous, the kind of girl you see on garage calendars, and Mrs. Starr, though in her forties, was still a good-looking woman: in fact, the kind I have often preferred, with a light in her skin and a body full to the ultimate but not spilling over. She could look like a queen but still feminine. She wore a perfume that made my head spin. It was hardest to avoid her. Billie was a little unreal, and the kind that maybe prefers to have you look rather than touch. She always gave a show if you wanted one. At one time or another I saw every part of her without trying, since she was always in the bathroom or sitting on the bed, doors open, taking the hair off her legs or whatnot, always grooming.

"But Mrs. Starr was fully dressed at all times. I never saw her leg above the knee. Even when she came to my room in her nightclothes—she slept on the living-room sofa and listened late to the radio after everybody else had gone to bed, and at least once it blew a tube and she thought it was a fuse and asked me to look in the box—her robe was frilly but decent and you could see only the collar of the lace nightgown. I saw this when I switched on my bedside lamp—so obviously the main fuse hadn't blown, and I looked in the box on the kitchen wall and they were all O.K. Then I went into the living room to tend to the radio, and she asked if I would just use the flashlight and not put on the lamp because the sofa made up like a bed was an eyesore.

"I found a tube that was almost entirely out of the socket, like somebody had been fiddling with it, and I put it back in. Sitting side by side on the couch, our knees bumped together; that perfume was overpowering. I almost lost control, but managed to get out of the room and in the hall, where the light was on. I ran into Betty, who looked as always pure as a child in her light-green pajamas. I guess she was on her way to or from the bathroom. She was like an angel, come to save me; because I might have gone back even yet. I know she was still suspicious after I told her the truth about the radio. Betty always understood me: she knew I was still a long way from organizing my energy. The next day was the first time I tried to have my organ removed."

"And at the clinic they referred you to me."

"No," Detweiler said, "that was at least the third time."

"You had tried twice before?"

"At least. I was really serious about it. . . . I'll tell you an interesting thing: Mrs. Starr, who looked soft and voluptuous, was actually very strong and rather hard when it came to killing her. Billie, on the other hand, was the yielding one."

"Were you punishing them for having attracted you, tormented you?"

"Certainly not. By killing them I was at last giving them a use."

"That's funny," said Dr. Brixton. "I believe you told Mr. Melrose that you strangled Mrs. Starr because she was making noise, and then Billie out of compassion, not wishing her to find her mother's body."

"And I told Tierney I went there to kill Betty, and I told the district attorney's detectives the killings were premeditated. I have said a lot of things to a lot of people."

"Which is the truth?"

"All, and none. The act is the truth, really. Everything else is language. You can't ever expect to Realize an act in words: what you are talking about is talk. The medium of action is Time, and what can you say about that?"

"Well, Joe," said the doctor, "I wish you had continued to come to me for treatment. I believe this tragedy could have been avoided. Not only have three innocent, decent persons lost their lives, but you are in danger of losing yours. Legal procedure in this state is antiquated, really medieval. Its test for criminal responsibility is criminally inadequate. The district attorney is out to get your head. He has political ambitions. He would like to be the next governor. The yellow press is trying to corrupt the minds of potential jurors by printing analyses of your character by bogus 'experts' who have never seen you—all of course concluding you are legally sane.

"I'm not sure that even Mr. Melrose clearly understands the situation. Society has a responsibility to people like you. It is a social problem, not a legal one or not even medical in the narrow sense. The first time you came into a public clinic with your request to be emasculated, you should have been given adequate psychiatric treatment. You were sick, Joe, and you are sick now. You should be in a hospital, not in a jail. It is we who are guilty of the crimes of which you are accused."

Dr. Brixton had developed some spirit while making this comment. He stayed gray all over, but his voice had force, an almost brutal authority that frightened Detweiler.

"Oh no!" Detweiler cried in terror. "Oh no, you don't, Doctor. Don't try to take my killings away from me!"

Detweiler had not suspected that Dr. Brixton would try to swindle him. When he had talked with the psychiatrist some years before, he had believed him a harmless sort of man in whom the energizing currents ran slowly, a person of no ambition, else why would he practice a profession the subject of which was unreality. But that was before the killings. Now he recognized Brixton as potentially his most dangerous enemy, much more ruthless than Mr. Melrose and with an additional malice of which the lawyer was innocent, having, as Brixton had not, the structure of law to check him. Detweiler was aware that in psychiatry there were no rules at all.

He had a number of subsequent sessions with Brixton, but he was careful to restrain himself when it came to philosophical speculation, which the psychiatrist would only use against him.

Finally the day came when the doctor said he had enough data from which to write up a report for Mr. Melrose, and he shook Detweiler's hand and said: "Goodbye for now, Joe. I'll see you in court."

"Why?"

"I'll be a witness for the defense."

Detweiler was staggered by the implications of this. "You don't mean to say you will tell the judge and jury about the operation I was trying to have done?"

Brixton said: "Now calm yourself, Joe. You are in terrible danger. We must do what is necessary to save your life. Surely you can endure a little embarrassment with that end in view."

"It isn't embarrassment, Doctor. *I* can stand the facts of life. But have you no decency? There will be women in that courtroom." The jail barber was overdue, and Detweiler's hair was too long for his taste. In his agitation now, a fine lock swung down over his left eye. He tried to rip it from his scalp, but that proved too painful to accomplish. He said: "You keep mentioning my 'terrible danger.' The only danger I am in is from your obsession with filth."

Then Mr. Melrose said he would bring still another psychiatrist, and Detweiler put his foot down.

"I really must protest, Mr. Melrose. Why in the world must these people be brought into the case to establish a plea of legal insanity? You have explained the difference to me between that and medical insanity; apparently there are maniacs by medical definition who could be judged liable at law. Therefore what is essential here is the legal aspect, not the psychiatric. So why can't we deal with lawyers instead of doctors?"

"As usual, Joe, you ask good questions, but the trouble is that you are too rational. You do not allow for the perversity of civilized institutions: you do not consider the tendency of any one discipline to encroach upon another, perhaps merely out of envy."

"Now, don't be cynical, Mr. Melrose."

"Sorry, Joe. I was just temporizing while endeavoring to think up a feasible answer; killing time, you might say."

Detweiler grinned appreciatively. Then he said: "Please don't worry. Everything will come out all right. You'll see." He sighed. "I'll even talk to your next psychiatrist."

Melrose brightened. "That might help, Joe. You see, it is more persuasive to have several witnesses give similar testimony."

"I understand that," said Detweiler, "but I could conceive of a situation in which one man told the truth in opposition to fifteen liars, imperfect observers, or whatnot."

"I could cite illustrative examples," Melrose responded in agreement. "And as often as not, the perjurers were my own defense witnesses."

"Come now. You are being too hard on yourself."

"I have never asked a witness to commit perjury," Melrose said reflectively. "Or implied that I would welcome it. Nor has a potential witness come to me with such an offer. It is curious, perhaps, but we both pretend, even in private, and without a suggestion of irony, that he is telling the truth. I say 'pretend,' but maybe I am pretending now that it is pretense. At the appropriate moment I believe."

Detweiler was impressed. "I suppose you can be permitted some cynicism, then, in your off-moments. Everybody needs a certain amount of relaxation."

Melrose said: "But of course perjury seldom plays a role in the testimony of so-called expert witnesses. It is only too easy for both defense and prosecution to find honest authorities who oppose each other diametrically in regard to the same phenomenon, even in such a supposedly exact science as ballistics. And when the human element enters, consistency goes right out the window. Dr. Brixton, for example, believes that a man who has tried to get himself mutilated can be held responsible for no subsequent act however criminal. I wager that the prosecution psychiatrists will find the same fact utterly negligible."

"Yes," said Detweiler, "there is only one area in which all

men agree, willy-nilly; one constant factor; one dimension in which we all have the same measurement: Time. Have you ever thought that only in Time are all men equal? Every sixty seconds all living things grow one minute older. There is no exception and no appeal. In that regard everybody is an expert, a professional."

Melrose shot the dazzling linen cuffs that emerged from his gray, chalk-striped jacket. He was a lawyer, trained not to show his feelings except as a device. Detweiler could not say what influence, if any, he was exerting on Melrose: but he had hope. He worried more about the lawyer than any of the others. Tierney could take care of himself. Dr. Brixton was nourished by the shameful reminiscences of his patients. But poor Melrose had nothing but his pleas. He went eternally through the world speaking on behalf of the accused. To Detweiler that seemed most unhealthy. He saw now that he had been wrong to try to kill Melrose; had he been successful, another Melrose would have taken the job, and the first would have died, his misapprehensions intact.

The Starr women had expected nothing better of him than death. If he would not love them, he would at least strangle them. Women crave some form of intimate attention—which is also why Betty got married behind his back.

But Melrose was a man, manifestly incapable to act for himself. Forever pleading in the name of another, defending killers, unable himself to kill.

"I once heard," Detweiler said diplomatically, "that all lawyers want to become judges."

Melrose's defenses came up. He said: "Don't try to run my life, Joe."

"I was just thinking, you have saved a lot of people from

punishment. Maybe you should take your turn at punishing."

"Once, early in my career," Melrose said, "I witnessed an execution. I had not defended the man. His counsel was one of the senior partners of the law firm for whom I worked. I went out of what I told myself was a serious, professional curiosity: I should know precisely what it was to lose a capital case. Notice the 'I.' A trial is always a competition between lawyers, for which the alleged crime provides an excuse. The 'defendant,' the 'state,' are assumptions, and interchangeable. But the man who is strapped into the electric chair is real, so actual, palpable, that when the current goes through him he turns red, then blue; smoke rises from him; he stinks of burning flesh. He writhes. Were it not for his bonds, his convulsing muscles would hurl him across the chamber.

"The judge who sentences a man to this is a homicidal maniac."

"Then," Detweiler said, "he must be found not guilty, according to the M'Naghten Rule. I begin to understand that principle now. Without it there would be total anarchy."

Chapter 18

TIERNEY'S affair with Betty was still underway as spring dried off into summer. It was by now starkly genital. She never heard from him during the curse, but he always appeared the day after it ended, when they could make love without protection and with impunity. He was very conventional, deplored stunts, special positions, and was troubled if any article belonging to Arthur was visible to him as he prepared to enter her. Yet he insisted on using the bedroom, the bed of the conjugal house. Once they had gone to a city hotel in a deteriorating neighborhood and obviously used by streetwalkers, but the proprietor knew Tierney from the days when Tierney put the bite on him as a precinct detective and gave them the best accommodations, gratis, discreetly. But Tierney could not perform. It seemed he preferred to violate the sanctity of the home.

She found it utterly boring to have a cop as a lover, and

tolerated the situation only because by contrast it gave Arthur greater value. She and Tierney were criminals, and Arthur represented the law. He was not, however, an enforcer or even an investigator: after that single encounter with Tierney he subsided into trust, faith, or whatever you might·wish to call it but cowardice. It had taken bravery for him to face up to Tierney, and Tierney's having thrown him to the carpet (for more than a month he had displayed a blue bruise on his fat elbow, the point at which he first touched the floor) in his own home, would have crushed the spirit of a lesser man.

But Arthur took moral nourishment from the incident. Betty remembered some old Greek legend concerning a wrestler who was easily thrown, but once he hit the ground he absorbed indomitable strength from the earth and was instantly on his feet again: a peculiarity which tended to discourage opponents. He was eventually defeated by Hercules, who lifted him into the air and squeezed him until he capitulated.

Arthur had become physically aggressive. Astounding Betty, he had tried to pick a fight with a man at the movies. In the row ahead this man had been commenting loudly to his wife. Arthur ordered him to desist; the man made a rude reply; Arthur invited him outside, and he shut up forthwith. Another time Arthur had stuck his head out the car window and cursed a fellow driver for cutting him off.

Arthur himself did not, consciously, interpret his change in style, in character, as a gain. He saw it rather as the necessary answer to the challenges of a world which was forsaking reason for violence.

"I have tried to be patient, to be tolerant," he said. "God knows. But what's the point if at any moment a lousy maniac can grab you by the neck and choke you dead?"

He seemed to give no credit to the struggle with Tierney, but Betty happened to know that that broke the ice, because she knew Arthur thoroughly, as a good wife should know her husband. The corollary was that Arthur did not know her at all, also as it should be. Women must be mysterious in a world in which men are physically superior. He had no suspicion of her illicit activity. Tierney's firm denial sufficed, for either Arthur's old character or his new. The old Arthur accepted a man's word; the new, with its Machiavellian sense of power, believed that the man who possessed superior force had no need to lie.

But Betty was not deeply interested in husbands or lovers at this time—she kept on with Tierney out of habit, apathy, his own wants—but an audience. The newspaper series had stimulated and not appeased her appetite for self-expression. The real story was yet to be told. The cruelest disappointment of her life had been provided by the degenerate who posed as a book publisher. She still half-believed in his professional authenticity, despite Tierney. He had spoken so well. Never mind his perversions: she could survive them. She had a history of such survivals: her father's odd ways, her sister's exhibitionism, her mother's relationships with the boarders, the first of whom had been an aggressive woman named Isobel. One, and only one, had Betty ever got for herself, Joe the sexless eccentric, soon to become a homicidal maniac.

One day she called Alloway, the reporter. He sounded eager to hear her proposition and, though she offered to meet him downtown, insisted on coming out to the "wildest suburbs."

She sat next to him on the couch and said: "If I don't have a book in me, no one does. I can't understand why no publisher has got in touch. I have always heard they besiege anyone who has got into the news."

Alloway's eyes roamed over the furniture and carpet. "It's somewhat different than I expected. I expected to see more fluff and pink, dotted swiss, shellacked bronze plates and a ceramic panther on the mantel, you know." He giggled and said: "I'm joking."

Betty remembered Arthur's suspicion of Alloway. The reporter's irrelevancy was something new, perhaps rude, but she couldn't be bothered.

"You must know the ropes in publishing," she said. "What I propose is this: you and I collaborate again, only this time what I say goes. I mean a full-length book, where we can stretch our arms."

"Sure," he said, "Might I ask you for a drink?"

He already smelled of liquor, and his gaze was still irresponsibly going to the drapes, the ottoman, the tole lamp on the end table. But she complied.

"Nothing for yourself?"

She said: "I want to talk business."

"So do I." He drank half the glass.

"Here's the way I see it. This time I'll write the whole thing, first, myself. Do you call that a rough draft? Then you take it, read it, give me your critique, then together we'll whip it into polished form. You'll also take care of the business end, publishing contract, and so on. I know nothing of these things. We'll split the royalties fifty-fifty. Deal?" Being hard, realistic, man-to-man, Betty thrust her hand at Alloway.

Instead of taking it, he put his own right hand on her left breast.

"I would never have had the nerve if you hadn't called," he said, still not meeting her eye. "And even then I had to get drunk. I dreamed of this so long I could not believe it would come true."

Betty rose calmly, and easily, for his hand merely rested against her and did not clutch, and standing staunchly before him, said:

"Get out of here, you drunken scum."

The next day a poison-pen letter arrived, addressed to Arthur. Betty opened it, as she did anything that looked personal, and read:

Dear Sir,

This has gone on long enough. Your wife is entertaining "gentlemen callers" in your absence. That was neither here or there till now, but today one of these individuals came out of your house in a highly inebriated condition and vomited on the sidewalk in full view of my two young children who were rollerskating there at the time. I don't intend to stand by and let this neighborhood become a slum.

A Friend

Betty destroyed the missive forthwith and told no one—not Arthur, assuredly not Tierney—of the letter, the visit, or the project. Twice she had been betrayed foully by persons privy to her dearest secret: it must not happen again. She had learned that to enunciate a special interest was to expose a weakness, to display a target for those whose ambitions are also out of the common run. Merely because she wanted to write a book, the bogus publisher assumed she would go down on him and Alloway was emboldened to assault her. Writing was apparently a kind of crime, even the threat to commit which created other malefactors from nowhere. She remembered she had shown her poetry to Joe Detweiler. There was some sinister force to language.

Betty was pleased that both Arthur and Tierney found their pleasure in her, but with neither of them had she ever reached a climax. Nor, for that matter, with anyone else. But not all she had to tell was sensational. She had within her a great unrealized potential, brief glimpses and resonances of which could be apprehended when she stood barefooted in the surf as gulls wheeled high above, or awoke at the chattering of birds at dawn on a spring morning and saw another new sun. Little white boats on the river; a vivid geranium in a window ten stories above a gutter full of waste; a broken doll in a trashcan; a straw-hatted horse pulling a cart: contrasts, similitudes, correspondences, echoes, the gamut of qualities, the relations between things and people and animals, the living and the dead. She saw much and had related little. She, who never felt so lonely as when joined with a man in the act of love, had a lover's passion for life in all its forms: there was as much truth in a fallen leaf as in sex and murder and their male perpetrators.

Eventually, using the energy and courage of defiance, she found it possible to sit down before a sheet of paper and take pen in hand. The whiteness of the foolscap was oppressive; the instrument too hard, smooth, erect; the chair exerted pressure against her sacrum; she itched all over. She knew what to write; the problem was how, given an inability to use the first person. She could say "I" with abandon, but could not inscribe it upon the nullity of the blank paper. That was the first revelation: the utter lack of community between the written and the real, when both were personal. Life had another grammar than language, though words were alive and living had its verbal features. "When I was thirteen, my father tried to rape me." This statement was as clear, as direct, as true as she could fashion it, impeccable in talking-turkey syntax and brass-tacks

314

vocabulary, this being no subject for the obscenity of circum-
locution—yet as a characterization in words of the event in
time, it missed the mark.

She had been awakened in the middle of the night. She
smelled whiskey. A hand groped at her lower belly. Perhaps a
dream-hand; or a real one fondling a dream-belly, which was
preferable. She wanted it to stay in reality while she dreamed,
but then it must forget so that she could remember. A dream
must be private else it was actual, and the actuality of her body
was disgusting. She approved of the hand, which was knowledge-
able, authoritative, and enormous, and she could control it with
her will: go here, go there, and it went, obedient yet prideful,
seeking to please from strength and never weakness. Up it went
to cherish the cones of her bosom, then back down to worship at
the original shrine, a dutiful pilgrim. And she put out her own
right hand to make verification, and found herself clutching her
own left wrist. That was the terror against which she cried out.

But her father was there, in the room. He said instantly:
"Shh, you'll wake Billie."

She whispered: *"Who are you?"* meaning, what are you
doing, and he understood and said: *"I came to close the window.
It is snowing in."*

"Have you been drinking?"

"Yes."

"I can smell it."

He stood by her bed, breathing heavily, making fumes.

She said: *"Why don't you go away?"*

"You called me."

"I had a nightmare."

"You better button your pajamas and pull up the covers,"
he said, *"or you'll catch cold."* He sounded bitter.

She said: *"I'm sorry to have bothered you."*

He answered, very bitterly: *"You just leave me alone."*

The rape was implicit in this experience, though perhaps, probably, he had not even touched her. What was true had not happened; therefore to be literal was to lie. Most of the story Betty had to tell was of a like nature: the truth that had not occurred, the history of that which had no time. But she was not dishonest. She could not represent this narrative as a personal confession, autobiographical, taking its chronology from the standard calendar, recording local names and habitations. To speak truly she must invent, construct, distort, and prevaricate.

So Betty began a novel and found her fluency, and the more she wrote, the less was her heroine a self-portrait. The name was Margaret, and Margaret had a will of her own. Her father was handsome and had his gallant side, and she could not hate him for violating her, no matter what the pressure applied by Betty. He was often drunk on rare wines, and he brought her gifts of jewelry and lace. Ill health and financial reverses completed his ruin, which had begun in the hostility of an avaricious wife, whose sexual appetites were evident but ambiguous. One day Margaret's father opened his wrists with a razor blade and perished in a rush of gore.

The novel was in every way an improvement over life; fiction, unlike experience, being capable of conclusions. In the fictive household Margaret's father was replaced by a rent-paying guest named Pauline, an old friend of Margaret's mother and a blatant invert who lost no time in making advances to both girls. Margaret's sister, a vain, empty-headed creature named Rosalie, perhaps succumbed: at any rate, the fur flew and Pauline soon departed.

Whereas in life, the friend of Betty's mother, Isobel Gauss, had been, like Betty's father, provably guilty of nothing. Coming home from school, Betty often found Isobel with her mother. They usually sat at a great distance from each other, both smoking heavily. Betty had once counted eight cigarette-ends in Isobel's ashtray, all burned down to the nub, unusable for her own experiments.

Another time, Isobel came out of the bathroom and crossed the hall to peek in at Betty, who was reading a movie magazine on the bed.

"Excuse me," Isobel said. "I thought you were Billie."

Betty smiled hypocritically: Billie's opinion of Isobel was negative. Billie was then fifteen and disapproved, for reasons of health, of persons who smoked or drank.

"I have insulted you, I think," Isobel said. She had a soft, fruity face though her body, while full, looked hard, as if it might, struck with a metal implement, clank. Betty had never made physical contact with Isobel. Fortunately Isobel was not a kisser or hugger. She had been married once, long ago, and in a state of alleged happiness when her husband of four months, driving home alone through the rain, executed a slide of but twelve feet, which might have been exhilarating on the apron of a deserted airfield: he was, however, adjacent to a fragile safety rail on the harelip of an embankment. Isobel henceforth lived in the absence of men and was, moreover, a critic of that sex, Betty knew from her mother, though anyone could have skidded in the rain.

Betty was mildly interested in Isobel's unfairness and felt a certain affinity with her because of the smoking. In the cellar of the building Betty would secretly puff on cigarettes stolen from her mother's pack. The janitor had caught her once, beside the boiler, remonstrating in his middle-aged, heavy-set, Slavic voice. Though in appearance the classic type of molester, he turned soddenly away from her defiance and belched at the water gauge.

Isobel said: "Are you curious to know what I mean?"

Betty blushed, twisted back to her reading. Isobel seldom addressed her, and never before when coming directly from the bathroom.

She said: "No." She heard no sound, yet when she looked Isobel was gone. After a while Betty wandered into the living room, where her mother sat beside an empty coffee cup, pencil in hand, notepad on the chair arm.

"Peas or stringbeans?" asked her mother, though not of her and neither of Isobel, who was not in evidence. Then: "Where is Isobel?"

Betty rarely looked at her mother, whose presence she had for a year or so now found embarrassing.

"I don't know," she sullenly answered.

"Isn't she in the bathroom?"

"How do I know?"

"Aren't you friends?" Betty's mother dyed her hair black, wore it close, with bangs. She was shortish, and at the distance of half a city block, might have been a husky schoolgirl. She was not overweight but wide-built, broad-shouldered for a woman, or perhaps not even that, really: it might have been the thrusting way she walked, she being one of those persons in whom manner takes precedence over matter. Close up, especially when seated, she was in no sense physically formidable, rather vanished into or merged with the environment as to body, establishing herself exclusively by moral means. Which, in addressing herself to Betty, took an interrogatory form. To answer one question was to receive another, in a nonsensical progression, touching nowhere on communication.

Betty said "Yes."

Her mother asked: "Isobel isn't famous for her patience, is she? She doesn't remember how it is to be a young girl. She sometimes expects to find her own type efficiency in everybody else, her own way of striking to the mark. And she is disappointed then. She is a genius at business."

"Pardon?" Betty asked idly. Isobel owned and operated an agency which supplied domestics to those who could afford them; certainly nobody in the social circle of the Starrs. Her mother often mentioned Isobel's yearly gain in precise figures, while Betty writhed at the bad taste of it. She was too old to be impressed by numbers, and too young to associate them with material realities. She had no idea of what her family paid in rent, for example, except that it was too much, like the costs of all necessities, always; and the Starrs were ever short of funds by definition. Her mother had once said, with a desperate gaiety: "If we were millionaires, we would still be broke." Her mother was given to making statements that defied reason, thereby excluding other people, though it may have been her purpose merely to torment them. For she was hardly a big spender. Betty often wore Billie's hand-me-downs.

Betty received no answer now. Her mother stared at the notepaper for a moment and then asked: "Or broccoli?"

Betty went to look for Isobel and found her in the back bedroom, still at this time the quarters of Betty's father—her mother even then slept in the living room. Now Betty saw a terribly ugly thing: Isobel's rumpled, off-white girdle, lying on top of her father's little desk. On this narrow piece of unpainted furniture he kept a table radio, an alarm clock, a few

dogeared westerns and self-help books: improve your personality, learn accounting at home, collected wisdom of the sages.
In the middle drawer of the single pedestal containing two
shallow and one deep, was a sex manual written by an M.D.,
illustrated with cross-section diagrams of penis and vulva, but
if he kept a store of condoms, Betty had never found them, nor
any literature unconditionally dirty. Betty had a school friend
named Eunice Pell whose Daddy received by mail, in plain wrap-
pers, a dozen fish skins at a time and kept them, in a diminishing
supply, in a bureau drawer beneath his clean handkerchiefs,
along with a filthy comic book professing to reveal what famous
cartoon characters did behind the frames of the newspaper strips.
Betty was utterly indifferent to such representations, insofar as
they were supposed to arouse her; but she valued their implication as to Mr. Pell and to men in general, whose sex did not
distinguish between reality and appearance.

There was Isobel's girdle. Isobel herself lay on the bed, her
shoes, with their sensible thick heels, underneath it.

She said soberly: "Made myself comfortable. Can't breathe
in that armorplate except when standing. My advice to you:
always keep your little tummy firm as it is now."

Betty asked: "Are you moving in?"

"Do I have your permission?" Isobel rubbed her toes together, the nylon rasping as if she walked through a bush.

"*My* permission?" At this Betty uttered a shrill laugh, almost
a neigh, signifying her preposterous deficiency. Over no creature, in no situation in all the vast universe did she possess an
ounce, a molecule, of power. In all equations she was zero.
Even Eunice Pell, a stupid, homely, pustular girl, yet privy to her
father's secrets, had a more vivid sense of being.

"It means a lot to me," said Isobel, but did not try to catch her eye. Instead she rolled up on a hip and backed it towards the wall, providing a cove, a sitting place for a visitor, on the narrow bed. She made no further invitation, and Betty would not accept this as such. The thought of approaching Isobel on her own volition was repugnant. She would have complied if asked; she must, having no power and no responsibility. She was only a young girl.

"Where will my father live?" she asked the heavy woman on the sagging bed.

"Yes, well," said Isobel, now with a sudden, yearning glance. "Did your mother fail to mention?" She flattened her hips, skirt straining, and rose upon a shoulder. "In my office building they needed a janitor, or should I say custodian. I obtained this position for him or anyway put in a word. It comes with quarters, basement but nice: little bedroom, toilet, and stall shower, maybe a hotplate for soup and coffee. Has to reside there because of nighttime maintenance: keep the boiler on, watchman duties, early trash removal, and so on. I'll tell you Andy was grateful. I only did what I could. He's not a well man, dear, and should have his cough checked into. I hope you girls take your chest x-rays yearly."

Billie had two wonderful pearlike breasts, but Betty still had grown no bosom worthy of the name, wore a brassiere only so that the backstrap would show through a thin blouse. She supposed that men looked for this, all the more so if nothing was displayed in front. She was tall for her age and had older ways, could handle a cigarette as if smoking were habitual to her, listened serenely to conversation without squirming or picking at her hair. Undoubtedly she was taken as older than her numerical years. High-fashion models had no more chest than she.

"So that leaves this room empty," said Isobel. "Why not

sublet my own apartment? I thinks, make a profit on it and pass part along to your Momma as boarder here." Isobel's cheeks grew fatter as she pressed her chin into her neck. "A lot can be done with this room. Do you sew, dear? And can help me stitch up some curtains? Oh, we will have fun, we women."

Betty's mother spoke from the hallway. "*Here* you are, you two, here you are." She made it sound as if she had had to search, as though they were in hiding from her. "Could I break this up?"

"We're great friends already," Isobel said in archness, peering intensely, meaningfully, at Betty, a look for which there was no foundation. "She's been making me feel at home. Has offered to help with the curtains. Wasn't that nice?"

In an abrupt gesture Mrs. Starr thrust the grocery list at Betty, swiftly, crisply, militarily precise, a dispatch to carry through enemy lines by a courier hitherto untried, but the only one around.

Never again did Betty come that close to Isobel; never was she asked; never did she catch Isobel in compromising circumstances with any living being. In a few months Isobel moved away without clamor or evident ill will and was seldom mentioned thereafter. Then began the series of male boarders, of which Joe Detweiler had been the last while Betty was in residence.

So much of life was tendency, likelihood, possibility; that which might have been, could have, would have, perhaps was, perhaps not. Only Joe Detweiler had acted decisively, had leaped the gulf between supposition and occurrence. Betty had underestimated him, but then she was sane and he was mad. For this reason she had long since ceased to think of the real Joe, incarcerated, or even as he had been when a boarder at the Starrs'.

Her own creation, possession, named Noel Phillips, was a sensitive young painter who fell in love with Margaret, and from there on, Margaret exercised absolute control over the narrative. Betty had no force left, could only listen. She had not suspected that the imagination was an even more ruthless authority than time. So her novel, heretofore violent, ended with no commotion whatever, reversing the living events which had presumably been its source, and omitting, denying the murders which in life had been at once so climatic and so senseless. Margaret and Noel, in the end, simply fled out into the world, there being no further story in requited love.

Summer was done when Betty finished writing her book, and by then she no longer saw Tierney. The break had come one hot August afternoon when, on pulling his sweating body off hers with the noise of loosening adhesive tape, he went into the bathroom across the hall and, without closing the door, made water loudly. No doubt he had done this before, but the heat of the day, the airless, westward-facing bedroom with the beige blind made orange by the suppressed sun, and the smell of Tierney's perspiration—not unpleasant, but strange: like roasted peanuts—exaggerated the effect. She was suddenly furious that this crude cop should be using the private toilet in her home, and when he emerged to climb into his striped shorts, she noticed for the first time how disgustingly he was haired from clavicle to groin, not an unbroken mat, but in clumps, as if it had been patchily sprayed on.

She rolled over, face in the pillow, exposing her beautiful behind, perfectly formed, the only portion of her body of which she was vain. She was luring Tierney to display his worst, and was not disappointed. He reached over and smacked her on the right buttock, then slipped his shirt on over his head, like a sweater: he never unbuttoned it all the way, nor did he usually take off his socks. Thus he was extremely quick in doffing and donning his attire, which furthermore he always arranged as near as possible to the bed, sometimes on a chair, sometimes the floor, with his pistol uppermost. For months he had first put on both underwear and trousers, gun at belt, before going to the bathroom, as if she might rifle his pockets in the interim.

He had now got to dashing in, taking his pee, and returning swiftly. Once dressed he would be very leisurely about returning to wash. He might insist she go first. Coming back she would see him sitting in his jacket, necktie in place, on the edge of the bed, perusing his notebook. Before he left he would plunge in, closing the bathroom door this time, and run the water, presumably rinsing his part: he took no shower, even in scorching weather.

Tierney's post-sex ritual had never thrilled Betty. But there was no good way for a man to clean up afterward, except perhaps Arthur's discreet and utter silence: he decently refrained from going to the toilet for an hour or so, though he apparently washed himself thoroughly and with dispatch—there was no good way, because of the universal male implication that the act was defiling. How vulnerable they were all made by their external genitalia; men could not even run properly unless it was strapped down. Tierney for example when naked would be no match for the weakest clothed criminal.

"Tierney," she said, rolling over on her back, "policemen are always scared, aren't they?"

He slipped the loop of the tie, which had not been unknotted, over his head and under the already buttoned collar. He seemed to take no offense at the question.

He said, as if it were self-evident: "They might get killed. That's what is different about the job."

"I didn't mean that kind of fear," said Betty, watching him close his fly. "I mean scared to the core, scared of being wrong, of being foolish, of being disobeyed, scared of life. In fact, the only thing you are *not* frightened of is being killed, else you wouldn't have taken the job."

"Well, I don't know," Tierney said genially, indifferent to the subject of the moment as he always was after sex. Even this, to Betty, was evidence of fright; she was fond of her theory. She had, however, not made a place for Tierney in her novel, for the obvious reason that there were no murders in that narrative. Thus he had no ideal role for her. He was stuck in reality, hairy and urinating. And scared.

But she had misinterpreted his mood, which he now revealed to be neither genial nor indifferent. He repeated: "Well, I don't know who is scared and why, but when there is shit to be cleaned up we come with our shovels and when the job is done we hear we stink."

"And you do," Betty averred. "And you're too scared to admit it."

"Call me up next time you are in trouble."

"I will," she said, "and you'll come."

Unobtrusively he had grown furious. Now he conspicuously took himself in hand and asked: "Why are you pushing me all at once?"

"It just occurred to me," Betty replied, "that in six months I have never got anything from you but your lust, and that's not unique. I could get that from the garbageman." With unprecedented fairness, she gave him a moment at this point to be nasty and ask if she had. But, perhaps because of his numerous professional opportunities to work off his venom, Tierney was not verbally malicious. He continued to stare morosely in Betty's direction.

"You have never even given me one flower," she said. "No, nor so much as bought me a drink when we met downtown, before or after."

Tierney blinked and felt his pockets as a man does when he is dressed and ready for the road: keys, change, sap, handcuffs.

"You don't even talk to me," said Betty. "When I think of you, I feel two hands pulling down my pants."

Tierney ran his little finger into his ear and twisted, grimacing.

Betty said: "A whore at least gets paid."

Tierney replied earnestly: "Not by police officers. They do it for free if you don't run them in."

Betty said: "You disgust me. You have always disgusted me." But she could see she wasn't denting his thick hide. He had jerked only when she touched the nerve of his profession. He was personally impervious.

He shrugged and said: "I'll call you."

She said, without hostility: "All right." And heard him go downstairs and out the door. The fact remained that Tierney was always ready to pull down her pants, ready to use her, ready to leave when he was done. He could be relied on, predicted absolutely. Being so singleminded, he really caused her no trouble at all. Obviously, from his point of view, she had an established value, was to him as reliable as he to her. Thus, at almost no cost, she had because of him both kinds of experience of life: give and take. She would not miss him if he never appeared again, but on the other hand, he could return whenever he wished.

In this situation there was a natural justice according to which Betty's adultery was only technical.

No living person knew of her book. She might not even offer it for publication and so expose herself to more assaults on the spirit. Its composition had enabled her to re-create herself, to use time as her own invention, to control experience. All else was vanity.

She now dreaded only one thing: testifying against Joe Detweiler. If only Tierney had shot and killed him while Joe was trying to escape: the triumph of professional violence over amateur. As a writer she had an eye for symmetry, form: it was the only defense against horror. She felt she would die if forced to return to murders and murderer, the killing time. But the law insisted on it. Trial was scheduled for September, and in three sessions with assistant district attorneys she had given extensive pretrial testimony.

She would at any rate not want her book published before the verdict was reached. For vanity did assert itself after all. It might be basically irrelevant, but it was normal, human. She sent her manuscript to a publisher whose name appeared on the spine of a cookbook, a volume, as it happened, that her mother had given her on the marriage to Arthur.

Surprisingly enough this publisher proved neither bogus nor perverted, nor did he act as a principal, but rather assigned an editor to write Betty with cautious interest and an invitation to lunch.

Betty judiciously picked the shrimp from her hollowed tomato; nevertheless, one slipped off a tine and fell to the tablecloth, lay there exuding pink sauce. It was the physical influence of the editor, whose plate was surrounded by a fall of saltstick crumbs, grains of rice creole, small stuff. Having dropped anything of substance, he retrieved and swallowed it. He was young and nervous and shrewd.

He said: "You found a way and a meaning. I read about the case of course and was fascinated *of course* and terrified! Terrified because the murders were essentially meaningless, nonsensical. He had nothing against your—well, excuse me, it must have been awful for you.

"What do you, who have suffered, think we should do with these people? Treat them? Put them out of their misery? Is vengeance the answer? Who knows how many Detweilers are at large in this city. If society could get to them before they get to us." He ate a forkful of wilted, french-cut green beans. "You rightly eliminate the crimes from your novel. Let's not mention them any more. We rejected a nonfictional treatment, an idea submitted by a newspaper reporter for a sensational quickie, to be in the bookstores two weeks after the trial ends."

Betty said: "That wouldn't be Alloway?"

The editor's brow flexed. "Right—oh, he said he knew—"

"That fucking son of a bitch," said Betty in a monotone. "He's queer, you know." But she saw he didn't know, and now that he did, he was frightened. Tierney was not alone in being scared; most other men joined him. Betty's theory grew more and more all-embracing. But it had no place for Detweiler.

"Well, the hell with him," the editor said bluffly, trying to live up to Betty's example. "As you might have gathered, we want to publish your book as a novel, as literature. The association with the unfortunate real-life events could be accidental. They couldn't, in your development as the person you are, no doubt, but I mean insofar as the book is a worthwhile piece of creativity. And I'll say now that I believe you could have been a writer had the murders never taken place."

Betty was overwhelmed. Like everyone she had an ideal statement to hear which from others she was ready to wait a lifetime: to hear that she was invulnerable to experience, that her worth was intrinsic.

Concealing her emotion, she said simply: "Yes. That is why I don't want to use my own name or any other reference to the case, the crimes, the trial. I don't want to trade on that."

The editor seemed to shiver. "Uh-huh," he said as an impatient waiter slid a green salad, glistening with oil, under his elbow. "You don't? I see. Well . . ."

"You agree with me?"

"I certainly do." He lowered his elbow within a centimeter of the salad, then suddenly raised his entire arm and brought it down upon a clean patch of tablecloth without mishap, without looking. "If the author-editor relationship is right and true, both are of one mind. . . . I agree. But I wonder." He stared around at other diners, past them and into the bar beyond, where it was night at midday. "I wonder about my publisher. He is in business to sell books. I also wonder about our obligation?" His eyes suddenly swooped to Betty. "Yours and mine. To see that the book gets read. What, finally, would it matter if a reader was attracted on the basis of sensationalism? The book is not trash. You see what I'm getting at? Better to have vulgar advertising and a quality product than the other way around, like that men's clothing store that runs chummy conversational ads, the soft sell in extremis, appealing to men of intelligence and good will, then you go to the store and find the rudest salespeople in town." He grinned, but his eyes were hangdog.

What a change from Tierney. His interest in Betty seemed so exclusively intellectual, so unselfish, and she was gratified by his example of a men's clothing store, as if they were a couple of guys.

"In short," he said, "if we can attract to this book thousands of readers who come for the wrong reasons, what cause is hurt?"

Chapter 19

The second psychiatrist, a Dr. Metcalfe, younger than Brixton and Melrose but older than Detweiler, had no undue interest in sex. However, Detweiler was suspicious of him in the beginning, thinking he might be tricky, so the killer responded rather sullenly at first.

METCALFE: *Why did you kill the Starr women and the boarder?*
DETWEILER: *Because of love.*
M. *Love?*
D. *What?*
M. *I asked you if the motive was love.*
D. *Where did you get that idea?*
M. *From you, just now.*
D. *Oh.*

M. *Well?*

D. *Yes.*

M. *Yes what?*

D. *Now, Doctor, you've got an answer. Just hang onto it; otherwise we won't get anywhere.*

M. *You won't explain your answers?*

D. *I'll be glad to. But what you must accept is that between a question and an answer, and an answer and an explanation, Time intervenes. You must not assume that, standing on the platform in the same place while the train moves rapidly along, you can step on board at will.*

Dr. Metcalfe suddenly looked very keenly at Detweiler and asked: "Which one is Will?"

"Pardon?"

Metcalfe said: "I just thought you might recall the old joke of the sergeant and a buck private he had ordered to 'fire at will.' The private asked: 'Which one is Will?'"

Detweiler nodded carefully. "The sergeant ordered the private to shoot this Will, and the private was making sure he aimed at the right fellow. I see what you mean. But I was using 'will' to mean volition, not as a person's name."

METCALFE: *So was the sergeant, but the private thought he meant a man. That is the joke.*

DETWEILER: *Oh, a joke!*

M. *Do you like jokes?*

D. *When I can recognize them, but I usually can't.*

M. *Why not?*

D. *Because they usually depend on a confusion, I think. Like this one. A choice of alternatives. You must choose one, and yet still remember the other. I don't have a very good memory.*

M. *Your choice was certainly clear. You assumed the sergeant was directing the private to shoot at a human being. You were not apparently shocked by a command of this sort.*

What would you have done had you been the soldier?

D. *I would probably have asked the same question. That's why I did not understand it was humor. To establish the situation with two military men, whose profession is to shoot the enemy, and one of them holds a loaded gun and is ordered by a superior to fire it—well, it is hardly shocking or in any way unusual that the target would be a person, an enemy.*

M. *Do you think the sergeant would refer to an enemy by an intimate, diminutive form of the enemy's first name, like "Will"?*

D. *It might be in a civil war, when enemies are often members of the same family or dear friends. Or Will could be a fellow soldier, a military prisoner being guarded by the private. He tries to escape, and the guard must shoot him, even though he knows him by his first name. Anyway, I am known as "Joe" around here. If I were trying to escape, someone would probably say: "Fire at Joe."*

M. *You are awfully ingenious, Joe. Do you think you are different from most other people?*

D. *Well, if I am, then I shouldn't be the one to say it, God knows, either morally or legally.*

M. *God. You believe in God?*

D. *I could not have killed those three people without God's faith in me.*

M. *You felt you were doing God's will?*

D. *Look here, it isn't easy to take human life.*

M. *I have read some of your earlier statements and know you are much occupied with Time. Are Time and God synonymous?*

D. *Oh, no. God is not Time. To kill Time is to know God.*

M. *Joe, would you say yourself that you were crazy?*

D. *As I said before in answer to the other question, I can't answer that, because to do so I would have to stand outside myself, because the frame of reference for such a judgment is exterior to the person being judged. Anyway, that is not my job, but yours. Do you think I'm crazy?*

M. *I don't think you are a mad dog slavering at the mouth, a weird monster, or anything of the sort. But I do believe that you can be proved insane from the legal viewpoint.*

Detweiler shrugged goodhumoredly. "Why?"

"To put it briefly at this point," answered Dr. Metcalfe, "because I believe you think you are God."

"That's not precise, but I won't argue," Detweiler said. "And it should be added that I think you are too."

"I am also crazy?"

Now Detweiler laughed. That was the kind of joke he could appreciate.

"No," he said. "You are also God."

Detweiler made good friends among the guards, who did him favors—brought thicker portions of stew, extra soap, changed his towel frequently—though he no longer asked anything special as had been his wont when first arrested; he was relaxed now. Mr. Melrose continued to drop around, which Detweiler appreciated because he knew the lawyer had other cases. In fact, he expressed concern that Melrose might be wasting time on him, which was quite another thing than killing it.

Melrose said: "Don't worry, Joe. I can look after myself."

Detweiler asked: "I've been wondering, are you all alone in the world?"

"No," said Melrose, "I have several young lawyers who work for me, as well as an office staff."

"I meant, outside your job."

"I'm a bachelor, if that's what you mean."

"Like me," said Detweiler. "Or me as I was on the outside.

I guess you can't call a prisoner anything but a prisoner. Do you know a lot of girls?"

"I'm afraid that when you get to my age, you know girls but they don't know you, at least not in the way they did when you were younger. Nowadays I choose a woman for decoration. I get an infantile pleasure from eating in expensive restaurants, accompanied by a conspicuously beautiful, elegant young lady. This pleases me aesthetically and also has a practical use: it is often mentioned in the gossip columns, which are read by potential jurors, making men jealous and annoying mature women. These reactions are however often merely superficial. In some deeper area of the soul they are favorably impressed, and take it as evidence of my potency."

Melrose shrugged and went on: "The girls always understand their role. Beautiful women are born with an innate understanding of publicity. I never make a pass at them, and they never expect one. Even in my days as a bedroom athlete I seldom made love to unusually decorative girls. They lie there like a salmon mousse."

The lawyer peered at Detweiler and ceased to smile. He said: "I apologize. It is sadistic to speak of women to a man in confinement. Please forgive me."

"I brought up the subject," said Detweiler. "I haven't seen a woman in ever so long, and I like to hear about them."

"Well, you'll see a lot next week," Melrose said.

Detweiler raised his brow.

"The trial," said Melrose. "Your trial, Joe. It begins next Monday."

"Already?"

"It's September, Joe."

Detweiler said: "You could have fooled me. The weather

must be unseasonably warm. I still wear only my shirt when they take me outdoors for exercise. I could have sworn I had been here only a month or two. I remember it was cold when I was arrested, and then spring came and the air got warm. And that's about it. I haven't noticed much change since. You know, on the outside, the equinoxes used to get to me: I would get indigestion and my face would break out every spring and fall. That just goes to show you."

Melrose looked puzzled.

Detweiler explained: "Being in jail. How much it's done for me." He could have told the lawyer more, but he respected Melrose's wish not to be trusted. Detweiler was growing ever nearer to the accomplishment of a full-scale Realization. "I'm sorry to have made you sorry about talking of girls. I don't miss sex."

"I do," said Melrose. "Being deprived of it by Time is perhaps harder to accept than by imprisonment."

"You no longer feel the desire?"

Melrose shook his leonine head. "I no longer have the patience."

Neither had Tierney. He never again got in touch with Betty after that midsummer argument—which had not been an argument in the sense of disagreement on established issues. He did not answer her attack on him as a lover; she made no response to his defense of the police force. They had come together in the first place through accident. In no way did she represent his considered taste in women, but you had to be a pragmatist in matters of illicit sex, taking what came along or doing without: he had a job to do.

As to that job, he expected to be transferred back to a

precinct shortly after election. A shake-up was due in the Department, and Shuster intended to cop out into retirement. Whatever else could be said about Shuster, he had been Tierney's protector, had brought him to Homicide, had sent up good reports on him. That this had done Tierney no over-all service was not Shuster's fault: Tierney had thereby been added to the shitlists of Shuster's powerful enemies, though Tierney was certainly as Irish as anyone in the ruling hierarchy.

The only conspicuous recent stink in Shuster's squad had been provided by Matty, and the lieutenant had managed to get that reported, in the only paper which mentioned it, as an accident that happened when Detective Matthias had been cleaning his weapon. Matty resigned from the force as soon as he came out of bandages with half a face. Tierney had not seen him since, but heard Matty was working partner in an uptown cigar store and on good terms again with his wife.

But other squads were under fire—seven bank robberies had occurred in one district throughout the summer, and no arrests had yet been made; thrice had a tailor shop been held up, diagonally across the street from a precinct house; narcotics pushers did business openly on certain street corners; the commander of the state police accused the city force of poor cooperation on some jurisdictional matter. These were among the charges made by a candidate for the city council. They were of course denied by the police commissioner and ignored by the incumbents. But hard after Election Day would come a host of transfers and superficial reorganizations—if the party out of power lost as usual. If they won, there would be more publicity and less actual change in the Department. Oddly enough. So said Shuster, who was apolitical. Tierney would miss him.

"You're going to have lots of time on your hands," he told

the lieutenant. "One of my wife's uncles retired last year without making any plans to keep himself occupied, and—"

"Don't tell me," Shuster said. "He got a heart attack while cutting the grass for the third time that week, or while shoveling snow back onto the sidewalk so he could shovel it off again. I know all those stories. Me, I've got plans. I'm going to hang out at the public library and look up the skirts of high-school girls doing their assignments. Then I'll play cards Wednesday afternoons with the Old Lady and her pals. And every night I'll have a nice hot cup of cocoa. If that gets boring I know a cemetery that needs a night watchman: I'll sit down on a gravestone at midnight and eat my sandwich, and if I die I can be buried right on the job."

All this while Shuster was looking at photographs of a body some kids had recently found while swimming in a local river. "The thing I will miss most about this job is the floaters," he said. Floaters were notoriously difficult to identify if they had been in the water for a time. Shuster hated every floater personally. He was reading a description of the corpse's clothing. "How did a floater get a handmade shirt? No laundry marks? If it was tailor-made the store will have a record. Think you'll ever wear tailor-made shirts, Tierney? In a pig's ass you will. I read the other day about What's-his-name, you know that fag actor who always plays detectives." Shuster could never remember a celebrity's name. "It says he has his *handkerchiefs* tailor-made. How about that? Nothing's too good for his snot."

Tierney said: "The store identified that shirt as one they made for a T. C. Livingston. He's a stockbroker. His wife said the laundry lost it the first time it was sent."

"The boogie girls who work for laundries steal them blind," Shuster said, "and give the loot to their studs. But this floater's

Caucasian." He squinted at the photo. "Isn't he? Hard to tell, black as he is. The bastard." He stared at Tierney. "What's Livingston's wife like?"

"About thirty-five and—"

"I meant in the sack," Shuster cut in. "These rich broads, they have it in the same place as a working girl, don't they?"

Tierney said: "Tie was from one of those two-for-a-dollar shops. No label on the coat, ripped off."

"Floaters always do that," said the lieutenant. "Before jumping in."

"This one was knifed first."

"I know," Shuster said. "He told the perpetrator, 'Do you mind ripping out my lapels before you throw me in? I want to give Shuster a hard time.'" The lieutenant spoke as if he believed this literally. Floaters always brought his paranoia to a head. He dropped the photograph at last, and said: "What happened? Did Bayson's husband throw you out on your ass?"

"For a man who has as many enemies as you, Lieutenant," Tierney permitted himself to say, "you must also have some friends."

"Informants aren't friends," Shuster answered. "As you damn well know." He glared at Tierney in rare, brief, but genuine hatred. "You're not the only one who got a lot of gash when he was young."

This gave Tierney an opportunity to tell Shuster what he otherwise would not have dared to. "Lieutenant, I'm going to miss you."

"You're damn right you will," Shuster said with sufficient ungraciousness to show he was pleased. "Without me you'll soon be back in a uniform."

Occurring at a rate of two a day, more than 250 murders

339

had been committed in the city since Detweiler's arrest, including negligent and nonnegligent manslaughter, though not manslaughter by vehicle. Detweiler had got more publicity than the average perpetrator, the average, if there was one, being some low-income individual who shot or stabbed a friend in, or just having departed from, a neighborhood bar. There was also great reason to believe that many murderers went unpunished, their crimes undetected or misinterpreted. Many floaters had died by drowning pure and simple, showing no wounds: whether they fell in or jumped or were pushed would never be known. Occupying a subway track as a train came along was another popular form of dying; whether the victim had jumped of his own volition or been given a boost by an enemy or merely an overanxious, impersonal crowd, was difficult if not impossible to determine. Shuster had no grudge against a subway loser, though: they usually carried identification.

All the same, arrests were made. Of reported homicides about 90 percent were solved in one way or another. Only two days before, Tierney and his current partner, a detective named Herron, had collared two suspects in the murder-by-beating of a minor official in the longshoremen's union. These individuals, if they were ever brought to trial, were prepared to plead justifiable homicide in self-defense, having taken the precaution to wrap the stiff's fingers around a switchblade knife. Some wino had stumbled on the body, lifted the knife, and tried to hock it. But the pawnbroker blew the whistle on him and the precinct detectives kicked him around a little, which is always done to winos because they expect it and unless they get it will remain sullen and uncommunicative, and sit around stinking up the place, with yesterday's crap in their pants. This little sideshow, however, had no substantive reference to the main event.

340

Tierney and Herron, and everybody else on the Force, could identify the perpetrators of every crime of violence committed on the docks: the Calise Brothers, an organization of persons few of whom were actually brothers and only two of whom were actually named Calise, and neither of them had ever got so much as a parking ticket their lives long. They owned trucking companies, soda-bottling plants, linen-supply services, and provided hat-check girls for luxury restaurants, enterprises of record. Their maintenance of order on the piers went without written documentation or municipal franchise, but was an operation a good deal more efficient than the linen service, which often returned scorched napkins.

Ordinarily the police did not bother either of the actual Brothers about one routine corpse who turned up among the refuse cans behind a dockside café, but Tierney got a rebellious hair in his ass, thinking about Shuster's impending retirement, so he called up the bottling-works Calise, Dominick J., alias "Big D.," though nobody called him that but the newspapers.

After the expected delay, Tierney was put through. Calise spoke in a bland baritone.

"I trust you are calling to inform me you have apprehended suspects in the repeated burglaries in my warehouses," he said.

"I'm with Homicide," said Tierney. "We picked up two boys who work for you."

"Did they state that?" Calise asked ominously.

"You know better."

Calise laughed and said: "O.K. But I never heard of you. Hang up and I'll call you back." He was well within his rights: anyone could pretend to be a police officer on the telephone. So he dialed Headquarters, asked for Tierney in Homicide, and was back on the line.

"Do you know Vito Scarfiotti and Anthony Maio?" asked Tierney.

Calise said: "All Ginzo names sound alike to me, but I'll turn you over to my personnel manager. I certainly don't keep up with every employe who runs a bottle-washing machine."

"How about those in specialized jobs?"

"You mean like homicide? I don't kill no one, Mr. Tierney. My soft drinks are pure. A bacteriologist takes samples of every batch. The competition made that one up about the dead mouse found in a bottle of our cola."

"These men never worked for you in any job whatever?"

"I told you I would have it checked out," Calise said impatiently. "I don't get fresh with a policeman. If everybody respected the law like me, you would be out of business. I'll put my personnel manager on the matter and he will get back to you day after tomorrow if not later today."

"Tomorrow a holiday for you?"

"No, but you'll be in court for the Detweiler trial, won't you?"

"I thought you never heard of me."

"You'd be surprised the imposters who call this number," said Calise. "I thought maybe Detweiler might once of drank a bottle of my soda and you was trying to make me for aiding and abetting. I want to see him burn. I hate psychos! Listen, give Jimmy Shuster a kiss for me."

There was no reason to believe the greeting was sinister. In his long career Shuster had met most of the local racketeers, and mobsters always prided themselves on knowing a detective's first name and using it if they were clean or certain they could not be proved otherwise.

Shuster now asked Tierney what was happening in the waterfront case, and in the course of his report Tierney quoted Calise's friendly remembrance.

"Yeah," Shuster said. "He likes me. He wants to hire me as chief of security for his enterprises. Been a number of burglaries around the plant, and a lot of tablecloth thefts from his linen service. Sort of consultant job. I wouldn't have to go in every day."

"You are taking it?"

"I might," Shuster said, "I just might. But one thing I know for sure: you are not going to make him for this waterfront homicide."

"You are telling me to lay off?"

"Tierney, Tierney, you dumb mick," groaned Shuster. "The day you make Dom Calise for even a misdemeanor I'll gladly give you my pension. So why bother with him? Go over to Missing Persons and find who lost this prick floater. Do something useful."

Melrose was making his last visit to Detweiler, preparing him for the trial. He said: "I still haven't made up my mind whether to put you on the stand."

Detweiler said: "You can't get out of it. I'll be the only one in court who was at the scene of the crime."

"It is your right not to testify," the attorney explained. "Because of the presumption that you are innocent. I thought you understood that, Joe. You don't have to prove anything. The burden is on your accusers. Now, the reason why I am in something of a quandary is that knowing you as I do, I am afraid you might want to make a speech. The judge won't permit you to do that. You will be allowed only to respond to questions."

"I can handle it all right," Detweiler said. "What about those psychiatrists you sent around, and the detectives before that, and the sessions I've had with you. I haven't done any talking other than question-answering since I came to this place."

"That I appreciate, but your answers are often not to the point—or at least not what the court would so consider. Well, we'll see how it goes. I alternate in my opinion. Sometimes I think you would be the most effective witness in your own behalf. There is a rhythm to any trial. I prepare a case as thoroughly as I can, but the trial is the ultimate reality, the focus of energy, a work of art, but transient, unknown beforehand, irrecoverable afterward."

Detweiler said: "Like every moment of life."

"No," said Melrose. "Not like any other. We could not endure such a succession of moments without a rise and fall. *We* couldn't and we cannot really understand anyone who can. Nevertheless, you may be interested to know that the lunacy commission appointed by the state has found you sane. Without talking to or even seeing you. You have also been pronounced sane by the newspapers, tried, and found guilty."

Detweiler shook his head. "It looks as if you're all alone, Mr. Melrose. You talk of 'we,' but nobody else agrees with you."

"Doctors Brixton and Metcalfe do. But your point is well taken, Joe. I would not want it otherwise. The district attorney is going to try this case. He has never faced me before. Time and again he has sent in some young assistant to be mangled. But he thinks he can make it now, with the support of public opinion. Moreover, he could use a victory. He intends to run for governor one of these years."

"He has the right appearance for it," Detweiler said. "I would probably vote for him if I could. I have never got around to voting though, because I have never lived long enough in any one place to establish residence. Have you ever thought of running for public office, Mr. Melrose?"

"Would you vote for me, Joe?"

"I don't think so, with all respect. I think you are too private."

Melrose laughed till his eyes ran.

"That wasn't criticism, but rather description," said Detweiler.

"I know that," Melrose said, wiping his face. He sighed. "Well, Joe, win or lose you'll soon be leaving here."

"And I certainly will miss it," Detweiler said with feeling. "I don't imagine there are many jails as nice as this one. But then, as you always say, I am legally still considered to be innocent, so the confinement is designed merely to hold me for trial. I expect prisons, where you are sent for punishment, are hardly as comfortable. That would be ridiculous: everybody would be fighting to get in, with three hot meals a day and unlimited opportunity for cogitation."

"I should say the common opinion of this place is much less generous than yours. My other clients have regarded it as the Black Hole of Calcutta. But don't you worry. If the verdict is favorable to us, you'll probably be committed to a hospital, and you will be weaving baskets and working with clay and eating quite a lot of your favorite Jello."

"I'm finished with sculpture," said Detweiler. "But I'm sure willing to try basketry. . . . What if you lose?

"I refuse to consider that."

"Come on, Mr. Melrose. If the district attorney has the courage to try a case against you, you can show some nerve too."

Melrose started. He said "I'm sorry, Joe. You're right. . . .

Then you will be taken to prison and put into a cell in death row and, if I have exhausted every legal device without success, you will be strapped into the electric chair and a current of electricity sufficient to cause death shall be passed through your body and continued until you are dead."

"And God have mercy on your soul," said Detweiler.

Chapter 20

BETTY AND ARTHUR were met by a crowd of reporters and cameramen at the entrance to the court and had their pictures taken again and again for TV and the papers and were the targets of shouted questions, e.g., "How's it feel to testify against your ex-boyfriend?" "Think Detweiler will burn, Betty?" "You going on the stand, Arthur?" Some of these same newsmen had waited outside their house and followed them in from the suburbs.

Naturally Betty was their main interest, and soon Arthur found several reporters between himself and her. Someone near him touched his elbow and said "Hi, Arthur."

It was Betty's father, who had got this far unnoticed by the newspapermen, though he also was a celebrity or should have been.

"Hello, Father." Arthur had never called him that before.

But he had not seen him since the night of the murders. Arthur's great change had taken place during those months. He had matured. He no longer considered so many alternatives, but took action when it was called for. He had ceased to worry incessantly over what was just in an abstract way, but he was more a man of honor than he had ever been in the days when he killed time by weighing choices, and he gained more respect from other people.

"I was sick at the time of the funeral," Starr said. "I never got in touch since because I didn't think she would forgive me."

In the old days Arthur would have assured him otherwise, but now he said: "You're right. She hasn't."

"She always hated me," Starr said. He had his ashen, freshly shaved look. His clothes seemed soiled though they may not have been. Arthur believed the same might be true of Starr's life in general.

Arthur felt an impulse and, in his new style, instantly acted on it. "Father," he said, "here you go." He pushed at him a folded bill.

Starr recoiled, they being now at the margin of the crowd where maneuver was possible. "I got funds," he said. "I'm doing a book on the case. Do you know who with?" He had begun to crow. "Alloway, the guy who did Betty's series."

"Watch him," Arthur said. "That's my advice."

"He's all right," said Starr. "I seen the contract. We split fifty-fifty. . . . You going to testify? I always liked Joe. He treated me right. I guess he's crazy—" He looked furtively about. "The D.A. guys told me not to say that. But he was nice, a real nice guy. You don't find many. Of course you have been real decent too, Arthur. And you did not murder anybody.

Hey, I hear this Melrose can be mean in cross-examination. I need a shot of something."

They shook hands, and Starr managed to slip the bill out of Arthur's fingers without acknowledging it. He slunk off, heading away from the court.

Arthur moved towards Betty. The newsmen stood their ground and had to be shoved aside, which they made no show of minding. But the last one he encountered, the reporter in Betty's immediate presence, who was scribbling in a notebook, protested. He used a fountain pen, and he dropped it in the scuffle. It was stepped on and crushed.

Arthur had not meant to do that. But when the reporter, inconsolable, shoved him back, he intentionally struck the man in the eye and as the newsman went down, kicked him. Then Arthur seized the camera from a nearby photographer and hurled it to the pavement. A colleague of the stricken fetched one of the uniformed policemen who guarded the entrance of the court. Arthur raised his fist to smite this officer, but before he could get in a blow the cop subdued him with a nightstick.

So Arthur was booked for resisting an officer, assault, and other counts. All of which the D.A.'s office had quashed several days later, but Arthur did have to pay for the broken camera.

On their way back to court from the precinct house, Betty told Arthur: "I'm proud of you."

Arthur shrugged: He said: "I just can't stand the kind of pushing around you get every day in this city. The rudeness, the boorishness, the conspiracy of ugly little people to make life as ugly and little for everybody as it is for them. Respect is a rarity. You have to beat it out of people." He winced and touched his midsection, where the cop had given him a taste of the nightstick, following which he had capitulated. "Have you ever noticed that only the weak say violence is senseless?"

Betty was not interested in the subject, but she agreed about the scarcity of respect. She said: "You know who always had it? Joe Detweiler."

Arthur was somewhat jealous. "Of course I never really knew him."

"Maybe he'll be found insane. That's his only hope. I don't want to see him die, and God knows *I* am the one who suffered for what he did."

"You know, in some primitive tribes they didn't officially punish murderers, the society, that is. The offended parties, the surviving relatives, were expected to deal with the criminal, as being the ones who had suffered the loss."

"O.K.," Betty said, "but revenge is illegal here and now, so don't go trying anything. I want my baby to have a father who is not in jail."

Betty had got pregnant some weeks before, long after the last time she had been intimate with Tierney. And she had had no lovers since. She felt sisterly towards the young editor, who had certain girlish traits though he was not exactly queer: showed sullen hurt if she resisted his suggestions on the rewriting of her book, had a womanly hard vanity as opposed to the soft self-admiration of men—yes, soft, Tierney had been soft; like most men he could not take criticism. Whereas she and the young editor had frequent spats, made it up over cocktails or the telephone or in notes, giggled and made faces at each other, and then soon were at it tooth and nail again. "Too bad you're already married," he said. "We would make a great pair." But he did not mean it in a sexual way.

Betty had not yet found the nerve to tell him of her pregnancy: she feared it would dull what was so piquant in their relationship.

Tierney was obliged to accompany Detweiler into court. They had not seen each other since the grand-jury indictment.

"Hi, Joe," Tierney said.

"Tierney!" said Detweiler. "I have something to tell you of the utmost importance."

"We'll talk about that later." Appearances in court were what Tierney liked least about his job. For hours you had to wait around at the pleasure of lawyers, whom, whether in the service of prosecution or defense or on the bench, he mistrusted and feared. His work, in which at any time he might be killed, ended in this: endless language. Like all city policemen, but unlike most other persons who practiced dangerous professions, Tierney often remarked bitterly to himself that he might get killed. Other risk-takers—human flies, racing drivers, secret agents—seldom mentioned this eventuality lest the thought bring on the event. But cops used it as a moral nightstick with which to batter law-abiding civilians: we might get killed for you, yet you give us little money and less respect: in reality, *we* are *your* victims. Unlike an acrobat treading the high wire over no net, Tierney saw the audience as immortal, himself transitory.

He had an impulse to tell this to Detweiler, because Detweiler was crazy and could not use it against him, but suppressed it for the same reason. Anyway, there wasn't time.

What Detweiler wanted to discuss with Tierney was that he saw Mr. Melrose and Mr. Crews shaking hands and talking in a very friendly fashion, though they were supposed to be enemies. He assumed it was against such an eventuality that Melrose had warned him not to trust his counsel. For Melrose had consistently spoken of the D.A. with dislike and contempt. Detweiler believed Tierney could explain the situation, but Tierney would not talk now. He seemed frightened. Perhaps in the high-ceilinged room, with its various levels of dark wood and odd odor—like stale cookies—he lost his power. He took Detweiler to the defense table and melted away.

It was then that Detweiler achieved his Realization. The contrast must have done it: he had not had any large space around him since he entered jail, no space that was ultimately contained, for, unlike the exercise yard, the courtroom was roofed, indoors, and yet had magnitude, and a good many people were moving about, undoubtedly to a purpose but to all appearances doing nothing, shifting papers, coughing to the echo, murmuring; someone blew an empty nose like a horn: utter nullity, as opposed to the rich sense of the jail, where space and time were perfectly correlated: mealtimes, mopping the floor, exercise, mental deliberation.

The remarkable character of the Realization was that *Detweiler was present in this time and place, every feature existed as always except it was otherwise, including himself, Daniel M'Naghten on trial in London in 1843 for the murder of Sir Robert Peel's secretary. Mr. Melrose wore a wig, as did Mr. Crews. All spoke with English accents. The judge, also bewigged, was addressed as "your worship." M'Naghten stood in a high place, isolated, admitting his supposed target had been Sir Robert. His barrister spoke against the thundering charges brought by the Crown ...*

"You can sit down now," Melrose whispered to Detweiler. "Sit down, Joe! Do you hear me?" He finally had to apply force, and there was laughter in the courtroom. Which might be all to the good, being a genuine demonstration of the defendant's difference from other men, to which the normal responded initially with amusement, which is founded on embarrassment, and embarrassment is the first step towards horror.

Melrose intended to horrify the jury to the degree that its members would be purged of other emotions: vengeance, pity for the victims, and especially, the yearning to see justice done. A dangerous game indeed, for Crews would obviously be trying for the same effect, towards another end. Crews's was a routine mind, a politician's imagination. He was trying Detweiler only for the murders of Billie and Appleton, and thus admitting he had no case against the defendant for the strangling of Mrs. Starr, for which there was no evidence of premeditation. That was to say, the first killing in chronology, the first Detweiler had ever been known to commit, the only life owned by Mrs. Starr, the death which was the direct cause of the two which followed, was being ignored by the state.

What Crews intended to show as peculiarly horrible, and deserving of punishment by execution, were only those homicides which had allegedly been deliberate: Detweiler had had a motive for killing Billie and Appleton, one any normal person could recognize as rational. Irrespective of why he strangled Mrs. Starr, he had killed the others so as to eliminate them as witnesses. So the district attorney would seek to prove.

As a lawyer Melrose was obliged to show at least a superficial respect for reason: it was a kind of code, like the traffic laws, which one tended to observe habitually but abandoned without declaration in an emergency, and all his cases were emergencies, all crimes, all arrests, all trials. Though premeditation in itself was not necessarily either reasonable or normal, if it came to that. He could prove as much to any twelve human

beings who understood the English language, and more impor-
tantly, he could make them remember it beyond the prosecutor's
rebuttal and the judge's instructions.

"If a deed is insane in the commission, can the planning of it
be sane? I will explain my point"—Melrose often appeared
pedagogical in his summations and usually tried to usurp the
bench's function and give instruction in the law, until ordered
to desist: juries like to be taught, crave acknowledgment of
their state of holy ignorance. Crews was the type of prosecutor,
Melrose knew from his preparatory reading in transcripts of the
D.A.'s past performances, who might erroneously assume it
would flatter a jury to treat its members as one's peers, but few
men could bear that obligation in these circumstances. Juries
were neither compassionate nor cruel; they were merely human.

"I will explain what I mean, and it is not 'I' or 'mine,' but
justice and decency and sense and humanity"—nevertheless,
Melrose would accompany these remarks with idiosyncratic
gestures, odd motions of his bladed hands, wrists screwing,
striding about and halting at inconsequential moments, movements which could not be other than personal. *He* was the point
he made, and he asked incessantly: Do I speak, dress, and move
as though I could lose?

"If a human being, for example, living in our place and time
and culture, plans to kill another man, roast his thigh, and sit
down at a table and eat it with gravy, mashed potatoes, and
string beans, is he not mad? Must he actually devour such a
loathsome repast before we who are more fortunate can con-
clude he belongs to a different order of creatures than we?
And then what? My learned friend no doubt would say destroy
him like a piece of filth. But even more learned men, as I
believe I am safe in saying the distinguished prosecutor, who

tempers his splendid talents with modesty, would agree, have said it is medieval, if not Neanderthal, to kill what we do not understand. Easy enough to do when one has the power, and all is well again—

"—until that terrible day when you look down and *see the next cannibal at work on your own leg.*"

In his summations Melrose preferred to speak at length about another, and worse, crime than the one with which his client was charged. When he eventually returned from cannibalism to the stabbing or shooting at issue, the latter was considerably devalued.

He was not worried about what Crews would do to establish premeditation. The D.A.'s case was certainly going to be weak when it came to Appleton's killing, which had manifestly been committed in self-defense. Which left the strangling of Billie.

Melrose had a special feeling about Billie. Ordinarily he never took an interest in the victims of a client, especially if they were deceased. To put it simply, they were not his business except insofar as their existence, or the disposition of their remains, was inimical to his defendant, in which event Melrose would do his best to destroy their reputations, expose them as bogus or greater scoundrels than the accused—the deceased Appleton, for example, the forgotten man in this case, had not been forgotten by Melrose, whose investigators dug up dirt on him: a minor role in some PX scandal during a tour of Army duty; a short-lived career, two decades earlier, in semipro boxing, not criminal but useful to the defense of a man who had killed him, a prize-fighter's hands being classified at law as deadly weapons.

But Billie was different. For one, she had been beautiful. The many extant photographs banished all doubt of this: it could not have been faked that often. Honey hair, grape eyes, peach cheeks, a body like a gastronome's larder. Nowadays if Melrose believed a woman edible she had reached the summit of his tastes. He could not be said to have fallen in love with pictures or a corpse. Nor would the real Billie, resuscitated, have been his meat. Much too vulgar. But the thought of it, the ghost of it in the photographs, the slightly opened mouth, the archness of her breasts, the suggestion in her smile of a wickedness that could be imagined only by the utterly innocent. She had been too pretty to work as a call girl, too frivolous to model legitimate underwear, too lazy to aspire to the stage and she slept with the wrong people.

Melrose was sorry she had had to die. It was just that the crucial charge against Detweiler was for Billie's murder. Crews would try to pack the jury with men, unattractive men who never had access to a Billie Starr except in the torn pages of a barber-shop magazine, sensible men who would not forgive Detweiler for the madness in which he strangled and did not make love to her.

On the other side, Melrose would want women jurors, to hate Billie in the grave and feel compassion for the boyish Detweiler. But whatever the composition of the panel, Melrose would horrify them. In this he would be quite sincere, for he was himself horrified by Detweiler. The defense psychiatrists, Brixton and Metcalfe, practitioners of the most simple-minded of the professions, the fools' science, saw Detweiler as the victim—of a self-castration complex, of religious delusions, of mythological terms, obliteration-yearnings, infantile power-dreams, of fantasies, disordered desires, warped communications, but ultimately, of course, of Society. Had he only been treated at an early age. . . . So with them too, Time was of the essence. In effect they agreed with Detweiler that he had no choice on Christmas Eve last but to kill three persons.

Inevitability conditioned by chance: that was Time, that was death, that was Detweiler, that was reality, and that was horrifying. Adequately to represent Detweiler one must be divine. Melrose, relentlessly human, intended to win this trial, but it would be sacrilegious to say in so doing he would conduct an appropriate defense. The murder of defenseless Billie was indefensible. He could only plead that Detweiler was mad, as in representing a tubercle bacillus he could but asseverate that it was lethal.

No, no example sufficed. Detweiler could not be likened to a germ, or a deadly weapon, or a wild animal, or a hurricane. He did not seek to degenerate, was not an inanimate thing, or hungry, or an inchoate force. He was a human being without definable purpose or profession or motive.

Detwelier was a man. He was mad. He was a madman. What Melrose found most horrifying was that his own high art would be to no avail: he must simply, even humbly, present the truth.

With this recognition Melrose was claimed by a strange serenity. Usually as a trial opened he perspired adrenalin as he waited to put his fangs into living flesh, his eyes and ears were hyperesthetic though his head was buried in briefs and jury lists: he could identify all significant persons throughout the courtroom and translate their whispers, read the judge's mood in the reflection of light from His Honor's glasses and anticipate the prosecutor's case in such detail he might have conducted it for him.

But now the defense counsel sat calmly awaiting the descent of the clerk's hand into the receptacle from which he would

withdraw the name of prospective juror number one. If accept-
able to defense and prosecution this person would probably
become foreman. The panel could elect another member for the
job, but rarely did, preferring that fate choose the individual
who must finally stand erect and announce the verdict. This
man, or woman, then, was most important of the twelve, the
only one with a title and not a number. Melrose had been known
to spend hours and exhaust all his challenges to get the right
foreman. He knew the precise weight of any authority.

Now, for once, he would not strain to hear the name, to
watch the man walk into the box—you could learn a lot from
a walk and a taking of a seat and the riding up of a suit
jacket, throat-clearing, lip-licking, arrangement of hands—he
would see but not peer, appreciate but not press, question but
not grill, and accept whomever. Detweiler was insane. Any
citizen would understand that, irrespective of his temporal
prejudices, in view of the terrible alternative: that he himself
did not exist.

The clerk brought up a slip and began to read it aloud:
"Wilfred T.—"

Detweiler stood up again. Melrose observed this without
anxiety, as if he had no responsibility in the matter.

Detweiler said, addressing the court: "I have done it! Do you
hear me? I have succeeded."

"No," said the judge, "you must observe the proper procedure here." He waved a finger at the ceiling. "Mr. Melrose,
will you please advise the defendant . . ."

Undoubtedly he supposed this a trick of Melrose's and refused to be excited by it—such was Melrose's interpretation, for
the lawyer's mind continued active though his will was quies-

cent. But at last he took Detweiler's elbow, saying: "Joe, you must sit down."

"I am sorry I forgot to say 'Your Honor,'" Detweiler told the judge. "I don't want to do the wrong thing. I respect procedures and institutions. Without them we would all be adrift. I have reason to appreciate this in the most personal way. Until I was put into jail I was never able to collect my thoughts, and until I was brought to this trial I never accomplished anything of a positive nature despite grievous efforts.

"God knows, I even killed three people. But the legal system is extraordinary. To be brought to justice! All this marvelous organization, so reasonable and yet compassionate, serious, grand, and precedented. Men live and die, laws change, civilizations rise and fall in the inexorable movement of Time. But justice is not transitory in concept though particulars alter through the centuries. In ancient times thieves were executed, traitors drawn and quartered, murderers beheaded. Today our punishments are not so severe, but we have not ceased to believe that theft, treason, and murder are wrong and that their perpetrators should be brought to justice!"

Detweiler spoke intensely, but his voice had no resonance and Melrose doubted that the prospective jurors, seated in the first rows, could hear him. The judge leaned forward and cupped his right ear. He was sixty-five years old and still touched up his light-brown hair so that no gray showed, which indicated more patience than vanity. Melrose had appeared before him on other occasions and tested this patience; it was not indifference.

But he was not ready as yet to lower the boom on Detweiler. The district attorney had been caught unprepared. His assistants were staring at him, but his own head was cocking first towards Detweiler, then at the bench. Finally he rose in almost innocent astonishment and wailed: "Your Honor!"

Melrose's thumb and forefinger met each other through Detweiler's elbow; but he was clutching only the arm of the coat.

Detweiler went on: "Out in the world, try as I would, I could not get a firm grasp on experience. I was incessantly distracted by the spectacle of mankind in motion, noise, color, the flow of all the different kinds of energy. I really started choking Mrs. Starr so that I could gain a moment's peace in which to think. But she was urgent. . . . Well, you know the rest. Despite what Mr. Melrose says, I believe I should be punished for that."

Judge Hardesty removed his glasses. "Son, if you want to change your plea you must do it in the proper way. I cannot allow you to deliver a monologue in this court. Now, if you so admire the process of justice, I ask you to sit down and let it take its course."

"I will, Your Honor. I just want to say that I did it here, only here. It is a great moment for me. I Realized M'Naghten and his trial—incomplete but authentic. And it was not memory or merely imagination based on something I read, because I had never heard of him before Mr. Melrose explained the position of the law on insanity. The recovery of reality! I can do it now at will. I have much work before me, but I can do it. Do you see what that means? I can bring them back: Mrs. Starr, Billie, and Appleton. On the one hand I killed them, but on the other, they are not beyond recall. This is an overwhelming joy."

At this point Melrose found it possible to get Detweiler back into his chair. Then he apologized to the court.

The judge asked Crews and Melrose to approach the bench. "Mr. Melrose," he said, "I think I don't have to say I cannot tolerate this sort of thing. But I'm saying it anyway in the event that you were as embarrassed by it as the court, that it was not a calculated device of yours."

"I give you my word it was not," Melrose said.

"I accept it. Now I want to ask whether you can henceforth control the defendant."

"Your Honor, he is mad."

"You are saying you cannot?"

"I say I don't know. If he could kill three persons on the spur of the moment—"

The district attorney interrupted, speaking so indignantly that at first Melrose could not appreciate the sense: "Yes, and if he is acquitted by reason of insanity and committed to an institution, you'll have him out next year on a writ, maintaining he has regained his sanity under treatment. This murderer will be back walking the streets and we won't be able to touch him until he kills again."

"As God is my witness, I do not want that," said Melrose. "I would rather see him executed."

Crews stared at Melrose in amazement. "So you can be human?"

"Human?" Melrose asked in his own astonishment. "What a choice of words. Is it 'human' to send a poor lunatic to be burned?"

"I have an obligation to the people of this state. I know you view that with your customary cynicism, but I have it, I'm sorry. I believe in it sincerely. The lunacy commission reported that Detweiler is sane insofar as the term has legal application."

"Without examining him in person," Melrose replied. "You saw him in action just now, John. Do you really believe the jury will think he is in his right mind? Look at him, sitting there.

He is back in his Realization, as he calls it. I don't know what he'll do next. He might try to strangle me, if he decides I need it. He tried once before. He believes he is God, or at least divinely directed. Do you really want to have him electrocuted?"

Crews did not turn to look at Detweiler. When the D.A. had referred to the alleged humanity of Melrose, he had meant his own, to which he was working up. It had taken Melrose a while to perceive this. And even yet the defense counsel was not prepared for Crews's magnanimity. He listened wearily to the routine expression of academic indignation, with no suspicion that it might be but the prelude to a kind of surrender.

Crews was saying: "I resent the implication that I am a sadist and enjoy executions. I merely try to do my duty. As it happens, I am opposed to capital punishment, but so long as the law stands, I will, I must—"

"When you are governor," Melrose said, "you can put through a bill for its abolition."

"Gentlemen," said Judge Hardesty, "may I suggest you get off the ad hominem pot?"

"All right," Crews said. He would not look at Melrose. Nevertheless he colored as he spoke. "I will accept a plea to second-degree murder."

The judge shrugged. "And how do you feel about that, Mr. Melrose?"

Melrose had an almost sexual loathing of favors done to or for him. Now that he had this unprecedented evidence of Crews's humanity, he was inclined to question it, label it as expediency or cowardice. Honoring little that had not been won in battle, he preferred to interpret the compromise as Crews's bleating admission that the state had a feeble case for Murder One.

Melrose smiled sardonically. "I'll have to talk to my client."

The judge called a recess, and Detweiler and Melrose went into a conference cell behind the courtroom and discussed the proposition.

"Well, this is something new," said Detweiler.

"You understand it then," Melrose said. "You are back with us and not in 1843?"

"Oh yes. Realization doesn't occur automatically. It requires the full force of the will. One doesn't just go into it without preparation. Sure, I am Joe Detweiler and you are Mr. Melrose, and you are proposing that I make still another compromise. First I agreed to plead not guilty because of insanity, and now I am asked to plead guilty to a lesser charge. The killings, however, haven't changed. So why do the accusations? *I* haven't changed, at least as I existed at the time of the killings, because any moment of Time is immutable. If I Realize that time, it will be repeated exactly as it happened originally. If insane, then insane. If sane, then sane.

"You made every effort until now to establish my insanity. I don't hear any mention of that in this new proposal. Now I am to be considered in my right mind, but guilty of something else."

Melrose knew he could not win an argument from Detweiler. He, the great advocate, had never scored a point on his own defendant. He could not control him, he could not advise him, he could not defend him in any sense of the word.

"What can I say, Joe? That is Law. Men do what they can with it. It's not like the multiplication tables, in which five times eight is forty every time, all times. Because men aren't numbers—" He broke off, regarded Detweiler for a moment, and resumed angrily: "No, that isn't correct. Often they *are* numbers, of course. The law is supposed to represent the interests and needs of the public, the common good, but that is to speak in numbers. More people oppose murder than favor it, so it is wrong. It is wrong to drive without a license plate on your car because more legislators voted for the bill that made that requirement law than opposed it. And those men are in office because more citizens voted for them than for their opponents.

"Civilization as we know it is statistical. I once heard that explained as having its origin in the Renaissance, when values became quantitative and secular."

He scowled at Detweiler and resumed: "To hell with that subject, and to hell with you. I'm sick of trying to save your life. I'm sick of discussing the matter with you. I'm sick and I'm tired and I'm old. The only thing that would save *me* at this moment is to go into that courtroom and make such an ass of Crews that his political career will be set back ten years. He is an utter mediocrity, a vain, pompous, sanctimonious idiot whom I wouldn't hire as a law clerk. Yet he will inevitably be the next governor of this state. I could do it. I have that God-given opportunity. He has no case. He is suggesting this change of plea to make the best of a bad job."

Detweiler said: "But you think we should take his advice?"

Melrose continued to look angry. "I labor under an awful obligation, Joe. I am obliged to look after the best interests of my client. I take this as my divine duty, the execution of which will save my immortal soul. It is something beyond good and bad, love and hatred, and even death. It is my profession."

"Yes," Detweiler said, "a man's work is holy. I agree with that."

"The judge will sentence you to prison. You can work there. You'll like it."

"But what gets me is if you are so sure you could win as it stands, why don't you want to go ahead with first-degree?"

"Because I'm not God," said Melrose. "I might drop dead before the trial was finished."

Representing the defendant, Melrose entered a plea of guilty to second-degree murder. He spoke briefly and not at all passionately of the crimes, of the psychiatrist's assessment, of Detweiler's theories and of his history. He made no general remarks about lunacy in or out of the legal meaning, but stayed ruthlessly particular. He asked justice for this one man, his only client on trial.

Crews then spoke of the heinousness of the murders, of Detweiler's signed confession, of the learned judgment of the lunacy commission that he was sane in the terms of the statute. He talked at length of his duty towards the people of the state who had entrusted to him his office. They must not be condemned to walk their streets in fear and trembling, to celebrate their holidays in the shadow of the lurking murderer.

Melrose remembered that Judge Hardesty had a kidney condition as he watched the jurist shifting about on the bench. Apparently he had not relieved himself during the recess. Finally the judge chose a moment when Crews was taking a breath to ask whether the prosecutor intended to move for denial.

Crews assumed an injured look and reluctantly recommended that the court accept the plea.

Then the judge looked down at Detweiler. "Son," he said, "you may say something now if you wish. But I hope you will be brief and succinct. We do not have time for a long speech."

Detweiler sprang to his feet. "The way I see it, Your Honor, well, it all boils down to this." He seemed to wait for a signal to go on.

"All right," the judge said, squirming. "Make your point."

Detweiler nodded. "To this," he repeated. "Each man kills Time in his own way."

Chapter 21

A WEEK LATER Detweiler was sentenced to life imprisonment. At prison he was given an immediate and thorough examination by the staff psychiatrists and, found to be insane by their standards, was transferred to an institution for the confinement of felonious lunatics.

Melrose got a letter from him at Christmas time.

Dear Mr. Melrose,

Forgive me for not writing sooner. As you might suspect, I have been very busy here, and not just with basketry, bead-work, etc.—have done no modeling in clay because as you know I am finished with image-making. The doctors are kind and generous though of routine mentality.

I want to thank you for putting up with me so long, and to apologize for the trouble I caused you. You are the most intelligent man I have ever known and I am better for our conversations. Your remark about quality versus quantity, for example,

*and the change brought about during the Renaissance. That is
the crux of the matter. Time is qualitative, not quantitative.
That is the key to Realization.*

*So at this Yuletide my fondest wish for you is that someday
your brilliance might be accompanied by Hope. Time is old,
but it is also forever new.*

*Well, pleasant as it is to talk on, duty calls and I must get
back to work.*

Your friend,

JOE DETWEILER

Melrose replied:

Dear Joe,

*I was touched by your letter, as I have always been touched
by your concern for me. I assure you that I, too, found our
conversations extremely rewarding. I shall be interested to hear
more of the progress of your work.*

*Now some news. I have been offered an appointment to the
bench. Oddly enough, our old opponent, Mr. Crews, was instru-
mental in bringing this about. If you recall, you and I once
talked of whether I wanted to be a judge. I said then that I
did not have the courage for the job. I have since changed my
mind, or perhaps my heart. I have accepted. I could not have
done this without your moral support.*

*May I wish you a Merry Christmas and a Happy New Year,
and you will understand when I call myself your client as well
as*

Your friend,

HENRY W. MELROSE

Though he knew it was not a joke, Detweiler laughed anyway when he received this missive. He had also written to
Tierney.

Dear Tierney,

I never did get a chance to speak to you again after the trial. I wanted to ask you for a favor. Will you please convey to Betty Starr my sympathies. I really went up there last Christmas merely to wish her season's greetings and give her a little present of a stuffed squirrel. I know I told you I intended to kill her, but that was not literally true. It was mainly to encourage you at the time, because your duty was to interrogate me and you weren't getting anywhere. I could never harm Betty. She is my ideal, and I still love her.

Now, as to yourself, I hope you know I value our friendship and think of you often. Please be careful. Your job brings you in contact with many dangerous people, and you must not let your attention stray.

Every good wish.

Sincerely,

JOE DETWEILER

Tierney was carrying this letter in his pocket as he entered a telephone booth in a midtown drugstore and dialed Betty's number.

"Tierney," he said. He did not try to anticipate his reception.

"Hi!" Betty sounded friendly.

It suddenly occurred to Tierney that it might be bad taste to mention the season. Today was Christmas Eve again, the anniversary.

He said: "I thought it was time to check up on you."

"Oh." She sounded cautious.

"Can you talk?"

She laughed. "Arthur's still at the office party, feeling up the secretaries. What do cops do on Christmas Eve?"

"I have the day off for a change. I'm doing some shopping."

"Gifts for the wife and kids?"

He grunted an uncomfortable affirmative, this reference for some reason causing him to feel more guilt than had the physical adultery.

Then she said brightly: "I'm pregnant." He knew an even greater unease, but refused to ask when or by whom.

She said: "And I've written a book."

"It sounds like you are making out all right."

"Yes," Betty said, "and don't worry. You're not mentioned in it."

Tierney hung up, went out into the crowded street, and wandered along looking in the windows of sporting-goods stores. His son had asked for a basketball, but Tierney resented being told what to buy. It was alien to the spirit of Christmas. He stopped before an eye-catching display of knives, a dozen or more, stuck by their points into a large ball of cork, a sort of porcupine. All types, clasp, Scout, throwing, sheath, including a stiletto of the kind he had once taken away from a suspect who had presented its business end to his belly. Tierney had got a citation for that arrest.

The individual standing next to him at the moment was a male Caucasian, age approximately twenty-five, height about five-ten, weight one-forty, dark brown hair, bad complexion, no hat, wearing a red-and-black wool jacket.

It was Tierney's day off, but policemen were never excused from duty. He observed this individual, who stood too long before the knives while other window shoppers came and went, and would not move to facilitate anyone's passage. Tierney himself wanted to get beyond, to the cameras, but he could not move around this individual because of the traffic entering and leaving the store.

"Let me by here, fella," he said. "You're not going to buy a knife. You might hurt yourself."

The individual turned and looked yearningly at Tierney. Tierney smiled in a tough but genial way.

"Come on," he said, and the individual swiftly brought out from under his shirt an eight-inch hunting knife and pushed its blade into Tierney's entrails.

Tierney felt it only as a pressure, a shove. The keen blade penetrated his clothing, skin, and bowels too quickly for pain and cleansed itself on the way out through the coat. So he saw no blood. For an instant he still believed the man was merely showing the weapon to him.

Then the knife was back in his body again and he lay upon the sidewalk and the assailant knelt beside him, stabbing him everywhere, and there was panic in the Christmas crowds. He could not move, yet he remained conscious and strangely not uncomfortable in the warm bath of his own blood.

The nearest traffic cop arrived and shot the assailant in the chest, neck, and head. The fourth bullet missed the target and hit the shoulder of a woman shopper, maiming her for life: so she claimed in the subsequent suit against the city.

The assailant died before Tierney, his brains across the sidewalk and halfway up the show window. A number of policemen were there when the ambulance arrived, and one had reached into the mess of Tierney's coatfront and got out his badge and slashed wallet. Tierney recognized nobody. He was put on the stretcher and lifted into the vehicle. He heard somebody say the inevitable, "Here's the pile of garbage," in reference to the assailant's corpse.

He remembered he had forgotten to pass Detweiler's message on to Betty, though that had been his alleged reason for calling her. Nor had he made the most of Detweiler's warning. But then nobody had to remind him he might get killed at his job.

The assailant turned out to be a psycho with a long history of treatment. The Department gave Tierney an inspector's funeral.

At his hospital, eating Jello, weaving baskets, and Realizing all manner of historical incidents, Detweiler failed to learn of this incident. He never had kept up with the news.

END.